M000251770

Crossing the Line
The Daniels Brothers, Book 3

By

Sherri Hayes

Crossing the Line
By Sherri Hayes

Copyright © Sherri Hayes, 2017
Originally published by The Writer's Coffee Shop in 2014

e-book ISBN: 978-0-9985652-2-4
Paperback ISBN: 978-0-9985652-3-1

Cover Photo and Design: Sara Eirew Photographer
Layout Design: Riane Holt

All rights reserved. No part of this book may be reproduced, scanned, or distributed in any printed or electronic form without permission. Please do not participate in or encourage piracy of copyrighted materials in violation of the author's rights.

This is a work of fiction. Names, places, characters and incidents are the product of the author's imagination and are fictitious. Any resemblance to actual persons, living or dead, events or establishments is solely coincidental.

Other Books by Sherri Hayes

Finding Anna series
Slave
Need
Truth
Trust

Daniels Brothers series
Behind Closed Doors
Red Zone
Crossing the Line
What Might Have Been

Serpent's Kiss series
Welcome to Serpent's Kiss
Burning for Her Kiss
One Forbidden Night

Single Titles
Strictly Professional
A Christmas Proposal

Summary – Crossing the Line

Detective Paul Daniels has spent four and a half years mourning the loss of his wife. He's been doing his best to raise their daughter, Chloe, with the help of his in-law's. When they inform him right before Thanksgiving that they're going to be moving over two hours away, Paul finds himself without anyone to watch Chloe while he's at work. Little did he know that meeting his baby brother's girlfriend and her sister, Megan, would change everything.

Megan Carson took a few wrong turns in her life, but she was doing her best to get back on track. When Paul mentioned his need for someone to watch his daughter, she quickly volunteered to be his live-in nanny. It didn't take long for Chloe to work her way into Megan's heart, and not much longer for her to realize that she was falling in love with Chloe's dad.

Dedication

This book is dedicated to my readers. Their love for these characters that live in my head never ceases to amaze me. Thank you all for your continued support.

Acknowledgments

A lot goes on behind the scenes before a novel hits the shelves. My beta, Riane, and my editors Wyndy and Andrea helped make Paul and Megan's story the best it could be. Thank you, ladies.

Chapter 1

"Did you see me, Daddy? Did you see me?"

Paul Daniels bent down and lifted his five-year-old daughter, Chloe, into his arms. "I did."

He gave her his best smile, not that she noticed. Chloe was too excited to pay much attention to anything for long. Paul thought nothing could top the excess of energy his little girl displayed the day Chris and Elizabeth called to ask her if she'd be their flower girl. He'd been wrong. Three months ago, Chloe had been full of questions about the unknown—she'd never been to a wedding before. Today, she was bouncing off the walls, and her smile matched his new sister-in-law's in pure joy.

It was as if he hadn't commented at all.

"And Eliz'beth's dress is sooo pretty. Isn't it pretty, Daddy?" Chloe didn't wait for his response this time either, before she continued. "Now she's my aunt." She concentrated to make sure she got it right. Megan had been working diligently to help Chloe improve her speech before she started school in the fall.

Paul searched the crowd of people bustling into the reception hall for the woman in question, as Chloe squirmed wordlessly making her desire to be put down known. He lowered her feet to the floor, and watched as she slipped in between two wedding guests while he continued to scan for Megan.

Megan was the younger sister of his baby brother Gage's wife. Paul had met her when she'd come to Thanksgiving with her sister.

Little had he known what a savior she'd turn out to be. She'd brought life back into his house. Life that he hadn't realized was missing.

She'd rescued him when he'd been in desperate need of someone to watch Chloe. Hours before he'd loaded Chloe into the car to set off for the holiday with his parents, his in-laws had announced they were moving almost two hours away. For four years, they'd lived nearby and were able to take Chloe whenever he was called in to work. His job as a homicide detective meant that he could be called out at all hours, and he couldn't leave his young daughter alone. Megan had fit the bill by offering to move to Indianapolis and into his house as a live-in nanny. She'd saved Paul from having to spend countless hours searching for an alternative.

As if knowing the direction of his thoughts, Chloe weaved through the people in her path until she was beside her nanny. Megan smiled when she caught sight of the little girl, and she circled her arms around Chloe's shoulders, lifting her off the ground, and twirling. They were both laughing—happy. The two of them had clicked from the beginning, and his chest clenched almost painfully watching the two of them together. It should have been Melissa standing there twirling Chloe, but he couldn't be upset that it was Megan. She'd put her life on hold for them—helped them out when they'd needed it most. Paul wished he could be as carefree.

His brother, Chris, wanted to give his fiancée, Elizabeth, the wedding of her dreams, right down to the ceremony being held in a quaint little church not far from where they lived in Springfield, Ohio—and it was. Elizabeth had walked down the aisle in a long white gown, his brother in a tux. Everyone who meant something in either of their lives was present. It was . . . perfect.

Unfortunately, it brought back too many memories for Paul. Memories that were raw and painful. Almost fifteen years ago, he'd been where his brother was—marrying the love of his life. He didn't begrudge Chris and Elizabeth their happiness. No, he was grateful. His brother had had a rough time of it after his first marriage fell apart. For Paul, it was a sharp reminder that he no longer had his wife at his side. She'd been taken from him by a drunk driver.

Starting to get choked up, Paul cleared his throat, and made a beeline for the bar. He didn't drink often, and never when he had to drive afterward, but tonight he didn't have to go anywhere but upstairs to his hotel room. Chloe was here, of course, so he couldn't go overboard. He just wanted to numb some of the pain.

Paul leaned his elbows on the bar as he waited for the petite blond bartender to finish with the drink she was making for another guest. He thought the guy standing patiently waiting for his drink was one of Chris' employees. Paul was also fairly certain that the guy was single by the way he was openly eyeing the young woman from head to toe. She was pretty— Paul wasn't blind, after all. Unfortunately, there was no spark. There never was. Not since his wife, Melissa.

Six months after Melissa's accident, he'd tried. He'd left Chloe with Melissa's parents and gone out to a club. It had been loud and he'd felt out of place, but he'd met a woman he found attractive and went for it. They'd ended up at her place an hour later, clothes on the floor, with him hovering over her.

He hadn't been able to go through with it, though. As he reached for a condom, he'd seen Melissa smiling up at him, her chest vibrating as she attempted to suppress her mirth while he fumbled trying to roll the rubber down his erection. It was an old memory, from when they were teenagers, but it had stung all the same. He'd gathered his clothes, dressed, and apologized, leaving the woman, whom he only knew as Karen, lying naked on her bed staring after him.

The bartender handed over the drink she'd made, and then turned to Paul without giving the other man a second glance. Looked like he wouldn't be getting that after-closing booty call.

She turned to Paul and smiled. "What can I get ya?"

"Scotch. Neat."

Her smile got wider. "Coming right up, handsome."

Paul glanced over his shoulder, and caught sight of his mom and dad. They appeared to be engrossed in a conversation with two people he didn't know. His dad looked in Paul's direction, and Paul quickly turned back around. The last thing he needed was his dad zeroing in on his less-than- festive attitude.

The bartender placed the half-full glass of scotch down in front of him. She made sure to lean in a little closer than normal. "Here you go."

"Thanks." Paul picked up the glass and took a drink. It burned as it went down his throat, which was good. Anything was better than the knife twisting in his gut.

"So how do you know the bride and groom?"

Not wanting to be rude, Paul answered her. "I'm the groom's brother."

"Older or younger?"

Paul laughed, before backing away. "Thanks again for the drink."

He made it halfway to the corner he'd scoped out as a decent hiding place, before he was waylaid by his brother, Trent. "Hey, man." Trent looked down at the drink Paul had in his hand, and raised his eyebrow.

"Something wrong?"

"I was going to ask you the same question. Since when do you drink anything but beer?"

"I like to mix it up sometimes." Paul didn't add that those "sometimes" usually involved his wedding anniversary and the anniversary of his wife's death. Chris' wedding didn't fall on either of those occasions, but Paul was making an exception.

"Since when?"

After taking another sip of his scotch, Paul narrowed his eyes at his younger brother. "Did you have a reason for coming over here other than to give me a hard time?"

Trent frowned, but let it go. For now, at least. "Megan and Chloe were looking for you. Chloe wants some pictures of you, Megan, and her together. Chris and Elizabeth don't have a problem with it, but they wanted to make sure it was okay with you before they agreed to anything."

The last thing Paul wanted to do was pose for more pictures, but there were very few things he'd deny his daughter. Pictures of the woman she'd grown extremely close to over the last four months wasn't one of them. "It's fine."

Again, he saw that look of doubt cross his brother's face. "Okay . . ."

Paul ignored Trent's curiosity. "Where?"

"Out in the lobby. The photographer has been taking some pictures in front of the fountain."

Not waiting to see if Trent would come up with more questions regarding his odd behavior, Paul took off toward the fountain.

Before entering the lobby, he took one last gulp of his scotch, feeling the heat. He could do this. For his daughter, he could do this. Setting his now empty glass down on a nearby table, he plastered a smile on his face, and went to find Megan and Chloe.

***

Megan Carson held tight to Chloe's hand as she continued to flutter about without a care in the world. They were in the lobby waiting on Paul. At least, Megan hoped they were waiting on Paul. It hadn't escaped her notice that he'd been tense all throughout Chris and Elizabeth's vows. And a couple of times she noticed him getting a look on his face. She couldn't help but wonder if he was thinking about his wife.

He'd smiled and laughed along with everyone else, but she could tell his heart wasn't in it. She now knew him well enough to know the difference. And she'd guess his family did, too. Although, technically, Megan was his family now as well—ever since her sister married his brother.

Chloe squealed, and pulled harder on Megan's arm. "Daddy!"

Releasing the little girl's hand, Megan stood back and watched Paul scoop up his daughter. Seeing them like this gave her a warm feeling. He smiled at Chloe, and this time it didn't look fake or forced. Then again, whenever it came to Chloe, Megan didn't question Paul's love or willingness to do anything for her. Chloe was the apple of his eye—a tangible reminder of his dead wife.

"I was told there's a picture that needs to be taken out here." Paul tickled his daughter's sides.

She giggled. "Yes, Daddy. I want a picture with yous, and mes, and Megan."

Paul glanced down at Megan, and she took in his warm brown eyes. She loved when they sparkled with joy, as they did in that moment. No one could do that to him but Chloe. Not his mom or his brothers. Not even her. No matter how much she wished otherwise.

The photographer approached them with his camera hanging from a strap around his neck. "Ah, good. Everyone's here, yes?"

He quickly corralled them into the correct position, with Megan and Paul flanking Chloe as the three of them sat on the edge of the fountain. To an outside observer, they'd look like a normal family. Appearances could be deceiving, though, and in this case, they were way off. Megan was Chloe's nanny, nothing more. She took care of Chloe when Paul was working, making sure she had everything she needed, and that the house wasn't a disaster when he came home.

That was where it ended. Occasionally, Paul would allow Megan to cook dinner for them, but it was rare, and usually only on days when he knew he wouldn't be home until after six. Paul took taking care of his one and only child seriously. She was his responsibility, and while he allowed Megan to take over when he had to leave, he didn't take advantage of her presence in their life— although sometimes she wished that he would.

With the pictures over, Chloe ran back into the reception with an announcement that she was going to find her grandmother— Paul's mom— leaving Paul and Megan behind.

"Thank you."

She looked up at Paul. He towered over her, at just over six feet to her much shorter five foot five. "You know I'd do anything for Chloe."

He was ultra-serious again. "I know, but you don't have to. You're not working tonight."

Megan frowned. He had that melancholy look she noticed crossed his features all too frequently. "Are you all right?"

It was Paul's turn to frown. "Of course. Why wouldn't I be? It's my brother's wedding."

His answer didn't ease her concern. Paul was a good guy—the best guy she'd ever met in her twenty-three years. He put every other man who'd crossed her path to shame, with the exception of Gage and the rest of his brothers and father. The Daniels men had certainly upped her standards in the opposite sex.

"I don't know. You just don't seem like yourself tonight."

Paul waved off her observation. "It's been a long day, that's all."

Yes, it had been a long day. Megan and all the other Daniels women, including Chloe, had met at the spa a little after eight that morning. They'd all gotten their hair and nails done while the guys did whatever guys did to get ready for a wedding. Since then, they'd all been going strong. Megan didn't think that was the problem, but she let it go. For now. "It *has* been a long day."

In what seemed like an effort to steer her away from any further questioning, Paul held out his arm, and motioned toward the reception. She took a deep breath, and smiled, allowing him to deflect. Whatever was going on with him today, she figured it had to do with his wife. One thing she'd learned about Paul in the four months she'd known him was that he was still very much in love with Melissa. It didn't matter that she'd been dead for over four years. She was still alive in his heart.

Once back inside, Megan was hijacked by her brother-in-law, Gage. "Would you please talk to your sister?"

Megan laughed. "What's up, Becca?"

Her sister, Rebecca, gave her husband a disapproving headshake. "Nothing, except Mr. Overprotective here doesn't think I can do anything on my own."

"I'm trying to be a gentleman." Gage huffed his response, but at the same time, he wrapped his arms around Rebecca's middle, pulling her up against him. It still amused Megan to see how Gage had changed since falling in love with her sister. He'd gone from the cocky playboy to the overprotective husband and daddy-to-be.

Rebecca leaned in to him. "I do *not* need for you to walk me to the bathroom. I'm not a child." She paused. "And before you say it, I'm not going to get sick. I haven't had a bout of morning sickness in over a week."

Gage kissed her temple and inhaled. "I'm sorry, beautiful, but you know how much I worry about you."

Megan watched her sister—her sister who could take down a man three times her size with her bare hands—melt in her husband's arms. "I guess you two don't need me anymore, then?"

They both chuckled, and Rebecca stood to her full height. "Of course I do. You, I don't mind accompanying me to the ladies' room."

Before she knew it, Rebecca was pushing her toward the bathroom. "Hey, slow down."

Rebecca stopped and released Megan's arm. "Sorry. It's just . . ."

"He's driving you nuts?" Megan laughed.

"It's not funny. You'd think I was terminally ill or something, instead of pregnant."

Although she knew Gage's attentiveness was probably getting to her overly independent sister, she also knew that Rebecca loved the attention. It was something Megan and Rebecca had lacked growing up—Rebecca especially. "You know you love it." Megan paused. "And him."

It took a few seconds, but then a soft smile brightened Rebecca's features. "It's sad, but I do. I know I shouldn't, but to know that he'd drop everything for me and the baby, no matter what, is a pretty amazing feeling."

"Yeah, I bet. I mean, we didn't have that growing up. He's going to be a great dad."

Rebecca glanced back to where Gage was now talking to his father and Trent. "He really is."

The talk of dads sent Megan's mind drifting back to Paul, and she immediately began searching the crowd for him.

"Looking for someone?"

Megan turned back to face her sister. "Huh? What?"

"I asked if you were looking for someone." Rebecca had a strange look on her face, and Megan knew Rebecca was going into big sister mode. It was the last thing she wanted.

"Not really."

Her sister frowned. "Is something going on I should know about?"

Now Megan was confused. "Like?"

"I don't know. I mean you've gone four months without chasing after a guy. That's a record for you."

Megan rolled her eyes. "Thanks."

"I didn't . . . I didn't mean it like that. I worry about you. I want you to find a nice guy—someone who will treat you well. I don't want to see you hurt again."

"I know. And when I find him, you'll be the first to know."

Rebecca reached up to brush a strand of hair away from Megan's face. It was something she'd done since Megan was little—a motherly gesture from the only real female authority figure Megan had ever known. "Come on. Let's get to the bathroom before I burst. I think I drank way too much water earlier."

Following her sister, Megan took one last look around trying to spot Paul, but she didn't see him anywhere.

Chapter 2

Paul didn't manage to stay under the radar for as long as he would have liked. Unfortunately, there were only so many places he could hide without leaving the reception entirely. That meant his family was able to find him without too much difficulty.

After leaving Megan, he'd ambled back over to the bar and got another drink to nurse. He needed to take it easy. No matter how bad the pain got, he didn't want his daughter to see him falling down drunk.

He made it about a half hour at his lone table in the corner, sipping his second glass of scotch and nibbling on some food, when Chris and Elizabeth found him.

"Congratulations." Paul tipped his glass to the bride and groom.

"Thank you." Chris held tight to his new bride's hand, and his smile was bright enough to light up the whole room. Paul remembered that feeling. He remembered holding his new wife in his arms—their first dance—their first kiss as husband and wife. Everything.

He was going to need another drink.

Elizabeth was the one to bring Paul out of his memories this time. "So I was wondering if maybe you'd like to dance?"

"Worn your new husband out already?" Paul attempted the joke, but it felt dead to his own ears.

Chris, luckily, didn't seem to pick up on it. Paul supposed his brother was too caught up in the joy of his wedding day, which was exactly as it should be. "Pfft. Not hardly. I'd dance with her all night if that's what she wanted. Aunt Claire, however, wants a dance."

Paul smiled. He wasn't feeling it, but he could pretend. He was good at that. "Sure. I'd love to dance with my new sister."

Reluctantly, Paul left the remains of his scotch on the table, and took Elizabeth's hand. Sure, he could have downed it like he did before, but if he kept doing that he wouldn't be able to walk soon. Plus, Chris might have noticed, and that was the last thing he needed. On the whole, Paul preferred beer, but he would have to down a case of beer to get that numb feeling he was looking for tonight. Scotch was more efficient.

Elizabeth held onto his arm until they reached the dance floor. They danced in relative silence, until he saw some of the happiness drain from her features. "Something the matter?"

She tilted her head to the side. "I was going to ask you the same thing."

Obviously he hadn't been hiding his emotions as well as he'd thought. "I'm fine. Good. My little brother got married today, and I happen to think the woman he chose is perfect for him."

She smiled, but the concern didn't leave her face. "Thank you for saying that, but what about you?"

"Like I said, I'm fine."

Elizabeth seemed to think about it for a moment, and he was really hoping she would drop it. He should have known better. "Does this remind you of your wife? Of your wedding?"

Paul shrugged, not wanting her to make a big deal out of it. "Some. It is a wedding, after all." He didn't add that when Elizabeth had walked down the aisle in her white dress he'd had a flash of Melissa walking toward him on their wedding day.

"I'm sorry. I wish I could have met her."

He nodded. "She would have liked you."

Elizabeth smiled. "I'm sure I would have liked her, too."

Although he didn't mind talking about Melissa to a certain extent—he talked about her often to Chloe—given the events of the day, he didn't think he could handle a long drawn-out discussion. When the song ended, Paul politely thanked Elizabeth for the dance, and went in search of his mom. He needed a few minutes to himself . . . away from everyone . . . but he didn't want to just up and leave without telling anyone either. That would only invite more questions from his family that he didn't want to answer.

He found his mom sitting near the buffet table. Chloe sat next to her, stuffing her face with a piece of bread and some chicken. "Hey, Ma."

"Da-mee!" Chloe's words were muffled around her food.

"Don't talk with your mouth full." His daughter didn't look fazed by his reprimand, and went back to eating.

"I was looking for you earlier."

Paul pulled out a chair beside his mom, and sat down. "Elizabeth wanted a dance."

Marilyn Daniels smiled at her oldest son. "I'm so happy for Chris. He should have married Elizabeth the first time around."

"That would have been difficult since Elizabeth was still married to someone else at the time."

His mom waved the comment away. "You know what I mean. Elizabeth should have been his first."

Paul couldn't argue with that. None of the family had been crazy about Carol, Chris' first wife. That should have been a big clue right there. Unfortunately, Chris found out the hard way that she wasn't the right woman for him when he caught her in bed with his best friend. Paul counted his blessings that he'd never had to experience a betrayal like that. He and Melissa had been childhood sweethearts. She'd been his first, and he hers.

"Paul?"

Blinking, he refocused on his mom. "Sorry. What were you saying?"

She glanced over at Chloe, and then back at him. "Chloe and I were talking about her having a sleepover with Grandma and Grandpa tonight, but I told her we'd have to make sure it was okay with you first."

"Please, Daddy? Please?" This time Chloe made sure to swallow first before she began pleading.

"Sure. We aren't leaving until around noon tomorrow, anyway."

"Yay!"

His mom laughed, and Paul managed a smile. "I was actually coming to find you to see if you could watch Chloe for a bit. I need to run up to the room for something."

"Of course."

"Did you need me to bring down some clothes for her while I'm up there?"

"Nah. We're good. I've got a T-shirt with me she can wear. You just enjoy yourself tonight. I've got Chloe."

"Okay."

"Thank you, Daddy." Chloe jumped up off her chair and hugged Paul's legs.

He hugged her back. She was growing up so fast. "You be good for Grandma and Grandpa, you hear?"

She smiled up at him. "I promise."

Bending down, Paul kissed the top of his daughter's head before walking away. He knew he could have asked Megan to keep an eye on Chloe for him, but he'd told her to take the night off and enjoy herself. She deserved it with all the overtime he'd been working lately.

As Paul headed toward the entrance, he paused and looked over the crowd. Everyone was having a good time, as it should be. He narrowed his eyes a little when he saw Megan talking to that same guy who'd been trying to chat up the bartender.

Shaking it off, he moved on. Megan was a big girl. She could take care of herself.

He looked away, and his gaze honed in on the bar once more. Chloe was spending the night with his parents, so he was free for the rest of the evening.

Throwing caution to the wind, Paul turned on his heel, and ambled toward the bar to get a bottle of scotch to keep him company up in his room. He already knew it was going to be a long night, and he was still feeling way too much. Chloe wouldn't be there, so there was no reason to hold back. He was going to get drunk. Maybe then, he could stop feeling for a while.

***

Megan saw Paul slip out of the reception hall. She was talking to a guy named Kevin. He was nice enough, but she couldn't help compare him to Paul. On top of that, she'd met plenty of guys like Kevin before. He was looking for someone to warm his bed and, for once, Megan wasn't interested.

When a half hour passed and Paul didn't return, Megan politely excused herself from the conversation she'd been having. She'd thought Paul was going to the bathroom or something, but she was starting to worry that something else was up. Knowing Paul would never leave Chloe, she went in search of the little girl.

As she began pressing her way through the crowd, Gage snuck up beside her. "Do you want to dance?"

"You mean you're willing to leave Becca's side for that long?"

Gage clutched his chest as if she'd wounded him. "I'm not that bad."

She snorted. "You really are."

"Now you sound like your sister." Gage was frowning, which only made Megan laugh more. "Okay, fine. She sort of told me not to come back for at least fifteen minutes under threat of bodily harm. Not that I'd mind exactly, but Chris might take issue if she pulls one of her self-defense moves on me in the middle of his wedding reception."

"I'm surprised she hasn't kicked your ass yet."

His eyes lit up, and he smirked. "Who says I don't like it when your sister gets a little frisky?"

"Eww!" Megan feigned revulsion. In truth, she was ecstatic that her sister had finally met her match. Gage fawned all over Rebecca, but he also didn't let her push him away. He refused to let her hide behind that wall she'd built up because of her and Megan's parents. Megan understood. She had walls of her own. That didn't mean she didn't want what Rebecca had finally found with Gage. Of course she did. Megan wanted to be loved and adored and cherished. She just didn't think it was in the cards for her.

"Come on. Please?" Gage pouted, making Megan laugh harder. He could be such a goof sometimes.

"Sure. Fine. Come on."

Gage danced with her for two songs, and then said he needed to go check on Rebecca. Megan knew her sister was more than capable of taking care of herself. But she also knew that it was useless telling Gage that. She would love to be a fly on their wall sometimes to watch her sister put the big burly football player in his place.

Shaking her head, Megan wandered over to the buffet tables. She'd eaten some of the smaller stuff earlier, but after dancing her stomach was demanding nourishment. Filling her plate, she looked around the room for some place to sit. She spotted Gage and Rebecca immediately, but they looked to be in the middle of what

Megan had learned to be foreplay for them—other people called it fighting. The last thing she wanted to do was get in the middle of that. If experience was anything to go by, they'd be sneaking up to their room soon to take out their aggression in other more sexual ways. Thank goodness her room was nowhere near theirs.

The bride and groom were across the room, eating and chatting with some of their guests, while Trent and his dad, Mike, were a few feet away. The Danielses were social people, and she liked them. A lot. It was just that she didn't know them very well. The two exceptions to that were Paul— who was MIA—and Chloe, so when she spotted the little girl with her grandmother, Megan strolled over to join them. "Mind if I sit?"

"Of course not."

"Me-gan, I'm eating chicken."

Megan smiled, and picked up her fork. "Is it good?"

Chloe nodded in an exaggerated fashion as she shoved another piece of chicken in her mouth. They'd been working on eating with utensils, and Chloe was decent at using the kiddie ones, but the normal-sized forks that they had at the reception were a bit much for her tiny hands.

"How have you been, Megan? I haven't seen you since Gage and Rebecca's wedding."

Megan swallowed the bite of food she was chewing before answering. "Good. Keeping busy. Rebecca talked me into taking some online classes."

"Oh, that's a great idea. Do you have a degree in mind?"

"Not really. I've always been interested in art, so maybe something to do with that. I don't know yet."

As if Marilyn and Megan weren't in the middle of a conversation, Chloe interrupted. "Guess what, Megan? I'm going to sleep in Grandma and Grandpa's room tonight. We're having a sweepover."

Not able to hide her smile, Megan reached for her drink. "You mean a sleepover? That sounds fun."

"Yep." Chloe was nodding again. "A sleep-over."

The next five minutes or so were spent listening to Chloe tell Megan all about the sleepover she was going to have with her grandparents, including the movie they were going to watch, and how she was going to get to stay up really, really late. It was impossible not to smile. Chloe put her whole heart into everything she did, and from what Megan had observed while living with Chloe and her father, the little girl was very much like her mother.

Those thoughts led right back to Chloe's father. Paul still hadn't returned, and Megan was beginning to worry about him. Had something happened with work? Or was it the wedding in general? The look on his face earlier reminded her of the one he'd get whenever she'd pass by his bedroom and catch him holding the picture of his wife in his hands. Paul was a great guy, and she didn't like seeing him hurting.

As Megan finished her food, she chatted back and forth with Marilyn. Every now and then, Chloe would interject a comment or share a story. When Mike Daniels, the patriarch of the Daniels family, approached the table, Megan decided it was time to go in search of Paul. She said her goodbyes, and kissed Chloe on the cheek, before going to find her sister.

Rebecca could, of course, read her like a book. "Oh no. What's wrong?"

Luckily, Gage wasn't around. "Nothing's wrong. Where's your husband?"

"He went to get me some more food. Stop deflecting."

"I'm not deflecting." It was sort of a lie, but not really. She knew that if she told her sister she was going to look for Paul, Rebecca would tell her husband and soon the entire Daniels clan would be off in search of him. Megan knew Paul wouldn't want that.

"Then why do you have that look on your face?"

"Maybe because I'm tired?"

"Uh-huh."

Not wanting to fight with her sister, Megan got to the point. "I just wanted to let you know that I'm heading up to my room. It's been a long day, and I'm ready to crash."

"Oh. Okay."

Rebecca looked torn for some reason. "What?"

"Nothing."

"Becca?"

"I saw the way you were looking at Paul earlier."

"Okay. And?"

"And . . ." She sighed. "Is something . . . you know, going on with you two?"

Megan's mouth fell open. She felt it, and she had no control of it at all. Her and Paul? Sure, he was attractive. Okay, more than attractive. But he'd never shown any interest in her that way, so even if she wanted to, which she kind of did, she wouldn't push herself on him like that. He and his family had taken Rebecca and Megan in, embracing them as part of the family. Plus, Paul wasn't over his wife. Megan knew that, above all else. "No. Why would there be? Besides, just because you're getting your freak on all over the place doesn't mean everyone else is."

Rebecca let out a relieved breath. "All right."

As if a lightbulb went off in her head, Megan narrowed her eyes at her sister. "What? You thought that just because he's a man and I live with him now that there has to be something going on?"

"I didn't say that."

"No. You didn't, but you implied it. I'm not a little kid anymore, Rebecca."

"I know. I'm so—"

Megan waved off her apology. "I'm going to my room. I'll see you tomorrow."

"Megan?"

Megan continued walking, and she was glad to hear Gage asking Rebecca what was wrong. He would keep her sister from following her. Megan knew she'd have to deal with Rebecca tomorrow, and that was fine. Right now, however, she needed some space. And to find Paul.

Something in the back of her mind told her to let it go—to leave him be. Megan pushed it aside and told herself that she just needed see that he was all right. Then she could go up to her room, find some cheesy romantic movie on television, and fall asleep.

Chapter 3

Megan looked everywhere she could think of, even walking outside to see if she could spot him talking on his cell or something, but she came up empty. He was nowhere to be found, and after twenty minutes of searching, she decided to head upstairs to her room. She figured he had to come back eventually, right?

As soon as Megan stepped inside her room, she kicked off her shoes. High heels made your legs look great, but they were killer on your feet.

Next to come off was her jewelry, and then finally, her dress. She'd dressed up more than usual for Chris and Elizabeth's wedding—more sophisticated, too. The dress she'd chosen was knee length, perfectly conservative, and had cute ruffled sleeves. To be honest, she was dressed more like her sister than she was herself. On most days, Megan preferred jeans and T-shirts, although she also liked skirts that showed off her legs. She might only be five foot five, but she had nice legs. Why not flaunt them?

She padded into the bathroom in her bare feet, figuring she'd go ahead and get ready for bed. When she emerged ten minutes later, she found the kitty cat pajamas she'd brought with her—since moving in with Paul and Chloe, she'd had to make adjustments to her sleepwear—and put them on.

Megan was about to crawl into bed and see what she could find on television when she heard what sounded like something crashing to the floor next door. Jumping up, Megan went to the door connecting her room with Paul's. He'd gotten them adjoining rooms to make it easier for Chloe, but since the little girl was with her grandmother, Megan knew the noise had to be coming from Paul.

"Paul? Are you all right over there?"

No answer.

"Paul?"

Still nothing.

Without stopping to think, Megan turned the handle on the door. It wasn't locked, and it opened easily.

She peeked inside, and what she saw had her scrambling across the room in a hurry. Paul was balanced—barely—against the dresser that supported the television. He looked as if he'd just come from the bathroom, and he was drunk. Not a little drunk, but can't-walk-straight-or-talk-without- slurring-his-words drunk. She'd never seen him like this.

"Meg-Meg-an." He sighed, and attempted to raise his arm toward her as she wrapped her arm around his waist. He was twice her size, and in his current condition, he was dead weight.

With little help from him, Megan moved him a few feet over to the bed. He plopped down so hard he bounced.

Once she was fairly sure he wasn't going to topple over, she glanced around the room. That was when she noticed the bottle of scotch on the coffee table. Most of the bottle appeared to be gone, and as there was no one else in the room, she had to assume he'd drunk it all himself.

"Will you be okay for a minute?"

"Su-sure." Paul smiled up at her, and she felt something flutter in the pit of her stomach.

Stop it, she told herself, as she marched back into her room to get some ibuprofen.

He was still where she left him when she returned with something for the headache he was bound to have come morning. She took one of the glasses provided by the hotel into the bathroom to fill it up with water, before returning to stand directly in front of him. "Here. Take these. If you drank as much as I think you did, then you are going to have one massive hangover in the morning."

Without comment, or protest, Paul downed the pills like they were candy. She handed him the water, and he drained that within seconds as well.

When he was done, she took the glass from him, and went to

refill it. Again, he drained it when she brought it back to him. Once he polished that one off, Megan set aside the empty glass. She couldn't help but wonder what had brought this on, although she was pretty sure she knew.

Megan was lost in thought when she felt Paul's fingers brush the outside of her legs. At first, she thought it was unintentional, but then he got bolder and flattened his palms so that they were bracketing her waist. She could feel the heat of his hands through her clothes. Megan knew she should push him away—he was drunk, after all—but she couldn't. She wanted to see what he would do.

"Always wear . . . most in . . . testing . . . p . . . jamaszzz."

She swallowed. He noticed her pajamas? Since when? "I like cats."

"Mmm." Paul slipped the pads of his thumbs under her shirt, and began making circles against her belly. It was incredibly intimate—more intimate than a lot of the sex she'd had. This felt different. It was different. This was Paul. He wasn't like the guys she normally hung out with.

"Paul?" Her voice cracked. Why did she feel as if this was her first time?

Again, he ignored her, and this time he leaned forward, pulling her closer. He lifted her shirt, exposing her stomach, and pressed his lips against her skin.

Megan reacted in the only way she could, by placing her hands on his head, lacing her fingers through his hair. What was happening?

Paul continued upward with his exploration—pushing her shirt out of the way as he went—until he reached her breasts. He cupped each one, filling both his hands, and began kneading and lifting them. Her nipples hardened, and she felt her body react in other ways. She knew she should stop him, but she couldn't. Megan had dreamt about this . . . how it could happen . . . but she'd never imagined it would be like this.

He eased her left breast into his mouth and began sucking on it as though it was his life source. Megan moaned. She was a woman who liked sex, and it had been almost five months. No matter how wrong she knew this was, if he was willing, she wasn't going to say no.

Hearing her pleasure, Paul released her breast, and leaned back on the bed, pulling her down with him. He cupped the back of her head, and a second later, his mouth was covering hers—his tongue pushing against her lips—begging, demanding entrance.

She opened her mouth, and his tongue surged inside, licking and caressing. Megan could taste the alcohol on his breath, but she also tasted him—something that was uniquely him. Even with Paul being drunk, she could tell he was a good kisser. He angled her head exactly the way he wanted it as he continued his assault on her mouth.

Megan felt him snake his other hand down her body and into her pajama bottoms. He didn't waste any time going for what he wanted. She gasped as his fingers found just the right spot between her legs. Her body was overheating. She just . . . she just . . .

Suddenly, he stopped kissing her and his hand stilled. The fingers that were tangled in her hair dropped onto the bed.

She opened her eyes and looked down at the man beneath her. His eyes were closed, his mouth opened, and he was snoring softly.

Well, that's a first.

Not ready to extract herself just yet, Megan reached up and caressed his face. He'd said *her* name. He'd known it was her. If nothing else, he'd known who she was. If she never got another opportunity to have him, she at least knew that he wasn't completely indifferent to her. He found her attractive—at least on some level.

Leaning down, she pressed a soft kiss to his parted lips before removing his hand from her pants. Megan knew she needed to go, but she didn't want to leave him with his feet hanging off the side of the bed.

It took some time, but eventually she was able to get his feet up onto the mattress and him into a position where she was confident he wouldn't fall off in the middle of the night. His head was near the foot of the bed, and his feet at the head, but it worked nonetheless.

Satisfied she'd done the best she could, Megan debated whether or not to sleep on the couch in his room or go back to her own. It was a hard decision, but she reasoned that he probably wouldn't want to be babied come morning, so reluctantly she went back to her room. The only concession was that she left the adjoining door open.

Curling up in her bed, Megan looked toward the open door. What would have happened if Paul hadn't fallen asleep? Unfortunately, she might never know.

***

It sounded like someone was scraping their nails on a chalkboard, and what Paul wanted more than anything was for them to stop. His head was pounding, and the noise wasn't helping. He cracked open one eye and quickly closed it again, as the sun shining through the window only made things worse. How much did he have to drink last night? He couldn't remember. From how he was feeling, though, it was a lot.

As gently as he could, he sat up. The pounding in his head increased slightly. He took a few deep breaths until he was sure his head wasn't going to fall off, and then made his way into the bathroom to relieve his bladder.

After taking care of business, he took a long look in the mirror. His eyes were bloodshot and he had dark circles beneath them. He looked as if he'd been to hell and back, and he felt that way, too.

Making his way back out into the room, he shielded his eyes as best he could as he walked across the room to close the heavy curtains. Once they were pulled tight, blocking the light from outside, the pounding in his head decreased a little more. Not willing to take the chance, however, Paul went to his bag and dug out some painkillers.

Downing them easily, he glanced at the clock. It was already after nine, which meant Chloe and his mom would be calling soon. He needed to clean himself up. Paul didn't want his daughter to see him like this.

Thoughts of his mom calling brought his mind back to what woke him in the first place. He went to retrieve his phone from on top of the nightstand near the bed, and sure enough, he had one missed call. It was from his partner, Janey Davis.

Dialing into his voice mail, he listened to her message. There had been another homicide last night. The third one in six months, all with the same MO: young woman, in her late twenties/early thirties, found in her home with her throat and wrists slashed.

With the first one, they'd thought it was a possible suicide, but the cuts were too clean and the angles wrong. Add to that the difficulty of slashing both one's throat and wrists. When the second victim turned up with identical cuts along her throat and wrists, it was obvious they had a killer on their hands. With victim number three, the higher-ups were going to start wanting answers.

Knowing he needed a shower before he called Janey back, Paul tossed his phone down on the bed, and went to grab some clothes. That's when he noticed the door between his and Megan's room was open. He strolled over to the door and peeked in. Megan was still asleep, curled up in her bed with the blankets tucked under her chin, and her hair in complete disarray.

A flash of his hand cupping the back of her head, her green eyes fully dilated staring back at him, filled his vision for a split second, and then it was gone. He shook his head, not understanding where the image came from. Nonetheless, it was enough to cause a reaction below his waist.

Knowing he needed some distance, Paul scurried out of the doorway and back into his room, quietly, yet firmly, closing the door behind him. He really needed that shower, and now he knew it was going to have to be a cold one—an ice-cold one, from the looks of it. Where had that image come from, and why now?

Paul felt much better after his shower, with one exception. He couldn't seem to get that image of Megan out of his head. It made no sense to him. She'd never looked at him that way before, and he'd never touched her like that. The flash made no sense to him, but he couldn't shake it. And every time it popped up, all his efforts to calm himself were for naught.

Knowing he needed a distraction, as soon as Paul was dressed, he dialed Janey. She picked up after the first ring. "Up late partying?"

He snorted, and felt it from his head to his toes. The medicine had helped his headache, but that didn't mean it had gone away completely. "Hardly."

"Oh, man. I need to show you how to party right, then, Daniels."

Paul chuckled. "Thanks for the offer, but I think I manage just fine."

She made a noise through the phone that sounded a lot like the raspberries he blew on Chloe's stomach from time to time. "Suit yourself. You know you're always welcome to come out with us anytime, though."

His partner and some of the other detectives from the station regularly invited him to come out with them after a shift, but he'd always made the excuse that he had to get home to Chloe. He had no idea how he would dodge that once she got older, but for the moment, it worked. None of them pushed, except for Janey, and he figured that was because she knew he was only using Chloe as an excuse.

Janey and Paul had been partners for five years. She'd been there when he'd lost Melissa, so she knew all the ups and downs he'd gone through. Janey knew more than most when it came to how much he still grieved for his wife, because she was there beside him every day.

Wanting to change the subject, Paul brought up the reason she'd called him in the first place. "Another victim turned up last night?"

"Yeah. Everything was the same as the other two, right down to the angle of the cuts. This guy knows what he's doing. Doc says he's confident now that the cuts were made by someone with a medical background."

It was something the medical examiner had brought up with the other two victims they'd found, but he'd been reluctant to go on record with it. Apparently, with this third victim, he felt he had enough evidence to support his theory.

"I suppose that narrows it down some. It will give us a place to start, at least."

"Anything is better than what we've had to go on so far."

That was the truth. This was one of the more frustrating cases he'd worked on in his fifteen years with the Indianapolis police department. There were no prints at the scene and no DNA left by the killer. There were no obvious signs anyone but the victim had been in the house at the time of death.

"When are you heading back?"

There was a knock on the door that joined his room to Megan's—the one he'd closed about thirty minutes ago. "We should be back tonight." He paused. "I've got to go. I'll call you when I get back and we can talk about a game plan."

"Don't sweat it. Enjoy your family time. I'll see you bright and early tomorrow morning."

The door cracked opened, and Megan peeked through. Her hair no longer looked as if she'd had someone running their fingers through it. Paul swallowed. "Okay. Sounds good."

Janey hesitated. "You sure you're all right?"

Paul's gaze never left Megan's. For some reason, he couldn't look away. "Yeah. I'm good."

Before Janey could interrogate him any more about his strange behavior, Paul disconnected the call. He set the phone down on the nightstand, feeling strangely uncomfortable as Megan opened the door further and stepped inside his room. She'd dressed, and was wearing an outfit he'd seen her in several times before. Why, then, did seeing her bare legs peeking out from beneath her skirt bring with it a flash of having those legs bracketing his hips?

"I didn't mean to interrupt your call."

He shrugged. "It's okay. Janey was only calling to give me an update on things."

"Oh."

When Megan didn't say anything more, he turned away from her and began to gather his things in preparation for their departure. "Are you about ready to go? I figure we can meet Chloe and my parents downstairs for brunch before we head out."

She didn't respond right away. "Paul?"

"Hmm?" He didn't look up, feeling the need to concentrate on what he was doing and not on her.

"Do you remember anything from last night?"

That made him stop. He looked over at the bed, and then to the coffee table where the bottle of scotch sat, almost empty. "I guess I drank a little too much."

She didn't comment.

Paul didn't remember getting into bed last night. And, given the door had been open this morning, he figured Megan, at the very least, must have checked on him. Maybe she'd even helped him to the bed. Either way, she was clearly concerned. "Thanks for checking on me. I usually don't go that overboard."

Megan took two steps toward him and then halted. He met her gaze and there was something there—behind her eyes—something he couldn't understand. Before he could ask her, however, she turned around and headed back toward her room. "I'll get my things and meet you in the hall."

He watched her disappear through the door, closing it behind her. For some reason, he felt as if he'd done something wrong, but for the life him, he couldn't figure out what it was.

Chapter 4

Megan tried her best to pay attention to what Chloe was saying as she sat next to her while they ate. As Megan had asked, Paul met her in the hallway outside their respective hotel rooms and they rode down in the elevator together. He didn't say anything on the way down, but she could feel him looking over at her from time to time. It was tense, and Megan knew why, even if he didn't.

They met Chloe and her grandparents downstairs in the lobby a little after ten. The little girl was wearing a new outfit Megan had never seen before. Megan guessed that Marilyn had been more prepared for last night's sleepover than she'd let on. It was cute, and very Chloe.

Paul loaded their luggage into the vehicle since he, Megan, and Chloe would be leaving immediately after brunch, and then joined the rest of the group in the hotel's restaurant. It didn't escape Megan's notice that Paul sat as far away from her as possible, even though the chair right beside her was empty. Was he remembering, or was it only in response to the obvious tension that was hanging in the air between them? She couldn't be sure.

Chloe recounted everything she could remember about the wedding, the reception and, of course, her sleepover with her grandparents, more than once. Each time, she added something she'd forgotten the time before. Concentrating on what the little girl said was difficult, though, since Megan's mind was still firmly set on what had happened with Paul the night before and what had—or hadn't—happened this morning.

She was acutely aware of Paul on the other side of the table. She knew every time he took a drink of his water, or rubbed at his temple, trying to relieve the hangover she knew he must have. It took everything in her not to say or do something, but she knew he probably wouldn't appreciate it. Especially in front of his family.

They were about halfway through their meal when Trent, Gage, and Rebecca joined them. Trent pulled out the chair beside Megan and plopped down. "Morning, sunshine."

Trent was a flirt, and normally Megan would laugh at his antics. She didn't have it in her this morning.

He, of course, noticed. "What happened, and whose ass do I need to kick?"

Luckily, he'd leaned in and said it so low that no one around them heard him. The last thing she needed was her sister picking up on her less than stellar mood. "Nothing. And no one's."

His frown told her just how much he didn't believe her.

She tried again. "Really. I just . . . didn't sleep all that well last night."

Trent looked her in the eye, still frowning. He looked over at Paul and then back to her as his frown increased. Everyone pegged Trent as the jokester of the family—he was the least serious of the four brothers, usually—but Trent was observant. He leaned in and whispered in her ear. "All right. But if you need to talk, I'm here, okay?"

Megan nodded. She tried to smile, to let him know she was really fine, but it was beyond weak.

When she glanced across the table after her brief exchange with Trent, she noticed Paul watching her. He was observant as well, but in a different way. But the look on his face wasn't that of a detached cop. Maybe Paul remembered more about last night than he was letting on. He'd never minded Trent flirting with her before.

Seconds after that thought crossed Megan's mind, Paul's expression cleared, and he turned to engage his father in conversation. It was as if nothing had happened. Whatever Paul's reaction to Trent's private chat with her was, he seemed to have successfully tucked it away.

The rest of the meal was relatively uneventful. That is, if you discount Gage not being able to take his hands off her sister. Before

Gage, she had never witnessed Rebecca giggle like a schoolgirl. Megan had no idea what Gage was doing underneath the table, but whatever it was had her sister in a very good mood. It wouldn't surprise Megan if they were late to check out of the hotel.

As everyone was saying goodbye to one another and preparing to set off, Marilyn walked over to give Megan a hug. "You take care of yourself, and if you need extra time to study, you make sure to speak up."

Megan didn't know what to say. Her mother had never been nurturing in the traditional sense—not nurturing at all, really. It had always been Rebecca who watched out for Megan—always her sister who made sure Megan had something to eat, or gave her that disapproving look when she made the wrong decision. When Megan was a teenager, she had sometimes loathed her sister for it. Okay, sometimes she still did, but after spending so much time with Chloe, Megan was beginning to understand.

"Call me when you get there?" Megan glanced over to find her sister standing next to her. Marilyn backed away, giving the sisters a moment together to say their farewells.

"Sure."

Rebecca frowned. "I'm sorry if I overstepped my bounds last night, but I always worry about you. I can't help it."

Megan had completely forgotten about what her sister had said the night before. Ever since she'd strolled into Paul's room last night to check on him, she'd had other things on her mind. "I'm good. Really."

"You know you can talk to me, right?" Rebecca paused. "And I'll try to just listen and not tell you what to do."

That made Megan chuckle.

Rebecca pursed her lips. "You're right. That's not going to happen. I can try, though."

Megan gave her sister a big hug. "I love you, Becca."

"I love you, too, Megan," Rebecca whispered as she hugged Megan back.

Gage came up beside Rebecca, and Megan released her hold on her sister. It took all of two seconds for Gage's arm to wrap firmly around his wife's waist, his hand resting on her barely visible baby bump. "Did you get some rest last night?"

Megan rolled her eyes. "Not you, too?"

He feigned innocence. "What?"

She shook her head, leaned up to give her brother-in-law a kiss on the cheek, and then turned to go. "Take care of my big sister."

"Megan?"

Megan should have known Rebecca wouldn't let her go that easily, so she glanced over her shoulder, and winked. "Don't do anything I wouldn't do."

Taking full advantage of the embarrassment she'd caused her sister, Megan walked swiftly across the room to where Paul was standing with Chloe and his parents. Before she could say anything, Paul did.

"Are you about ready to go?"

"Yep."

Paul said a quick goodbye to his parents, and allowed Chloe some last minute hugs to her grandparents, before the three of them headed for the car. He remained silent until he had Chloe buckled into the backseat, and was situated behind the wheel.

He maneuvered the car out of the parking lot and onto the road, driving toward the interstate. They had roughly a two-hour drive in front of them. Normally their trips between Ohio and his home in Indianapolis were filled with conversation. Sometimes they'd play *I Spy* with Chloe, if her nose wasn't in a book or playing with her Barbies. During those periods, she and Paul would normally pass the drive chatting about whatever came to their minds. Once, they'd ended up discussing the age-old argument of which came first, the chicken or the egg. It was silly, but it passed the time.

"You okay?"

She kept her eyes forward, not looking at him, and released a frustrated sigh. "I'm fine."

He didn't ask again, and she was glad. Every now and then, she felt his gaze on her, but she ignored it and appeared to be engrossed in watching the road. Megan didn't want to lie to him, but she had no idea how to even begin to bring up what had happened between them last night, and how much he might or might not remember about it. Add to that the fact that they were going to be spending the next two hours in a vehicle with little ears that could hear anything they said and any conversations that needed to happen weren't possible at the moment.

Besides, Megan had to figure out how in the world she was

going to bring up the subject. It wasn't as if she could come right out and say, 'Hey, do you remember making out with me on the bed in your hotel room last night?'

Okay, she could, but she didn't think that would go over really well. Paul was an incredibly private person. Although he was open with his daughter—and even Megan, to some degree—she was pretty sure if she confronted him with it straight out, he'd clam up. At best, he would shut her out. At worst, she'd be out of a job.

Paul was important to her, and after what had happened, Megan knew that on at least some level, he felt something for her, too. Maybe it was just physical attraction. It was possible. Megan knew that she was attractive to the opposite sex, and it might have only been that which had prompted last night's reaction from Paul.

Even as the thought crossed her mind, Megan didn't believe it. Yes, he had been trashed. No, he didn't remember what he'd done, so he probably wasn't thinking rationally.

Megan knew all of that, and she was ashamed to admit that she had personal experience with getting plastered and not remembering what you'd done the next morning. Paul wasn't like that, though, and she couldn't see him going up to some random woman and initiating something like that just because he was out of his mind drunk.

Maybe she was deluding herself, but she didn't want last night to have happened because she was convenient. She wanted him to want her for her, and she was positive that they would have had sex if he hadn't fallen asleep. Megan wanted more than just sex from Paul, however. The problem was she didn't know if he'd ever be able to give her more than that. He still loved his wife. How could Megan ever compete with that?

***

Paul tried his best to concentrate on the road and not the woman sitting beside him in the passenger seat. His hangover lingered, but he was able to ignore it for the most part. It wasn't nearly as bad as it had been a few hours ago. What he couldn't ignore was the growing feeling that something was bothering Megan, and that he'd somehow had a part in whatever it was.

The entire drive home, he tried his best to recall what had occurred the night before. He remembered going back to his room, removing the plastic covering off one of the glasses the hotel provided in the room, and sitting down on the small couch with his bottle of scotch. Gradually, as he drank, the pain had begun to dull. Memories of Melissa—their wedding, their life—flooded his vision, but he was detached from it. Seeing her face didn't bring with it the twisting in his gut.

He swallowed, and blinked several times, forcing his concentration back on the highway in front of him. The last thing he needed was to get distracted while driving.

With that in mind, Paul pushed through what he could remember of the previous night, and pressed his consciousness for what wasn't so readily available. He squinted as if that would somehow help, but all it did was serve to nudge his headache closer to the surface once more. How was it possible he couldn't remember? Not even as a teenager had he drunk enough to cause memory loss. Surely there had to be something he could do to bring what had occurred back to him.

He kept trying even though it only increased the pounding in his head. The image of Megan standing over him, her eyes full of desire, kept surfacing in his mind the harder he tried to push through the fog in his brain. For the life of him, he couldn't figure out where it had come from. Megan had never looked at him like that before. He was sure of it. But there was something about it that seemed more real than a dream. What happened last night?

By the time Paul pulled into his driveway, he wasn't any closer to solving the mystery. The last thing he could positively remember was picking up the bottle of scotch to pour himself yet another drink, and almost dropping it. At that point, he'd decided that maybe he'd better stop.

That's it. That was the last thing he remembered. What happened after that? At what point did Megan come into his room? Had she found him on the couch and helped him to the bed, or was he already there? Had he said something to her? Done something to offend her?

Or . . .

Paul didn't allow himself to finish that thought. Shaking his head as if that would somehow clear his mind, he went back to his previous contemplation. He and Megan weren't incredibly close, but he'd thought they'd become friends of sorts. They talked, were cordial to one another. She knew about Melissa, and about the drunk driver who killed her. Of course, she didn't know everything that had happened that night—why Melissa had been running to the store to get diapers at three in the morning.

Paul squeezed his eyes shut to block out the memory, and the guilt. No, Megan didn't know all the ugly details, but she knew enough.

Redirecting his thoughts back to Megan, some of the tension in his shoulders eased. There'd been a few nights he'd come home late, needing to unwind, and the two of them had sat around the kitchen table and played a few hands of poker together. Even after spending hours at a crime scene, talking to witnesses, and going over evidence, she could make him laugh. Megan was . . . fun.

"Can I get out now, Daddy?"

Paul glanced in the rearview mirror at his daughter. She was shifting impatiently in her booster seat. Although Chloe knew how to get out of her seat, he'd drilled it into her that she wasn't allowed to unbuckle herself without asking first or him telling her it was okay. It was a safety thing, and the last thing he wanted was something to happen that would cause him to lose Chloe, too. He didn't think he could bear that.

"Yes, you may get out." The second he gave his approval, Chloe had the seat belt unfastened, and was darting out the door toward the house.

Megan opened her car door and went around to the back of the vehicle to start unloading the luggage. Sighing, Paul joined her while Chloe ran around in circles in the yard, releasing her pent-up energy.

They worked together to unload the bags. Once everything was out of the trunk, Megan hitched her bag over her shoulder, and began walking toward the house. Paul thought about stopping her, but then again, what would he say? Sorry if I said something I shouldn't have last night? That didn't sound like much of an apology. Besides, he was still perplexed by the flash of her heated gaze.

He let her go, and picked up his own bag, as well as Chloe's. "Come on, Chloe. Let's get inside and I'll get us some lunch."

"But I'm not hungry!"

"Chloe." Paul was not in the mood to deal with one of her tantrums.

Her lower lip pushed forward, and she crossed her arms as she stomped toward the house. Paul shook his head and followed her inside.

Lunch was a quiet affair. Chloe was still pouting because he'd made her come inside, and Megan appeared to be completely engrossed in a book she was reading. It gave him time to think about what he needed to say to her, because he knew he had to say something.

"May I go play now, Daddy?"

Paul glanced down at Chloe's plate. Most of her food was gone, so he nodded, and opened his mouth to give her the okay. Apparently, his nod was enough, as Chloe didn't wait for him to utter the words before she took off, running up the stairs to her room.

Once Paul was confident they were alone, he turned toward Megan. Again, he opened his mouth to speak, but nothing came out. Not because Megan subverted him in any way, but because he still had no idea what he was going to say to her.

She looked up at him and caught him staring. "Something wrong?"

"No." He shook his head and stood, taking his plate to the sink. Why was this so difficult?

"Oh." She almost sounded disappointed. "Were you planning to go into work today?"

He glanced at her over his shoulder as he rinsed off his plate. "No. Why?"

Megan shrugged. "I thought maybe I'd head to the mall if you're going to be here."

Paul smiled, and it felt as if a weight was lifted off his shoulders. "Sure. Go. Have fun."

She paused as if she was going to say something, but she must have changed her mind. "All right. I'll run up and say goodbye to Chloe before I leave." At the door, she paused, and faced him. "Did you need me to pick up anything while I'm out?"

Something clenched in his chest. "No. I'm . . ." He cleared his throat. "I'm good."

"Okay. See ya in a few hours." She smiled at him as she skipped through the doorway, and bounded up the stairs.

Alone, Paul placed his hands on the counter, and looked out the window overlooking the sink into the backyard. He'd been granted a few hours, and he needed to use them wisely. He ran over the events of last night in his mind once more. But like before, everything went blank before Megan's appearance in his room.

He heard her come back downstairs, and shortly after that, the front door opened and closed. The sound brought to mind earlier that morning when he'd peeked into her room to check on her—of her lying in bed—and again he felt those same stirrings in his groin.

Where was this coming from, and why now? Megan had lived with them for months, and not once had he reacted this way. Sure, she dressed a little sexy sometimes, and of course he noticed. How could he not? But she was twenty-three and single. Wasn't that what twenty-three-year-olds did?

Paul rubbed his eyes with the palms of his hands and sighed. He had to stop thinking about it. Later, after Chloe went to bed, he'd talk to Megan. Maybe, after he got some answers, the strange reaction his body was having would go away.

Needing a distraction, Paul finished cleaning up and made his way upstairs to find Chloe. She was in her room, playing with her dolls.

He knocked on her door, and she looked up. "Mind if I join you?"

Chloe seemed to consider his offer for a second, and then picked up one of her dolls, handing it to him. "You can be Ken."

So for the next few hours, Paul sat up in Chloe's room playing dolls with her and having a tea party, all the while trying not to think about a certain conversation he needed to have with her nanny.

Chapter 5

Megan ran her hand along the rack of clothes until her fingers brushed against something she liked. Removing it from the rack so that she could get a better look, she held it against herself, and smiled. She'd long finished gathering the personal care items she needed. This wasn't about need at all. This was about want.

On the long drive back to Indianapolis, Megan had done a lot of thinking—both about the previous night and that morning. Paul wanted her. At least, on some level he did. She was convinced of that. He'd said her name. He'd known it was her. Not his dead wife.

Plus, that morning at breakfast—that look he gave her—when he saw Trent whispering in her ear. Had he remembered something? The vibe coming off him had been one of annoyance. It wasn't as if Trent had never flirted with her before. Usually, he laughed it off the same as she did. Trent was only being Trent. Something had changed. At least, she hoped it had.

With all the thinking she'd done, Megan decided to play to her strengths. Maybe the mature thing would be to sit down and talk to him about what happened, but she was afraid Paul would try to dismiss it. Megan couldn't take that.

During the four months Megan had known him, she'd never seen him go out on a date—never seen him take interest in any woman. From what she gathered from little things he and his family said, Paul didn't date. At all.

Of course, Megan didn't know if that extended to booty calls or not, but she had a feeling it did. Paul didn't strike her as a one-night-stand kind of guy, which was another reason she thought what happened in the hotel might mean more than just him scratching an itch.

Tossing the pajamas over her arm, Megan rifled through the racks until she found two more sets of cute pajamas that she liked, before checking out. If Paul found her attractive, she was going to use that to her advantage. A girl had to try, right?

It was dark by the time she got home. She smiled when she saw that Paul had left the kitchen light on for her. It was amazing how little things like that could make her feel warm inside. No one but Rebecca had ever cared enough about her to leave the light on. Not even her parents.

As she reached the bottom of the stairs, she could hear voices coming from the second floor, and realized that Paul must be giving Chloe her bath. The little girl was becoming more and more independent and she wanted to bathe herself, but Paul insisted she was still too young to be left alone. As a compromise, after running the bath water to the correct temperature, Paul would sit on top of the toilet seat and read a magazine while Chloe had her bath. Megan was waiting for the day when Chloe would cease to allow that much from her father. She was growing up. It was only a matter of time before she became fully aware of the differences between boys and girls.

With extra care, Megan tiptoed up the stairs so she didn't disturb them. She should have known better than to think she could pass by the bathroom undetected. Paul glanced up, and Megan paused, waiting. For what, she didn't know. Their gazes held, and his forehead furrowed in concentration.

Her heart began to pound. Did he remember?

Chloe squealed, breaking their connection. He averted his gaze back to his daughter, and Megan took the opportunity to make her escape.

Once inside her room, Megan closed and locked the door. She rushed over to her bed and dumped out the contents of her bags. Putting everything away except for the three new pajamas, she considered her options.

The first one had a cute little T-shirt type of top and boxer short bottoms. They were blue with bunny rabbits all over them. She remembered the way Paul went right for her legs, which was why she'd gone for all shorts-type selections.

Her second pajama set was more grown-up looking than she normally went for, but she wanted to be prepared for anything. Megan had no idea what Paul liked. It was lavender and had a spaghetti-strap top that dipped low. She didn't have a lot up top, not really, but she wasn't flat either. The bottoms that came with the outfit were much shorter than the others.

Megan picked up the last outfit. The bottoms were pink, with little red and white hearts—most likely left over from Valentine's Day. It was paired with a simple light pink tank top. She'd liked it as soon as she saw it. Megan only hoped Paul didn't think it was too much, with the hearts and all.

Deciding to take a chance, Megan put on the tank top and heart shorts. Aside from the hearts, it wasn't all that unlike what she normally wore to bed. She was hoping that while he'd notice, he wouldn't immediately become suspicious. He was a cop, after all.

After taking a look in the mirror, Megan opened her bedroom door, and peeked out into the hallway just in time to see Chloe barreling toward her. Megan bent down to brace herself for impact. Even then, she had to put a hand down on the floor to keep from falling backward.

"Are you going to help Daddy read me a bedtime story?"

"I can, if you want me to."

Chloe nodded, took hold of Megan's hand, and led her down the hall to her room, leaving Paul to follow. Megan glanced over her shoulder, and found Paul smiling. She smiled back. This was the Paul she knew—the one who loved his daughter above all else.

Inside her bedroom, Chloe released Megan's hand and walked over to her bookshelf. She selected the book she wanted and then climbed into her bed. Paul sat down on one side of Chloe, and Megan on the other. They each took turns reading a page until the little girl was yawning and rubbing her eyes.

Paul closed the book, and Chloe started to whine.

"Time for bed."

"But, Daddy . . ."

He didn't say anything, but his look spoke volumes. Chloe lowered her eyes and huffed a little, before lying down and closing her eyes.

Paul leaned over and kissed her on the forehead. "Good night, sweetpea."

Chloe kept her eyes closed tight. "Good night, Daddy."

Megan followed suit, giving Chloe a kiss on the forehead, and saying good night.

The little girl yawned. "G'night, Meg-an."

Megan smiled and ambled out of the room with Paul. She was so caught up in the bedtime ritual they'd taken part in that she was completely caught off guard when Paul reached out, stopping her from continuing.

"Could we talk?"

She met his gaze, and her heart began to race. It wasn't what she saw in his eyes, it was what she didn't. He had what she called his "cop face" on. His expression was devoid of emotion, and he looked as if he were gearing up for a battle of some sort. Was that because he'd remembered what had happened between them? Megan didn't know, and she wasn't sure she was ready to find out.

Unfortunately, running wouldn't help her cause, so she answered in the only way she could. "Sure."

He nodded and turned abruptly toward the stairs. She followed him to the kitchen.

Paul didn't sit down, so Megan didn't either. Instead, she stood right inside the doorway with her back against the wall. She might even have lifted her leg a little and arched her back, to make her chest stick out a bit more.

He strolled over to the far side of the room and leaned back against the counter, facing her. For the longest time, he didn't say anything, and neither did Megan. She was tempted, but she wanted to find out what he'd say first.

After a long, drawn-out silence, Paul cleared his throat. "I wanted to talk to you about last night."

Megan nodded, afraid that if she spoke, she'd give something away.

Paul took a deep breath and looked her in the eye. "I wanted to say that I'm sorry."

She paled. "You're sorry?"

He nodded. "Yes."

Megan felt sick to her stomach, and she saw something flash across his face before he schooled his features. "You remembered?"

Paul shook his head. "No. And I'm sorry about that, too. I can't tell you the last time I blacked out like that from drinking too much. It shouldn't have happened, and I'm sorry."

The churning in Megan's belly subsided a little, but anxiety rapidly took up residence. "So you don't remember what happened?"

She said it more to herself than to him, but he answered her anyway. "No."

Megan swallowed and pushed herself off the wall, walking toward him. He watched her with an eagle eye. She knew he was wondering what she was doing, and to be honest, she was wondering the same thing herself.

When she came to a stop in front of him, she stood closer than they'd ever been before, with only one exception. He looked down at her, and she hoped he liked the view that included a nice display of the tops of her breasts. Just thinking about Paul and her breasts together brought back the memory of his hands and mouth on them. Her body heated at the memory.

Licking her lips, she searched his eyes for any recollection. "You kissed me."

His eyes grew wide with shock, and he tensed. Other than that, he didn't react in any way to her bombshell.

Megan decided to push the envelope a little by filling in the gaps for him. She wanted to touch Paul, but she was afraid it would spook him. "I heard a noise, so I went to check on you. You'd bumped into the dresser, and almost knocked the television over, so I helped you to the bed."

The vein in his throat pulsed rapidly, but he remained silent.

"You don't remember any of this?"

"No." It sounded as if it were a struggle for him to say that one word.

She sighed and reached up to touch his face. Paul leaned back, evading her hand. Megan tried to hide how much that hurt, but she knew he saw it anyway.

Before she could regain her equilibrium, Paul sidestepped her, putting some distance between them. She wanted to grab hold of his arm, and pull him back to her, but she didn't. It would have been too much to ask for him to take her in his arms and pick up where they'd left off.

***

He'd kissed her? That was impossible. But even as that thought crossed his mind, Paul knew she was telling the truth. Once again, the sight of Megan perched above him filled his mind. This time, it took on a whole new context.

Megan wasn't lying.

Paul flexed his fingers, unsure what to do with himself. He was in uncharted territory. This wasn't like the woman he'd picked up in that club four years ago. He knew Megan. She lived in his house, for crying out loud. It wasn't as if he could up and leave.

Chancing a look at Megan, he could see the hurt in her eyes. He could tell she was trying to hide it, but she wasn't doing a very good job. He felt like a cad. She'd said he'd kissed her, not the other way around. *He'd* initiated the kiss. *He'd* changed things between them. It was his fault.

He closed his eyes, and took a deep breath before opening them again. Megan looked so small as she stood there in his kitchen in her shorts and tank top. His heart was beating wildly in his chest, as he knew what he said next would hurt her. It was the last thing he wanted, but he knew it needed to be done. He still loved his wife—would always love his wife. There was no future for him with anyone else.

"I was out of line. I'm sorry." He paused. "I still love my wife, Megan. Nothing can happen between the two of us."

She was quiet for several seconds, and then he saw her press her lips together and straighten her shoulders. "Why?"

Paul looked at her with slight disbelief. "Did you miss the part about me still loving my wife?"

"No. I didn't miss it. I know you still love Melissa." Hearing his wife's name twisted the knife that seemed to be permanently lodged in his gut.

When he didn't add anything, she continued. "Why does that mean nothing can happen between us? Don't you think she'd want you to move on? Find someone else?"

"I can't." Paul met Megan's gaze and shook his head. "I'm sorry. You have no idea how sorry I am, but I just can't."

Without giving Megan time to respond, Paul said good night, and bounded up the stairs. He was running away, he knew that, but it was either that or break down in front of her—and to Paul, that would have been worse. Talking about Melissa to Chloe was one thing. Discussing her with Megan was something altogether different. Paul didn't want to think about why that was, exactly. He knew he might find answers he didn't want to know.

Paul woke up the next morning feeling as if he hadn't slept at all. It had taken him hours of tossing and turning before he'd finally drifted off, and then when he did, he was tortured by images of Melissa *and* Megan. In one dream, he'd been lying in bed with his wife, talking . . . kissing. It was a pleasant dream, and one he had often.

But as he leaned in to give Melissa a kiss, the dream changed and it was no longer Melissa in front of him. It was Megan. He'd woken with a start, panting, and stiff as a board.

Sleep was impossible after that.

The smell of coffee filled the kitchen as Paul pulled Melissa's mug out of the cabinet. He'd found it in the dishwasher the day after her funeral, and he'd been using it ever since for his morning cup of coffee. It made him feel close to her somehow, as if a part of her was still with him when he started his day.

Before his wife died, Paul always drank his coffee black. He figured if he was going to drink the caffeinated beverage then it shouldn't be doctored to make it taste like something else. That was before, though.

Paul opened the refrigerator and removed the milk, setting it on the counter. Once the coffee pot stopped percolating, he filled his glass three quarters of the way, and then topped it off with milk— just like Melissa used to drink it.

After putting the milk away, Paul sat down at the kitchen table and picked up the morning paper he'd snatched from the driveway as soon as he came downstairs. This was his routine, and routines were good. Unfortunately, Paul couldn't focus on the words in front of him. It was as if he were reading some foreign language instead of English.

Frustrated, he tossed the paper down on the table, and massaged his temples. What was happening to him?

The sound of footsteps on the stairs caused him to glance up. Seconds later, Megan appeared. She was still wearing her pajamas from the night before. The bottoms only covered about a quarter of her leg, which meant there was plenty left over for him to see. Megan wasn't tall, but her legs were long, and for a moment, Paul wondered what it would feel like to have them wrapped around his hips.

Startled by the direction of his thoughts, Paul shot up out of his chair and nearly spilled what was left of his coffee.

"You okay?"

Paul noted the concern in her voice. Unfortunately that wasn't helping whatever it was that seemed to be happening to him. To them. No, to him. There was no *them*. "Yeah, I'm fine."

She looked at him intently for a long moment, and then strolled past him to the counter to get herself some coffee. Paul clenched his eyes closed, and forced himself to breathe. He needed to get out of there.

Clearing his throat, he turned to face her, but she had her back to him. Unfortunately, that gave him a clear view of her backside. He averted his eyes quickly as his body began to betray him. "I'm going to head to work early this morning to catch up on some paperwork."

Megan turned around, holding her coffee against her chest. His eyes narrowed in on her breasts. "All right."

He knew he needed to go—get out of there, but his feet refused to move.

"Paul?"

"Yes?"

She laid her cup down on the counter, and stalked toward him. Okay, maybe stalked was too strong a word, but that was how he felt at the moment. His feet were glued to the floor by some unknown force, and she was walking toward him. His brain was telling him to run as fast as he could in the opposite direction, but his limbs weren't cooperating.

Megan came to a stop in front of him. Without pause, she placed her right hand in the center of his chest, and met his gaze. "Why are you running away from me?"

He swallowed. "I'm not."

By the look in her eyes, she knew he was lying. "Yes, you are."

"Megan . . ."

"Paul."

Wrapping his fingers around her wrist, he removed her hand from his chest, and took a step back. "I told you last night that this couldn't happen, and I meant it."

"I'm not agreeing to that." He could hear the stubborn determination in her voice.

"You're going to have to."

"Why? Give me one good reason why this can't happen."

Her eyes were fierce. He could see the fight in her. "I'm still in love with my wife. I can't . . . I can't give you anything."

Megan's eyes softened a little. "I know you still love Melissa."

"Good. Then you understand why nothing can happen between us."

She stepped closer, eating up the space he'd put between them. "No. I don't. Why does that mean you can't give me anything?"

Megan leaned forward, brushing her breasts against his chest, causing him to suck in a breath. "What are you doing?"

"Proving a point."

"Which is?"

She looked up at him. "You want me, Paul Daniels, whether you want to admit it or not."

Before he could respond, Megan leaned back, gave him a coy smile, and slid around him. She disappeared up the stairs, leaving him dumbfounded. He didn't want another relationship. Not with Megan. Not with any woman.

He did want her, though. She was right about that. Or at least, his body did. The evidence was visible if anyone happened to walk into the kitchen at that moment.

But it didn't change anything.

Leaning his head back against the wall, Paul took several deep breaths until he felt his body was back under control. Work. That was what he needed to take his mind off Megan and whatever was happening between them. There was a serial killer out there, and he knew from experience that whoever it was wouldn't stop until they were caught.

Before his thoughts were invaded once again by Megan, Paul raced up the stairs to get ready for work. Megan was young. She probably just had a crush on him or something. It would pass.

He repeated that mantra all the way to the station, trying to convince himself that it was true. Paul didn't want to think about what it would mean if it wasn't. Megan lived in his house, and he hadn't been with a woman in nearly five years. He didn't know how long he'd be able to resist her temptations. Paul didn't want to hurt her. He cared about Megan, but he also knew he could never give her anything more than his body, and she deserved so much more than that.

Chapter 6

Paul breathed a sigh of relief when he entered the station. People were milling around, going about their tasks even at the early hour. It was familiar. Safe.

He bristled. *Safe*. Since when had that become what was most important to him? He used to be willing to take risks. Used to do it all the time for his job. How many people had told him and Melissa that they would never last, yet they'd been married for more than ten years when that drunk driver ran her off the road. More than that, they'd been happily married. With a newborn baby.

Chloe had changed things for them, but not in a bad way. They'd cherished the little girl who had blessed their lives. Melissa had difficulties getting pregnant, but after five years of trying, they'd brought a beautiful baby girl into the world. Unfortunately, Melissa had only been part of Chloe's life for six months before she was taken away from both of them.

Thinking about Chloe brought him back to Megan. As he sat down at his desk, Paul replayed the conversation he'd had with his daughter's nanny. He'd had women come on to him over the years—more so since becoming a widower—but none of them had sparked anything in him. This morning was different. There had been a spark, and he wouldn't lie to himself. It scared him on a deep and primal level.

After Megan sauntered out of the kitchen, it had taken a good ten minutes for his erection to go down. No woman had done that to him with such ease since Melissa. She used to be able to look at him, and he'd be up for whatever she had in mind.

"You're here early."

Paul looked up as his partner slid into the desk across from him. "I wanted to go over the new files."

Janey glanced down at his desk and raised one eyebrow. "Were you expecting those files to magically appear in front of you?"

He shrugged and reached for the stack of folders on the corner of his desk. "Very funny, Davis."

Leaning back, she gave him a once-over. "Something happen at your brother's wedding I should know about?"

"It was a wedding." He tried to concentrate on the report in front of him.

"That doesn't mean nothing happened."

Paul continued to look down at the files as if they held all the secrets in the universe.

When he didn't elaborate, Janey sighed. "You're sure?"

"I am." He looked up and gave her the best smile he could muster. "So catch me up. What's the latest on the newest victim?"

Janey spent the next hour bringing Paul up to speed on the case. He'd only been gone for four days, but there had been a lot of new developments within that time. This newest victim was twenty-eight-year-old Casey McMurphy. She was a flight attendant, newly married, and had no children.

The similarities between this victim and the first two were few. Apart from each of the women being around the same age, and all being home alone at the time of the murders, nothing else matched up. They'd been searching for a connection between the first two victims, but had come up short thus far. Paul was hoping they would be able to find something to tie the three women together. Once they knew how the killer was selecting the victims, they would have a better chance at catching him or her.

In his absence, Janey and one of the other detectives had interviewed Mr. McMurphy, but Paul wanted to see the crime scene for himself. Throughout the drive, Janey kept glancing over at him.

"What's on your mind, Davis?"

"I was going to ask you the same question, Daniels."

He pulled into the McMurphys' drive and turned off the engine. Paul opened his door and exited the vehicle without a word to his partner.

Janey sighed and unfastened her seat belt. "Fine. I get it. You don't want to talk about it."

They strolled up to the house in silence, and Paul took the time to observe his surroundings. It was a nice neighborhood. He heard dogs barking from the house next door and there was a sprinkler going a few houses down. Nothing stood out to him as being out of the ordinary.

Paul rang the doorbell, and after several minutes, a young woman answered. She looked to be around Megan's age, but she was shorter. The woman was even wearing a short skirt, showing off her trim, athletic legs.

He quickly put a stop to the direction his mind was heading. He was working, and he needed to concentrate. Whatever was going on, or not going on, with Megan and himself wasn't what he needed to be focusing on at the moment.

"Hello?"

They flashed their badges. "Is Mr. McMurphy home?"

The woman froze for a moment, and then seemed to come out of it, stepping back to allow them inside. "H-he's in the kitchen. Let me . . . let me go get him."

Without another word, she scurried out of sight. Paul gave a questioning look to his partner, and she shrugged, letting him know that she didn't know who the woman was either.

While they waited, Paul looked around. The house was simple, but nice. In fact, what stood out to him the most was the lack of clutter or anything else that made the house looked lived in. Granted the McMurphys didn't have any children, but there should still be evidence of the two people living there. If there was, he couldn't see it from where he stood.

Evan McMurphy walked into the room looking as if he hadn't slept in days. His eyes were bloodshot, and he had dark circles beneath them. "Detectives?"

Janey took the lead. "We're sorry to bother you again so soon, Mr. McMurphy, but I wanted to introduce you to my partner, Detective Daniels. He was out of town this weekend, but he and I will be handling your wife's case."

Paul extended his hand. "Hello, Mr. McMurphy."

Evan McMurphy shook Paul's hand and nodded.

"Detective Daniels wanted to get a look at the crime scene for himself. It shouldn't take more than a few minutes."

"Sure. Of course."

Janey led Paul down a long hallway to the back of the house. The sunroom remained blocked with crime scene tape. Although the forensic unit had already been through the room from top to bottom, it hadn't been cleaned yet.

As he walked around the room, Paul noted the small similarities between this murder and the others. Opening up the file, he compared the position of the victim's body with the others. The killer not only positioned each of the bodies in a similar way, but where the women were placed in the room was the same. It was almost as if the killer had used a tape measure to find the exact center, and place the body in that spot. "Whoever this person is, they are big on details."

His partner nodded. "I agree. It does look like this one may have struggled a bit more than the others, though." She pointed to a vase lying on the floor—its contents spilled out on the beige carpet. With the other two victims, nothing had been out of place. There had been no sign of a struggle at all. It was as if whoever it was walked in, did their business, and left.

Paul worked his way over to the large French doors along the back wall. There was no sign of forced entry. He opened the door, checking for any evidence that the lock had been picked. There were some scratches, but they could have come from general wear.

He shut the door, and found Janey looking over the contents on the desk. "Hopefully she fought her attacker enough for us to get some DNA."

After speaking to Mr. McMurphy again, he officially introduced them to his friend, Sarah Cartwright, although Paul got the impression there might be more there than just friendship. At least, on her part. Then again, he might be seeing things that weren't really there. The whole thing with Megan was throwing him off, and he didn't like it.

He and Janey canvassed the neighborhood, talking to anyone who was home, hoping someone had seen a stranger lurking or a car hanging around prior to the murder. As with the others, no one appeared to have seen or heard anything unusual that night or anytime leading up to it.

Returning to the car, Paul pulled out of the drive and turned toward the station. "What do we know about Mr. McMurphy?"

Janey shrugged. "Early thirties. Works as a CPA downtown, and at a local community college teaching accounting two nights a week. I didn't get any bad vibes when I spoke to him the first time. Or this time, for that matter."

Paul nodded. "What about the woman?"

She cocked her head to the side and raised her eyebrow. "My first impression?"

"Of course."

"I think she has a crush."

"So you don't think there's anything going on there?"

Instead of answering him, she countered with her own question. "Do you?"

He shrugged. "I don't know. Maybe."

They spent the rest of the drive lost in their own thoughts. Paul was beginning to get frustrated. There were three dead women and little to no evidence to lead them to the killer. He knew that sooner or later whomever it was would slip up and leave something behind that would tie them to the crimes—they always did. Paul only hoped more women didn't have to die before that happened.

***

Megan spent her day playing with Chloe and getting some general housework done. When she'd first moved in, Paul was reluctant to let her do much of anything around the house. He was fiercely independent, and for whatever reason, he felt it wasn't Megan's responsibility to do anything beyond taking care of Chloe.

Chloe was much like her father. She liked to sit in the corner and read her picture books or play on her LeapPad. It left Megan twiddling her thumbs with nothing to do. When she'd explained this to Paul one night, he admitted that it might be helpful if she could do some minor house cleaning in her downtime. He still did his own laundry, but she took care of her own and Chloe's, along with vacuuming, dusting, and cleaning all but the master suite. That was Paul's space, and she got the impression very early on that it was off-limits. It was even rare for Chloe to go in there.

Even with the added chores, it didn't always keep her busy

during the hours Paul was at work. That's why she'd decided to go back to school. Two days a week, she would log on to the school's website, and download her assignments. Eventually, if she decided to pursue an arts degree, she'd have to take some classes on campus as well, but by then Chloe would be in school.

There were a lot of things Megan was starting to regret about the last five years of her life. Growing up, her sister, Rebecca, had constantly been on her case about school. When Rebecca left for college, she had called Megan every day to make sure she stayed on top of her classes and wasn't slacking off.

Back then, Megan hadn't appreciated what her sister did. In fact, she'd resented her for it most of the time, and had only done what Rebecca asked because she hadn't wanted to deal with the fallout. As soon as Megan graduated, though, she knew she had to get away. Unlike her sister, Megan had no interest in continuing her education, which is why as soon as she graduated, she took off with the first guy who offered.

For five years, she bounced from guy to guy, hoping that one of them would love her, but they never did. Not for long, anyway. No matter how sweet they were in the beginning, they always showed their true colors eventually.

When she caught her last boyfriend in his friend's garage snorting cocaine, she'd had enough. After growing up with her parents, and her dad's drug problem, she refused to be in a relationship with someone who did illegal drugs. Megan could party with the best of them, but even she had her limits.

Moving in with Paul and Chloe had changed Megan's life. It was a fresh start—one she desperately needed. She moved into the guest bedroom, stopped partying, and concentrated on herself for a while.

Megan closed the window on her computer screen, and went to check on Chloe. She found her exactly where she'd left her over an hour before— sitting on her neon pink beanbag in the corner of her room, reading. "Chloe?"

The little girl reluctantly looked up from her book.

"Are you hungry? I can make you a snack."

She appeared to consider the question for a moment. "Can I have app- ules? And teese?"

They walked . . . well, Megan walked and Chloe hopped, down

the stairs to the kitchen.

Before Megan handed the food over to Chloe, she worked with the little girl on her pronunciation. Apples were easy once Megan sounded it out for her slowly. Cheese was a little more difficult.

"T-eese."

"No. Listen to the first part of the word closely. Ch. Ch. Can you do that?"

"Ch."

Megan smiled. "Good. Now add it to the rest of the word. Ch-eese."

Chloe repeated the word exactly how Megan said it. "Ch-eese."

"Great job!" Megan handed the little girl the apples and cheese, and gave her a kiss on the top of her head, before taking a seat on the other side of the kitchen island.

Chloe dug into the cheese and apples, holding one in each of her little hands. "Meg-an, why doesn't my daddy have a girlfriend?"

Megan choked on the drink of water she was swallowing. "Um. I don't know."

"Allie says that her daddy has a girlfriend. And Debbie says if there is no mommy that daddies have to have a girlfriend to take care of them."

Not knowing how to respond, Megan said nothing for several minutes.

"You take care of me and Daddy. Are you Daddy's girlfriend?"

Megan's chest clenched. "No. I'm not."

Chloe frowned. "But . . . what if I want you to be?"

Strolling over to Chloe, Megan brushed the hair back over the little girl's shoulders, tucking it behind her ears. "It doesn't work that way, honey."

"Why not?"

Megan sighed and gave Chloe a small smile. No matter how much Megan wanted to be exactly that, Paul's girlfriend, it wasn't only up to her. "It just doesn't."

Chloe opened her mouth, ready to ask another question, but luckily the phone rang, interrupting the inquisition. It was Marilyn Daniels, Chloe's grandmother. After a brief conversation with Paul's mother, Megan handed the phone over to Chloe. Within minutes, the two were involved in a conversation that revolved around summer vacation.

Giving them a little privacy, Megan busied herself cleaning up the remains of Chloe's snack. Chloe was set to spend a month this summer with her grandparents—two weeks with Paul's parents, and two weeks with her mother's parents. Paul had brought it up a couple of weeks ago, letting Megan know she'd be free to visit her sister or go on vacation herself during that time.

Megan had thought about it. She had a little money saved up since Paul paid for almost all of her living expenses. Even if she didn't have money, she knew Gage, her new brother-in-law, would pay for a plane ticket if she asked.

Money wasn't the problem. The problem was that she didn't want to leave Paul. Sure, she'd love to spend some time with Rebecca, but her sister had Gage. Megan knew he'd take care of Rebecca and make sure she had everything she needed. He practically worshipped the ground Rebecca walked on. Plus, the two of them were like a couple of animals. She wasn't sure she could take being in the same house with them for a month while they were all over each other. Especially when she was currently sex deprived herself.

Chloe hung up the phone and raced over to stand beside Megan. "Can I go play?"

"Sure." Without wasting another second, Chloe took off up the stairs, leaving Megan alone.

Tossing the rag she'd been using into the sink, she followed Chloe. Maybe come the end of May, Megan wouldn't have to worry about whether or not she should leave and give Paul his space or not. Maybe, just maybe, a certain five-year-old would get her wish and her daddy would get a girlfriend.

***

Paul pulled into his driveway a little before six. He could have worked longer. He could have worked all night, since they were no closer to solving the case than they had been this morning, but he didn't want Megan to think he was running away. Again. That, and he'd only missed tucking Chloe into bed a handful of times over the last four-and-a-half years. He wasn't willing to sacrifice precious time with his daughter because he didn't know how to deal with his sudden attraction to her nanny.

Megan was in the kitchen prepping dinner when he ambled through the door. He cleared his throat to get her attention. "Hey."

She looked up, smiling, the same as she always did when he came home from work. "Hey."

He relaxed a little when she went back to what she was doing and made no mention of what had happened that morning. Throughout the day, images of Megan had popped up in his mind. These weren't things he remembered happening, but they felt real—more real than a dream—and Paul was almost positive they were from the night of Chris and Elizabeth's wedding. That, or her declaration that morning had triggered some very vivid imagery.

Chloe ran in from the other room and hugged his legs. "Daddy!"

Paul swung her up in his arms and kissed her cheek. "Hi, sweetpea. How was your day?"

His daughter proceeded to tell him all about her day, including the phone conversation she'd had with his mother, while she helped him tear the lettuce apart for a salad. To be honest, Paul had nearly forgotten about Chloe's month-long vacation with her grandparents. Normally, he counted down the days until he had to give her up for a month to share her with the four other people who loved her almost as much as he did. Even though it was still two months away, he'd barely thought about it.

He wasn't a fool. Paul knew the reason for that had to be Megan. She'd changed things for both of them. Their house was happier with her in it. Chloe liked having her here, and so did he.

That didn't mean he wanted a relationship with her.

Dinner was filled with random conversation about nothing in particular, and as the evening wore on, Paul relaxed even more. Chloe asked several questions about Janey, which he found somewhat odd, but his daughter was very curious. Sometimes it took people a while to pick up on that because she often kept to herself, but Chloe noticed things most adults would dismiss or ignore. He wondered if she'd follow in his footsteps and become a detective, or if she'd opt for something safer.

After putting Chloe to bed, Paul lingered for several minutes before trudging back down the stairs to the living room where he knew Megan would be waiting. He refused to run away again. She'd surprised him the first time, throwing him off-kilter. This time he was prepared.

At least, he hoped he was.

Megan was curled up on the couch, wearing another pajama set that he didn't recognize, with her feet tucked up underneath her. She was watching something on television. It was casual and completely normal for Megan at this time of night, but for some reason his gaze zeroed in on the skin peeking out below her very short shorts. He could almost feel how soft and silky it would be beneath his hands.

Paul quickly averted his eyes, but not before realizing that he'd been caught staring. Megan smirked at him, as he took a seat across the room, trying discreetly to adjust himself. She knew what she was doing to him. Paul only wished that he understood it.

"Did you want to play some poker?"

He took a few moments to consider her question and if there could be a hidden meaning behind it before answering. They'd played cards—mainly poker—many times before. It was her favorite game, and while he'd never played competitively, he and some of the guys at the station used to get together on occasion and play a few hands. "All right."

Megan smiled, and it twisted something deep in his stomach.

She jumped up from the couch, and strolled across the room to get the cards. His gaze went directly to her ass as it swayed back and forth with each step she took. He had to close his eyes to keep himself from looking. Otherwise, the problem in his pants would become much more pronounced, and there would be no way he could hide it from her.

Less than a minute later, he heard her not far from him, shuffling the cards, and figured it was safe to open his eyes. Boy, was he wrong. Megan sat not two feet from him near the corner of the coffee table. She was up on her knees, her arms pressed firmly against her sides as she manipulated the cards. The position pushed her breasts up, giving him plenty to look at from his angle above her.

Coughing, Paul swiftly lowered himself to the floor, hoping that the new angle would help. It did in some ways, but didn't in others. Megan wasn't wearing a bra, and he could see the tips of her nipples pushing against her pajama top.

Looking up to the ceiling, he took a deep breath.

"You ready?" Megan asked, bringing his attention back to her.

He nodded, not trusting his voice.

They played five hands before he decided to head up to his

room, and he lost every single one because he was so utterly distracted. Something had to be done. There had to be a way to reverse whatever made this happen.

As he lay down in his bed that night and closed his eyes, the flashes he'd had earlier in the day morphed into memories. Paul groaned as he relived what he knew was no longer a dream. He didn't have to imagine how soft Megan's skin was along her thighs—he knew. He'd felt it himself.

By the time everything replayed in his mind, he was hard, and knew there was no way he was going to be able to get to sleep anytime soon if he didn't do something.

Throwing off the covers, he headed into his bathroom for a very long, very cold shower.

Chapter 7

Megan pulled her car up in front of Chloe's best friend, Debbie's house. Chloe was bouncing in her seat, barely able to contain herself, wanting out of the vehicle as soon as humanly possible. "Can I get out now, Megan?"

"Yes, you may."

By the time Megan unbuckled her seat belt and exited the vehicle, Chloe was already at the front door, ringing the bell. Debbie and Chloe had a playdate scheduled, which meant that after Megan dropped Chloe off, Megan was free for the next two hours. She was still contemplating what to do with herself.

Before she could go any farther with her thoughts, Debbie's mom, Tessa, opened the door.

"Hey." Tessa smiled down at Chloe. "Debbie's—"

A delighted squeal was heard inside the house, followed by little feet coming down hard on the tile floor. Not two seconds later, Chloe took off into the house.

Tessa and Megan looked at each other and started laughing. "I wish I had their energy."

Megan nodded, agreeing with Tessa. "I wish I had half of it."

"Oh please, you're only what? Twenty?"

"Twenty-three."

Tessa waved her hand in dismissal, as if to say the three additional years weren't important. "You're still a baby. Wait until you're my age."

Although she kept a smile on her face, Megan grimaced. She knew Tessa didn't mean anything by it. In fact, she thought Tessa might mean it as a compliment. If not for Paul, Megan might have taken it that way herself.

"I'll pick Chloe up around five, if that's okay."

There was another squeal in the background, and Tessa shifted to look over her shoulder before refocusing her attention on Megan. "That should be fine. The girls usually settle down after a few minutes and go play in Debbie's room. Hopefully, I can get some work done around the house."

"Call me if you need me to pick her up early."

Megan waved goodbye, and walked slowly back to her car. It wasn't anything fancy, but at least it was hers. When she'd first come to live with Paul and Chloe, she didn't own much of anything, and most certainly not a car. But with Paul working all day, and some nights, she needed to have a vehicle to drive both herself and Chloe around.

As she slid behind the wheel, she remembered that first weekend when Paul took her to look for a car. They'd left early in the morning, dropping Chloe off at her grandparents so she wouldn't be bored all day. It was the first time Megan and Paul had truly been alone together, and the day she began to get to know the man that he was.

Starting her car, Megan pulled away from the curb, and headed back home. She figured she'd spend her free time getting some of her schoolwork done, and relax. It was Friday night, and so there would be no dinner to prep. Paul always brought home pizza, and they all sat around the living room and watched a movie. Considering there was a five-year-old in the house, however, most of the movie selections were of the Disney variety.

As Megan was walking into the house, the phone started ringing. She rushed across the room to answer it. "Hello?"

"You sound like you're out of breath. Is everything okay?"

Megan laughed. "Hello to you, too, Becca."

"Sorry."

Shaking her head, Megan strolled over to the kitchen table, and took a seat. "That's okay. I love ya anyway."

"Thanks." She could almost see her sister rolling her eyes. "But you didn't answer my question."

Megan sighed. "Yes, I was out of breath. I was just walking through the door when you called. Chloe had a playdate this afternoon."

"Oh."

"What? You thought it was going to be something more sinister?"

"Not exactly—"

"Maybe you leaving the FBI wasn't such a good idea, sis. What? PI work not exciting enough for you?"

"Hardy har har. Laugh it up. I'm allowed to worry about you, you know."

It was Megan's turn to roll her eyes. "Yes, I know. You remind me of that fact often enough."

Rebecca was silent for a long moment. "Am I really that bad? Gage says I need to relax, that the stress isn't good for the baby."

"You should listen to him, and no, you aren't that bad. *Most* of the time. You're my big sister, and you've looked out for me all my life. I get it. Maybe having a baby of your own will give you someone else to focus on."

Instead of getting a snarky comeback from her sister, Rebecca remained silent.

After several minutes, Megan began to regret her comments. "I'm sorry if I hurt your feelings, Becca. You know I didn't mean anything by it, I—"

"No. It's okay. You're right. Gage tells me the same thing all the time. He says . . . he says I worry too much about you. But I can't help it."

It was then Megan realized her sister was crying. "Becca?"

Rebecca sniffed. "I'm fine. It's these crazy pregnancy hormones. I start crying, and I can't stop."

Megan didn't know what to say to that, so she said nothing.

Eventually, Rebecca seemed to get a hold of herself. "So, the reason I was calling . . ."

"Yes?"

"Gage says that Chloe always spends time with her grandparents during the summer. I was thinking maybe you could come stay with us for a while."

Megan bit the inside of her cheek, worrying it. She'd been trying to figure out what to do for the past three weeks. Chloe was set to leave in a little over a month, and yet Megan was no closer to making a decision. "I don't know. I mean, don't you want to spend time with your new husband?"

"Gage has training camp all summer. He's gone ten hours a day, five days a week."

"But you have your work."

"I work mostly from home these days. Plus, I run the Nashville office, remember? I can take time off whenever I want."

Once more, Megan didn't respond.

"You don't want to come."

"I didn't say that."

"You didn't have to." Rebecca's voice changed, and Megan knew what was coming next. "Do you have a new boyfriend?"

"No."

"What then?"

For some reason, Megan's patience went out the window. "Why does there have to be a reason? Why can't I just want to stay here? I like it here. I'm happy here. Why does there have to be some ulterior motive?"

Rebecca said nothing, and after a while, Megan thought that maybe her sister had hung up. "Becca? I'm—"

"Hello?"

"Gage?"

"Megan?"

Megan cringed. "Yeah, it's me. Is Becca okay?"

"I don't know. I'll call you back later, all right?"

"Okay."

By the time Megan hung up the phone, she felt like crap. She shouldn't have yelled at her sister. Rebecca was being . . . well, Rebecca. And it wasn't as if Megan hadn't given her reason to question her. Besides, her sister wasn't completely off target. No, Megan didn't have a boyfriend, but the reason she didn't want to go did revolve around a guy.

Sighing, Megan leaned over, resting her head on her arms.

"You should go."

She snapped her head up, and came face-to-face with Paul. "What?"

He cleared his throat. "You should go spend some time with your sister."

The look in his eyes was guarded, and she knew the real reason he wanted her to go. For the last three weeks, she'd been teasing him mercilessly. She hadn't missed the bulge in his pants every night before he headed up to bed, or the extra showers he'd been taking. If she had to guess, she would bet they were cold ones.

Megan stood and walked toward him. The muscles in his throat constricted as he swallowed. He looked nervous.

Coming to a stop a foot in front of him, Megan looked up, meeting his gaze. This was dangerous. For her, anyway. She was the nanny, and at any point, he could send her packing. The fear was there, but she pushed it aside. If that happened, she'd deal with it— she'd have to. But what was the alternative? Do nothing? Keep things as they were? She couldn't do that. Not when she thought there was a possibility for more.

She licked her lips, and she didn't miss how his gaze flickered down to take in the movement of her tongue. "You're home early."

"I'm on call this weekend, so I cut out a couple hours early." His voice sounded rougher than usual, and she reveled in the reaction he had to her. It had gotten more pronounced in the last few weeks. She was hoping that meant she was wearing him down.

"Oh. I see."

He glanced behind her. "Where's Chloe?"

"She's over at Debbie's. I have to pick her up around five." Megan inched closer.

Paul eyed her cautiously. "What are you doing?"

Megan played innocent. "I don't know what you mean."

He swallowed. "Yes, you do. You need to stop this . . . this game."

She reached up on her tiptoes, bringing their lips within inches of each other's. "This isn't a game. Not to me."

Closing the remaining distance between them, Megan pressed her lips against his.

***

Her soft lips made contact with his, and he nearly lost it. For the last three weeks, Megan had done everything she could to tempt him. At night, she ran around the house in pajamas that gave him glimpses of what he was denying himself—parts of her that he knew he'd once touched and kissed.

If that weren't enough, she'd taken every opportunity she could find to casually touch him or brush up against him in some way. It was driving him crazy, and he found himself aroused almost constantly whenever she was near. Paul couldn't take it anymore. She was killing him. He grabbed hold of her arms, ready to push her away, but then her warm hands pressed against his sides, and she moaned as her tongue licked along the seam of his lips.

No longer thinking, Paul pulled her tight against him and took control of the kiss. It was full of frustration, lust, and a need he didn't understand. He plunged his tongue inside her mouth. The kiss was almost violent as teeth, lips, and tongues fought each other for dominance.

Megan didn't fight him. If anything, she encouraged him. She dug her fingers into his skin, anchoring herself.

Needing her closer, Paul released his hold on her forearms, and palmed her ass. The move not only brought her flush against him, but it also gave him the leverage he needed to lift and move her. Megan eagerly embraced this new position, and wrapped her legs securely around his waist.

A few steps forward and he was able to set her down on top of the kitchen table. He didn't relinquish his hold on her, however. If anything, he pressed her tighter, letting her feel what insane things she did to his body.

Paul couldn't think properly. All he knew was that Megan was in his arms, hot and willing, and he wanted her. Trailing kisses down her neck, he leaned her back, and began edging her sweater up to reveal the amazing breasts he knew she had underneath.

Once Megan realized what he was trying to do, she reached down and quickly pulled the sweater up and over her head. She tossed it behind him somewhere, seeming to care as little as he did where it landed.

He grazed his thumbs over her hardened nipples that were still shielded by her lacy bra. She arched into his touch, encouraging him.

Brushing one cup out of the way, he wasted no time sucking her breast into his mouth and licking it. Megan moaned, and he could feel the heat between her legs increase.

His heart was pounding in his chest. It was loud. And it sounded . . . not right.

Somehow, through the foggy haze of Paul's brain, he registered that the pounding wasn't, in fact, coming from him. Someone was at the door.

He froze.

Paul straightened and took a step back. His gaze never left Megan where she was sprawled out on his kitchen table, her clothes in complete disarray, and one naked breast pink and swollen from his attention. He was rock hard, his body already protesting the loss of heat and pressure.

Megan opened her eyes, searching. "Paul?"

She sat up and reached for him.

He shook his head. "Someone's at the door."

A confused look crossed her face, and whoever it was knocked again, this time on the kitchen door. Megan scrambled to her feet, and snatched her sweater up off the floor while straightening her bra. With a sly smile, she slipped the sweater back over her head. "Aren't you going to see who it is?"

Shaking his head to try and clear it, he went to answer the door.

His partner, Janey, stood on the other side of the doorway, looking somewhere between worried and irritated. "There you are. I was starting to think I'd have to send out a search party."

"Sorry. I was . . . I didn't hear you at first."

Janey pushed her way past Paul, and handed him a folder. "This came in right as I was about to walk out the door. I thought you'd want to get your hands on it ASAP. It's the DNA results from the third murder victim." Janey paused when she noticed Megan standing across the room. "Oh, hi, Megan."

"Hello, Detective Davis."

There was tension in the room, and Janey seemed to pick up on it. She looked from Paul to Megan, and then back to Paul again. For several minutes, no one said anything, and guilt began to take root. Less than five minutes before, he'd been ravishing his nanny on the kitchen table. Nope. Not a thing to feel guilty about there.

Paul cleared his throat, and rubbed the back of his neck. "I'll read through the files tonight after Chloe goes to bed."

Nodding, Janey moved back toward the door to leave. "Call me if you need anything, or if . . ." She paused, and glanced briefly over at Megan. ". . . if you want to talk."

"I will. And thanks for the file."

Janey acted as if she couldn't get out of his house quick enough, and he knew she suspected what she'd nearly walked in on. Paul shut the door firmly behind her, and turned to face Megan. She was standing with her arms wrapped protectively around her waist.

"Don't say it," she whispered.

He closed his eyes and sighed. "Okay, I won't."

"Good."

Looking over at her, his heart clenched with his next words. "But that doesn't change anything."

She shook her head. "How can you say that?"

"Megan—"

"No! You can't stand there and say that you feel nothing. You're attracted to me. Admit it."

Paul leaned back against the doorjamb, feeling as if there were a twenty- pound weight on his chest. "Yes, I'm attracted to you."

"Then why won't you give us a chance?"

Looking at her standing in his kitchen, the way she had her body positioned, she looked young—younger than twenty-three. "We would never work."

"You keep saying that, but I want to know why." He opened his mouth to reply, but she interrupted him. "And don't say it's because you still love your wife. I know you love Melissa, and you always will. I'm okay with that. And I don't see what that has to do with us. She's not here. I am."

Paul listened to Megan's speech, and watched as she squared her shoulders waiting for his response. He averted his eyes, and took several slow, deep breaths. "A part of me died that morning the patrolman came to tell me Melissa had been pronounced dead at the scene. They didn't even bother taking her to the emergency room. She went straight to the morgue."

He found Megan's eyes again, and there were tears glistening in them. "I'm sorry," she whispered.

His heart clenched painfully, seeing that he was causing her pain. It had to be done, though. She needed to understand. "You're young. You deserve to find a guy who will be able to give you what you need . . . what you deserve. I'm sorry, but I'm not him."

Before she could say anything else, Paul opened the door behind him. "I'll get Chloe, and then we'll pick up the pizza before we come home." He paused. "You should call your sister back and apologize. Tell her you're coming to visit. The last thing you want to do is leave a rift between you and the ones you love. You never know when you won't have the opportunity to take it back."

With those parting words, Paul walked out the door leaving Megan standing in the kitchen. He hated hurting her, but she'd left him no choice. There couldn't be a *them*. Kissing Megan had made him feel alive. She made him feel as if he deserved to be loved again.

He didn't. The last words he ever said to his wife weren't ones of love. They were ones of frustration and anger.

No. There was one thing Paul was sure of. He didn't deserve a second chance. Not after the way he'd royally screwed up the first one. If it hadn't been for him, Melissa would never have been out that time of night in the first place, and she'd still be there with him. Chloe would still have her mother. They'd be a family.

As Paul drove toward Debbie's house, he brushed away a few stray tears. He needed to pull himself together. The last thing he wanted was for Chloe to see him crying. She'd want to know why, and it wasn't something he could explain to her.

All he had to do was make it another five weeks. Then Chloe would be off with her grandparents, and Megan would be at her sister's. Maybe the distance would be good for all of them, and Megan would realize that he wasn't the right guy for her. It was his only hope, because he didn't know how much longer he would be able to resist her if she didn't.

Chapter 8

Megan stood staring at the door Paul had exited minutes before. The last words he'd spoken to her echoed in her head over and over again. He didn't think he could be the man she needed . . . deserved. How was that possible? Paul was the best man she'd ever met. He loved his daughter and would do anything for her—for his family as well.

Before she could dwell on it too much, the phone rang, and she blindly answered it. "Hello?"

"Hey, Megan. It's Gage."

That brought her quickly out of her musings. "Is Becca all right?"

"Yeah, yeah. She's fine. She's lying down at the moment."

"Oh. Okay." It wasn't like her sister to take naps, but maybe that was part of the whole pregnancy thing, too. It wasn't as if Megan was used to being around pregnant women.

Gage cleared his throat. "Look, you can tell me to butt out, or whatever, but Rebecca was really hurt when you said you didn't want to visit. She thinks she . . . we've done something to make you feel as if you aren't welcome."

"No, it's not . . . that."

"Then what?"

Megan sighed. She didn't want to lie, but she couldn't exactly tell the truth. "I'm not crazy about leaving Paul alone for an entire month."

"Why?"

"No reason."

Her reply was too quick. "What's wrong?"

The tone in his voice was the same she'd heard from Paul a time or two. Luckily, those times had all involved Chloe and not her.

She decided to be vague, but honest. "I think Chris and Elizabeth's wedding affected him more than he's admitting."

"How so? Did something happen? Did he say something?"

Megan hesitated. "No. Not exactly. It's more what he hasn't said." She paused. "Maybe I'm reading too much into it. I don't know."

But she did know. Megan knew what Chris and Elizabeth's wedding had done to Paul—knew that he'd gotten himself so drunk he couldn't remember what had happened. And given what he'd admitted to her only moments before, she was betting that his grief had more of a hold on him than anyone realized.

"Maybe I should call Ma."

"No!" Megan nearly bit her own tongue. An outburst like that wasn't going to help her cause in the slightest. "No. I mean, if he wants to talk about it, he will, right? I don't think it's good to force it, and I don't think he'd appreciate it if your parents got involved."

Gage didn't respond right away, and when he did, he didn't sound happy. "I suppose you're right. Paul's always the one taking care of everyone else. He doesn't really like it when people stick their nose into his business."

She breathed a sigh of relief. "Exactly. But you see why I don't want to leave right now."

"Why didn't you just tell your sister this? I'm sure she would have understood."

Megan released an exasperated sigh. "Because I really didn't want to say anything to anyone, nosy."

He laughed. "Okay, okay. I won't pry. But your sister does want to see you. What if you come out for a week or something? Surely Paul can survive without his housekeeper for one week."

"I'm not a housekeeper. I'm the nanny."

Gage made a dismissive sound. "Tomato, tamahto." He paused. "So will you come? I'll even set up the first floor bedroom for you so you don't have to hear us."

"Pfft. That would work if you two kept it in your bedroom."

He laughed.

"Well?"

She leaned back in her chair, and picked a nonexistent piece of fuzz off her sweater. One week. Megan didn't want to leave Paul at all, but she had to admit that she did want to see her sister. "Okay. I'll come for a week."

"Great. I'll have Rebecca call and the two of you can get everything arranged. We'll pay for your plane ticket, and pick you up at the airport."

"You don't have to do that."

"We want to. You're family, remember?"

Megan hung up a few minutes later, and she instantly felt guilty. She shouldn't have said anything to Gage. It wasn't any of his business or anyone else's, but if she hadn't told him, then he and Rebecca would have thought she was intentionally avoiding them.

Glancing up at the clock, Megan realized that almost a half hour had passed since Paul walked out. He and Chloe would be back with the pizza soon, and Megan had no idea what mood he'd be in when he returned. One thing she knew for sure, however, was that she had to find some way to make Paul understand that he was the right guy for her. How she was going to do that, though, she had no idea.

***

Tessa smiled when she saw him standing on her front porch. "Oh, hi, Paul."

"Hello, Tessa. How are you?"

She chuckled, and stepped back to allow him to enter. "Same as usual. You know how it is, chasing after a five-year-old all day."

It was his turn to laugh, although it was halfhearted. He couldn't get his mind off what had happened with Megan. Of course, lately he couldn't seem to think about much else.

Paul followed Tessa as she led him down the hall to Debbie's room, where the two girls were playing. They heard the adults enter, and looked up from their dolls.

"Daddy!" Chloe trilled, jumping up and running over to greet him.

He picked her up, and hugged her tight. Chloe was the only thing in his world right now that made sense to him. She was his one constant. "Hiya, sweetpea. How was your afternoon? Did you have fun with Debbie?"

"Uh-huh. We played with her new dollhouse. It's pretty, isn't it, Daddy?"

Chloe pointed to the large, three-story dollhouse they'd been playing with when he'd walked in. "Wow. It's big."

She nodded, and then glanced behind him. "Where's Megan? I want to show her Debbie's dollhouse."

Paul set Chloe down on her feet . . . more as a distraction. "You can show her another time. We're going to pick up the pizza for tonight and meet her at home. You can tell her all about it then."

Her lower lip jutted out in a pout. "But I wanted to show her."

"You can show her next time. Go say goodbye to Debbie."

Chloe lowered her head, and trudged back over to Debbie. "Bye, Debbie."

Debbie stood, and gave Chloe a hug, which she returned.

They said their goodbyes and Paul helped Chloe into the backseat of his car. Once he was satisfied that Chloe was strapped in securely, Paul walked around to the driver's side and got in. As he pulled away from the curb, his frown deepened. He couldn't let whatever was happening with Megan affect his relationship with Chloe—he couldn't. "What do you say we order the pizza, and then go to the park across the street while we wait?"

"Yay!" Chloe kicked her legs in excitement, and a huge smile lit up her face.

He could do this. He would do this. Megan was just Chloe's nanny. Nothing more.

***

Megan was at her computer when Paul and Chloe got back with the pizza. They were almost an hour later than she'd expected them to be. She was beginning to get worried as it was growing dark outside, but Megan figured that Paul needed to put some distance between them after their heated make-out session. She knew that it had certainly thrown her for a loop. The last time he'd been drunk, and she'd been unsure of his motivations. This time it was all him, and boy, was it ever. Just thinking about it again was making her warm all over.

Chloe came bounding up the stairs to get her for dinner. The little girl was all aglow about Paul taking her to the park, telling Megan how he'd pushed her really high on the swing.

As they entered the living room where Paul had laid out the pizza, Megan skidded to a stop, and all moisture left her mouth. Paul was bent over at the waist, facing away from them, the khaki dress pants he typically wore to work pulled taut against his backside. Megan wasn't normally one to get turned on over any one part of a man's body, but as with everything else, Paul was different. Over the last few weeks, she'd fantasized about his mouth, his hands, and she was sure that his ass would be starring in a few of those fantasies in the very near future.

They ended up watching *Finding Nemo*. It was one of Chloe's favorites, and in the last five months, they'd watched it at least twenty times. Megan could almost quote it word for word. At one point, Chloe had her mouth around a piece of pizza and said, right along with the characters, "Remember: rip it, roll it, and punch it," before taking a large bite with a huge smile on her face. Megan and Paul had shared a look, and chuckled silently.

Those were the types of moments she loved—the ones where they were both in this bubble—sharing something between them. It usually happened around Chloe, but then again, there weren't many times when they were together and Chloe wasn't around.

Once the movie was over and the pizza demolished, Paul took Chloe upstairs to bed while Megan cleaned up downstairs. After their "moment" when Chloe quoted Squirt from the movie, Paul had studiously ignored her. Not in a rude way, but in a way that let her know that he didn't want to interact with her if it wasn't necessary. That hurt, but she'd known all along that he was fighting whatever was going on between them. She had to keep telling herself that was all it was.

With everything back to normal in the living room, Megan headed upstairs to say good night to Chloe. To her surprise, Paul stood when she entered. "I already read Chloe her story." Then he turned to his daughter. "Say good night to Megan."

"Night, Megan."

Her chest clenched painfully as she bent to kiss the little girl good night. "Good night, Chloe."

Paul strolled by Megan, leaving the room, and she moved to

follow him, turning out the light as she went.

By the time she'd stepped out of the room and closed the door behind her, he was halfway down the hall. "Hey."

He stopped, and wheeled around to face her.

When he didn't comment, she squared her shoulders, and walked forward. He didn't back away, but the way he held himself didn't encourage her either. "I wanted to let you know that I decided to go visit my sister while Chloe is with her grandparents."

She watched as some of the tension left his body. "Good." He cleared his throat. "That will be good for you. And her."

Megan nodded. "I'll only be gone a week."

He opened his mouth, but she cut him off.

"They're newlyweds. Work or not, they need their time and space. Especially with the baby coming."

He released a shaky sigh, and she wondered what was going through his mind. "You should stay the whole month."

"No."

He quirked an eyebrow at her. "No? Why not?"

Megan took a step closer to him, and he paled. "You're not getting rid of me that easily, Paul Daniels. I know you think you aren't good enough for me for some insane reason, but if you think that's going to stop me, you've got another thing coming."

"Megan . . ."

She shook her head. "I don't want to hear it. I've known you for five months now and I refuse to believe that you aren't the man you appear to be."

"And what kind of man is that?" A small smile pulled at one side of his mouth, and she was happy to see at least something break through the unmovable façade he was displaying.

"A good one. You're kind, loving, and honorable. You're a good cop, and a great dad. And . . ." She hesitated.

"And?"

"And you're one hell of a kisser."

To her surprise, Paul stepped forward. He raised a hand to cup her face, and then brought his lips down to graze the side of her ear. The heat from his palm spread down her neck, and her breath caught in her throat waiting to see what he'd do.

"That doesn't mean I'd make a good mate for you. It just means I'm good at faking it."

A second later, Paul released her. She looked up at him, stunned, and unsure what to make of his declaration.

"Good night, Megan."

Before she knew it, he had slipped into his room, leaving her staring after him. Again.

Sighing in frustration, Megan marched into her room. She wanted to slam the door, but knew she couldn't because of Chloe. Instead, she threw herself on her bed and screamed into her pillow. This was one of those times when she needed a best friend or a big sister to talk to. Although she knew she could talk to Rebecca, she didn't think her sister would be all that helpful, given the situation. Rebecca would think Megan had a crush and tell her that she needed to find a hobby or something, and get over it.

Things weren't that simple. What she felt for Paul wasn't merely a crush. She'd had crushes before. Lots of them. All those guys, boys really, that she'd followed all over the country—they were crushes. She'd seen what she wanted to see in them, not who they really were.

Changing into her pajamas, Megan crawled into bed, and grabbed the book she'd started earlier in the day. The problem was she couldn't concentrate on a single word she was reading. She closed the book, and tossed it onto her nightstand.

Sinking down lower in the bed, she raised her knees and hugged them to her chest. She was tempted to go knock on Paul's door and throw herself at him, but she didn't think that would get her what she wanted. Not in the long run, anyway.

Megan didn't sleep well that night. Her thoughts were filled with Paul and how to get him to open up to her. After what he'd said the day before, she was sure something had happened between him and his wife. Something he was ashamed of, maybe?

She dressed, and headed downstairs as she usually did. Paul was sitting at the kitchen table going over the file Janey had dropped off.

"Morning."

He glanced up, and then immediately back down. "Morning."

Trying not to take it personally, Megan went to get some coffee, and then joined him at the table. "Did you have any plans for today?"

"Since the sun is shining and it's not raining, I figured I'd do some work outside in the yard. Besides, I need to stay close to home since I'm on call."

Megan nodded and took a sip of her coffee. "Maybe Chloe and I can work on the flower beds. She was talking about all the pretty flowers the last time we were at the store."

"I'm sure she'd like that." Although he was talking to her, Paul never took his eyes off the papers in front of him.

"Can't you look at me?" Her voice was soft, and it was impossible to disguise the hurt she felt.

Paul closed the folder, and faced her.

"Thank you."

They sat staring at each other for several minutes before Paul got up and refilled his coffee. He didn't return to the table. Instead, he leaned against the counter. It was clear to her that he was putting physical distance between them on purpose.

"I'm not giving up, you know."

His knuckles turned white as he gripped his coffee mug so hard she thought he might break it. With his mouth set in a hard line, he met her gaze. "I know."

Chapter 9

Paul was called out late Sunday night. He knocked on Megan's bedroom door, letting her know where he was going before taking off. She'd been groggy and rumpled, and looked way sexier than she had a right to. He was positive seeing her like that would only serve to add content to his new and rather arousing dreams the next time his head hit the pillow.

The homicide that night was of the standard variety, and they had the suspect in custody before they'd finished going through the crime scene for evidence. Even still, it meant Paul didn't get home until dawn. He was coming through the door when Megan appeared at the bottom of the stairs. "Are you just getting back?"

He closed the door, and locked it behind him. "Yeah."

She yawned and stretched, raising her arms above her head and molding her top against her chest. He quickly looked away. Luckily, she wasn't awake enough to notice.

Paul cleared his throat. "Still tired?"

"Yeah."

Laughing, he walked over to start the coffee pot.

When she realized what he was doing, Megan took a seat at the kitchen table, and rested her head in her hands. "I don't know why. Besides you waking me up last night, I slept pretty good."

Neither of them said another word until Paul brought a steaming cup of coffee over to her. "This should help."

Picking it up, she took a deep breath, and then a cautious sip.

She sighed, and smiled up at him. "Thank you."

Paul smiled back. "I'm gonna check on Chloe, and then catch a few hours' sleep."

Megan took another sip of her coffee, and then nodded. "I'll keep her downstairs once she wakes up so you can get some rest."

"Thanks."

He headed toward the stairs, but she stopped him. "And Paul?"

"Yes?"

This time the smile on her face wasn't so sleepy and innocent. "Thanks again for the coffee."

Even with his desperate need for sleep, Paul couldn't help but respond to that twinkle in Megan's eye. She knew what she was doing. He'd give her that. Before he did something he would regret, he trotted up the stairs trying to remain quiet and not wake his daughter.

After a quick glance in Chloe's room, he closed her door, and headed down the hall. Once inside the privacy of the master suite, he strolled over to his bedside table. He removed his gun and holster, putting them away, and then ambled into the bathroom.

When he returned to the bedroom, he walked directly over to his nightstand, and picked up the picture of Melissa he kept there. He inhaled a shaky breath, and released it. "What's happening to me?"

She didn't answer, of course.

Paul lowered himself to sit on the edge of his mattress, clutching his wife's photograph with both hands. "Why now? Why her?"

He paused as the scene from downstairs replayed in his head. "Why?"

Kicking off his shoes and removing his tie, he lay back on the bed, his head on the pillows. For the longest time after Melissa died, his life outside of his job and Chloe didn't make sense. It had taken him years to begin to feel somewhat normal again—like he wasn't missing an arm or a leg.

People always told him that things would get better in time. He hadn't believed them. But they'd been right, in a way. Although he never went a day without thinking about his wife—missing her—the time and distance had made it easier for him to cope. It was as he'd told Megan. He was good at faking it. As the years passed, it was easier to smile and act normal even if he didn't always feel that way.

He traced the curve of Melissa's cheek with his index finger.

"She's twenty-three and very persistent." Paul paused, and closed his eyes. "I don't know what to do."

Turning, Paul laid Melissa's picture on the pillow beside his head, and stared at the beautiful woman who gave birth to his daughter. A part of him wished that she was here to tell him what he should do. The logical part of his brain, however, knew that if Melissa were there with him, he would never be in this type of situation. Megan would never be part of his life. Not in the way she currently was, anyway. She'd just be his baby brother's sister-in-law—someone he saw from the outside looking in, but never had too much contact with.

His eyes began to close as he continued to gaze at Melissa's image. Deciding to give up the battle, he sighed and allowed the exhaustion to take him.

***

Megan had a huge smile on her face as she continued to sit at the table and drink her coffee. She was wearing him down. Megan knew it. She only had to have patience. Not her strong suit, but she could do it. For Paul, she would do just about anything.

A half hour later, she was in the living room watching some television when Chloe came creeping down the stairs. She was rubbing the sleep from her eyes when she spotted Megan on the couch. Without a word, Chloe padded across the room to where Megan sat, and climbed onto her lap. Wrapping her arms around the little girl, Megan kissed the top of her head, and flipped the channel to some cartoons.

Eventually, Chloe began to wake up more. "Where's Daddy?"

"He was called into work last night, so he's upstairs sleeping. That means we need to play quietly downstairs for a while and let him rest."

"Did someone die?"

Megan nodded. "Yes, I think so."

Chloe seemed to think really hard for a while. "Why?"

"Why what, honey?"

"Why did they have to die?"

Megan brushed a strand of hair away from Chloe's face. "I don't know. Sometimes bad things happen."

While Chloe considered that, Megan decided it was time to change the subject. "Why don't we go into the kitchen and get you some breakfast, and then we can play a game or something?"

"Okay."

Seeming to have completely forgotten their conversation, Chloe slid off Megan's lap and ran into the kitchen.

Four hours later, a freshly showered and shaved Paul sauntered into the living room where Megan and Chloe were playing Candyland. Megan saw him first. "Feeling better?"

Before he could answer, Chloe chimed in, "Daddy, do you want to play with us?"

Paul walked over, and knelt down beside his daughter. "I'd love to, sweetpea, but I've got to go into work for a few hours."

Chloe pouted.

He sighed. "Maybe we can play some tonight after dinner, okay?"

"Okay." She still sounded disappointed.

Megan picked up a card, looked at it briefly, and then moved her little plastic man. "Will you be home around the usual time?"

"I should be."

"Okay." She gave him a sweet smile, and gently brushed her hand along the side of his thigh. "We'll see you at dinner."

Paul cleared his throat, and stood. It took all Megan had in her not to do a happy dance when she saw how he quickly turned away from his daughter to hide any reaction he was having. "Be good for Megan, Chloe. I'll see you tonight."

"Okay, Daddy." Chloe went back to concentrating on her game.

Paul moved to the door, and after telling Chloe she'd be right back, Megan followed him. He paused with his hand on the doorknob, and by his stance, he knew she was right behind him. She waited for a moment to see if he'd turn around, and he did. The look on his face made her want to giggle. She suppressed it, though.

"I wanted to thank you again for the coffee this morning. It was a lifesaver."

"You're welcome."

Megan glanced over her shoulder, making sure Chloe was still out of sight in the other room before she stepped closer to him.

He clenched his fists, but other than that, he didn't budge.

Inside she was grinning like a Cheshire cat. "After you went upstairs this morning, I got to thinking."

Paul swallowed. "About?"

"Tessa mentioned to me a few weeks ago that Debbie's been asking if she and Chloe can have a sleepover."

"A sleepover."

She shrugged, not wanting to make too big a deal of it. Yet. "Yeah. We'd drop Chloe off in the afternoon or early evening, and then pick her up the next morning. They'd play, watch movies, eat junk food. You know, girl stuff."

He looked over her shoulder toward the room Chloe was currently occupying, before returning his gaze to Megan. "I guess that would be okay. If Chloe wants to."

This time Megan didn't hide her smile. "Great! I'll let Tessa know."

Paul nodded, and started to leave again.

Megan stopped him. "So I was thinking . . ."

"Yes?"

"Since Chloe will be gone for an entire evening, I was thinking maybe you and I could do something. Go out." As soon as the words left her mouth, Megan's nerves skyrocketed. She might appear confident, but really she was scared to death.

"Go out?"

"Yes."

He closed his eyes, and sighed. When he opened them again, he was wearing his cop face. "You're a lovely girl, Megan, but I don't think that's a good idea."

"How will you know unless you try? We try."

Paul shook his head. "Look, I need to get to work. Why don't you . . . stop by around five, and the three of us can go out tonight? Get out of the house."

It was Megan's turn to sigh. "Fine. We can do that, but the three of us going to dinner isn't what I had in mind."

"It's all I can offer you, Megan. I'm sorry."

"You keep saying that."

"Because you don't seem to be listening."

"Megan?"

She turned toward the little girl's voice for a second, but it was long enough for Paul to make his escape. Megan gritted her teeth in frustration, and went to help Chloe.

***

Paul couldn't get out of there fast enough. She'd asked him out. On a date. At least, that's what he assumed it was. He was a little rusty at those types of things, but he was pretty sure that was her intention.

Knowing Megan, he doubted his little brush-off was going to stop her for long. The woman was relentless.

It would be easier if he didn't feel anything for her, but damn it, he did. More than he wanted to admit.

That didn't change anything, however. He still wasn't right for her. Even if the thirteen-year age difference was taken off the table, they were in very different phases of their lives. Megan was going back to college, trying to find her way in the world after being sidetracked for almost six years. Although he knew she adored his daughter, that didn't mean she was ready for a long-term commitment.

Stopped at a red light, Paul realized where his thoughts had gone, and shook his head trying to clear it. He couldn't go there. It wasn't fair to her, or to Chloe.

A little voice inside his head reminded him how it had felt to kiss Megan. To hold her in his arms—feel her soft skin beneath his hands, his lips—

The car behind him honked its horn, and Paul looked up to find that the light was now green. Cursing, he pushed his foot on the gas, and continued on to the station. He was going to have to figure something out fast.

He strolled into the station about ten minutes later.

"Hey, you made it in."

Paul reached for the coffee pot before answering his partner. "Yeah. It's amazing what a few good hours of sleep can do for you."

With his coffee in hand, he followed Janey back to their desks.

"The report's in your in-box. I looked it over. Seems fairly straightforward to me."

He took a sip of his coffee. "Yeah, it was. Perp dropped his wallet trying to get away, and went straight home afterward. We had him in custody quickly."

Janey shook her head. "There are some pretty dumb criminals out there."

"Yes, there are." He couldn't disagree with her. Most cases were solved because criminals made mistakes. Some of them were small and easily missed if the detective wasn't paying attention. Others, like the one the previous night, were blatantly obvious. "Makes our jobs easier, though, when they're stupid."

She nodded. "Now if only our serial killer would lend us a helping hand and do something equally stupid."

Paul couldn't agree with her more. "At least we now have DNA. That's something."

"It is. Doesn't help, however, that the guy isn't in the database."

The DNA the coroner lifted from one of Casey McMurphy's fingernails confirmed their serial killer was a male. But what Paul wanted to know was what had made Mrs. McMurphy fight back when the other two victims had not? "Anything new come in on the case?"

"Not really. I've been combing through our three victims' backgrounds. Again. This time I'm looking at shopping patterns, routines, anything that might put all three women in the same place. We need to find out where this guy is selecting his victims."

He nodded and took another sip of coffee. "It would be nice if we got lucky and could figure it out before he set his sights on another woman."

"Unfortunately, we are probably running out of time. I'd say we're due for a new body to turn up soon."

Paul knew Janey was probably right. Their first victim had turned up two weeks before he'd gone to his parents' for Thanksgiving. The second was found almost two months later. With the discovery of yet a third victim, also found almost two months after the one previous, a pattern had been established, and their two months was nearly up. It was one of the few things that aided in the apprehension of such psychopaths. They had an order of things, and most of them meticulously stuck to those rituals—even if, in the end, it was their downfall.

For the next hour, Paul finished going over the report from the previous night. He'd been the lead detective on the scene, so it was his responsibility to make sure all the i's were dotted and the t's crossed. He was about done, when he realized he needed some clarification on a few details from the first officer on the scene.

Paul looked around the room before focusing on Janey. "Have

you seen Officer Rollins?"

"Not recently, no."

Pushing away from his desk, Paul went in search of the patrol schedule. Since Rollins was working last night, there was a possibility that he was home in bed. Sure enough, Rollins had the next twenty-four hours off.

Paul sighed, and went in search of the patrolman's contact information. He wasn't going to sit on the report for almost two days until he could track Rollins down.

Ten minutes later, Paul returned to his desk and picked up his phone. It rang several times before a groggy voice picked up. "Hello?"

"Officer Rollins?"

"Yeah?" The voice sounded measurably clearer.

"It's Detective Paul Daniels down at the station."

"Oh, hi." Paul heard movement, and he figured Rollins was getting up out of bed.

"You were the first officer on the scene of last night's homicide, were you not?"

"Yeah, I was. Is something wrong?"

"I want to go over a few details of your statement with you."

There was a grunt on the other end of the line. "Ah. Yeah. Okay."

Paul glanced up at the clock. It was already after two. "I'll be here until around five. Can you make it in before then? I want to clear this off my desk today."

It took a moment for Rollins to answer. "Sure. Give me forty-five minutes, and I'll be there."

"See you then."

He hung up the phone, and noticed Janey giving him a look. "What?"

"Being a little hard on the guy, aren't you?"

"Just trying to get this dreaded paperwork done."

"Hmm. This doesn't happen to have anything to do with a certain nanny that lives at your house, does it?"

"Megan? No. Why would completing a report have anything to do with her?"

"I wasn't talking about the paperwork itself. I was talking about the tone you took with Officer Rollins. And don't think I missed the tension between you and your nanny the last time I showed up at your house."

"I don't know what you're talking about." Paul stood. "I'm going to see what I can wrestle up from the vending machine. Do you want anything?"

Janey chuckled and shook her head. "No. I think I'm good."

Paul nodded, and went in search of something to fill his rumbling stomach. He should have known better than to think Janey wouldn't have noticed something wasn't right between him and Megan. She was a detective, after all. It would be more unusual if she hadn't noticed.

As promised, Officer Jay Rollins strolled into the station forty-five minutes later. He was freshly showered and wearing street clothes. Considering what Janey had said, Paul figured he should make nice. "Thank you for coming in. I appreciate it."

Rollins pulled up a chair beside Paul's desk, and opened the file Paul handed to him. He quickly scanned over the information. "Everything looks accurate. What more did you need?"

They were minor details, granted, but Paul knew from experience how the tiniest facet could become a huge deal when a case made it before a judge. Once Paul explained the additional information he needed, Rollins went in search of a computer so that he could adjust his section of the report.

Rollins returned at a quarter till five with the file and his updated statement.

"Thanks again."

"No problem."

Officer Rollins turned to leave, and a lightbulb went off in Paul's head. "Hey, Rollins?"

"Yeah?"

"You're single, correct?"

A questioning look crossed Rollins' face. "Yes."

"No girlfriend?"

"No. Why?"

"My daughter and her nanny will be here in a few minutes, and we're going out for dinner. I was wondering if you might like to join us."

"Are you trying to set me up with your nanny, Detective?"

Paul shrugged, trying to keep it casual.

"How old is she?"

"She's . . ." The words died in his throat as he saw Megan across the room. ". . . here."

Officer Rollins turned to follow Paul's gaze. No more than two seconds passed before Paul heard Rollins mutter, "I'm in."

Chapter 10

Megan was seriously contemplating violence as she sat across from Paul. When she and Chloe arrived at the police station, she'd been surprised to find out that it wouldn't only be her, Paul, and Chloe going out to dinner. A patrolman, Officer Jay Rollins, was joining them.

At first, she hadn't thought much of it. He was a colleague of Paul's, and she figured they were friends, or needed to talk shop, or whatever. That theory quickly went out the window once they were seated at their table. Paul made sure that she and Officer Rollins—Jay—were sitting beside each other. Jay even pulled out her chair for her when she went to sit down.

She was further convinced that the whole thing was a setup when Jay began asking her all about herself, and not in a casual, friendly way. He also, aside from a few interactions when they were ordering, had pretty much ignored Paul and Chloe—focusing solely on her. Megan felt as if she were on a blind date, only no one had bothered to give her a heads-up in advance.

To his credit, Jay appeared to be a nice guy. He was cute, with sandy blond hair and blue eyes, and he had an infectious smile. Six months ago, she might have been interested, but as he continued to talk, her mind would drift back to conversations she'd had with Paul. If it was a topic they'd talked about, she'd remember what he'd said or done—if he'd laughed, or taken a firm stance on the opposite side of the argument.

Jay seemed determined not to upset her. No matter what she said, what position she took on a particular subject, he smiled and nodded. Where was the fun in that? Where was the passion? She loved verbally sparring with Paul. From the beginning, he'd valued her opinion, even if he didn't always agree with it. Up until she'd made her feelings for him known, he'd never treated her as anything other than an equal.

That was why she was currently fuming. Paul had done this on purpose because she'd asked him out. Did he not understand that she didn't want to date just anyone? She wanted to date *him*. Truthfully, she wanted a lot more than that, but she could be patient. Really, she could. She only wanted their relationship to move forward, no matter how slow the pace.

Unfortunately, for most of the meal, Paul studiously ignored her and Jay. He spent most of dinner talking with Chloe, and helping her color the menu the hostess gave her. It didn't matter how many glares Megan sent his way. Paul appeared oblivious. It was as if he'd put on blinders and could only see what was directly in front of him. She understood him wanting to show his daughter some attention, but Megan knew that wasn't what was going on.

After dinner, Jay walked close beside her out to the parking lot—his arm occasionally brushing against hers. Paul had rushed Chloe to the car, and Megan knew it was to give her and Jay some privacy, which did nothing to quell her ire.

She was trying not to be rude to Jay, but it was proving more and more difficult with every step. The last thing she wanted to do was lead him on.

"I'd like to see you again. I have this Friday night off—maybe we could go out to dinner, just the two of us."

Megan stopped, and turned to face him. She waited until she was positive Paul and Chloe were inside the vehicle and out of earshot. "Thank you for the offer, but I can't. I'm sorry."

"Oh. All right." He sounded disappointed. Megan hadn't thought she'd given him the impression that she was interested, but apparently, she had— at least, on some level. Either that, or he'd purposefully misread her polite responses.

She looked up at the sky, and cursed Paul for putting her, and Jay, in this situation. This whole thing was his fault—him and his crazy notion that he wasn't good enough for her.

When Megan lowered her gaze back to meet Jay's, he was watching her with a note of curiosity. She'd seen a similar look from Paul many times. "You're a nice guy, Jay, and if things were different, then maybe, but . . ."

"I thought . . ." Jay cleared his throat. "Daniels said you weren't seeing anyone."

Megan sighed. "I kind of figured."

"But you are."

She had to give him credit. He caught on fast.

"It's complicated."

Her body language must have given something away because Jay glanced briefly over in Paul's direction before returning to look at her. "You and Daniels? But why . . ."

"Like I said, it's complicated."

He sighed, nodded, and leaned in to give her a kiss on the cheek. "If you change your mind, you know where to find me."

Megan gave Jay a weak smile, and watched him cross the parking lot to his car. The fact that she felt guilty for having to let a perfectly nice guy down easy only fueled her anger more. She turned, marched the short distance to the car, and hopped inside, not once looking in Paul's direction.

On the ride home, Chloe was quiet—too quiet—especially considering how close it was to her bedtime. Although she was a good kid, she was still a five-year-old, and it wasn't uncommon for her to get cranky when she was off her routine. Dinner had taken longer than it should have, and on a normal night, they'd already be tucking her in bed. The one time Megan peeked over her shoulder at Chloe to check on her, she'd been holding her baby doll against her chest in one hand, and rubbing her eyes with the other. Megan decided that Chloe must have tired herself out beyond being cranky.

That was until they arrived home. Usually Chloe was the first one out of the car unless Paul told her to stay in her seat. This time, both Paul and Megan had exited the vehicle, yet Chloe hadn't moved.

Paul went to get her, and that's when the tantrum started. Chloe kicked and screamed when he carried her into the house and up to her room. Megan followed close behind in case he needed help. She might be upset with Paul, but that didn't have anything to do with Chloe.

They worked together to put Chloe's pajamas on her, and to get the little girl into bed. In the six months Megan had been Chloe's nanny, she'd never seen her act out like this. Chloe was firmly told by her father that there would be no story tonight because of her behavior. He tucked the blankets around her, kissed her forehead, and headed for the door.

Megan followed suit, kissed the little girl's forehead, and then turned to go. As she began to back away, however, Chloe grabbed hold of Megan's jacket, and clung to it as if her life depended on it.

"Chloe, what's wrong?"

"Are you gonna leave, Me-gan?"

Kneeling down so that she could be on eye level with Chloe, she brushed hair off the distressed little girl's forehead. "I'm just going downstairs, honey. It's all right. You'll see me in the morning."

"You promise?" The words were said around sobs.

"I promise."

Chloe wrapped her arms around Megan's neck. "Love you, Megan."

Megan returned the hug, and then tucked Chloe back in bed. "I love you, too, Chloe. Now get to sleep before your daddy comes back in here."

In response, Chloe closed her eyes tight, and pretended to already be asleep. Megan chuckled silently, shaking her head as she turned off the light, and strolled out of the room.

As soon as the door was closed behind her, Megan took a deep breath, and headed downstairs where she knew she'd find Paul. With each step she took, the anger, and an increasing amount of hurt, pounded through her veins. Was the idea of dating her so terrible that he'd stooped to setting her up behind her back?

She descended the stairs into the kitchen, but Paul wasn't there. After checking the living room, she confirmed that he wasn't in there either. Glancing back up the stairs, she considered that he might have gone directly to his room, but quickly dismissed the thought. His door was open. If he'd been in there, she would have seen movement . . . heard something.

Determined to find him, Megan opened the back door to see if he'd gone outside for something. She was about to close the door again when something caught her eye. Squinting, she realized it was Paul, sitting in the backyard on the wooden swing that she'd never seen him use.

Zipping up her jacket, Megan softly closed the door to the house and crept almost silently across the yard. She lowered herself into the seat beside him, and tried to gather her thoughts. As much as she wanted to yell at him for what he did, she didn't think that would get her anywhere.

***

After leaving Chloe's bedroom, Paul practically ran down the stairs and out the back door. He'd needed air, space, something, so it didn't feel as if every breath he took weighed a thousand pounds.

Somehow, he found himself on the swing in his backyard. He remembered putting it together for Melissa. She used to sit and watch him mow the lawn, an iced tea in one hand, and a huge smile on her face—her long legs tucked beneath her. He missed that smile.

Paul was deep in thought—memories—when he heard the back door open. He didn't have to look to know it was Megan. Part of him wanted to hide from her. He could easily have held perfectly still and she would have been none the wiser to his presence.

His subconscious must have had other ideas. Without thought, his knees bent just enough for the swing to rock, drawing her attention.

He stopped the swing and waited. The closer she came, the faster his heart beat in his chest. Whether he liked it or not, he was attracted to Megan, and seeing her tonight with another man hadn't changed that. If anything, it had made it all that much worse.

She sat down next to him—her thigh pressing ever so slightly against his. It took everything in him not to twist to the side and take her right then and there. He'd somehow thought that seeing her with Rollins, giving her another option, would solve all their problems. Paul couldn't have been more wrong.

Throughout dinner, he'd kept his focus on Chloe, but he'd heard every word that both Rollins and Megan had said to each other. He imagined her smiling at his jokes—Rollins touching her in subtle ways just to gauge her reaction. It was maddening on a level Paul was entirely unfamiliar with.

Although he'd been hoping they would hit it off, and Rollins would ask her out, he hadn't been prepared for what that would mean. Against his will, he'd turned his head just in time to see Rollins give Megan a kiss. Paul couldn't tell from his angle whether it was on the lips or the cheek, but either way it caused a wave of jealousy to overtake him.

Silence enveloped them as they sat motionless on the swing. Paul had so much he wanted to say to her, but he didn't know if he could, or even should, share what he was feeling. Setting her up with Rollins had been a mistake. He knew that now.

"Why?" Megan's voice cracked, drawing his attention. Her jaw was locked tight, but he couldn't tell if it was from anger or if she was trying to keep herself from crying.

Paul didn't need to ask what she was referring to. He already knew. "I'm sorry. I shouldn't have—"

"No. You shouldn't." This time her tone was clipped, and there was no disguising how upset she was.

He didn't know what to say, so he stayed quiet.

She must have realized he wasn't going to respond. "Is it because I asked you out? Is the idea of dating me so horrible . . . so outrageous . . . that you felt you needed to set me up with someone else?"

Paul closed his eyes, and sighed.

"No. You don't get to do that. You don't get to push this under the rug and act like it didn't happen. I need to know why? Why did you do it?"

Leaning forward, he clasped his hands together, and rested his arms on his knees. "I'm not right for you, Megan. I've tried . . . I've tried to tell you. I'm sorry, but I can't be what you need. Rollins . . . I thought . . . maybe . . ."

"Is this about what happened with Melissa?"

He didn't answer.

It was her turn to sigh. "Whatever happened, I know it can't be *that* bad."

Before he knew what was happening, Megan had her hand on his arm, and the spot where she touched him tingled. He wanted more. As much as he knew he shouldn't . . . couldn't . . . want more, he did.

When Megan spoke again, her voice was barely above a whisper. "Jay asked me to go out with him Friday night."

Paul's chest contracted almost painfully, and he lowered his head. It was what he'd wanted to happen—what was meant to happen. So why did he feel as if he was going to be sick?

"I told him no."

He snapped his head up to look at her. "Why?"

She looked him square in the eye. "You know why."

They sat staring at each other for a long time until he looked away. Even with everything going on, even with their topic of conversation, Paul wanted to kiss her. How messed up was that?

He heard her let out what sounded distinctly like a huff, and the swing jerked a little as she removed her hand from his arm. Paul knew she was frustrated. If their situations were reversed, he supposed he would be, too.

Running a hand over his face, he took a deep breath, and looked out across his backyard. "I was called out around ten o'clock."

The moment the words left his mouth, it was as if he could feel a change in the air around them. Megan stilled to the point that, for a moment, he thought maybe she'd stopped breathing. He took a chance, and glanced in her direction. Her eyes were wide, and she held her posture rigid. She was waiting.

Paul returned his gaze to the darkness of the yard, unable to look at her or anyone else as he relived the worst night of his life. "The victim had been brutally raped and murdered. It was a gruesome scene . . . the worst I'd had to deal with since becoming a cop."

He let that hang in the air for a minute before continuing. "By the time we went over the crime scene and talked to the woman's family, it was nearly three in the morning when I walked through the door. Melissa was awake. She'd just put Chloe back down after a feeding."

Closing his eyes, he tried to push back the memories—to keep them from taking over, pulling him into the past. "I wasn't in a good mood. I was grumpy, and stressed, and angry for what had been done to that young woman. She was only eighteen, and he'd nearly torn her to shreds before killing her."

He looked down at the ground although he couldn't see much. The moon hung low in the sky, casting a heavy shadow. It fit the mood of their conversation, he supposed. "When I'd left the house earlier, Melissa noticed that we were almost out of diapers, and asked if I could pick some up on the way home. With all that happened, I'd forgotten."

To her credit, Megan didn't comment. She sat quietly and listened to every word of his confession.

"When she brought it up, I exploded. I don't know if it was the exhaustion or the stress . . . either way, she didn't deserve my anger. We'd fought before, of course. We'd been together for fifteen years. But this was different. I accused her of not appreciating what I did for her and our family. I was . . . I was mean about it. I said . . . I said things I shouldn't have. Things that, to this day, I wish I could take back."

The swing moved, but Paul didn't have it in him to look in Megan's direction to see what she was doing—how she was reacting to his revelation.

He cleared his throat, and finished what he'd started. If he was going to spill his guts, then he wasn't going to hold back. "Our fight ended when I yelled at her that she should just go get the damn diapers herself. She grabbed her purse off the counter, swearing that she'd do just that, and stormed out the door."

After a long pause, he whispered, "She never made it to the store. A mile from our house, a drunk driver ran through a stop sign and broadsided her. She was pronounced dead at the scene."

"I'm sorry."

Paul snorted. "I don't deserve your sympathy, Megan. I lost my wife because of my own stupidity—I cost my daughter her mother."

"No. You didn't."

Not wanting to argue with her, Paul stood. Keeping his back to her, he took a deep breath, and uttered the words that made him feel as if he were sticking a knife into his chest and twisting. "You should go out with Officer Rollins. I don't deserve a second chance."

Before she could reply, he walked back into the house. Hopefully, now she'd see. He wasn't the man she thought he was.

Chapter 11

Megan sat outside thinking about everything Paul had told her, until the cool night air finally drove her inside. He'd left the lights on for her, but when she went upstairs, she noticed his door was closed. Knowing he wouldn't welcome her intrusion into his private space, Megan reluctantly trudged into her room and got ready for bed.

It was only as she was drifting off to sleep that what Chloe said resurfaced in her mind, and Megan wondered what had prompted the little girl's sudden fear. So much had happened in the last five hours that it was difficult to tell what had caused the outburst. She knew she'd have to talk to Paul about what happened. No matter what was going on between them, they couldn't let it affect Chloe.

Megan didn't get much sleep that night which, considering how her evening had ended, wasn't a big surprise. Deciding she needed as much mental armor as possible, she took the time to get herself dressed and primped before going downstairs.

When Megan sauntered into the kitchen, she found Paul sitting at the table, reading the paper and drinking his morning cup of coffee. He didn't glance up or acknowledge her arrival in any way, but she knew he was aware of her by the way he hesitated for a moment as she walked behind him.

After getting her coffee, Megan pulled out a chair, and sat down to his right. She took a sip of her coffee. "Paul?"

He glanced up. From the look on his face, he appeared to be preparing for battle.

Although she knew they needed to talk about what he'd shared with her the night before, they needed to talk about Chloe more. "After you left Chloe's room last night, she said something to me. I've been thinking about it, and well, I'm worried."

This got his attention. "What did she say?"

"She asked if I was leaving."

Paul sat up straight. She had his full attention. "Why?"

"I don't know for sure, but I have to assume that it had something to do with what happened at dinner."

"Megan . . ."

She met his gaze. "Don't. We'll talk about last night, but not now. Not when Chloe is going to come downstairs at any minute. My biggest concern is that she thinks I'm going to just up and leave her."

"You don't think I'm concerned about that, too?" He stood, and took his cup to the sink. "I'll talk to her."

"I don't think that's a good idea."

He turned abruptly to face her. "Why not? I'm her father. It's my—"

"But it's *me* she thinks is leaving. She needs reassurance from *me*, Paul. Not you. Not on this."

The sound of little feet descending the stairs ended their discussion. Seconds later, a sleepy-eyed Chloe waddled into the kitchen.

Paul crossed the room, and lifted her into his arms. She clung to his neck, burying her face against his shoulder.

He carried her over to the counter, and proceeded to grab the supplies he would need for her breakfast before depositing her into a chair, and placing the items before her. She timidly glanced up at Megan, scooted her chair a little closer to where Megan was sitting, and then picked up her spoon to begin eating her cereal.

Megan looked questioningly at Chloe as she drank her coffee and nibbled on a muffin she'd snatched off the counter. Chloe stared intently at her cereal, but would pause every now and then as if she were waiting for something.

"Good morning, Chloe."

Chloe peeked up at Megan. "Morning."

Although Chloe wasn't typically a morning person, her mumbled greeting wasn't normal.

Glancing over at Paul, Megan saw him frown. At least he realized that she wasn't exaggerating the issue.

Megan turned her attention back to Chloe. "Chloe?"

She waited until she was sure she had the little girl's full attention.

"Honey, last night you asked me if I was leaving. Do you remember?"

Chloe nodded, and Megan thought she saw a note of fear in Chloe's eyes.

"Can you tell me what made you think that I was leaving?"

Chloe looked toward her father.

Paul tried to reassure her. "It's okay, sweetpea."

She still looked unsure.

Megan reached out, and placed her hand over Chloe's where it lay on the table. "No one's mad at you, sweetie. We're just trying to understand."

Chloe lowered her eyes. "You were mad at Daddy."

"Just because your dad and I don't always agree, doesn't mean I'm going to leave, Chloe. Grown-ups disagree sometimes."

"But that man. He . . . he kissed you." She said the last part in a conspiratorial whisper.

Megan sighed, and slid off her chair so that she could kneel down next to Chloe. Taking both the little girl's hands in hers, Megan tried to be as honest as she could. "I can't promise you that I'll never leave, Chloe, but I don't plan on going anywhere anytime soon, okay?"

"Okay."

There was still a little uncertainty in Chloe's reply, and Megan knew the little girl needed more assurance. "Do you think I can get a hug?"

Chloe didn't hesitate. She circled her tiny arms around Megan's neck, and squeezed tight. "I love you, Megan."

Megan hugged her back. "I love you, too, Chloe."

***

Leaving for work that morning was more difficult than usual. He wanted to stay and comfort his little girl. Paul knew he wouldn't be able to protect Chloe from every emotional, or even physical, obstacle she would face, but as her father that desire was there.

As he'd said goodbye to Chloe, giving her an extra-long hug, he didn't miss the pointed stare he'd received from Megan. He knew she held him responsible for Chloe's reaction, and in all honestly, Megan was probably correct. Paul was the one who'd invited Rollins to have dinner with them. Paul was the one who'd set everything up, including what led up to the kiss Chloe witnessed. It was his fault—at least most of it.

Paul parked his car outside the station, and took a moment to compose himself. As much as he needed to figure out what was going on in his life at the moment, he also had cases to work and a serial killer to catch.

He got out of his vehicle, and was halfway across the parking lot when he caught sight of Janey striding toward him. The look on her face told him that he wasn't going to like whatever it was she was about to tell him.

"We've got another victim."

Turning on his heel, they returned to his vehicle, and drove to the crime scene. He needed to get his head in the game, and figured the best way to do that was to begin gathering the facts. "What do we know?"

"The victim is a twenty-six-year-old female named Shelly Otis. Her roommate found her about an hour ago when she came home after a night shift."

"Anything else?"

"Not much. Since we're fairly sure this is another victim courtesy of our serial killer, they're waiting on us."

It didn't take them long to arrive. The victim's house was only about ten minutes from the station, in a middle-class subdivision. Paul noted that the surroundings were eerily similar to those of the other victims. Everything about the neighborhood was normal, average. There was nothing that made this place stand out. Was that a key to how this guy chose his victims?

"It looks like the others."

He glanced over at his partner. "Yeah. I was thinking the same thing. Could be a clue."

Janey snorted. "If it is, that he's choosing his victims based on them living in nondescript subdivisions . . . that's about as helpful as knowing he likes the color yellow."

Paul smirked. "Maybe he does."

She shook her head. "So not helpful, Daniels."

He released a harsh laugh, and then exited the vehicle. Janey followed, and they showed their badges to the patrolman positioned in front of the house, before going inside.

The forensics team was still doing their thing. Paul and Janey took a brief look at the crime scene, and Paul noted that it was in line with the others. The victim was lying in the center of the room, with her wrists and throat slashed. Blood pooled on the carpet, and stained the pink polka-dot bikini she wore.

Paul glanced out the window into the backyard, looking for any sign of a pool, and noticed what looked to be a hot tub roughly five feet from the house. "Do we have time of death?"

The ME looked up from where he was positioned over the body. "More than ten hours, so I'd say last night some time."

Nodding, Paul moved toward the door. He and Janey headed down the hall to where they'd been told the victim's roommate was waiting.

Sitting on the couch in the living room was a young woman who looked to be in her mid to late twenties with long reddish brown hair. She was staring off into space, face and eyes blotchy from the tears she'd been shedding. This was the part of the job Paul hated the most. It was hard to stay detached when coming face-to-face with the victim's friends and family. It always brought back memories for him.

Since the roommate was female, Janey took the lead. It was an unspoken agreement between them. "Katherine Bates?"

The woman turned abruptly, looking almost shocked to see them standing a few feet in front of her. "Yes."

Janey smiled. "Hello, Ms. Bates. I'm Detective Davis, and this is Detective Daniels. We need to ask you a few questions."

She glanced down, toying with a tissue. "Okay."

"When was the last time you saw your roommate?"

"Last night, before I left for my shift at the hospital. Shelly was in her room."

Janey moved to sit next to her on the sofa. "I know this is difficult, but do you remember seeing anything out of place when you left the house?"

She shook her head. "No. I was . . . I was running late, and

I . . ." Tears started streaming down her cheeks, and it took several minutes for her to compose herself.

The rest of the questioning went in a similar vein. She didn't know much. She hadn't seen anything. What's more, she and Shelly often worked opposite shifts, so she didn't have a lot of information on Ms. Otis' daily routine. They wrote down what she did know, and gave her their cards in case she thought of anything else.

After leaving Ms. Bates, Janey and Paul spoke to a couple of neighbors who'd been home the night before. Like the others, though, no one remembered seeing anything out of the ordinary. Paul and Janey still had no idea how this guy was getting into the homes of his victims without anyone seeing anything, or there being any sign of forced entry.

They stopped for lunch on the way back to the station.

Once they'd placed their order and their server had retreated to the kitchen, Janey turned her attention on him, an amused look on her face. "So how did dinner go last night with Rollins?"

He groaned. "I don't want to talk about it."

Janey laughed. "That bad, huh?"

Paul sighed. "You could say that."

"I could've saved you the trouble and told you that before you went."

"What part of 'I don't want to talk about it' did you miss?"

This only added to Janey's mirth. "Like it or not, that nanny of yours is smitten with you. And I doubt she appreciated you trying to throw another man in her direction."

He took a sip of his soda. "Is this one of those times when I tell you to butt out and you completely ignore me?"

She leaned forward and smiled. "Yep. It is. I've known you for five years, Paul, and I've never seen you rattled by a female. Heaven knows, I've witnessed women flirting their little hearts out more times than I can remember, but you've barely registered it. Megan Carson is different, whether you like it or not."

Paul said he didn't want to talk about it, and he didn't, but if anyone would understand it would be Janey. "I'm not—"

"Do not say you're not ready. It's been five years, Paul. Don't you think it's time you got back on the horse, so to speak?"

That wasn't it, but he let her assume that it was so she'd let the subject drop. Janey didn't know about his argument with Melissa the night of her death. He'd never told her. He'd never told anyone.

Until Megan.

***

Megan made it a point to spend extra time with Chloe that day. She tried to reassure the little girl as much as she could that she was there for the foreseeable future—for as long as Paul would allow her to be.

They read a couple of books together, and even made some brownies for dinner that night. As the day progressed, Chloe seemed to relax. It was one problem Megan could cross off her list.

She was still irritated with Paul. They needed to have a long talk, but she knew that doing so with Chloe around was tricky. Sure, Megan could wait until the little girl was asleep, but there was always a chance that they'd be interrupted.

There was also a possibility things could get heated—and not in the good, take-me-to-bed-and-have-your-way-with-me kind of way. Megan had every intention of making Paul realize that he was not responsible for what had happened to Melissa. Knowing what was keeping him from pursuing a relationship with her was equal parts frustrating and incredibly sad. It was obvious that he'd been beating himself up over this for the last five years, and Megan's heart hurt for him. She wanted to fix it.

At five o'clock, Megan and Chloe headed into the kitchen to start dinner. Paul would be home soon, and Megan had no idea what kind of a mood he'd be in. He knew her well enough to know that she wasn't going to let something like this go, but Megan also wasn't naïve. She knew it wasn't going to be easy.

They heard a car pull into the driveway, and Chloe scrambled down from her stool to wait by the door. Paul sauntered in a few seconds later. He hoisted his daughter up into his arms, and hugged her tight—a little tighter than was normal. That was when Megan noticed the tension—the stress— radiating from his body. Something had happened today at work. And as much as Megan wanted to hash it out with Paul, she knew tonight wasn't the night for it. She'd have to bide her time and wait.

For his part, Paul tried to put on a good show. He kissed Chloe on the cheek, and then lowered her back to the floor. "Something smells good."

"We're making chicken fa-fa—"

Chloe scrunched up her nose. Megan knew she was trying desperately to remember the rest of the word. "Fajitas."

"Fa-heat-taas." Chloe gave Paul a huge smile before rejoining Megan. "Did you want to help us make them, Daddy?"

Paul strolled over to stand on the other side of Chloe. "Sure. What is it that you need me to do?"

For the next half hour, they worked together to chop vegetables, marinate chicken, and warm tortillas. When there was nothing more Chloe could do to help with the food, she announced that she was going to set the table. It was haphazard, and Paul ended up with two spoons and no fork, but that was okay.

Chloe was all about helping—she'd been that way from the time Megan moved in. Sometimes Megan wondered if it was Chloe's way of supporting her dad. She might not be aware of the guilt he was carrying—the hurt—but kids were very perceptive. They picked up on things that many adults dismissed. Maybe this was her way of trying to comfort her father.

When they sat down to dinner, Paul was quieter than usual. He smiled at the appropriate times, and asked Chloe about her day, but there was something off.

Megan waited until Chloe was tucked into bed before bringing it up.

They were sitting downstairs watching television—or, she was watching television. Paul was staring off into space somewhere. "Paul?"

He glanced over at her, blinked, and then sat up a little straighter in his chair. "Yes?"

She could tell by his posture that he was bracing himself. "Is everything all right? I mean, you seem . . . I don't know. Worried? Stressed? Did something happen today?"

Paul released a breath, and she figured he'd been waiting for her to start in about their conversation the night before. They would talk about that, but not when he was like this. "Just work, that's all."

Megan scooted closer. She was on the couch, and he was in the recliner almost two feet away, but she needed to be closer to him. "A case?"

He nodded.

She wanted to reach out to him, but she didn't know if her touch would be welcomed. "Is it . . . I mean, I had the news on earlier. They said there was a woman found dead in her house."

Paul sighed, and closed his eyes. "I can't . . . I can't talk about the case."

Megan decided to throw caution to the wind. She reached out, spanning the distance between them, and covered his hand with hers.

He jerked, but didn't pull away.

They sat like that for several minutes before he opened his eyes and looked at her. He didn't say anything at first, but some of that haunted look he'd had before was gone. "I should get some sleep."

He stood, and she retracted her hand.

Paul hesitated.

"If you ever need to talk, Paul, I'll listen."

He didn't look at her. "Good night, Megan."

She watched him stroll out of the room and disappear up the stairs. Dropping her head back against the couch, Megan sighed. He'd allowed himself to take comfort from her. That was something, right? Rome wasn't built in a day, and Megan had a feeling that breaking down the walls Paul had built around himself was going to take some serious work on her part.

Pushing herself up off the couch, Megan turned off the lights, and headed up the stairs. Tomorrow was another day, and somehow she knew that once Paul got some rest, his defenses would be back up in full force.

Chapter 12

Megan couldn't have envisioned the chaos of the next few weeks if she'd tried. One of the other detectives had a death in the family, which meant Paul and all the remaining detectives had to pull extra shifts. If that weren't bad enough, as things were returning to normal, some of the officers came down with the flu. As often happens, the illness slowly spread through the department. It was only a matter of time before Paul came down with the bug.

The week before Chloe was supposed to leave for a month away with her grandparents, Paul arrived home one evening looking paler than usual. Megan knew almost immediately something was off. When Chloe ran over to greet her father, instead of picking her up, he hugged her against his leg, and ruffled her hair.

"Chloe, can you get the milk out for me?" Megan asked.

The little girl nodded, and raced across the room to get the milk.

While Chloe was busy, Megan edged closer to Paul. "You caught it, didn't you?"

"I'm fine."

"Uh-huh. Sure you are." Megan shook her head, and took the milk out of Chloe's little hands.

Paul cleared his throat, and Megan could hear the strain. "What are we having?"

"Pork chops."

"I helped season them, Daddy." A big smile stretched across Chloe's face. She was still completely unaware of her father's plight.

He smiled in response, but it didn't reach his eyes. "You're such a great helper."

Megan knew by the way Paul was acting that he had to be feeling pretty bad. "Why don't you have a seat? Dinner will be ready in a few minutes."

"I told you, I'm fine. What do you need me to do?"

Placing her hands on her hips, Megan fixed him with a hard stare. She didn't say anything, but he got the message loud and clear. He pulled out a chair and sat down.

Megan, with Chloe's help, brought everything to the table. As Megan lowered herself into a chair, she placed two painkillers down on the table near Paul's hand.

He glanced down at the pills, and then up at her. She thought maybe he would try to argue with her, but instead, he reached for the pills, and popped them in his mouth. "Thanks."

Throughout dinner, Megan made a conscious effort to keep Chloe occupied. Normally the little girl was all about filling her father in on what she'd done with her day, but Megan didn't think Paul was up for conversation at the moment. Eating seemed to be taking a considerable effort all on its own.

When they were finished, Megan asked Chloe if she'd help her put the food away and load the dishwasher. "Why don't you go upstairs and get into bed? Chloe and I will clean up."

To her surprise, Paul didn't argue.

He was halfway up the stairs when Chloe realized Paul was no longer in the kitchen. "Where did Daddy go?"

Megan bent down so she was on eye level with Chloe. "Do you remember how your daddy told you that some people at work were sick?"

"Uh-huh."

"And you know how sometimes when you're around people who are sick that you get sick, too?"

She scrunched up her nose in concentration. "Daddy's sick?"

Megan brushed a strand of hair off Chloe's face. "I think so. Which means we need to let him rest as much as possible, okay?"

"Okay."

Smiling, Megan stood. "Do you think you can help me load the dishwasher?"

Chloe nodded, eager to help.

For the rest of the evening, Megan kept Chloe downstairs so that Paul could rest. It wasn't until bedtime that things got a little dicey. Paul always tucked her in when he was home, and she couldn't understand why he couldn't that night. It took some work, and an extra story, but Megan finally got Chloe to settle down and close her eyes.

Before heading to her own room, Megan decided to check on Paul. She knocked lightly, and when he didn't answer, she cracked the door open so she could see inside. He was curled up on his side, his eyes closed, and the covers pulled up tight to his chin. The urge to go to him was strong, but she resisted.

She almost had the door closed when she heard him call her name.

Reopening the door, she stepped inside. "Yeah, Paul, it's just me."

He rolled over, and sat up a little. "Chloe?"

Megan strolled closer. "She's in bed. I had to bribe her with an extra story."

A small smile pulled at the corners of Paul's mouth. "She'll do anything to get an extra story."

Megan chuckled. It was true. Chloe would do almost anything for a story. There had been times when she'd asked Megan to make one up off the top of her head. Since Megan wasn't gifted in that way, she did her best to redirect the little girl's attentions. There were times, however, when it was impossible.

Paul coughed, and Megan momentarily forgot about Chloe. "How are you feeling?"

"Like someone ran a steamroller over my body."

Megan frowned. "Let me see if we've got anything in the medicine cabinet."

Megan ambled into Paul's bathroom. She'd only been in the space once before. Not long after Megan moved in with Paul and Chloe, the little girl had caught a cold. Paul kept all the medicine in his bathroom, out of Chloe's reach.

Like the first time, Megan was almost shocked by the difference between Paul and most of the guys she'd met. In her past experience, most men were slobs when it came to their personal space, with towels littering the floor and globs of toothpaste in the sink. There was none of that in the room she was currently standing in. The towel he'd used that morning was draped across the top of the shower bar, and the sink, with the exception of a few hairs from where he'd shaved, was clean.

Although Megan was tempted to explore some more—especially since she no longer saw Paul as only her employer, but a man she desperately wanted to get closer to—she went to the medicine cabinet, and found some cough syrup. Grabbing that, along with a glass of water in case he got thirsty during the night, Megan headed back into the bedroom.

Paul hadn't moved.

"I found some cough syrup for you. I didn't see anything specifically for the flu in there, so I'll have to go to the store and pick something up."

"Not tonight."

There was an edge of panic in his voice, and Megan immediately understood why. Even though she knew his reaction was irrational, it was also telling. "I'll wait and go in the morning, if that would make you feel better."

He took a sip of the water she'd set on the nightstand. "Thank you."

Megan sat down on the edge of the bed.

"What?"

She folded her hands in her lap. It was the only way she could keep from reaching out and touching him. "Nothing."

Paul sat up a little straighter. "Come on. You can tell me. I'm not *that* sick."

He punctuated his comment with another cough.

Megan reached out automatically to touch his arm, right above his wrist.

Instead of pushing her away, however, Paul gripped her hand and squeezed. "I'm okay. Or I will be."

She nodded, and for a few minutes, Megan sat and watched their hands pressed together. "Did you need anything? I can make you some soup."

As if the bubble had burst, Paul released her hand, and pulled the covers higher. "No, I'm good. I need some rest, that's all."

Megan stood. "I'll let you get some sleep."

She walked to the door, and stepped out into the hall. "Megan?"

"Yes?"

"Thank you. For taking care of me, I mean."

Megan smiled at him before pulling the door closed. She headed to her room, and stripped out of her clothes before padding naked to her bathroom. If Paul was sick, she knew she'd have to be extra diligent about keeping herself and the house clean. She'd also have to try to keep Chloe away from her dad for a few days while he recovered. The last thing any of them needed was for the little girl to fall sick days before she was supposed to go off with her grandparents.

***

Paul woke up the next morning feeling worse than he had when he'd gone to bed. He hated being sick. His mouth felt as though he'd swallowed a mouthful of cotton balls, and his throat as if it were lined with sandpaper.

He took a small drink of what was left of the water Megan had given him the night before, and winced as the lukewarm liquid slid down his throat. Paul had hoped a good night's sleep would have cured him, but that was wishful thinking on his part. Most of the department had come down with it.

With a groan, he fumbled for his cell phone, and dialed his boss. Once that was out of the way, he sent a quick text to Janey. She'd picked up that he wasn't feeling well when they'd parted ways the day before. Paul didn't think she'd be all that surprised that he wouldn't be going into work. Janey had only been back to work a week herself, after being out sick for four days.

It only took a minute or two for Janey to reply.

I got it covered. Call me if you need anything.

Everyone had been pulling extra hours trying to cover for those out sick. Paul would like to say those extra hours involved trying to catch their serial killer, but sadly, that wasn't the case. One day last week, he'd even had to go out on patrol because they were stretched so thin. Things were beginning to get better, people were coming back to work, and everything was getting back to normal. He and Janey had been hoping to sit down with their files today and reassess. It looked as though she'd be doing that on her own.

Heaving himself up out of the bed, Paul stumbled into the bathroom to take care of business and splash some cold water on his face. He looked horrible. It was difficult to say whether he looked worse than he felt or if he felt worse than he looked. Deciding he was too sick to care, he turned off the bathroom light and went back to bed.

Paul figured he must have fallen asleep again because the next time he opened his eyes, the sun was a lot brighter as it streamed in through the windows. He blinked, trying to shield his eyes, as a piercing pain shot through his head.

A light tapping noise on the door caused him more anguish, but it wasn't nearly as bad as the light.

He heard someone enter his bedroom, and pried his eyelids open against the light to see who it was. As much as he wanted to see his daughter, Chloe needed to keep her distance until he beat this bug or else she'd come down with it as well. It might even keep her from being able to go on her summer vacation with her grandparents, and Paul knew how much she was looking forward to seeing them. Melissa's parents had always been a huge part of Chloe's life from the time she was born—they'd only lived three miles away. With their move two hours north, Chloe had only seen them a handful of times in the last six months. It had been an adjustment. For all of them.

"Hey."

Megan stepped forward, blocking a good portion of the light. Some of the pain eased, and he released a sigh. There might also have been something else—calm, maybe—but he wasn't going to dwell on that. "Hey."

She must have noticed him squinting, because the next thing Paul knew, she was marching over to the windows and pulling the curtains closed.

"Better?" Megan asked as she returned to stand beside his bed.

"Yes. Thank you." He tried to sit up, and without him asking, Megan readjusted the pillows behind him. "You know you shouldn't get too close. You'll catch it, too."

"Well, if I do, you'll just have to take care of me then, won't you?" She sauntered across the room, and returned with a tray that held two pieces of toast and some tea.

Although he wasn't really hungry, Paul knew he needed to eat. He hadn't eaten much for dinner the night before, and if he wanted to kick this cold, he would need his strength. Why did every inch of his body have to ache?

Megan set the tray over his lap, and Paul picked up one of the pieces of toast. He was weak, and it irritated him. Paul was used to taking care of things, including himself. "I didn't ask you to take care of me. I'm perfectly capable—"

"Stop being a baby." Megan swiped his empty water glass from the nightstand, and strolled, unperturbed, into the bathroom.

When she returned with his refilled glass, she had a rather serious look on her face. "What?"

She set the glass down and crossed her arms over her chest. Even in his less than stellar state, Paul couldn't help but notice the way the motion pushed her breasts up, making them look fuller. Megan wasn't overly endowed in that area, but he had firsthand knowledge of how well they fit into the palm of his hand.

He suppressed a groan as his body reacted in spite of his condition.

Megan's expression softened, and she rushed to get him another dose of painkillers. She'd misinterpreted his reaction. That was probably a good thing. He didn't think he could fight her off right now.

Without argument, Paul swallowed the pills. "Thanks."

"You're welcome."

She didn't cross her arms again, which sent a wave of disappointment through him.

"Something on your mind?" He figured he might as well have her get whatever it was out of her system.

Megan met his gaze. She looked weary, but determined. "Cindy called this morning. Melissa's mom. She asked for you, and I told her that you were sick."

Okay, not what he'd been expecting. He opened his mouth to ask what she wanted, but coughed instead.

Megan handed him the tea.

He took a sip. It still felt as if there were tiny nails coating his throat, but at least it suppressed his urge to cough. "Thanks."

She frowned. "I'll add cough drops to the shopping list. I wanted to see if there was anything specific you wanted before Chloe and I head to the store."

"No. I don't think so."

"Okay."

Megan shifted her weight. She was nervous about something, and he figured it had to have something to do with her conversation with his mother-in-law.

"What did Cindy say?"

"Well, when I explained that you were sick, she . . ."

Paul waited for Megan to go on, but she didn't. "Did Cindy say something to upset you?"

He didn't think Cindy would do such a thing, but he guessed it wasn't out of the realm of possibility. When he'd told his in-laws that Megan was moving in with him and Chloe six months ago, Cindy and George had both been concerned—Cindy more so than George. To his knowledge, Cindy had never voiced those concerns to Megan.

"No. Not exactly."

Paul was trying to have patience, but given all he wanted to do was close his eyes and sleep for the foreseeable future, her stalling was grating on his nerves. "Spit it out."

Megan jerked at his tone, and of course, his gruff reply sent him into another round of coughing.

This time, she didn't hand him his tea. He guessed he deserved that. "Sorry."

"I know you aren't feeling well, and men tend to be babies of the highest order when they're sick, but that doesn't give you the right to be rude to me. I'm trying to help."

"I know, and I appreciate it. I do." Paul sighed. "What did Cindy say to you?"

"She said that since you're sick, she and George would come get Chloe early. That way, you could rest and get better faster. Plus, she said this way, hopefully Chloe wouldn't catch whatever you have."

"So when are they coming?"

Megan bit the inside of her lip. "They'll be here this afternoon."

Paul didn't know what to think. In a way he was glad they would be taking Chloe early. She was set to leave in five days, and if Janey's illness was anything to go by, it would take him nearly that long to recover, anyway. It wasn't as if he'd get to spend any real quality time with her before she left. Still, it was always difficult handing his little girl off for any extended period of time. "I guess this means you can head down to Nashville and visit your sister a little sooner."

Megan looked at him as if he'd grown two heads. "You think I'm going to go off and leave you here alone? When you're like this? Not a chance, mister. You aren't getting rid of me that easily."

"I'm a big boy, Megan. I've been sick before. I can take care of myself."

She shook her head like a disapproving parent, and strolled toward the door. "Chloe and I are going to the store. Eat your breakfast, and leave the tray by the bed. I'll come get it when I get back."

Without waiting for his response, Megan left his room, and closed the door behind her.

Paul leaned back against his headboard, and looked toward the ceiling. He was in some serious trouble. Megan's flight to Nashville didn't leave for five days. He'd been relying on Chloe being around to create a buffer between them. It had worked in the past. What was he going to do with her gone? He and Megan alone in the house together wasn't a good combination. Sure, he was sick, but unlike with Chloe, that didn't mean Megan would keep her distance—the last twelve hours had already proven that.

He took a drink of the peppermint tea Megan had brought with his breakfast, and sighed as the warmth coated his throat. Her taking care of him wasn't helping. Paul didn't get sick often. The last time it happened, his wife had still been alive, and Chloe hadn't yet been conceived. Melissa had brought him tea and juice and made sure his blankets and pillows were just so.

The memory of Megan adjusting his pillows caused a pang of longing in the pit of his stomach. There was one problem, though. He didn't know if he was longing for Melissa or Megan, and that brought him up short. The two women were so very different. How could he be having this pull toward Megan when, at the same time, he missed his wife?

It didn't make sense, but then again not much had made sense in his life for the last two months—not since Chris and Elizabeth's wedding.

Chapter 13

The moment Megan told Chloe they were going to the store to pick up some medicine for her dad, the little girl began asking questions. From the sound of it, Paul had never been sick—or at least, not that Chloe could remember. Chloe only had one parent left. She didn't want him to go away, too.

It was then Megan truly understood the little girl's freak-out when she'd thought Megan was going to leave. To think that one of the two people at the center of her world was going away, especially after she was already missing her mother in her life, was a scary prospect for a five-year-old.

The questions continued in the store. "What's this for, Megan?"

"It makes it so you don't cough."

Megan moved on to the next item on her list.

"What about that?" Chloe asked when Megan placed a box of tea in the cart.

It went on like that as they weaved their way through the store.

When they arrived home, Chloe helped Megan bring the groceries inside. Chloe was still worried about her dad, and Megan knew she would have to keep the little girl's mind off things until her grandparents arrived. Megan gathered what they'd need to make several batches of cookies. Chloe loved to bake, and they'd spent many hours in the kitchen making cakes and brownies over the last few months.

When Chloe found out what they were doing, her face lit up like it was Christmas morning. She rushed into the kitchen, grabbed her apron, and stood in the middle of the floor waiting impatiently.

Megan laughed. "Did you wash your hands?"

Chloe frowned, and ran into the small bathroom down the hall where there was a stool she used to reach the sink.

Hearing the water turn on, Megan used the time to unload and separate what they'd bought. She was almost finished when Chloe ambled back into the kitchen, wiping her hands on her little apron. "Can we make the cookies now?"

Megan attempted to hide her smile. "Not quite yet. We need to find a recipe first. Can you grab that book over there on the shelf that says cookies?"

Without waiting for any further instruction, Chloe went to the bookcase Megan indicated, the one where all the cookbooks Melissa had owned were stored. A couple of minutes later, the little girl brought the blue and tan book with the word cookies in big bold lettering. "I gots it, Megan. Now what?"

Chloe's eagerness was infectious. It was one of the things Megan loved about her. "I need you to sit down here at the table and find us a recipe for chocolate chip cookies. Do you think you can find all those words?"

The little girl nodded, and quickly took a seat, opening the book.

This time Megan didn't hide her smile. "I'm going to run these things up to your dad real quick, then I'll be back down and we can start making the cookies, okay?"

"I have to stay away so I don't get sick." Chloe repeated the explanation Megan had given her both the night before and again that morning.

It was also the explanation Megan had given Chloe when she'd explained that Chloe's grandparents were coming to pick her up early. Chloe had been torn. She missed her grandparents and longed to spend more time with them, but she was also afraid for her father. After several reassurances, and letting Chloe know that she could call her daddy anytime she wanted while she was with her grandparents, she seemed more at ease with the idea. Megan wouldn't go as far as to say she was excited. She only hoped Cindy understood that she would have to keep Chloe extra occupied for the next few days.

Megan knocked lightly on Paul's bedroom door before cracking it open to peer inside. He was lying in bed with his eyes closed, but as she walked into the room, he opened them.

"You're back."

"Yeah. I brought you some things I thought you might need." She handed him the bag and he took a look inside. Going through the grocery store, Megan had picked up anything she thought he might need, from things to settle his stomach to those proclaiming to help fight the flu.

He coughed and promptly pulled out the bag of throat lozenges. "Thanks."

"Did you need anything else at the moment? Chloe and I are going to make some cookies. I figure that will keep her busy until Cindy gets here."

"Good idea." Paul coughed.

She frowned, but after he assured her that he didn't need anything else, Megan headed back downstairs.

When she strolled into the kitchen, Chloe had already dug out the mixing bowl, the flour, and several measuring cups.

"Were you going to start without me?"

The little girl smiled up at her. "I's got everything ready, Megan."

Megan laughed and shook her head as she picked up the recipe book Chloe had left lying on the table. Sure enough, it was open to a recipe for old-fashioned chocolate chip cookies.

For the next three hours, Megan and Chloe worked side by side making cookies. Megan knew she and Paul would be eating cookies for weeks— even if Megan sent two to three dozen with Cindy. Baking had done the job, though. Chloe smiled and laughed freely. There was no sign of the furrowed brow that had been present early that morning.

At twelve thirty, Megan whipped them up a quick lunch, and then marched the little girl upstairs to clean up. While Chloe was washing her face and brushing her teeth, Megan packed Chloe's suitcase. Other than clothes and the stuffed bear she slept with, there wasn't much to take. Cindy and George kept toys at their house, and Megan had no doubts that more would be added to their collection over the next three weeks. Grandparents spoiled their grandchildren—or at least, that was how it was supposed to be.

Promptly at two, there was a knock on the door. Chloe ran to answer it, not waiting for Megan. With her grandmother here, Chloe was full of energy.

She wrapped her arms around Cindy's waist. "Grandma!"

Cindy laughed. "Oh, my. Let me have a look at you. I think you've grown two inches since the last time I saw you."

Megan brought all of Chloe's things downstairs, and then asked if she wanted to say goodbye to her dad. Without giving a verbal response, the little girl took off up the stairs toward Paul's bedroom. Megan was hot on her heels, but even still, Chloe reached Paul's door first. "Chloe."

At the sound of her name, she stopped, and looked wide-eyed at Megan.

"It's okay, honey, just try to remember your daddy is sick."

Chloe looked down.

Megan sighed, and knocked on the door before pushing it open.

Paul turned his head and opened his eyes. When he saw Chloe, he smiled. "Hi, sweetpea."

"Hi, Daddy." Chloe twisted her fingers together, and shifted her weight from one foot to the other.

"Cindy's downstairs, and Chloe wanted to come up and say goodbye before they leave," Megan said when she saw a crease beginning to form in Paul's brow.

"Oh." He glanced over at the clock. "I didn't realize how late it was. Did you get all your cookies made?"

"We made lots, and lots, and lots of cookies, Daddy. We's taking some to Grandpa."

"That's very nice of you. I'm sure he'll appreciate it."

Paul coughed, which led to another deeper cough.

Megan knew it was time for them to go and let Paul get back to recovering. "We need to say goodbye and let your daddy rest. Plus, I'm sure your grandma has lots of fun stuff planned for you. You don't want to miss that, do you?"

Chloe looked up at Megan, and she ran a gentle hand through the little girl's hair. There was so much in Chloe's eyes—more than there should be in someone so young. Two seconds later, Chloe practically hurled herself at her father's blanket-covered legs. She hugged him tight, and Paul reached down to brush his fingers along her forehead.

"I love you," she whispered.

"I love you, too, Chloe." She turned her head to look at him, but didn't let go. "Be good for your grandma and grandpa."

***

It nearly broke Paul's heart to watch as Megan coaxed Chloe away from him and out of the room. He could see she was torn. She wanted to go with Cindy, but she didn't want to leave him. Whether he liked it or not, Megan and Cindy were right. Chloe would be better off with her grandparents. The longer she stayed in the house, the more likely she'd get sick, too.

He must have drifted off to sleep because the next time he opened his eyes, it was dark out. His throat was dry, and he was starving. Paul figured it was a good sign that he was hungry. Maybe he would be back to work sooner than he'd thought.

Kicking the covers off him, Paul shuffled to the bathroom and then made his first trek outside his bedroom since coming home from work over twenty-four hours before.

It was after midnight and the house was quiet. Megan was asleep. She'd left her door open—something she didn't normally do—probably thinking it would be easier for her to hear him.

Paul was careful not to make too much noise as he crept down the hall, but he couldn't help but pause at her door. The room was clothed in shadow, but he could clearly see the outline of her figure lying in the bed. Megan was full of contradictions. He knew she came from a not-so- pleasant childhood, and yet she was great with his daughter.

She's great with you, too.

He closed his eyes and took a deep breath. As he inhaled, he caught Megan's scent. It was somewhere between lilac and cherry. He didn't know if it was a perfume she wore or what, but she always had a hint of it surrounding her.

Before he could get lost in memories, Paul backed away from the doorway, and continued downstairs to the kitchen. Everything was neatly put away, and he was easily able to find leftovers to warm up in the microwave. Megan was taking such good care of him, and it made what he was feeling for her that much more complicated. If it was only physical attraction, he could deal with that. But it wasn't only physical. He liked her. He enjoyed spending time with her.

As Paul sat in the darkened kitchen eating the soup he knew Megan most likely made just for him, he considered his options. He still didn't think he was good enough for her—or anyone, for that matter—but although Megan knew what he'd done, she didn't seem to agree. Could he give a relationship with her a chance? Would it work, or was he setting them both up for failure? He was thirty-six years old. She was twenty-three. Did they even want the same things?

All the questions were making his head hurt, so he decided to put off any more contemplation until he was feeling better. It wasn't as if anything could happen while he was feeling like he was, anyway.

Putting everything away, Paul trudged back up the stairs, and tumbled into his bed. He popped a few more pills and rolled over, closing his eyes against the pain. Everything else would have to wait until morning.

Over the next thirty-six hours, Paul began to feel somewhat normal again. He no longer felt as if he'd been beaten and left for dead. His muscles ached, but it was more like something one would experience after a good hard workout.

Megan took her role of caregiver seriously. She hadn't been pleased that he'd awakened the other night and gone downstairs for food. He'd been given a nice little lecture about letting people take care of him. Was that something all women learned how to do? Did they teach it in school or something? He could have sworn he'd received a similar lecture from both Melissa and his mother at various times in his life.

As it was, Paul didn't want for much of anything. Megan made sure he had food, water, cough syrup, pain medication, and anything else she thought he might need. The only problem with all her attention was that as he started to feel better, he began craving other things. She'd go to plump up his pillows and her breasts would come within inches of his face. There was a time or two when he came close to pulling her top out of the way and sucking one of her nipples into his mouth. Knowing exactly how it would feel and taste made it doubly tempting.

He'd been home for three days when his partner showed up bearing gifts.

"I thought you'd be climbing the walls by now."

Paul sat up as Janey strolled across the room. "Megan brought over the TV from her room for me to watch. Not much on during the day, but it's better than staring at the ceiling."

Janey sat down on the edge of the bed and handed him a thick folder. "I have to go to court this afternoon, so I thought I'd bring the file over for you. I looked at it until my head hurt, but I'm not finding many patterns."

"But you're finding some?"

She shrugged. "Just the usual. They all lived or worked within a twenty-mile radius, so most of them went to the same stores. There is overlapping, but nothing I can find that screams it may be the place they attracted the attention of a serial killer."

He opened the folder and paged through some of Janey's notes. "A pattern is a pattern."

"True, but I'm not finding anywhere all these women went a day, a week, two weeks before they were killed. It's possible this guy is picking his victims and then watching them until the time is right. If that's the case, it's going to make him harder to track. Considering he's killing about every two months, I have to think he's picking his victims with some degree of frequency."

Paul nodded. "I agree. There has to be a pattern. We just aren't seeing it yet."

Janey let him look over the file for a few minutes before she shifted her weight, getting his attention. "So. How are things going with the nanny?"

He rolled his eyes. "None of your business."

She laughed. "That good, huh?"

Paul grunted.

"A little piece of advice—"

"I don't need any advice on my personal life."

"Oh, but I think you do. Besides, I'm going to give it to you anyway, whether you want it or not." Janey looked over her shoulder, and then back to him. "If you like her, then you should go for it. Chloe likes her, and I've seen some of those looks she gives you. What do you have to lose?"

"It's not that easy, Davis."

"Why the hell not? Don't tell me you're not attracted to her."

"It's not—"

"Exactly. So suck it up and ask the girl out. You do remember how to do that, right?"

Paul snorted. "Yeah. I'm not that old and decrepit."

She patted his leg. "I didn't think so."

Janey stood and sighed. "As much as I'd love to stay and give you more grief, I need to get to the courthouse. Call me later if you need anything. Or if you find something."

"I will."

Paul spent the next several hours going over the case file. Janey was right. Although there *were* patterns, they weren't ones that stood out or screamed a connection. All of the women had been to the same grocery store in the last six months, but only three went on a regular basis, and one hadn't been to the store for four months before she was killed. While they would follow up on the lead, it was most likely a dead end.

When Megan brought his dinner, Paul set the folder aside. "Smells good."

Megan smiled and sat down on the bed. He could feel the heat of her body as it pressed against his leg. As usual, he was hyperaware of her.

"Is that what Detective Davis brought over earlier?" Megan asked.

He glanced at the file, and then took a bite of his food before answering. "Yeah. She's hoping maybe I can see something she's missing. Fresh eyes and all that."

"This is the serial killer?"

Although Paul didn't discuss the details of his cases with Megan, the murders had made the news, and she knew he had been assigned to the case. "Yes."

She nodded and bit the side of her lip.

Needing to touch her, Paul reached out and took hold of her hand. "What is it?"

She met his gaze. "Did you want me to cancel my trip? I can stay here. It's not a big—"

"No. Go. You need to spend time with your sister." He saw by the scowl on her face that she was going to protest. "And I need to catch up on the work I missed. With Chloe gone, I'll probably be pulling twelve to fifteen hour days for the next week."

Megan nodded. "All right."

Paul couldn't help the pull he felt toward her, and how right it felt to hold her hand like he was. A surge of warmth raced through his body, and he wondered if maybe he was making the wrong decision. Maybe he could try . . .

No. It would never work between them. They were too different, and he was . . .

Paul looked down at their hands intertwined together, and it was hard to remember his arguments. He had to hold firm. It was for the best. He had to keep telling himself that.

Chapter 14

Sunday morning arrived before Megan knew it, and she was packing up her things for her trip that afternoon. Paul was feeling much better, although his cough lingered. The last two days had been interesting. She wasn't sure what to make of Paul's apparent one-eighty.

Okay, so not much had changed. It wasn't as if he'd declared his undying love to her or anything, but he was different. When he'd joined her in the kitchen for dinner the night before, the wall that always seemed to separate them wasn't there. Maybe it was only the lack of Chloe's presence. Megan was trying not to read too much into it and get her hopes up.

"Are you about ready?"

Megan glanced up to see Paul's figure framed in her doorway. He'd gone into work for a few hours the day before, but was staying home this morning so that he could take her to the airport.

She smiled and made a final check of her suitcase. "I think so. If I forgot something, I'm sure Gage or Rebecca can run me to the store."

Paul strolled into the room as Megan zipped up her luggage. He picked up the suitcase and started for the door.

"I can get that, you know."

He looked back at her and smiled. "So can I."

Megan rolled her eyes. Since he'd started feeling better, Paul had been insistent that he could do for himself. She supposed this was his way at realigning the scales, so to speak.

It was nearly a half hour drive to the airport. Megan spent most of that time staring out the window and tapping her fingers against her leg.

"You all right?" Paul asked.

She turned her head to look at him. "Yeah. It's just . . . I've only flown once before. I guess I'm nervous."

Paul nodded. "It's been years since I've flown. I don't mind it, but it's not my favorite thing either."

"I was in Oklahoma. My boyfriend at the time wanted to go see one of his friends play in New York City." Megan's voice trailed off as she let that piece of information hang in the air. That time and place in her life felt like a lifetime ago.

"We took a trip to New York when I was a kid, but I don't remember much."

Megan nodded. "I don't remember much either."

Paul glanced over at her and frowned.

She shrugged. It wasn't as if she had tried to hide her past. "I remember the airport, and taking the subway to this rat-infested motel. Billy and his girlfriend were there. They'd brought booze, and . . ."

"And?"

"And . . . we partied. A lot." Megan tried to downplay it, hoping he wouldn't pick up on what could happen in a hotel room with two guys, two girls, and a whole lot of alcohol.

She should have known better.

"Define *partied.*"

His voice had an edge to it, but she couldn't tell if he was upset, hurt, or . . . well, she had no idea. Either way, she was determined to be honest with him. "We got drunk and fooled around."

"As in . . . had sex." This time she didn't miss how he gritted his teeth as he spoke.

"Yes."

Paul's knuckles turned white on the steering wheel. "Did you even use protection? What am I thinking? You don't even remember most of it. How are you going to remember if you bothered to use condoms?"

Okay, that ticked her off. She crossed her arms over her chest and stared him down. "Look, you knew about my past. I made no secret of how wild I used to be. I made some stupid mistakes. I know that. I don't need you telling me how dumb I was."

He was silent for several minutes. "You're right. I'm sorry. I have no right to make judgments. Especially on something that happened years ago."

Although she wanted to be mad, she didn't want to leave him for a week with an argument hanging between them. "Apology accepted."

They approached the exit sign for the airport, and Paul took a deep breath. "Gage and Rebecca are picking you up in Nashville?"

"Yeah. They're meeting me in baggage claim." Megan smiled. "I wonder how big Becca's tummy is now? All she had was a little bump the last time I saw her, but she's got to be bigger now."

"She's what—about six months along?"

"Yep. So she should have a belly for sure."

Paul laughed, and it was good to hear. Unfortunately, that segued into a coughing fit.

Megan dug into her purse and found a cough drop. "Here."

He took it and popped it into his mouth. His cough subsided as he pulled up to the curb at the airport. "How did you come to have cough drops in your purse?"

She smiled and shrugged. "You never know when they'll come in handy."

Paul shook his head, but he was smiling, so she knew all was good.

They both exited the vehicle, and he unloaded her suitcase from the trunk. He set it down on the curb and turned to face her. "Call me when you land?"

Megan nodded. "Take care of yourself while I'm gone, okay?"

"You do the same."

She knew she needed to go, but there was something stopping her.

Paul glanced up at something over her shoulder, and she could guess that it was the security guard coming to tell him he needed to move his vehicle.

Before she could overthink it, Megan closed the distance between them and planted a solid kiss on Paul's lips.

When she backed away, taking her suitcase with her, Megan couldn't help but revel in that little thrill she got at the stunned look on his face. "I'll see you in seven days. Don't forget me."

He chuckled. "I don't think that will be a problem."

Megan giggled, and waved as she walked through the glass doors. She would miss Paul, but more importantly, she hoped he would miss her. If he didn't, that meant he probably didn't feel as strongly for her as she did for him. It didn't mean he never would, but it would make what she wanted more difficult to achieve.

She got her ticket and made her way through security. It was a little different than she remembered. Then again, she hadn't been paying much attention to anything other than Dale the last time she'd set foot in an airport. She had been smitten with the wannabe rock star, and at the time, she would have followed him anywhere.

As she found a seat at the gate to wait on her flight, Megan mused over how much her life and her tastes had changed. Looking back, she had trouble seeing what exactly had appealed to her about the bad boys she'd followed across the country. But even as the thought crossed her mind, Megan knew. Freedom. That was what they'd offered her. Or, at least, that's what she'd thought they'd offered her.

Thinking about her past boyfriends brought Paul back to the forefront of her mind. He'd been shocked about her revelation in the car. Megan was sure there were other things about her past that would shock the pants off him as well. She had two rules: no illegal drugs and no violence. Growing up, she'd witnessed her mom being battered around a few times by her dad. It wasn't something she was willing to put up with. Thanks to her big sister, Megan never had to. Rebecca had taught Megan how to protect herself, should the need arise.

Megan snorted. She'd given her sister such a hard time over the years. Thinking back, Megan wondered how many times Rebecca had protected her and she'd been oblivious.

A woman's voice came over the intercom, announcing Megan's flight. She picked up her carry-on bag, and made her way onto the plane. Megan needed to find a way to express her gratitude for all her big sister had done for her. Considering how bratty a child Megan had been growing up, and their father's hot temper, Rebecca might have saved Megan's life.

*****

After leaving the airport, Paul drove directly to the station. It was Sunday, and as a seasoned officer, he was no longer required to work weekends unless he was on call, but he needed something to do. Saying goodbye to Megan was harder than he'd thought it would be.

Paul sighed as he pulled into his assigned parking spot outside the station. He kept trying to tell himself that going on a date with Megan wasn't a good idea. Then again, if they did go out on a date, if she could see they weren't compatible, that dating him wasn't all it was cracked up to be, then maybe she'd refocus her attention on someone else—a guy closer to her age, maybe.

A nauseous feeling settled in the pit of his stomach. He didn't like that idea either. The thought of seeing her with Rollins, or someone else like him, had Paul's insides tied up in knots. "It would be for the best."

He tilted his head back and closed his eyes.

Two sharp knocks on his car window jolted him upright. He glanced over to see one of the rookie patrolmen—Paul couldn't remember his name— staring back at him.

Paul rolled down the window.

"Everything okay, Detective?" the patrolman asked.

"Yes. Everything's fine. Is there something I can do for you?"

The young man shook his head. "No, sir. I happened to be walking by and noticed you sitting in your vehicle."

"Ah." Paul rolled up the window, removed his keys from the ignition, and opened the door. He stepped out onto the pavement and pocketed his keys. "Just doing a little thinking."

The officer nodded. "You're working the serial killer case, right?"

"Yes." Although Paul recognized the officer, he didn't really know the guy.

"I thought so."

Before the rookie could ask any more questions, Paul set off toward the building.

Of course, that didn't stop the officer from following. "Are you getting close to solving the case?"

Paul didn't answer until he was right outside the station door. He paused, and then faced the other man. "Why are you so curious?"

"Um. I—um."

"Do yourself a favor. You do your job, and let me do mine." Not giving the guy a chance to respond, Paul opened the door and went inside.

Paul didn't have long to ponder his conversation in the parking lot before Janey found him.

"Hey. I thought you might be in today. Is your nanny off to visit her sister?"

"Yes, *Megan* is off to visit her sister. I dropped her at the airport about twenty minutes ago."

Janey turned, attempting to hide a smirk. She wasn't all that successful, however. His partner had been abundantly clear regarding her feelings on his relationship status even before Megan entered the picture.

Needing to redirect her attention, Paul unlocked his desk and retrieved the file he'd stored there the day before. "You up for some legwork today?"

"You thinking of running down some of those leads?"

He nodded. "I figured we could hit some of the overlapping locations on our list."

With the case file tucked under his arm, Paul weaved through the desks, heading toward the station entrance with Janey following close behind. Not far from the door, he spotted the officer who'd cornered him in the parking lot. The guy was talking to another patrolman, one Paul had worked with for years.

"You okay?" Janey asked. "Not getting sick again on me, are you?"

Paul opened the door, and ambled out into the parking lot toward his vehicle. "You wouldn't get that lucky, Davis. Come on, we've got a case to solve."

They were leaving their second stop—which failed to yield any new information—when his cell phone rang. "Daniels."

"Hey. It's Megan."

He glanced down at his watch, and sure enough over two hours had passed since he'd dropped her off at the airport. "How was your flight?"

"Good. I sat beside this guy who sells advertising. He's in Nashville for some kind of convention."

A spark of jealousy surged through him, and Paul quickly clamped down on it. "Sounds . . . interesting."

She laughed. "Not really. He was nice enough, though. Oh, and he invited me to stop by the convention if I had time—he even gave me two tickets in case Becca wants to tag along."

"I see." Paul closed his eyes and tried to ignore his irrational response.

"Okay, well, I'm almost to baggage claim, so I should probably go. Becca texted that they were already in the airport waiting. I'll text you later, all right?"

"Have fun." His throat clenched as he spoke those two simple words.

"I will."

The phone went silent, and he removed it from his ear.

"Everything all right with your girlfriend?"

"She's not my *girlfriend*."

He climbed behind the wheel of his car, and Janey slid into the passenger seat. Starting the engine, Paul maneuvered out of the parking lot and headed toward their next destination—a nail salon. About halfway there, Paul chanced a look at his partner. She wore a knowing smirk. He decided it was probably better to ignore her, so he concentrated on what lay ahead. Questioning people, looking for clues, uncovering leads—those things he understood.

The nail salon sat on a side street not far from the local community college. Since it was Sunday, there wasn't a lot of pedestrian traffic, but Paul had to imagine that on a weekday the area would be hopping. There were restaurants along the main drag, as well as a few small specialty stores. Megan had been down to the college a few times to pick up textbooks and the like. He wondered if she'd ever been to any of the stores or restaurants.

"You coming?" Janey's question brought him back to the present.

"Yeah."

They spoke to the owner of the salon. She remembered two of the women, but couldn't recall seeing the other two. It was what they'd expected, but given what they were working with, they were hoping to catch a break.

Since they were in the area, they decided to take some time to inquire in some of the surrounding shops. Most staff didn't remember any of the women, but they got lucky when they stopped in a little pizzeria. The man behind the counter was fairly sure he'd seen three of the women in his restaurant. It wasn't a positive ID, but it was something.

After finishing at the pizzeria, they decided to call it a day. It was after five and most of the stores were starting to close. Overall, it had been a productive day, and they'd be back at it on Monday morning.

Since Paul was on his own, he dropped Janey back at the station, and then stopped off at his favorite Thai restaurant to pick up some dinner.

Nom, the owner of the restaurant, greeted him as soon as he walked in. "Paul. It's been a long time. Where have you been?"

"Been staying in a lot lately."

Nom smiled and came around the counter to give him a hug. "Ah. Well, good to see you."

Before Melissa died, they had frequented the restaurant a lot. Melissa loved Thai food. They'd gotten to know Nom and several of the staff over the years. "It's good to see you, too, Nom. How have you been?"

"Good. Good. Can't complain. You here to eat?"

Paul checked his watch. Chloe usually called him before Cindy began getting her ready for bed. "I was hoping maybe I could get something to go."

"Of course. What would you like?"

He gave Nom his order, and she disappeared through the swinging wooden doors into the kitchen. Taking a seat in the corner, he waited.

The food didn't take long, and soon he was on his way home. He was pulling his car into the driveway when he heard his phone beep, letting him know he'd received a text. His stomach did a little flip in response. Given Megan's promise to text him later, he knew it was probably her.

Somehow he made himself wait until he was inside the house before checking his phone. Sure enough, it was Megan.

I'm hiding in the basement.

He smiled. **Why are you hiding in the basement?**

They r in their bedroom. It was this, or ear plugs.

Paul laughed out loud as he removed his food from the bag and laid it out on the table. **That bad huh?**

U have no idea.

Although Paul had nothing against texting, it wasn't his favorite way to have a conversation. Hitting the call button, he waited for Megan to pick up.

Her laughter echoed through the phone. "I wondered how long it would take you to give up and call me."

He rolled his eyes. "So, other than hiding in the basement, how's your visit so far?"

"Not bad. They picked me up, and then we went to get lunch. Oh my goodness, Paul, Rebecca has the cutest belly. It's not as big as I thought it would be. It looks like she has a basketball stuffed inside her but we can only see half of it."

"Rebecca's pretty fit. That's probably why."

"Yeah, I guess. I mean she still runs every morning and stuff." Paul could almost see Megan shrug.

"That would do it."

"The house has changed a little, too. Becca moved her things in, of course, and then she took over one of the rooms on the first floor and turned it into an office. Oh, and the room across from their bedroom—the one Becca stayed in before—they're turning that into a nursery. It's covered in jungle prints."

Megan sounded happy, even if she had started the conversation off with a complaint.

"Glad you went?"

She didn't answer right away. "Yeah. I mean, there is no way I could stay here long-term if the last half hour is any indication, but . . ."

"But you missed your sister."

"Yeah."

The word hung in the air, and Paul could tell she wanted to say something else. Instead, she remained silent. He let it go, and asked another question. "So do Rebecca and Gage have any plans for you tomorrow?"

"Gage has practice, so I think Becca and I are going shopping. I tell you, this baby has done something to her brain. Becca never liked to shop. Ever."

A flash of Melissa coming home loaded down with packages after a full day of shopping filled his mind. "Babies change a lot of things."

"I guess I just didn't realize how much. Not that they didn't change things, but people. I mean Becca is still my bossy, overprotective sister, but she's different, too. I guess that's a good thing." Megan sighed. "So anyway, tell me about your day. What did you do after you dropped me off at the airport?"

They talked until Chloe called, and then Paul reluctantly said goodbye to Megan. He spent another twenty minutes on the phone with his daughter as she told him all about the day she'd spent with her grandma and grandpa. When he hung up, Paul realized he'd only eaten about half his meal. He'd been so caught up in his two phone conversations that he'd forgotten to eat.

Standing up, he carried his cold food to the microwave and shoved it inside. Although his stomach was rumbling, begging for food, Paul couldn't regret the way he'd spent his evening.

Chapter 15

"Sorry about last night."

Megan looked up from the stack of baby blankets she'd been perusing. Rebecca was holding a bottle with little yellow bears in her right hand, a sheepish look on her face.

"What are you apologizing for? Ditching me, or making so much noise I had to spend most of the evening in the basement?" Megan grinned to lessen the harsh impact of her words. She wasn't mad at her sister, but she hadn't relished spending three hours hiding in their basement either. It wouldn't have been so bad had she been able to talk to Paul the entire time, but she hadn't. As it was, she'd ended up watching reruns of *CSI*. It was the only thing decent she could find on television.

Rebecca placed the bottle back on the shelf. "Both, I guess. I mean we didn't mean . . ."

"You're still newlyweds. I get it."

Her sister rubbed a hand over her growing belly and smiled. "It's just, ever since I entered my second trimester I can't seem to control myself."

Megan snorted. "And you could control yourself before?"

"Okay, you're right. Gage has always been able to . . . well . . ." To Megan's surprise, Rebecca giggled. It was weird, but good, too. Her sister was happy.

"Yeah, I get it." And Megan did get it. Those two make-out sessions with Paul had her craving more of his kisses. She could only imagine what it would feel like to have him inside her . . . surrounding her.

Walking over to a rack filled with little socks, Megan sighed. She missed sex. Battery-operated boyfriends had nothing on the real thing.

Her sister threw a few items in their cart and continued down the aisle. Megan followed close behind, still lost in her thoughts, and wondering what Paul was doing right then.

"So are you seeing anyone?"

Rebecca's question brought Megan up short.

"Um. Not exactly." While she wasn't ashamed of her feelings for Paul, she had no idea how her sister would react to such information. Rebecca hadn't been thrilled when Megan made the decision to move in with Paul and Chloe in the first place.

Megan should have known her sister wouldn't let a vague answer go unchallenged. "What do you mean, *not exactly*? Is there someone you're interested in? You're not chasing after another bad boy, are you?"

"No. I'm not chasing after another bad boy." Megan sighed, this time loud enough for her sister to hear while she played with the button on the cutest little suit she'd ever seen.

Rebecca placed her hand over Megan's and squeezed. "I just want you to find someone who will love you and make you happy. That's all."

"I know. And I'm working on it. Promise."

They stood there for a long minute before Rebecca let go of Megan's hand and started moving forward again. Rebecca didn't say anything for a long time, but Megan knew her sister well enough to know that Rebecca's silence only meant she was choosing her words carefully.

For the next half hour, the two women weaved their way through the store, picking out a variety of items Rebecca and Gage would need once their baby was born. It wasn't until they were in the car and on their way back to the house that her sister broached the subject of Megan's love life again.

"Can you do something for me?"

"Becca, you know I'd do just about anything for you."

Rebecca grimaced, which should have been Megan's first clue.

"What?" Megan asked.

"Promise me that when you figure it out with this guy, whoever he is, that you'll bring him to meet me."

"Um—"

"Look, I'm not asking because I don't trust your judgment or anything, but . . ."

"But my judgment has sucked in the past."

Rebecca laughed. "Well, when you put it that way . . ."

Megan chuckled, and turned in her seat to give Rebecca her undivided attention. "I know you're worried, but don't be."

"Says the girl who ran off with a guy that she'd known for a week, and had me worried I'd find her in a ditch somewhere."

"Hey! I was eighteen." As much as Megan knew Rebecca was justified, it burned her when her sister threw her past in her face.

"And now you're only twenty-three."

Megan tried to keep her cool. It wouldn't do any good to yell at her sister. If anything, it would only make Rebecca think she was right.

Taking a deep breath, Megan waited until she knew she could respond without anger coloring her tone. "Becca, I love you, and I know you worry about me, but things are different. I've changed. You've changed. You have a husband now to worry about. And a baby on the way that's going to need all that protective mothering you're so good at."

Rebecca swiped at a tear that rolled down her cheek. "Is that your way of telling me to butt out?"

Megan smiled. "Kinda. Yeah."

For the longest time, Rebecca didn't say anything. She drove through the streets of Nashville, letting a heavy silence linger between them. As they turned onto Gage and Rebecca's street, her sister cleared her throat. "I can't make any promises—habits are hard to break—but I'll try not to be so overbearing, okay?"

Leaning across the center console, Megan placed a quick kiss on her sister's cheek. "Thank you."

Rebecca shook her head and laughed. "I still want to meet him. I mean, if he's important to you . . ."

"I promise that if things become serious then I will let you meet him."

While she could see that Rebecca wasn't entirely happy with the outcome, Megan was glad her sister seemed willing to let it go—at least, for now. They unloaded their purchases from the car, made some lunch for themselves, and then curled up to watch a movie in the theater room Gage had set up in the basement. It felt normal, something neither Rebecca nor Megan got a lot of growing up.

Around three o'clock, Gage bounded down the stairs, announcing that he was home from practice. His hair was still damp from the shower he took, and even Megan had to admit he looked good. As soon as Rebecca laid eyes on him, she pushed herself up from the couch, and ran over to him.

The amazing thing was Megan didn't know which one was happier to see the other. They both wore matching smiles, and as soon as they were within touching distance, they were all over each other.

"Hello, Beautiful," he whispered against Rebecca's lips a moment before his tongue disappeared inside her mouth.

Megan cleared her throat and stood. "I guess that's my cue to leave."

She went to brush past them, but Gage reached out a hand to stop her. "You don't have to leave. We can control ourselves."

"It's okay, really," Megan insisted. "I wanted to check out the pool, anyway. I'll change into my swimsuit and give you two some alone time."

As she headed upstairs, she heard Gage stop Rebecca from following. There was no way Megan would begrudge her sister her happiness, or even the great sex Rebecca was obviously having. It was difficult to witness, considering the current condition of Megan's love life, or lack thereof.

Megan swiftly changed into her bikini, grabbed a large towel, and slipped through the sliding glass doors out onto the patio. Gage had a decent sized in-ground pool. When she'd stayed at his house the first time, she hadn't gotten a chance to take advantage of it. She was determined not to make the same mistake this time around.

Throwing her towel onto one of the lounge chairs, Megan sat along the edge of the pool, letting her legs dangle in the water. It was warm. Not bathwater warm, but warm enough to confirm that the pool was heated.

Megan pushed off the side and jumped in. She held her breath as water surged over her head before she popped back to the surface. It had been years since she'd been swimming. Rebecca used to take her to the local YMCA whenever she could scrounge up enough money. They were some of the best memories Megan had from her childhood.

Leaning back in the water, Megan floated on the surface, letting the Tennessee sun warm her skin. Did Chloe know how to swim? Did Paul? Megan had never thought to ask, but she'd have to find out.

As typically happened when Megan began thinking about Paul, her thoughts turned to less innocent avenues. Her nipples hardened as she imagined him standing there all wet with nothing but swim trunks on.

She closed her eyes and groaned. Yes, she'd definitely have to explore that fantasy with Paul if the opportunity ever presented itself. Of course, she'd prefer if it were far away from prying eyes, and certainly from innocent ones like Chloe's. What Megan had in mind was more along the lines of X-rated.

***

Over the next four days, Paul and Janey systematically worked their way through all the leads on their list. They'd gotten several hits tying three of the four victims together, but never all four. It was frustrating, especially when the killer could already be targeting his next victim.

The one thing they were fairly certain of, however, was that the connection revolved around the campus area. Only two of the women took classes at the college, so it was a given they frequented the area. Casey McMurphy's husband worked on the campus, which would easily tie her to the area as well. The only unknown was the first victim. There was no record of her ever taking a class at the college, and the only positive ID they'd gotten on her in the area was from the man at the pizza shop.

The only hitch in this positive progress in their investigation was the vast area of the campus itself. If one included the immediate surrounding area regularly used by students and faculty, it was easily the size of a small town. There was also the consideration that more than ten thousand people passed through the area on any given day of the week. There were students, professors, campus staff, maintenance and lawn care workers ... not to mention all the owners and employees of the various businesses. While Paul and Janey had narrowed down their search, they were no closer to finding their killer.

After a long twelve-hour day, Paul dropped Janey back at the station to get her car, and then headed home. He popped a frozen pizza in the oven, too tired to whip up something more elaborate, and downed two glasses of water. Over the last few days, he and his partner had clocked more miles than he cared to count. It wasn't as if he were out of shape, but he also wasn't twenty anymore.

The timer went off, and he took his pizza out of the oven. Slicing it into four large pieces, Paul loaded one onto a paper plate, and ambled over to the table. He quickly devoured what was in front of him, and went to grab another. Halfway through the second slice, Paul realized what he was doing. It was almost seven, which meant Chloe was due to call any minute. It also meant that shortly after that, Megan would most likely be calling as well.

With both Megan and Chloe gone, the house felt empty. The funny thing was Chloe had been doing these trips to her grandparents since she was a year old. That first year it had been hard to let her go, but being able to chat with her every night had eased his anxiety. The first couple of days were always challenging, but after that, he was fine.

This time, it was different. While he eagerly awaited his daughter's phone call every evening, he found that wasn't the only conversation he was anticipating. Since Megan had been gone, she made it a point to call him every night. She'd tell him all about her adventures in Nashville with Rebecca and Gage, including a trip to a local bar where she'd danced with a couple of Gage's friends. He was man enough to admit that he was jealous. And that he missed her.

Paul didn't know what to do anymore. He still didn't see a relationship between the two of them working out, but it was becoming harder and harder to brush under the rug. Megan made him feel things he'd thought died with Melissa.

Before he could think too much about it, Chloe called. He spent roughly ten minutes talking to his daughter before Cindy got on the phone.

"Sometimes I don't know how you do it, Paul."

He laughed. "Do what?"

"Keep up with her. It seems the only time I can get her to slow down is to put a book in her hands."

"Now you know why she has an entire bookshelf full of books in her room. She'll sit up there for hours reading."

Cindy sighed, and he heard the sadness creep into her voice. "Just like her mother."

It was true. Chloe was a lot like Melissa.

The seconds ticked by with neither of them contributing to the conversation.

His mother-in-law broke the emotion-filled silence. "Paul, I want to ask you something, but I don't want you to take it the wrong way. The last thing I want to do is sound critical, but is something going on between you and Megan?"

He took a deep breath, but didn't answer.

"Now, I know when you first told me that she was moving in with the two of you that I expressed my concern, but Chloe has said some things and—"

"What has she said?" Paul racked his brain trying to think of things Chloe could have seen or heard. Nothing came to mind.

"It's not so much what she said, more how she talks of Megan. She thinks Megan is going to be around for the long-term. She's grown attached."

"And you think that's a bad thing?"

"I think it's a cause for concern, yes. Paul, she's already lost her mother. Now she's grown attached to another woman—a woman who lives with you—how is she going to react when Megan decides to move on? She's a young woman, Paul. Eventually, she's going to want to get on with her life. What's that going to do to Chloe when she does?"

"First of all, I don't think Megan would walk out on Chloe. It's true, Megan might leave one of these days." As the words passed through Paul's lips, he felt cold inside. "If that happens, we'll deal with it. Second, Megan has no plans to leave anytime soon. Should I deprive my daughter of a loving relationship with another woman because there is a potential for heartbreak in the distant future?"

Cindy didn't respond immediately. "I guess you're right. I just . . . I just don't want to see her hurt. Losing Melissa . . ."

"I know. But Cindy, Megan has been good for Chloe." Paul didn't mention how good Megan had been for him as well. "And as much as we both want to shield Chloe from hurt and heartache, there are going to be times when we can't."

Paul heard Cindy release a shaky breath. "I'm sorry I brought it up. It's none of my business."

"Cindy, we've always been open and honest with each other. I'm grateful for everything you and George have done for Melissa and me and especially all you've done since I've been trying to navigate this parent thing on my own. But Megan's role in our lives is a given, at least for the time being. As for the future . . . who knows?"

Paul's conversation with his mother-in-law ended shortly after that. Cindy was distraught and worried. He could understand that, but he also couldn't give her the concrete reassurances she was looking for.

Needing to wind down, Paul headed upstairs to take a shower. He brought his cell into the bathroom, just in case. If Megan called, he didn't want to miss it.

That in and of itself should have given him his answer, but stubborn as he was, he fought it. As the water pelted him, Paul replayed the original question Cindy had asked him—was Megan going to be a permanent fixture in their lives? Did he want her to be?

The answer came barreling at him full speed. Yes.

But what if it didn't work? What if she realized he was just a lonely middle-aged man with nothing to offer her?

He knew she wanted more from him than what they currently had. What he didn't know was exactly how much more she wanted. That brought up the question as to what he wanted. If he gave this thing with them a shot, where did he see it leading?

The more Paul thought about him and Megan as a couple, the more questions—the more doubts—surfaced. He glanced down the length of his body. Although he was in shape for his age, there was a little more fat around his middle than there had been five years ago. He'd seen most of her and she was taut and soft and . . .

Releasing a breath, Paul flipped the handle that controlled the temperature of the water all the way around to cold. He jolted as the frigid water hit him like daggers, but it made quick work of his growing arousal.

As he stood with his eyes closed, trying to calm down, his phone rang, and a split second later his heart was pounding in his chest. Paul swiftly shut the water off and stepped out onto the towel. He wiped off his hands, and reached for the phone. "Hello?"

"Hey. You sound out of breath. What are you doing?" Megan asked.

Paul quickly ran the towel over his body, and then wrapped it around his waist. "I just got out of the shower."

Megan released a sound that went directly to his groin.

So much for the cold shower.

Chapter 16

Paul didn't sleep much the remainder of the time Megan was away. He worked as much as he could, but in the end he came home to an empty house—one that felt emptier than he could ever remember it.

On Saturday, he put in another twelve-hour day, hoping to wear himself out enough so that he'd be able to get some rest. It didn't work. He tossed and turned the entire night. When he awoke on Sunday morning, he had a desperate need to see Megan. Their phone conversations weren't enough. He missed her smile, her eyes, the way her hair bounced when she laughed.

He was in trouble, and he knew it. For the last two days, he'd argued with himself as to whether or not he should take that leap of faith and ask her out. He still wasn't sure a relationship between the two of them would work. Megan was young and full of life. He . . . well . . . he was . . . not. The last thing he wanted was to bring her down—hold her back. Paul wanted her to be happy.

There was a part of him that wanted to see if he could be part of that happiness, but fear nearly choked him every time he thought of what could go wrong. What if he messed up again? He didn't know if he could survive that a second time.

But as much as he feared the possibilities, did he really have a choice anymore? Sure, he could keep things the way they were—or try to, anyway. Given their track record, he wasn't hopeful.

Paul could also ask Megan to leave. It would probably be the most logical option. He knew that. However, the thought of her not being part of their lives anymore turned his stomach.

He'd also thrown around the idea of dating someone else. Maybe what he was experiencing was a natural progression in the grieving process—his mind and body telling him it was time to move forward. Melissa had been gone for nearly five years. Although that option might discourage Megan, it didn't sit much better with him than the thought of her leaving.

The other alternative was for him to swallow his fear, ask her out, and see if it went anywhere. Maybe their connection wouldn't be as intense once he took the challenge away. Maybe, just maybe, they'd have a horrible time, and she would realize that he wasn't the man she thought he was.

As Paul drove toward the airport, he knew how unlikely a scenario that was. Megan had lived in the same house with him for seven months. She knew his habits, his likes and dislikes. She'd even seen him at his worst when he was sick in bed with the flu.

Five miles from his exit, he saw a sign advertising a twenty-four-hour market. Without giving himself time to overthink it, he took the ramp off the highway, and followed the signs until he found the small store. Inside, they had a variety of food and beverages for travelers, not much past the basics, but he was hoping they would have what he needed.

It didn't take him long to find what he was looking for. There sitting next to the front counter were three bouquets of flowers—one made up of a dozen red roses, and two with a variety of colorful flowers. It had been years since he'd asked a woman out. In reality, he hadn't formally asked a woman out since he was sixteen. He was a little rusty.

Paul eyed the roses briefly, but swiftly changed his mind. Melissa had loved roses, but they didn't feel right for Megan.

Of the two other flower options, one was primarily pink, and the other was mostly yellow. Both were pretty, but for some reason he was drawn to the yellow. They reminded him of sunshine.

After paying for the flowers, Paul drove the few remaining miles to the airport with the flowers lying beside him on the passenger seat. He parked his car in the parking garage, and headed toward baggage claim. On the way inside, he received a few stares from passersby. An older lady smiled at him, and he held tighter to the bouquet. He hoped he was doing the right thing, and that Megan would like the flowers.

The first thing he did once he was inside the airport was check to see if Megan's flight had landed. To his surprise, the board showed her plane had arrived five minutes ago. That did nothing to calm his nerves. Was he really ready for this? If she said yes, it would change things between them. What would happen if it didn't work?

Paul was still debating with himself when he saw her come down the escalator. She didn't see him at first. Her head was tilted down, and he could see her cell phone in her right hand. She furrowed her brow, and he instinctively took a step forward.

As if sensing him, she glanced up, meeting his gaze. A huge smile lit up her face, and all the worry he'd seen a moment ago vanished. She reached the bottom of the escalator, and rushed toward him. Without any hesitation, Megan dropped her bags at his feet, wrapped her arms around his neck, and hugged him.

What he felt in that moment was difficult to describe. A whiff of lilac and cherries filled his nostrils as her warm body pressed solid against his. He circled his arms around her waist and returned her embrace, enjoying the feel of her in his arms. She was home.

They stood there for several minutes, not moving. People went around them, not seeming to pay much attention to their reunion. Eventually, Megan pulled back a little so that she could see his face. "Hi."

Paul chuckled, and put some more space between them. "How was your flight?"

"Good."

Megan reached to pick up her bags, but Paul beat her to it. He hitched her backpack over his shoulder, careful not to crush the flowers. Extending his free arm, he offered them to her. "I got these for you. A kind of welcome home present."

She took them in both her hands and inhaled.

Paul held his breath, awaiting her reaction. Had he made the wrong choice? Should he have gotten the roses?

A smile tugged at her lips. "They're beautiful. Thank you."

"I'm glad you like them." Before he could say any more, a noise sounded from the baggage carousel, and they went to retrieve the rest of her luggage.

Twenty minutes later, they were in the car, and on their way home. Paul had made his decision. Buying her flowers had sealed it. He was going to ask her to go out with him on a date. One date, and then they would see how it went from there.

There was only one problem. He didn't know how to go about asking her. Should he do it now, or should it be something more romantic? Paul hated feeling so unsure of himself. He'd never felt this way with Melissa. Everything between them had been easy, especially in the beginning.

Of course, back then things had been simple. They were kids without any real responsibilities. Their first date had been to a school dance. He'd taken her out to dinner beforehand at a moderately priced restaurant, and then to the dance. After that, he'd driven her home. Simple. Uncomplicated. The exact opposite of his current situation.

"Something on your mind?" Megan asked when they were about halfway home.

He glanced over at her. She'd turned slightly to face him, and was holding her flowers gingerly in her lap. It was now or never. "I was wondering if maybe you'd like to go out with me Friday night."

Megan didn't respond right away, and he was back to paying attention to the road so he couldn't see her reaction to his question. "Are you asking me on a date?"

Paul swallowed hard. "Yes."

Again, she didn't say anything. This time he looked in her direction. She had leaned her head back against the headrest, and was staring at him intently. He'd expected her to jump at his offer, since she'd been the one to push for it in the first place. That's why her next question surprised him. "Are you sure?"

Since they were coming up on their exit, Paul waited until they were off the highway before he replied. But instead of answering her question, he asked one of his own. "What? Have you changed your mind? I thought . . ."

She shook her head. "No. I haven't changed my mind. But I'm curious as to what made you change yours."

As scared as he was, Paul figured he needed to be honest. "I did a lot of thinking while you were gone, and well . . ." He took a deep breath, and admitted something to her he hoped he wouldn't regret. "I missed you."

Megan laughed.

"What's so funny?" he asked.

"You mean, all I had to do was go away for a week? Here I've been trying to get your attention for months, and leaving is what does it?"

"Oh, trust me, you got my attention just fine."

She smirked. "Good to know."

Paul pulled into his driveway and turned off the car. "So?"

"So what?"

He tried not to let her see how anxious he was. "You never answered my question. Will you go out on a date with me Friday night?"

"Oh. That."

Paul tightened his hold on his keys, and he could feel the metal biting into his hand. "Yes. That."

Instead of answering him, Megan opened her door, and stepped out of the car. He followed, completely perplexed.

They both came around to the back of the vehicle to get her luggage, but when he reached for the handle, she stopped him. "Kiss me."

"What?" It had been a while since he'd asked a woman out on a date, but if memory served, the kiss came *after* the date.

"I want you to kiss me."

This time he detected a note of amusement in her tone. He wasn't sure if he should be annoyed or not, since she appeared to be having fun at his expense. "Isn't that supposed to come after the date?"

She shrugged. "Let's just say . . . this is my way of finding out if you're serious or not."

Paul stared at her for a moment, and then decided why not? It wasn't as if he didn't want to kiss her. In fact, it had been at the top of his list since the moment he'd laid eyes on her at the airport. He'd only been holding back because . . . well, he didn't know why exactly.

Stepping forward, Paul closed the distance between them, and cupped the back of her neck with his right hand. She tilted her head up and slightly to the left, leaning into his touch. Placing his left hand at her waist, he brought her closer until he could feel the heat radiating from her body. It had been over a month since he'd felt her soft and warm beneath his fingers.

Megan closed her eyes as he lowered his mouth to hers. For once, he didn't question it—didn't think about all the reasons why not. This time, he allowed the desire he'd been keeping a tight lid on to come to the surface.

***

When Megan issued her challenge, she hadn't known how Paul would react. He'd caught her off guard when he asked her out. The entire time she'd been in Nashville, she'd racked her brain as to what else she could do to try and break through the wall he'd built up around him. There was no way she could have known that her absence would be enough to push him out of his comfort zone.

As Paul's lips continued to move against hers, Megan gave in to the urge to touch him. Holding tight to the flowers with one hand, she used the other to grip the back of his head, pulling him closer. He seemed to like that. His fingers flexed on her hip, and he shifted them slightly. She moaned as he pressed her up against the car. With every second that passed, it was becoming more difficult to remember they were in public.

Paul ran his palm down her hip to cup her ass. The movement lifted her an inch or so higher, which brought her more in line with the hard length of him pressing aggressively against his jeans. She began rubbing herself against him, seeking friction.

He groaned, and ripped his mouth away from hers.

Megan didn't want their kiss to end. She tugged at his hair, trying to get him to pick up where he'd left off.

"We can't . . . do this here." His words were broken, spoken in between short, shallow breaths.

A car passed by as they stood clinging to one another, and Megan knew he was right. They were standing in his driveway in the middle of the day. Somehow she didn't think the neighbors would like it much if they began ripping each other's clothes off on the front lawn.

She buried her face in the crook of his neck, willing herself to calm down.

Even though Paul had stopped the kiss, he seemed to be in no hurry to let her go. She smiled, and placed a soft kiss at the base of his neck.

He chuckled. "What was that for?"

Instead of answering that question, she answered another. "Yes."

Unfortunately, this caused Paul to pull back so that he could see her face. "Yes, what?"

Megan smiled, and ran her fingers freely through his hair. "Yes, I'll go out on a date with you."

Paul threw his head back and laughed. The motion separated them further, and Megan let her fingers fall.

To her surprise, when he realized they were no longer connected, he grasped the back of her head with both hands, and gave her a swift, hard kiss. When he separated their lips, he didn't release her. "I missed you. I really did."

Reaching up, she ran her fingers along his jaw. "I'm glad to be home."

He kissed her again, and then took a step back. They unloaded her suitcases, and brought them upstairs to her room. There was a moment of awkwardness. Things were changing between them, and it seemed as if neither knew exactly what that meant.

After a few minutes of strained silence, Paul excused himself from Megan's room. She let herself fall backward onto the bed, and grinned so wide her cheeks hurt. Paul had kissed her. Willingly. Knowingly. They were going out on a date. A real, honest-to-goodness date. And he'd gotten her flowers. No guy had ever bought her flowers before.

Megan looked over to her dresser where she'd placed the bouquet. The flowers were beautiful. They reminded her of spring, of new beginnings, which was completely appropriate given the circumstances.

As she lay there, she began to wonder where he'd take her on their date. Not that the where really mattered. Paul was finally admitting that he felt something for her—that she wasn't only his daughter's nanny. Doubt crept up in the back of her mind, wiping the smile from her face. *Maybe he's just horny.*

No. She didn't believe that. If sex was all Paul wanted from her, he could have had that months ago. He'd always been the one to stop their physical encounters, not her. And he'd said he missed her. Not kissing her or making out with her. Her.

Pushing herself up off the bed, Megan flipped her suitcase open and unpacked her things. It took a while. She sorted through her clothes, throwing the dirty ones in the hamper. Rebecca had offered to let her use their washer and dryer, but Megan had brought plenty of clothes with her for the week, so she'd opted to bring her laundry home instead.

Once everything was put away, Megan headed downstairs to find some food. Rebecca and Gage had taken her out for a late breakfast before dropping her off at the airport. At the time, she'd been stuffed. That was nearly five hours ago.

When she came down the stairs, Paul was riffling through the cabinets. He must have heard her enter because he turned abruptly to face her, almost as if he were a child caught with his hand in the cookie jar. "I didn't see you there."

She walked over to the refrigerator and checked to see if she could find any leftovers. It was practically empty. Even when she'd first arrived, there had been a fair amount of food in the refrigerator. Besides the basics—milk, cheese, condiments—there were only two bottles of beer and a container that looked as if it held some sort of cake. "Where is everything?"

"Oh. I've mostly been eating takeout." He shrugged. "I've been working long hours, and since it was only me . . ."

That made sense. Needing something more than what was to be had in the refrigerator, Megan made a beeline for the pantry. She found a box of pasta and some sauce. It might not be all that creative, but spaghetti was easy to make and filling.

As she moved about the kitchen, Paul seemed out of his element. He stood leaning against the counter for a while, and then moved to sit in one of the chairs. She glanced over her shoulder to find him tapping his fingers against the table and staring out the window into the backyard.

"Everything okay?"

He snapped his head around to look at her. "Yeah. Yes. Everything's fine."

She finished making her pasta, and loaded a healthy portion onto her plate. "Did you want some?"

"No. I'm good."

She brought her plate over to the table and sat down. Paul looked uncomfortable.

After swallowing a few bites, Megan couldn't take it anymore. "Paul, what's wrong? And don't tell me nothing."

He rubbed the back of his neck and eyed her cautiously. "I guess I'm feeling a little lost."

"Lost? Why?" Megan asked, taking another bite of her food.

Paul sighed. "I'm not sure how this is supposed to work. Us."

"How do you want it to work?"

Megan could tell he was thinking about his answer, so she waited. The minutes ticked by as she finished her spaghetti and took her plate to the sink. When he still hadn't answered by the time she was done, she strolled over to him. Deciding to throw caution to the wind, Megan straddled his lap, sat down, and rested her arms over his shoulders.

"What are you doing?" he asked.

"Cutting to the chase." She brushed her lips back and forth across his.

Paul's breathing began to pick up. He closed his eyes, and took control of the kiss. Less than a minute later, he was running his hands up and down her back underneath her shirt, and his tongue was caressing hers. It wasn't as desperate as some of their make-out sessions, but that didn't make it any less hot.

This time it was Megan who pulled back. "That's how it works. This. Us."

He rested his forehead against hers. "I should probably tell you something."

She scraped her nails along his scalp, and she felt him shiver. "What's that?"

"I've never—"

"Don't even try to tell me you've never had sex before. You have a daughter, remember? That one won't work with me."

Paul chuckled and pinched her.

"Ouch."

"Serves you right. That wasn't what I was going to say."

She massaged the spot he pinched. It really didn't hurt. It was more the principle of the matter. "What were you going to say then?"

He brushed a strand of hair away from her face. "My wife—Melissa—is the only woman I've ever dated."

Megan's eyes went wide with shock. "Really? As in, ever?"

Paul nodded.

"Wow." She thought about it a moment. "What about sex? Was there anyone else besides—"

"No."

"Not even . . . after?"

He shook his head.

The primary emotion Megan was feeling was disbelief. Not that she didn't think Paul was telling the truth, more that she couldn't imagine someone as passionate as him going without sex for so long. Finding out his wife had been his only lover stunned her. Wow. Five years. Megan couldn't imagine.

"So does that mean you don't want to? Have sex, I mean. Is that why you never . . ." Megan held her breath waiting for his answer.

He was quiet for what felt like a really long time. "I tried once. About six months after my wife died."

This was good, wasn't it? I mean, it meant he wasn't saving himself for marriage or anything. "And what happened?"

Paul shook his head. "It's a long story, but needless to say I didn't try again."

"But that doesn't mean you don't want to, right?"

"I didn't for a long time."

Megan searched his face, hoping she wasn't misinterpreting what he was saying. She didn't think she was.

Standing, she reached for his hand. He hesitated for only a moment before linking his fingers through hers and following her up the stairs.

Chapter 17

Paul had a pretty good idea where they were heading, and yet he couldn't figure out if he was excited about finally making his fantasies a reality, or scared out of his mind. The closer they came to her bedroom, the less distinguishable the two emotions became. It was as if the fear and the anticipation had combined.

With their hands still linked, Megan dragged him across the threshold of her bedroom, and over to the nightstand. She opened the drawer and extracted a condom. Tossing it on the bed, she turned to face him.

He swallowed, and tried not to let her see how nervous he was.

She stepped closer, releasing his hand, and placed both of hers, palms down, on his chest. "You can say no."

The thing was he didn't want to say no. He'd been dreaming about Megan for the last three months.

Knowing he needed to show her that he was in this all the way—that he wanted this—he took hold of her hips, and drew her toward him. She sucked in a breath as their lower bodies connected. He was painfully hard, and more than ready. "I don't want to say no."

Megan smiled, and ran her hands up his chest and neck until her arms rested on his shoulders. Her breasts flattened against his chest, and Paul closed his eyes. He felt her breath on his face, and turned his head to meet her lips.

"Relax," she whispered.

Their mouths met in a tender caress. It wasn't desperate need, but a slow burn. There was an energy inside him that was increasing in intensity.

She slid her tongue along the seam of his lips, and he opened his mouth, allowing her to slip her tongue inside. He dug his fingers into the flesh of her ass, increasing the friction against his groin. His eyes rolled into the back of his head at the sensation. It was at that point instinct started to take over, and he began moving them closer to the bed.

When the back of her legs hit the mattress, Megan broke the kiss, and sat down on the edge of the bed. She immediately went to work on removing his jeans. "Take off your shirt."

Without stopping to think, Paul pulled the T-shirt over his head, and threw it somewhere a few feet away. By that point, Megan had unfastened his jeans and worked them halfway down his thighs.

She glanced up at him, a wicked gleam in her eyes. "Tighty-whities, huh?"

"They're practical."

Without taking her gaze from his, she ran a finger over his erection. He thought he was going to lose it. No one had touched him like that in five years. Paul felt as if he were dangling from a cliff, hanging on for dear life.

Then she went and did something he hadn't expected. Although, knowing Megan, he should have. She took hold of both sides of his underwear, and yanked them down to join his jeans. He stood there, fully erect, with his pants bunched down around his knees.

Paul was about to kick them off and out of the way, along with his shoes, when Megan sucked his length into her warm mouth. He released a strangled moan, and tangled his fingers loosely in her hair. It had been years. He'd forgotten how good it felt to have a woman's mouth on him.

He closed his eyes and enjoyed what she was doing with her lips and tongue. All too soon he felt his orgasm building. He didn't want her to stop, but if she continued, they'd never make it to the main event.

With great reluctance, Paul pushed her back. The cool air was a stark contrast to her warmth. She smiled up at him, licking her lips.

Paul kicked off his shoes and then finished removing his jeans. Leaning forward, he lowered himself onto the bed—his hands spread wide, bracing himself. She leaned back on the mattress as he towered over her. "You're wearing too many clothes."

She lifted her arms over her head and stretched, arching her back. "So why don't you do something about it?"

Reaching for the bottom of her shirt, Paul worked it up past her breasts, and she helped him ease it over her head. She wore a pale pink bra with little blue flowers. It was cute and innocent. A direct contrast to the hard nipples he could see outlined beneath the thin fabric.

Paul remembered what Megan's breasts felt and tasted like against his tongue. Pushing the material of her bra out of the way, he quickly latched on to her nipple, and drew it into his mouth. She held his head in place, pushing her chest up, encouraging him to take what he wanted.

And take he did. No matter how much he licked and sucked, he couldn't get enough. If not for the growing need he had to be inside her, he could have spent hours—days—lavishing attention on her breasts.

Megan rotated her hips, and Paul could no longer ignore the pulsing in his groin. Reaching down between them, he unbuttoned her jeans, and then unzipped them. She helped him push the denim over her hips and down her legs, letting them fall to the floor beside the bed along with her shoes. The only things that remained between them were her bra and panties, and even those seemed too much. Megan seemed to agree, and between the two of them, the offending items were gone in a matter of seconds.

He ran his hands down the length of her body, taking in its perfection. Her curves were subtle, but they were there. Paul wondered how they'd change after she had a child of her own, and then swiftly stifled the thought. That wasn't what this was about. They hadn't—

Megan touched the side of his face. "Hey. Where did you go?"

Shaking his head, Paul kissed her. "Nowhere. It's just been a long time for me."

"Ah, yes. Well, we can take care of that easy enough."

A second later, Paul was lying on his back, and Megan was climbing on top of him. He recognized the move she'd used as one commonly taught in self-defense classes. This was the first time he'd had it executed on him outside of the gym.

"Where did you learn that?" he asked.

She straddled his waist, trapping his erection beneath her. "Becca. She was big on making sure I could take care of myself."

"I'd say she did a good job, then. That was an expert m—" The word died in his throat as Megan started rocking against him. He dug his fingers into her hips and guided her movements.

"Did you want to talk, or did you want to do something way more fun?" Her voice held a playful tone, but he heard the desire there.

Grabbing the back of her head, he pulled her face down to his. This kiss was all tongues and teeth as they moved against one another. He could feel her heat against him, and he needed to be inside her.

Reaching for the condom he knew was beside them on the bed, he snatched it up and tore open the packaging. Megan sat up, and took it from his hands, scooting back a little so that she could roll it down his length. Once it was in place, she lifted herself up onto her knees, and held him in position while she lowered herself down.

Paul held his breath as her heat enveloped him. It had been so long that he'd almost forgotten how it felt to be inside a woman, to have her surround him completely. It was indescribable.

Megan released a soft moan as he filled her, and he could see the pleasure on her face. It was an amazing sight, and he wanted to see more—he wanted to give her more. Repositioning them slightly, Paul began moving. In response, Megan leaned back, bracing her hands on his thighs, and met each thrust of his hips with one of her own. It felt good. Right.

Unfortunately, Paul hadn't been intimate with a woman for five years, and all too soon he felt his orgasm approaching. The only way to stop it would have been to halt all movement, but that wasn't something he was willing to do. "Megan?"

She met his gaze—her eyes glazed over with her own arousal. "I'm . . ."

Before he could get another word out, she reached between them, and began pleasuring herself.

Paul groaned, and gritted his teeth. Watching her was making it that much harder to hold on, but he couldn't look away. It was the sexiest thing he'd ever seen.

With each brush of her fingers, she brought him closer and

closer to the edge. He was sweating, not only with the exertion of sex, but also from trying to hold his climax at bay.

The moment he felt her spasm around him, Paul let himself go, and with only a few more thrusts, he found his own release. It left him sweaty, and spent, and feeling better than he had in years.

Megan collapsed on top of him, her breathing heavy against his neck. He wrapped his arms around her back, and buried his nose in her hair. She still smelled like lilac and cherries.

***

All Megan's limbs felt as if they'd come loose at the joints. She'd missed sex, but even she could admit this was different. It hadn't only been about having fun—which, of course, it was—but it was more than that. This was Paul. And being able to show him how she felt without having to hold back was beyond amazing.

He shifted a little as he separated himself from her. Megan felt the loss, and wanted him back. In that vein, she started kissing his neck and shoulders, anywhere in easy reach. Lazily, she threaded her fingers through his hair, and massaged his scalp with her nails.

Paul chuckled. "Easy. I'm an old man, remember? I need some time to recover."

She smiled against his neck, and then propped herself up on her elbow to look at him. "So what you're saying is that you're going to need a few minutes before we go at it again?"

He brushed the backs of his fingers down her cheek, before rubbing his thumb along the curve of her lips. "I'm afraid it will take more than a few minutes."

Paul pulled her down for a kiss. It was fairly chaste considering they were lying naked together on her bed. Still, it had her pulse racing in no time.

Before she could get carried away, Paul ended it. "I need to go clean up."

The cold air hit her as soon as he left the bed. She watched as he strolled into her bathroom and disappeared from sight. Glancing down at their clothes on the floor, Megan wondered if she should get dressed. Normally, that's what happened after sex—well, unless she passed out drunk beforehand. That wasn't the case here. Plus, she really didn't want to get dressed. What she wanted to do was crawl into bed with Paul and stay there for the foreseeable future.

When Paul reentered the room, she was sitting up on the bed with her legs crossed Indian-style. He sat down beside her, and the awkwardness returned. She knew she needed to do something to fix it, but she wasn't sure how. They were in uncharted territory—for both of them.

She laid her palm face up on the bed between them. Paul hesitated for a moment, and then placed his hand on top of hers. He laced their fingers together, and gave them a squeeze.

They sat there not talking for several minutes until she shivered. He noticed. "Are you cold?"

Megan shrugged. "A little."

Paul stood, releasing her hand. She was regretting her confession until she realized what he was doing. He walked around to the opposite side of the bed and pulled the covers back. "Get in. I don't want you to catch cold."

She pushed herself up on her knees, and reached for the sheet and blanket. "Only if you join me."

He smiled. "That's the idea."

Megan scurried beneath the cool blankets, and her stomach did a little somersault when Paul slid into bed beside her. As soon as he was in, she snuggled against him. He held her close, and it felt natural. It was where she was meant to be.

They lay there for a long time, him tracing patterns on her back, while she played with the hair on his chest. Most of the guys she'd been with had little to no hair on their torsos. Paul's was covered with brown curls. Megan liked it. It seemed to fit him somehow.

"What are you thinking so hard about?" he asked.

She smiled, and twirled several strands of his hair around her finger. "I was thinking about the hair on your chest."

"Ah. I do have a lot, don't I?"

"You do. But I like it." Megan propped her head up to rest on her hand while she continued playing. "You know, this is the first time I've seen you without a shirt. Even when you were sick, you always wore a T-shirt."

"Habit. When Chloe was younger, there were a lot of nights I'd have to go into her room for one reason or another. It was easier to already have something on than to fumble around for clothes in the middle of the night."

"And before Chloe?"

"Um. No."

"So . . ."

He rolled onto his side to face her. "After I moved out of the college dorms, I got used to sleeping in the nude. Going back to pajamas was an adjustment, but it doesn't bother me anymore. It's all what you get used to."

"Do you think this is something you could get used to?"

Paul raised his eyebrows in question.

Megan didn't want to push, but she also remembered how unsure he'd been earlier. Had that all disappeared? "Us, I mean."

He searched her face, and then shrugged. "I don't know. This," he gestured between them, "is new to me—different."

"Because of your wife."

"Partly, yes."

She edged closer to him. "I know I said this before but I do understand that you'll always love Melissa, and I'm okay with that. But Paul, she's not here anymore, and I am. I want to be part of your life, and not just as your daughter's nanny."

Paul caressed her cheek with his thumb. "I hope you realize after this afternoon that I don't just think of you as the nanny."

Megan smiled, and closed the distance between them. "Good to know."

The kiss was teasing, and full of possibilities. She felt him growing hard against her hip. Megan was ready for another round.

When Paul leaned back, she groaned.

He laughed. "You know, I wasn't joking earlier. I'm an old man. I need recovery time."

She rolled her eyes. "You're not old."

Paul raised an eyebrow.

"Okay, you're *older*. That doesn't make you old."

"If you say so."

Megan pushed him onto his back, placed her hands on his chest, and rested her chin on top. "I do."

He was quiet for a long moment. "Did you have somewhere you wanted to go Friday night? I haven't been on a date in over five years. I'm a little out of my element."

She tilted her head to the side. "You still want to go?"

"On a date? Sure. Why wouldn't I?"

"It's just . . ." Megan gestured to their current nakedness.

"You thought because we slept together that I'd change my mind?"

Megan shrugged and looked away.

"My word. What kind of jerks have you been dating?"

She didn't answer.

Paul tilted her chin back to where she was looking at him again. She was somewhat embarrassed. Most of the guys she'd dated in the past weren't jerks exactly, but they weren't what you'd call gentlemen. They hung out and had a good time together, which often included some down and dirty sex. She had no idea what Paul was seeing as he looked at her, but she felt almost guilty. It was new, and she wasn't sure she liked it.

Hoisting her further up his body, Paul pressed their foreheads together so he was looking her straight in the eye. "Megan, I have no idea what's going on between us. This," he mimicked her gesture from before, "is only part of it. If all I wanted was a quick roll in the hay, I could have gotten that years ago."

"Of course you could have. You're hot."

He laughed. "You're not making this easy, you know."

Megan smiled. "Sorry."

"What I'm trying to say is that there's more to what's between us than physical attraction. At least, I think there is."

"Are you trying to say that you like me?" It was so easy to tease him sometimes.

"Possibly."

She bracketed his head with her forearms, and kissed the tip of his nose. "I like you, too. But what happened to you thinking you're not good enough?"

"Oh, I still think I'm not good enough for you. I messed up before, and there's no guarantee I won't do it again."

"You didn't mess up."

"Megan—"

She cut him off with a kiss—one she refused to end until she felt the tension in his body melt away. Releasing his lips, she began working her way along his jaw, and down his neck. "Think you're ready to go again, old man?"

Megan let out a squeal as Paul rolled them over. Heat flared in her body as his mouth blazed a trail down her torso to the space between her legs. For the next thirty minutes, Megan didn't think about much of anything, which suited her just fine.

Chapter 18

After their second round of amazing sex, they lay holding each other until they both drifted off to sleep. Over the years, Megan had learned to sleep almost anywhere and in any position. She also trained herself to wake up at a moment's notice. That's why when Paul began to jerk and twist beside her, she was instantly alert.

His eyes were closed, so she was fairly sure he was dreaming. From the look on his face, though, it didn't look to be something pleasant. "Paul?"

There was no change.

"Paul. Wake up. You're dreaming. Paul!"

Paul's eyelids flew open in panic, and he held his body rigid. The only exception was his chest, which continued to move up and down rapidly.

Megan had no idea what was going on, but she knew better than to touch him. That was a sure fire way to end up getting slapped or punched.

She decided to wait him out. It didn't take too long before he realized that there was no immediate danger. He shifted his gaze to the side, and noticed her for the first time.

"Did I hurt you?"

"No." Megan scooted closer. She'd been in a few situations similar to this in the past—one of the hazards of sleeping next to guys she didn't know all that well. On a scale of one to ten, this situation ranked low on her fear meter.

Paul sat up and held his head in his hands. Beads of sweat glistened off his back.

"Do you want to talk about it?" she asked.

He sighed and shook his head.

"Okay." Megan was at a loss. Something had happened and he was shutting her out. She knew this thing between them was new, but it still hurt.

Without looking in her direction, Paul threw the covers off him, and began gathering his clothes. Unsure what was going on, Megan followed his lead. He was finished dressing before she had her jeans halfway up her legs.

"Are you hungry?" He didn't wait for her to answer. "I'm going to see what I can dig up downstairs. Maybe call for a pizza."

Megan stood there completely dumbfounded as Paul rushed out of her room. What the hell was going on?

She finished putting her clothes back on and headed downstairs. Paul was sitting in the living room with phone in hand, talking to the pizza shop.

"Yes, I'd like a large supreme pizza. And can you put extra black olives on half of it?"

That made her smile. No matter what was going on, Paul had remembered she liked extra black olives on her pizza.

Paul gave their address, and then hung up. He set the phone down on the coffee table without looking in her direction. "The pizza should be here in about forty minutes."

"Okay." Megan leaned back against the doorjamb observing him. If she didn't know him so well, she would have thought she'd imagined what happened in her bedroom. He sat casually on the couch with his forearms resting on his knees. The only real giveaway was the way he held his shoulders. He wasn't as relaxed as he appeared.

Megan wanted to do something to make it better, but she was at a loss. She wasn't even sure what had happened beyond he'd had a nightmare of some kind. Was it work related? Was it about his wife? Either was a distinct possibility.

He reached for the remote and turned on the television. Apparently, he was planning to ignore the elephant in the room.

Megan decided to play along for the time being. Crossing the room, she sat down beside him, and tucked her feet under her.

Paul glanced briefly in her direction, but then went back to flipping through the channels. He settled on a sitcom.

They watched in silence, sitting side by side yet not touching, until the pizza arrived. Paul got up and paid for their dinner while Megan busied herself in the kitchen getting them something to drink. He brought the pizza to the table, and they both took their usual seats.

When Paul reached for his third slice, Megan decided she couldn't take it anymore.

"Are we just going to act like nothing happened?"

He stopped mid-chew, but didn't answer her.

"Did you have a nightmare? Was it about your wife?"

Paul dropped his pizza back into the box.

"I thought we were going to try and make this work between us. How can we if you shut me out?" Megan was trying to remain calm, but the way he was acting was beginning to scare her.

"It's not a big deal. It was only a dream." He sounded defeated.

Megan reached across the space between them, and covered his hand with hers. He stared at her with a blank look on his face. "I want you to talk to me."

He shook his head.

"Please."

For a long time, he said nothing. The silence was almost deafening. "Yes, it was about Melissa."

Megan breathed a sigh of relief. He was talking. Anything else she could deal with, but if this had any hope of working between them, they had to communicate. "Okay."

Although she wanted to know more, she decided not to push. Instead, she shoved away from the table, and walked over to put her arms around his neck. It was a simple gesture, but Megan recalled many times in her life when all she had needed was a hug and her world made sense again. She was hoping maybe she could give that to Paul.

At first, he didn't react. Then something changed, and she felt him release the tension in his body. He circled his arms around her and pulled her down onto his lap. She held on tight, and reveled in this new connection between them.

"Are you sure this is what you want?" he asked. "I'm not such a catch, you know. I have a lot of baggage."

She hugged him tighter. "So do I."

He leaned back so that he could look her in the eye. "I'm serious, Megan. I don't know how to do this with you. With anyone. Melissa was . . ."

"The love of your life."

Paul hesitated. "Yes. I thought I'd be with her forever."

Megan nodded. It wasn't exactly what she wanted to hear, but it wasn't as if she hadn't known. No man remained celibate for five years after losing a woman he wasn't over the moon about.

He snorted. "I'm not doing so well, am I?"

"You're doing fine. I knew what I was getting myself into." Megan tried to comfort him.

"What I don't understand is why you would want to?"

She framed his face with her hands, and placed a chaste kiss on his lips. "Because I think you're worth it."

He sighed, and rested his forehead against hers. "So what do we do now?"

"Well . . ." Megan straddled him and brought her mouth to hover above his ear. "We could finish eating the pizza you ordered, or we could do something more . . . fun."

Paul's chest vibrated against her.

Megan gave him the most innocent look she could manage. "What?"

"You have a one-track mind."

"I don't know what you mean. I was thinking if you were full of pizza, maybe we could play a game or something. That's all." She kept a straight face, but inside she was struggling to stay composed.

"Sure you were." His tone was serious, but she could see the twinkle in his eye. He was having fun. More importantly, the haunted look that had been plaguing him since he woke up had disappeared.

Reaching behind her, Megan tore off a bite of pizza, and popped it in her mouth. She made sure to lick her fingers nice and slow, teasing him.

It worked. His brown eyes dilated, and she felt evidence of his interest against the inside of her thigh. She repeated the process, and watched as his eyes grew perceptively darker.

When she went to take her third bite, Paul stopped her. "You're a tease, do you know that?"

Megan grinned. "Only if I don't plan to put out, which I do."

"Oh you do, do you?"

"Yep."

She ran her tongue along the seam of his lips, and he groaned. "Maybe we should wait."

"Wait for what?"

He sucked in a breath. "It's . . . Chloe . . ."

That got her attention. Megan glanced up at the clock and sighed. She sat up, but remained straddling his lap. Paul was right. Chloe would be calling any minute. It wouldn't do them any good to get all hot and heavy, and then have to stop in the middle to answer the phone. There was no way Paul would miss his daughter's call, and Megan would never ask him to.

***

Paul was having a hard time remembering why he couldn't take Megan back upstairs and bury himself deep inside her—a very hard time. When he made the decision to ask her out, he never imagined that less than two hours later they'd be in her bed. She was full of sexual energy, and it was all directed solely at him.

For his part, Paul couldn't remember the last time he'd had sex twice in one day. He and Melissa had a fairly active sex life, but they'd been together for fifteen years. The days of endless hours in bed where they were doing more than sleeping died off somewhere in their twenties. Neither had seemed to miss it, but now he was wondering if maybe they should have.

Megan took another bite of her pizza. "A penny for your thoughts?"

He followed suit, and reached for the slice of pizza he'd deposited back in the box earlier. It was a little awkward to eat with Megan sitting on his lap like she was, but he had no desire for her to move. "I was trying to remember the last time I had sex more than once in a day."

Her eyes grew wide.

"Don't look so shocked. When you get older, things change."

She scrunched up her nose.

Fortunately, that was the end of the conversation for the time being, as the house phone rang. Megan reluctantly got up, and he went to answer it.

They both took turns talking to Chloe. His little girl was having fun. She'd forgotten all about him being sick, and was busy enjoying the time with her grandparents.

He slipped out of the room when Megan took the phone, to give her a little privacy. It was also the first real opportunity he had to regroup after waking up from his nightmare. It wasn't the first time he'd had that particular dream. After Melissa died, he'd had it almost every night. Over time, it happened less often, but when it did, it was intense. Once, he broke his bedside lamp. And more than a few times he'd ripped his bed sheets.

When he woke up and realized he wasn't alone, it had terrified him. What if he'd hurt Megan while dreaming? He didn't know if he could live with himself. It was one more reason not to have a relationship with her.

There was one huge obstacle arguing the other side, though, and it was Megan herself. She was smart, sexy, and she made him feel more alive than he had in years. Megan had awakened a part of him he'd thought dead and buried. He wasn't sure he wanted to give it up. He wasn't sure if he could.

Megan found him in his bedroom. "Cindy wanted me to tell you to call her if you needed anything."

He smiled. "Thanks. Sometimes I think she's having a difficult time letting go. When they lived in town, I relied on them a lot. Even after all these years."

"That's understandable, I guess."

Megan remained by the door, and he realized she was waiting for an invitation to enter. He'd been somewhat protective of his bedroom. It was his space. The only time she'd come in without waiting for permission was when he was sick. Even then, Megan had been cautious. She'd brought him food and medicine, and she would retrieve items from his bathroom when he needed them, but that was all. Paul realized that if whatever this was between them had any hope of working, he was going to have to let her in. Not only to his personal space, but to everything else as well.

Paul sat on the edge of the bed and patted the space beside him.

Megan smiled and strolled into the room. She took a seat beside him and took hold of his hand. "I wasn't sure if you'd want me in here."

"I have been a little overprotective of my bedroom, haven't I?"

She shrugged. "A little. But I get it."

He grunted. "You let me off the hook too easy, Megan."

"What would you have me do, hmm? I won't fault you for loving your wife. It's not a competition."

"No, I suppose it isn't." He couldn't deny her logic, but it was almost too rational.

"Look, I won't say I'm not a little jealous sometimes. I mean, you loved her. But it seems petty to me to get upset with you over it. At least from everything you and your family have told me about Melissa, it sounds like she loved you just as much."

Paul took a deep breath to steady himself. "Thank you for understanding. I don't think most women would."

She squeezed his hand and laid her head on his shoulder. "Yeah, well, I'm not most women."

He laughed. "No. You most certainly are not."

They sat there for several minutes staring off into space before Megan spoke. "Does me being in here bother you?"

"No. I thought maybe it would, but it doesn't."

Megan hugged his arm. "Good."

"I don't know . . ." He paused. "I don't know if I'm ready to . . . sleep with you in here yet, though."

She smiled up at him. "But you still *want* to sleep with me, right?"

He brushed a strand of hair away from her face. "I do. But . . ."

"But?"

As much as he didn't want to talk about his dream, he knew if they were going to continue sharing a bed, he'd have to. She needed to know what she was getting herself into. If she chose to kick him out of her bed, then that was her decision and he'd respect it.

"Sometimes I have dreams—nightmares—like I did today."

Megan's expression turned serious. "Okay."

This was harder than he thought it would be. "Most of the time they revolve around the night Melissa died. I don't want to go into the details, but sometimes when I have them I get . . . violent."

"Violent how?"

He frowned. "I broke my lamp once. If you look closely at the base, you can see the crack where I glued it back together."

She looked over his shoulder at the lamp and then back to him.

"That's why you asked if you'd hurt me."

"Yes. I've always been alone when it's happened before. And the lamp hasn't been the only casualty. I've had to replace quite a few sheets as well."

When Megan didn't respond in any way, he became anxious. "I would never hurt you on purpose."

"I know that." She sounded somewhat insulted.

He sighed. "Anyway, I wanted you to know, and I'll understand if you don't want to take the risk."

Megan gave him a funny look. "Are you serious? You really thought I wouldn't want to sleep in the same bed as you on the off chance that you have another nightmare?"

"I could hurt you, Megan, and I wouldn't even be aware of it."

She sat up and turned to face him. "Paul, how much do you know about how I grew up?"

"Only what you've told me." Granted, that wasn't much. He knew it had been far from a fairy-tale childhood, and that her older sister, Rebecca, had pretty much raised her. Paul also knew that neither Megan nor Rebecca had anything to do with their parents.

"I guess I should probably fill you in, huh?"

"You don't have to—"

"Yes, I do. If I'm asking you to be open and honest with me, then I owe you the same."

He couldn't disagree with her there, and to be honest, he was curious.

Megan straightened her shoulders and took a deep breath. "My dad wasn't around when I was born. He was in prison."

Paul blinked, but didn't say anything.

"You see, my dad had a thing for drugs. Both using and selling. It was small stuff mostly, but he wasn't very good at evading the law. He was in and out of prison my entire childhood."

"I'm sorry." Paul felt as if he should do or say something, but he was at a loss. Being a cop, he saw situations like the one she was describing. It was rough enough to see from the outside looking in.

"To be honest, things were better when he was away. Mom was depressed and drank a lot, but other than that, things weren't bad. Becca made sure there was food in the house and that the bills were paid. She helped me with my homework and made sure I got to school on time.

"Everything changed whenever Dad was home. The first few days weren't horrible. He was happy to be out of prison, and he'd hug and kiss us—tell us he loved us, and that things would be different. At first, I believed him. Becca never did, though."

Paul tugged Megan's hand into his lap, and rubbed the inside of her wrist with his thumbs. He didn't know what else to do.

"About a week would go by, and then one of his friends would stop in to see him. They'd start drinking, and then the drugs would come out."

"Your father did drugs in the house in front of you?" Anger welled up inside him.

Megan nodded. "Becca always made sure to get us out of there if she could. Or at the very least, she'd stock up on snacks and water, and we'd hide in our room. I can't tell you how many blanket forts we made during those times."

It was then Paul understood the connection between Megan and her sister. He knew they were close, but the relationship had always seemed a bit unnatural. Now he knew why. Rebecca had been Megan's protector.

"It wasn't a great childhood, but Becca got me through it. I don't know if I would have made it without her."

Paul heard what Megan didn't say. There would have been no reason to hide if there was no danger. "Megan, did your father ever . . ."

"No. He never hurt me, although he used to knock Mom around sometimes. And I think he got to Becca once or twice. She never said anything, but once I saw some bruises on her arm that looked like fingerprints."

He'd heard enough. Wrapping her in his arms, he buried his face in the crook of her neck. "I'm so sorry you had to go through that."

She circled her arms around his waist and returned his embrace. "Paul, I didn't tell you all that to make you feel sorry for me. I'm not that little girl anymore."

Paul pulled back enough to see her face. "I know that."

Megan ignored his comment. "I told you because I wanted you to understand that I know the difference. You aren't a violent man, Paul, and I'm not helpless. Nor am I defenseless. If worse comes to worst, I can always go for the family jewels. That would wake you up, for sure."

She winked at him, taking some of the sting out of her threat.

"It really doesn't worry you?"

"Nope."

He smiled and let the warmth in his chest grow. Paul wasn't stupid. He recognized the feeling for what it was. He was falling for Megan, and all his reasons why they shouldn't be together—all the reasons why they couldn't work—were quickly becoming less and less important.

Chapter 19

Megan woke up alone this time. They'd made love again before going to sleep in her bed. Paul had been restless near morning, but he didn't thrash around as he had the day before. She had taken a chance and snuggled up to him. He settled down almost instantly.

She rolled over to look at the clock. It was a little after six thirty in the morning. Paul had to be in to work at eight, so he'd probably left her to sleep while he went to his room to get ready. Tossing the covers off, Megan threw on some clothes, and went in search of coffee.

As Megan measured out the grounds and started the coffeemaker, she couldn't stop smiling. She and Paul were dating. They were going to explore what was between them. Megan was flying on cloud nine, and she didn't want to come back down to earth anytime soon.

Arms circled around her waist from behind, and she leaned back into the warm chest crushed against her back. She didn't know if it could get any better than this.

Paul ran the tip of his nose along her neck. "Good morning."

"Good morning." She tilted her head to the side to give him better access.

He placed little kisses along her neck and jaw while he toyed with the skin along her belly beneath her shirt. She felt the heat grow between her legs. All he needed to do was say the word and she was ready.

His next words burst her bubble. "I need to get into the station early, since I took yesterday off."

She groaned, and he chuckled.

"You can't still be horny after last night," he said.

Megan turned in his embrace and wrapped her arms around his neck. He pulled her flush against his body, and whether he admitted it or not, she didn't think it would take much to get him going either. "I've got a newsflash for you, Detective. I have a pretty healthy sex drive."

He smiled. "Is that so?"

"Yes." She rubbed up against him seductively to drive home her point.

Paul sucked in a shaky breath. "You're going to be the death of me."

She released him, and stepped back. "Oh, but what a way to go."

He shook his head and adjusted himself.

Megan retrieved their mugs and poured them both a cup of coffee. He gave her a chaste kiss in thanks, and then they both took their places at the kitchen table.

"Do you think you'll be working late tonight?" she asked.

"I don't know. I'm waiting for some documents I requested. If they're delivered today, I'll probably stay late to work on them. Otherwise, I should be home around the usual time."

She nodded and took a sip of her coffee. "I'll go to the store today and restock the fridge. Did you have any requests for dinner?"

"You don't have to cook for me, Megan."

His statement confused her. "I cook for you all the time."

"No, you cook for us. Yourself, Chloe, and me. That's different."

Megan set her mug down. "No. It's not. Why are you so against me doing things for you? When I moved in, I had to fight you to do basic chores around the house. Now you don't want me to make dinner?"

"It's not that I don't want you to." Paul massaged his temple.

It hadn't been her intention to start their morning off with a fight.

"Then what is it? Please, help me to understand, because I don't get it."

He sighed and met her gaze. "I don't want you to feel as though you have to *do* things for me."

"And if I want to?"

"Why would you want to?" he countered. "You're twenty-three years old. You have your whole life ahead of you."

"Yeah. So?"

"So. I'm a middle-aged man with a five-year-old daughter."

Megan stared at him. She was starting to get angry. "Why does our age difference bother you so much?"

"Because I don't want to be the one that holds you back." With that, he pushed himself away from the table, and went to the sink to dump the rest of his coffee.

"Don't you think that should be my decision?"

He braced his hands on the counter in front of the sink and bowed his head. "Megan, do you understand what us being together means?"

"Yes."

Paul turned around to face her. "Are you sure? You're walking into a ready-made family. Once we've crossed that line, there's no going back."

"Don't you think it's a little late for that? Or are you regretting last night?"

He softened his voice. "No. I don't regret it. If anything, I want to drag you back upstairs and stay there with you for the next three weeks."

"So what's the problem?" She really wasn't understanding. If he wanted to be with her, and she wanted to be with him, what was the issue?

"In three weeks, Chloe will be back home. And she's going to realize things have changed between us."

"Of course she will. She's a smart little girl." Megan still felt as if she were missing something—something big.

Paul sighed and ran both hands over his face before letting them fall to his sides. "What I'm saying is that once Chloe finds out about us, her imagination is going to take off. She's . . . ."

"She's what?"

"She's going to start thinking that we're going to get married and that . . . that you're going to be her new mommy."

Megan tried to keep the anxiety out of her voice. "And that's not what you want."

"Argh. Why does this have to be so difficult?"

"I don't know." Maybe she'd read Paul all wrong. Maybe all he was looking for was someone to warm his bed every now and then. How could she have misread him so badly?

Something akin to a growl rumbled deep in Paul's chest, and he crossed the room in two long strides to where she was sitting. He hoisted her up by her arms to stand in front of him. "Please don't look at me like that."

"Like what?"

He framed her face with his hands, and she closed her eyes. "Like I've just killed your puppy."

She opened her eyes. "I don't have a puppy."

Paul ignored her comment. "I'm going to be honest, Megan. I don't know what I want. This thing between us—how I feel about you—it's new. And shocking. And I don't know what to make of it. But if it did work between us, then yes, I would want a future with you. A permanent one."

Megan smiled and leaned into his touch. "Me, too."

"You'd be willing to accept a ready-made family and everything that goes with it?" he asked.

"Yes."

"How can you know that?"

Megan placed her hands over the top of Paul's, and brought their faces closer together. "Do you trust me?"

It was his turn to look offended. "Of course I do."

"Then trust me to make my own decisions. I know what I'm getting myself into."

"How—"

She covered his mouth with her right hand. "Paul, I've known what I want for a while now. And I know everything that comes with it—Chloe, Cindy and George, your family. I want to see where it takes us. See if what I've been imagining—you and me—is possible. It doesn't scare me."

"It scares me," he mumbled under her fingers.

Megan smiled and leaned in to give him a kiss. "Don't be scared. It's just me."

He groaned and hugged her against him. "That's what scares me."

She laughed and kissed him again. Paul didn't make it to work early that morning.

***

Two hours later, Paul sat at his desk going over paperwork. Not only had he not made it to work early, he'd been almost an hour late. Granted, with all the weird hours he'd been working, he doubted any of the other officers would even notice the anomaly. Of course, his partner was the one exception.

"About time you showed up, Daniels."

He didn't bother looking up. "Overslept."

Janey rested her hip on the edge of his desk. "Didn't your nanny come home yesterday?"

"Yes, I picked Megan up from the airport yesterday afternoon. Which you know perfectly well, because I told you that's what I was going to do." This time, he shot her a piercing glare before returning to the file. Janey was a good partner, but she could be incredibly nosy. Maybe it was because she was a cop, but he didn't remember having the same problem with his previous partner, Doug. Then again, Paul and Melissa were already married by the time he and Doug had been partnered up. Maybe that was the difference.

"Uh-huh. And you're trying to tell me she had nothing at all to do with you being late this morning?"

"I was late. That's all. Can we drop it and get to work?"

She chuckled and sauntered over to her desk. "So tell me what you've got, Oh Great One."

Paul rolled his eyes. "I was thinking we could canvass the campus area again. Drive around. Talk to some of the pedestrians."

Janey groaned. "Do you really think spending another day driving around is going to garner any new information?"

"Do you have a better suggestion?"

"What about that list of employees and students the college was supposed to send over?" Janey asked.

Paul leaned back in his chair. "Still waiting on them."

She shook her head. "There's got to be something. Maybe we should talk to the families again."

"All right. That might be a good idea. Since we're fairly sure the campus area is where our killer is choosing his victims, they might help us narrow our search area."

He stood and grabbed his jacket off the back of his chair. They made their way to his vehicle, and headed toward the first victim's parents' home. Jessica Chase was single, living alone, so her parents and her best friend were their closest connection.

Less than a minute after they left the station, his phone beeped letting him know he had a message. Since he was driving, he ignored it. Janey, however, did not. She snatched the phone from the center console where he'd placed it.

"What are you doing?"

"Being inquisitive. You never get texts. Maybe it's important."

"I'm sure it's not." Paul said, hoping Janey would take the hint and return his phone to the console.

She didn't.

With a few swipes across the touch pad, his partner pulled up his text message. "I knew it!"

Paul glanced in her direction and frowned. It didn't take a genius to figure out the text was from Megan. She and Gage were the only two people who ever sent him text messages, and the last message Gage sent him had been months ago. But what did Megan text him that had Janey looking so smug?

"Care to change your story, Detective Daniels?"

Janey turned the phone so that he could see the screen. His heart skipped a beat, and he had to concentrate to keep from losing control of his car. There, on his phone, was a picture of a woman in her bra and panties—a bra and panty set he recognized.

His partner laughed at his reaction. "No comment, Detective?"

He swallowed, and tried his best to focus on the road. "Fine. We're . . . exploring our options."

She laughed. "From the looks of it, you'll be exploring a lot when you get home tonight. I guess that means you won't be working late anymore."

Paul shot her a look. "Do you think we could stick to the case and not my love life?"

Janey smiled and returned his phone to the center console. "At least you admit that you do have a love life."

He grunted.

"I'm happy for you. Really. And from everything I've seen, I think Megan is good for you."

"Are you finished?" he asked.

"For now."

They arrived a few minutes later at Jessica Chase's parents' house. Her father was outside working in the yard. Paul and Janey exited the vehicle.

"Good morning, Mr. Chase." Janey extended her hand to the older man.

"Detectives." Devlin Chase removed his gloves and met them in the middle of his yard. "Have you found new information about our daughter's killer?"

Paul shook the man's hand. "We were wondering if you and your wife had a few minutes to talk to us."

Mr. Chase was obviously curious, but he nodded. "Sure. My wife's inside."

Janey and Paul followed Mr. Chase inside the house. The closer they got to the kitchen, the stronger the scent of cinnamon and sugar became. It reminded Paul that he'd skipped breakfast in favor of other activities. Shaking his head, he did his best to dispel the memory of Megan's legs wrapped around his head.

"Detectives." Elaine Chase wiped her hands, and stepped around the counter.

To try and stay focused, Paul decided to take the lead. "Good morning, ma'am."

Mrs. Chase reached for her husband. "Did you find something?"

For most families, the worst part of an investigation was the waiting. They wanted closure so the healing could begin. "We wanted to ask you a few more questions."

"Of course." Mr. Chase wrapped his arm around his wife.

"Do you know if your daughter frequented the area near the local community college?" Paul asked.

The couple looked at each other before Mr. Chase answered. "I think she may have tutored someone there last year, but I don't know who it was."

"Trudi would probably know, wouldn't she, Devlin? She's probably at work." Mrs. Chase clung to her husband.

They asked a few more questions, and Mrs. Chase remembered that they'd found a better picture of their daughter, if they wanted it. The one the family had originally provided was a profile shot. There wasn't anything wrong with it, but sometimes profiles were harder for people to identify.

With the picture in hand, Paul and Janey got back in his car and headed for the restaurant where Trudi Olsen worked. There was one big advantage to visiting Jessica's best friend at her place of employment—he'd have the opportunity to get some much needed food.

By the time they were seated in Trudi's section, Paul's stomach was growling.

"Didn't you eat anything this morning?"

Paul didn't bother to look up from the menu when he answered Janey. "No."

She snorted. "I wonder why."

"Hello. My name is—"

Janey smiled up at Trudi. "Hello, Ms. Olsen."

"Um. Hello. What are you doing here? I mean, did you find something?" Trudi glanced over her shoulder.

Paul laid his menu on the table. "We were hoping to order some food, and maybe chat with you a bit if you have time."

"Yeah. Sure. Um. Let me get your order in, and then I'll let my manager know I need to take a break."

The restaurant was still serving breakfast, so he ordered a stack of pancakes, three eggs, and some bacon. It was a lot of food, but he was starving. There was no telling how many calories he'd burned off in the last twenty-four hours.

Trudi disappeared into the kitchen, and then returned less than ten minutes later with his food and Janey's coffee. As he dug into his breakfast, Trudi pulled up a chair, and sat down. "So what's up? Did you find something?"

Since he was eating, Paul let Janey run with the questioning. "We were hoping you could tell us about any connections Jessica may have had to the local community college, or the area itself. Her mother thought she remembered Jessica tutoring someone there last year."

"Yeah, she did. It was last summer." Trudi's eyes grew wide with concern. "You don't think that was somehow related to her death, do you?"

Janey patted Trudi's hands reassuringly where they lay clasped together on the table. "We're just following some leads. No stone left unturned— that sort of thing."

Trudi nodded.

Paul took a sip of his coffee. "Do you happen to remember the person's name she was tutoring?"

"I think his name was Scott. He was in a fraternity, I remember that. He invited Jessica to a couple of parties."

This could be the break they needed. Jessica had been the only victim they couldn't positively link to the campus area within six months of her death. "Do you know if she ever went to any of them?"

Trudi thought about it for a long moment before answering him. "I don't think so. To be honest, I think she was kinda glad when the tutoring was over."

"And why is that?" Janey asked.

"I think he was hitting on her. She had a boyfriend at the time, so she told him no."

Paul set his fork down on his plate. "He didn't take the hint?"

Trudi shrugged. "He was . . . persistent. Jessica said he never got physical with her or anything, but he was constantly flirting."

They wrote down all the information Trudi could remember about the young man Jessica had tutored the previous summer, as well as the name of Jessica's boyfriend at the time. This was the reason why one had to go over information dozens of times. Both he and Janey had specifically asked about boyfriends more than once, yet this was the first time they were hearing about Jessica's.

Hoping they could speed things up, when they left the restaurant, they made their way to the campus admissions office. The dean was extremely helpful, especially since they'd already sent over a warrant for records. By the time they left, they had a list of all the fraternities and their members. All they had to do now was find the Scott they were looking for.

Chapter 20

Paul and Janey spent the rest of the day back at the station going through the list of fraternity brothers the dean had provided. The Internet allowed them to get background on the eight Scotts they had on their list. By the end of the day, they had pictures of each of the men, along with an idea of each one's personality. It always amazed Paul how much information people shared on social media sites. On days like this, he was grateful. It made his job that much easier.

At five o'clock, Paul shut down his computer, and slipped on his suit jacket. Janey smiled, but didn't say anything.

The drive home was full of anxious anticipation. Megan had continued to text him periodically throughout the day. None of them were as provocative as the first—mostly small reminders she was thinking about him. Paul had to admit that they were a nice pick-me-up to his day.

He pulled into his driveway and turned off the engine. It was taking all he had not to rush into the house to find her like some sort of crazed madman. He hadn't felt like this in a long time.

As calmly as he could, Paul made his way inside. He glanced around the kitchen, but didn't see Megan anywhere. Closing the door behind him, Paul called out to her. "Megan?"

Her voice floated down from the second floor. "I'm upstairs."

His heart started racing as the possibilities of why she was upstairs flitted through his mind.

All his restraint went out the window as he ran up the stairs to find her. He was out of breath by the time he reached the top, but he didn't slow down. In three strides, he was at her bedroom door.

The sight that greeted Paul had him hard in a matter of seconds. Megan lay on the bed in nothing but the bra and panty set she'd texted him that morning. It was dark blue with lace trim—a striking contrast against her skin.

Megan sat up, resting her weight on her arms behind her. "Welcome home."

He released a shaky breath. "What are you doing up here?"

"I thought maybe we could have a picnic." She waved her hand toward a wicker basket he'd yet to notice sitting on the floor beside the bed.

Paul was trying to wrap his head around what he was seeing.

When he didn't move, Megan crawled off the bed to come stand before him. She reached for the lapels of his jacket, and pushed it up and over his shoulders. It dropped unceremoniously to the floor behind him. Next she went for his tie. "You're wearing way too many clothes, Detective Daniels."

As soon as she removed his shirt, Paul removed his gun and holster, grabbed hold of her waist, and crushed her against him. She gazed up at him with a look he was becoming very familiar with. Threading his fingers through her hair, Paul lowered his mouth to hers.

Megan enthusiastically kissed him back. If he didn't know any better, he would have thought she was attempting to crawl beneath his skin the way she rubbed herself against his body. She didn't hide that she wanted him, and it had his erection protesting against the confines of his suit pants.

Completely forgetting about food, he walked them back toward her bed. Megan scraped her nails along his back, sending shivers down his spine. He needed to be inside her already. Paul kicked off his shoes, and together they made quick work of getting rid of his pants and underwear—the only thing left between them were the scraps of satin and lace she was wearing.

Before he could remedy that, Megan broke away, and crawled backward onto the mattress. She had her back arched and her legs spread. He could see the evidence of her arousal seeping through her thin panties. Paul couldn't take his eyes off it.

"Did you change your mind, Detective?" she asked.

Paul blinked and adjusted his gaze up to meet hers. She was grinning. Megan knew exactly what she was doing to him.

In response, Paul narrowed his eyes, and launched himself onto the bed. He covered her body with his, and trapped both her hands above her head.

Megan giggled. "I didn't know you liked it kinky, Detective."

He attacked her neck with vigor—licking and biting at her flesh. "I'll show you kinky."

Something snapped inside him, and Paul shifted his hold so he could grasp both of her wrists with a single hand. With the other, he covered her breast and began tweaking her nipple.

"Paul."

The way she said his name was all the encouragement he needed. Paul continued to play with her breasts, but he was getting frustrated with her bra. It was getting in his way.

He let go of her wrists, and Megan seemed to know exactly what he wanted. She twisted to the side so he could reach behind her and unclasp her bra. They worked together to remove it, and then Paul went back to worshiping her.

While his mouth was busy, he used his hands to encourage Megan to wrap her legs around his waist. As soon as her heat was pressed up against him, he nearly lost it. "Now you're the one wearing too many clothes."

She laughed and dropped her legs. Reaching between them, Megan worked her panties down her legs. As she did this, however, she began scooting herself further up the bed—away from him.

Paul waited until the offending material was gone before diving forward to catch her by the hips. He pulled her back down the bed until she was where he wanted her.

Megan circled her arms around his neck and shook her head. "So impatient."

"Says the woman who sent dirty pictures of herself to my phone."

She smiled and ran her fingers through his hair. "Only one."

He groaned. "One was enough."

Using his neck as leverage, Megan pulled herself up to whisper in his ear. "You didn't like it?"

Before he could respond, she covered his lips with her mouth. Paul didn't fight it. He could admonish her later.

Everything happened rather quickly after that. There was kissing and touching. She fumbled around for a condom, and he quickly rolled it on. Then he was pushing himself inside her. Paul was lost in the need to possess every part of her. It was as if he couldn't get enough—couldn't get close enough to her.

She met him thrust for thrust, grinding her hips against him, seeking her own pleasure. It was a heady feeling, knowing she desired him as much as he did her.

Paul felt his climax approaching, and more than anything he wanted her there with him. Reaching between them, his touch edged her closer. Megan dug her nails into his shoulders, and she threw her head back. "Paul!"

Seeing Megan orgasm had to be one of the best things he'd ever seen in his life. She embraced her sexuality completely. It was enough to send him over the edge.

Megan laughed as he collapsed on top of her.

"Sorry," he said, rolling to his side.

She turned to face him, still smiling. "I don't think you have anything to apologize for."

Her gaze roamed down his length and back up again. There was a hunger in her eyes that did nothing to stop the blood that was pounding through his veins. Ten years ago, he would probably have been ready to jump her again.

"You're insatiable."

"Is that a complaint?" she asked.

It was his turn to laugh. "No."

She smiled. "Are you hungry?"

"Famished."

Megan reached across his lap and over the side of the bed to retrieve the wicker basket he'd noticed before. She pulled it up onto the bed, and rearranged herself so she was sitting with the basket on the mattress in front of her. One by one, she began removing the items.

Paul excused himself so that he could clean up. When he came back into her bedroom, he slipped into the bed, and got comfortable against the headboard. Every few seconds Megan would cast him a sly glance, but other than that, she focused on what she was doing. The more he watched her, the more it hit him that she truly seemed to want him, and not only in the physical sense.

"Are you all right?" Megan positioned herself beside him at the top of the bed.

"Yes." He suddenly had an impulse to kiss her, so he did.

She smiled and handed him a container. "There's little sandwiches, fruit, cheese, chicken—"

He cut off her list with another kiss. "It's wonderful. Thank you."

Megan shrugged. "I know you've been stressed lately with the case and . . . well . . . with us."

Paul reached for her hand and laced their fingers together. "I'll make you a promise, okay? I'll try my best not to stress about what's going on between the two of us. We have a lot to figure out in the next three weeks, but I'm willing if you are."

***

Paul's words were music to Megan's ears. She felt as if she'd been waiting to hear him say them forever.

She tilted her head up, and placed a featherlight kiss on his lips. "That's all I want."

He smiled, and for the first time Megan thought everything might really work out the way she hoped. Paul felt something for her—he was willing to give a relationship between the two of them a chance.

For the next several minutes, they busied themselves eating. She was biting into a chicken wing when Paul cleared his throat. "Janey knows. About us, I mean."

Megan swallowed. Did he not want his partner to know? "Okay."

"She saw your text this morning. The picture."

"Oh." Megan didn't know what to think. It was only a picture of her in her bra and panties. She wasn't naked or anything. Although taking a picture like that had crossed her mind, she knew Paul wasn't quite as adventurous as her, so she had toned it down. "Did you not want her to know, then? About us?"

He was quiet for a long minute. "I don't know. I guess I was hoping to keep it to ourselves for a while. We don't know if this is going to work, and once people start finding out—"

"It complicates things. I get it." And she did. He wasn't sure this was what he wanted. It would be easier if no one knew, in case things didn't work out.

What she was thinking must have shown on her face, and he jumped in to correct her assumption. "No. That's not what I mean."

"Then what did you mean? If you're ashamed of us, Paul, then this isn't going to work." The thought turned her appetite sour.

Paul made a frustrated noise, and laid the food he had on his lap off to the side before pulling her into his arms. "I'm not ashamed but, Megan, you have to understand that this is a big step for me. I want us to be sure that this is going somewhere before we announce it to the world. Does that make sense? Who knows, maybe you'll find out something about me that repulses you?"

Megan snorted.

He kissed the top of her hair, and she wrapped her arms around his torso. "Hey, it could happen. I'm not perfect."

She looked up at him. "I know that."

"I mean, look at this. Clearly, I could have done a better job explaining myself."

Megan shook her head. "That was my fault. I shouldn't have jumped to conclusions."

Being with Paul was a roller coaster of sorts. They had the friendship thing down, now they had to figure out if it could be more than that. He was right. It was going to take time.

"I've never been in a situation like this," Megan admitted.

She seemed to take him off guard with her comment. "What do you mean?"

"I've never been friends with a guy first."

"Never?" Paul looked somewhat horrified.

"Never."

"Well, I've already expressed my opinion of the guys you used to date." He reached once more for the food, and handed her one of the little sandwiches she'd made.

She took what he offered, and thought about what he said. "Does it bother you that I've been with so many men?"

They'd pulled the covers up around their lower halves, but other than that they were naked. Maybe it wasn't the right time to bring something like that up, but Megan had always been one to speak her mind, no matter the situation. Of course, it had gotten her into trouble more times than she could count.

"The truth?" he asked.

"Always."

Paul dropped his arms from around her, and he sat up a little straighter. Megan matched his posture. He clasped his hands together in his lap and met her gaze. "I try not to think about it."

"Because it does bother you." She knew they had to get it all out in the open.

"A little, yes."

Megan nodded, and bowed her head. Never before had she regretted the number of partners she'd had. "I figured it might. You've only been with one other person."

He sighed and reached for her again. She went willingly, needing to feel the security of his arms. "This isn't going to be easy, you know. We're very different."

"I know. I don't expect it to be easy. I've tried easy, and it's not all it's cracked up to be."

"How about we take it one step at a time? We have three weeks to see if we can make this work before Chloe comes home," Paul said.

"Right."

They went back to eating the food she'd made, but this time they kept one arm around the other. As they ate, they talked about their day. Megan had spent most of it doing laundry from her trip and going to the grocery store.

Most of the food she'd placed in the basket was gone, but neither of them seemed to have any desire to move from the bed. Megan rested her head on Paul's chest while he ran his fingers up and down her spine.

"Have you thought any more about where you'd like to go Friday night?"

Megan glanced up, and then went back to playing with the curly hairs at the base of his stomach. "Do you like to dance?"

He chuckled. "I haven't danced in years. Not since high school."

"So is that a no?" she asked.

"No. It isn't a *no*. It's an *I have no idea*. Do you?"

"I love to dance." Megan smiled.

"Do you want me to see if some of the guys at work can suggest something? I'm sure there's a club in Indianapolis where we could go."

She loved that he was willing to do something out of his comfort zone for her, but Paul wouldn't know what he was looking for. "I have a better suggestion. Why don't you let me take care of it? I've got time during the day with Chloe gone anyway, and I don't want to take time away from your case. I know it's important to you."

Paul kissed her forehead and eased them further under the covers. "I think I'm showing my age. It feels wrong for you to plan our date when I'm the one who asked you out."

Megan turned over on her belly so that her face was only inches from his. "Do you know how sweet it sounds to me that you actually care about that?"

He pushed the hair back from her face. "That's me. Sweet."

She smiled. "You are. Sweet, and sexy, and . . ."

"And?"

"And . . ." Megan trailed her palm down his chest, and wrapped her hand around his length.

"Megan? Maybe we should finish talking about this first. I mean, it's still early, we can—"

Megan cut off his protest with a bone-searing kiss. When she removed her lips from his, she went to work on his neck. She loved the way his body felt under her lips and hands. She loved his reactions. Everything about Paul was honest. He didn't pretend to be something he wasn't. No, he wasn't perfect, but she would take his imperfections over lies any day.

As Megan continued to lick and suck on the skin around his neck and shoulder, Paul threaded his fingers through her hair. She wasn't sure if he was trying to encourage her or stop her. Either way, Megan was loving it. "Go ahead. I'm listening."

He laughed, but there was no humor in it. "I can't think with you touching me like this."

She smiled against his neck, and took a section of his skin between her teeth, worrying it. "Sure you can."

Paul groaned. "What were we even talking about?"

Megan laughed and pushed herself up so that her forehead was touching his. "You were disagreeing with me finding you sweet and sexy."

"Was I?"

She nodded. "Uh-huh."

They stared at each other for several beats before Paul brought her face down to his. Megan always enjoyed kissing—mainly because it almost always led to other things. While she couldn't wait to make love to him again, she could also go on kissing him all night. It wouldn't be the same, but there was also something about it that felt as if they were connecting on a different level. Not only the kissing, but the touching—the caressing. The way he held her made her feel like she was precious to him.

Eventually, the kissing built to the point where they both needed more. Paul dug one of the condoms she kept in her bedside table out of the drawer, and they were soon connected in the most intimate way. They had a long way to go, and a lot of things to figure out, but she would take it. Paul was special. All she had to do was get him to see it, too.

Chapter 21

Megan stood on her tiptoes and wrapped her arms around Paul's neck to kiss him goodbye on Friday morning. The last three days had been good. Really good. They were beginning to settle in to being a couple.

"Unless something comes up, I'll be home a little after five." Paul held her close, showing no sign of wanting to let her go.

"I'll probably be upstairs getting ready."

He kissed her again, trailing one hand down her spine until he was cupping her backside.

She giggled. "You know you're going to be late if you don't leave soon."

Paul groaned and reluctantly released her. "I'll see you tonight."

Megan waved goodbye as he left. Tonight was their date, and she was beyond excited.

Once Paul was out of sight, she headed upstairs to finish getting ready for the day. She had a lot of things to do. Not to get ready for the date, but to keep herself busy so the day wouldn't feel as if it were dragging on forever.

Grabbing her purse, she locked up the house and made her way to her car. Her first stop was to the nail salon. Megan wanted to look her best for their date, so she was treating herself to a manicure and pedicure. She'd also bought a new dress for the occasion.

On her way out of the salon, Megan spotted Paul and Detective Davis across the street. She debated whether or not to make her presence known, but the decision was made for her when Paul noticed her. He looked confused. She hadn't told him she was coming down to campus, but it wasn't like she normally cleared her day with him ahead of time.

She waited as Paul said something to his partner and then crossed the street. "Hey. I didn't know you'd be here."

"I didn't know you'd be here either."

Megan had to press her hands against her sides to keep from reaching for him. He was working. It wouldn't be appropriate if she threw herself at him, would it?

Paul glanced over his shoulder and nodded in his partner's direction. "We're here working a case."

Megan smiled and held up one of her hands. She'd picked vixen red as her color to match the dress she'd chosen for that night. "Getting my nails done."

He raised his eyebrows. "Interesting color choice."

She knew she probably shouldn't, but Megan couldn't resist. Taking a step forward, she got close enough to whisper so only he could hear. "I thought it would look good later tonight as I'm running my hands all over your body."

Paul sucked in a breath and averted his gaze. "Tease."

Megan laughed.

"Are you on your way home, then?" He tried to discreetly adjust himself and divert her attention.

This only made her smile wider. "Not yet. I'm taking a summer class, and I need to stop by the bookstore to pick up a couple of textbooks."

He furrowed his brow. "Be careful, okay?"

"All right. Is there something going on?" she asked.

Paul hesitated, and she knew he was debating how much to tell her. She also realized that because he was choosing his words carefully, the answer to her question was yes.

"It's okay. I get it. You can't talk about it. I'll be extra careful. Promise."

He took a deep breath and released it. "Thank you."

Megan smiled, trying to ease the tension the subject matter had created. "I'll let you get back to work."

Paul seemed reluctant to leave, but then he nodded. "I'll see you at home."

She watched as Paul jogged back across the street to rejoin his partner. He waved to her and Megan waved back before she walked the short distance to her car. Slipping inside, she started the engine, and pulled away from the curb.

A few minutes later, Megan pulled into the small parking lot outside the campus bookstore and library. The two buildings were connected, which she loved. It meant that she could pick up her textbooks and any research materials she needed, all in the same stop. A win-win in her opinion.

On her way inside, Megan spotted Jay—the patrol officer Paul had tried to set her up with. He wasn't in his uniform, so she had to assume he was off duty. "Jay!"

He smiled when he saw her. "Megan."

Now that he wasn't being thrown at her as a possible suitor, Megan was genuinely happy to see him. "How have you been?"

"Good. You?"

Megan smiled. "I'm good."

Jay looked behind him at the library, and then back at her. "So are you a student here?"

"Yeah. I've been taking some classes online. I still prefer textbooks to the online manuals. There's something about being able to flip through the pages and highlight what I'm needing." Considering how much she loved technology, using electronic textbooks had never appealed to her. She had tried it with her first online class, but had ended up breaking down and buying the book anyway. This time, she decided she wasn't even going to bother with the online version.

"Ah. A woman after my own heart."

They both laughed.

"So what about you? Are you a student here, too?" Megan asked.

To her surprise, Jay blushed. "Yeah. I'm taking some classes in criminal psychology."

"That's great." Megan was truly happy for him.

"Do me a favor, though, will you?"

She was thrown for a minute by the change in his demeanor.

"Don't tell anyone that you saw me here, all right? I-I don't want anyone at the station finding out."

Megan didn't understand why he wouldn't want anyone to know

he was taking classes, but she figured that was his business. "Sure. I won't say anything."

He smiled. "Great. Thanks. Well, I'll let you get back to whatever. It was great seeing you again, Megan."

"You, too."

Jay breezed past her, and she resumed her way into the bookstore.

Inside the building, Megan located the classic art section, and began browsing through the textbooks. She knew what she was looking for, so it was only a matter of finding it.

A man wearing a red apron with the school logo on it approached her. "May I help you?"

She smiled and handed him the list of books she needed.

"Ah, yes. We've got those right over here." He walked farther down the aisle and stopped in front of a large display. One by one, he plucked the books she needed off the shelf.

"Thanks."

He smiled back at her. "That's everything except for the one on Da Vinci. It's in our library section. Would you like me to show you?"

The man's help was saving her a lot of time, so she nodded. "That would be great."

Megan followed him into the connecting building and up a flight of stairs. She was learning that most places tucked their arts sections into a corner, and the campus library was no different. She followed the man across the room to the back corner. It was a place Megan imagined she'd be spending a lot of time in over the next few years if she hoped to finish her degree.

It took a few minutes, but the man was able to locate the book on DaVinci Megan was seeking.

"Thank you, so much. You just saved me an hour of searching."

"No problem. It's my job."

She smiled as she flipped through the book.

When she closed it and looked up, she'd expected the man to be gone. Most employees disappeared quickly once they were no longer needed— off to help someone else or get back to their regular work. He remained standing roughly three feet away from her, shifting his weight from side to side.

He noticed her staring at him, and cleared his throat. "Um.

I . . ."

The man cleared his throat again. He appeared nervous. "I was wondering if . . . if maybe you'd . . . you'd like to . . . go out sometime."

Megan was completely caught off guard. "You're asking me out?"

He nodded.

Although the man was cute in a nerdish sort of way, her heart already belonged to another. "I'm sorry. I can't. I'm seeing someone."

He sagged his shoulders in defeat. "Oh. I understand."

Before she could utter another word, he was striding away from her. Megan was left feeling as though she'd done something wrong, when of course she hadn't. He'd asked her out, and she'd said no. So why did she feel so bad about it?

Trying to push what had happened to the back of her mind, Megan took her items to the front desk so she could check out. She had a date to get ready for. Tonight was to be about her and Paul, and having fun together. In many ways, this would be a first for both of them, and she wanted it to be special.

Taking her bag of books, she headed to her car. With every step, she became more confident about tonight and what she had planned. She couldn't wait to get their date started.

***

Paul was more unnerved by the sight of Megan than he should have been. He knew she took classes through the college, and he knew she'd been on campus before. For some reason, it had never crossed his mind to warn her to take extra precautions. Because of that, he spent the rest of the afternoon cursing himself. That, and as his date drew closer, the butterflies in his stomach were turning into something much more violent.

"Something bothering you, Daniels?" Janey asked when they finished talking with the president of the last fraternity house on their list.

He waited until they were in the car to answer her. "I just have a lot on my mind."

Paul pulled out into traffic and started toward the station. It was already after four thirty. He was going to be late. The good news was they were fairly sure they had found their Scott. He'd graduated the year before, thanks to some tutoring he received for a required math class. No one at the fraternity could remember the woman's name who had tutored Scott, but the timing fit. Their next move would be to track Scott down. According to his social media profile, he was still in the area.

Janey twisted in her seat. "About the case?"

"No." Paul debated whether or not to continue, but decided why not? "I have a date with Megan tonight."

"That's great. Where are you taking her?"

He shouldn't have been surprised at his partner's curiosity or her support. "I don't know. She offered to plan everything."

"Wow. I'm impressed. Somehow, I always pictured you as a take control kind of guy."

Paul grunted. "Normally I am. With Melissa I always planned our dates—even after we were married."

Janey nodded. "But with Megan, it's different?"

"Yeah. It is."

"That can be a good thing. As long as it's what you want." Janey leaned back in her seat and scanned their surroundings. They were passing through a residential area where there had been some recent break-ins. Although burglary cases didn't usually fall in their laps, keeping your eyes opened was a cop thing.

He was quiet until they turned onto the road that led to the station. "I like being with her. She . . . she makes me feel alive again."

His partner chuckled. "And for that reason alone, I would like her. Paul, you've grieved for Melissa long enough. It's time to move on. It's okay to move on. Don't you think that's what your wife would have wanted? For you to be happy?"

Paul nodded. It was the only response he could give since his throat constricted with the overwhelming emotion he felt.

As soon as the car was parked in its spot, Janey was out of the vehicle, and on her way inside the station. "Come on. Let's go get this paperwork done so you can get home to your hot date."

It took them over a half hour to log the necessary reports. Paul sent Megan a message to let her know he'd be late, and she responded with a quick, *I'll be waiting.* For some reason, Paul was expecting her to be agitated. She'd made plans, and his job was getting in the way.

Paul pulled up in front of his home at five forty-two. He was twenty-two minutes late.

Megan was coming down the stairs when he strolled through the door. "Hey. You're home."

She was dressed in a deep red dress that cut off around mid-thigh. It was fitted, and left very little to the imagination. He felt his lower half react almost instantly.

"You look amazing."

The smile that graced her features only made her more beautiful. She walked over to him, and gave him a soft, lingering kiss. "Thank you."

Seeing her like this made it easy to forget they had plans—plans that didn't include him ripping that dress off her. Paul had to remind himself that there would be time for that later. "Just let me go upstairs and change. Then we can go."

Megan showed no signs of being in a hurry. "Don't you want to shower? I don't mind waiting if you do."

"Yeah, I would. Are you sure you don't mind?" he asked.

She gave him another chaste kiss, and then walked over to the other side of the kitchen. "Not at all. We've got time."

"I'll be quick." Before he could be tempted any further, Paul raced up the stairs to his room.

It didn't take him long to shed his work clothes and hop in the shower. He did take some extra time shaving to make sure he didn't miss any unwanted hair. It was strange how much he felt like a teenager again. When you're with someone for so many years, you fall into a routine. They know you. You know them. The mystery fades. What's left is a level of companionship that can stand up to whatever the world throws at you. He missed that. But what he also found he missed was this—this edge of excitement, the unknown possibilities.

Finished grooming, Paul went to his closet to find something to wear. He opted for a dark gray dress shirt and a pair of light gray slacks. Paul debated on adding a tie, but decided against it. If they were going dancing, he wanted to be comfortable.

When he walked back downstairs, Megan whistled.

He laughed. "Thanks. Are you ready to go?"

"Yep. Ready when you are."

Paul offered her his arm. He led her to his car and opened the door for her. She pecked him on the cheek and then slid inside.

Once he was behind the wheel, Paul turned on the engine, and began backing out of the driveway. "Where to?"

She gave him directions, and they ended up about a twenty minutes from his house at a little Japanese restaurant. After waiting in the lobby about fifteen minutes, they were escorted to their table and given menus. It had been a while since Paul had been to a place like this. Having a small child often meant steering restaurant selections to places that served more kid- friendly items. He didn't see many of those items on this restaurant's menu.

"I thought this would be good. Different," she said.

He looked up at her and nodded. "I don't see many things on here Chloe would be thrilled about."

Megan chuckled. "I know. Could you imagine how she'd react to sushi?"

Paul snorted. "We'd probably draw a lot of unwanted attention."

The server came to take their drink orders. They decided to order some sushi as well for an appetizer. Paul had never had it before, but Megan said she loved it when it was done right. He was willing to give it a try.

"How in the world did you go through thirty-six years of life and not eat sushi?" Megan asked as their food started to arrive.

He shrugged. "Never had it growing up, and once I was an adult, the opportunity never presented itself, I guess."

She picked up one of the pieces of sushi and held it up to him. "It's tuna."

Paul opened his mouth and bit into the raw tuna and rice.

Megan waited for several seconds while he chewed. "What do you think?"

"It's different. Not bad. Just different."

Before she popped the remaining bit of tuna into her mouth, she pointed to the butterflied shrimp. "Give that one a try. If you like steamed shrimp, you'll like that one."

He did as instructed, and she was right. It was very similar to steamed shrimp, which he'd eaten numerous times at parties, dipped in cocktail sauce.

They finished off the sushi Megan ordered—some he liked more than others. The best part, though, was when she wanted him to try a new one and would feed it to him. He wasn't sure why he found that appealing, but he did. Maybe it was how her face lit up, or how she'd bounce slightly in her seat as she waited for his reaction.

By the end of dinner, Paul had to admit he was enjoying himself. The food was good and the company was even better. He and Megan had always been able to talk. Paul had feared that maybe changing the parameters of their relationship would alter that, but thus far, it hadn't. If anything, it had opened the conversation up more.

"You ready to go dancing, old man?" Megan teased as they ambled out of the restaurant.

He pulled her against him, and walked her backward until she was pressed against the cool metal of the car. At first their age difference had truly concerned him, but the more they were together, the more he realized that it wasn't an issue. Not for her and not for him.

"I'll show you old," he whispered a moment before his lips crashed over hers.

By the time they broke apart, they were both panting. He raised his eyebrow, waiting for her to retract her original statement.

Instead, Megan sidestepped him, running her palm over his crotch as she moved to the passenger side of the vehicle. "It's a good start. Let's see how you do on the dance floor."

Chapter 22

Paul was still shaking his head as he steered his car toward the club.

"You all right over there? Something wrong with your head?" Megan asked.

"My head is fine, you vixen. Other parts of my body—well, I'm not so sure."

She laughed. "You'll be fine. Besides, we're just warming up for later."

"Is that so?"

Before he could say anything else, his cell phone rang. It was after seven thirty, which meant it was most likely Chloe. He hadn't told his daughter, or Cindy, of his date with Megan. No one knew except his partner. It was easier that way.

"Can you answer it and put it on speaker since I'm driving?" he asked.

Megan reached for the phone and hit the necessary buttons. She propped her elbow on the center console, and held the phone up where it would pick up his voice. "Hello, sweetpea."

His daughter's voice resonated in the close confines of the car. "Hi, Daddy."

The conversation lasted for several minutes as Paul weaved through Friday night traffic. Megan sat stoically silent in the passenger seat, holding his phone. He saw her smile a couple of times as Chloe talked, but she kept her comments to herself.

When Chloe was finished, she passed the phone over to Cindy as per usual. Paul had told his mother-in-law that he most likely wouldn't be home when it was time for Chloe to call, so to phone his cell instead. Cindy hadn't asked, and he hadn't gone into detail as to why.

"How are things?" Cindy asked.

He glanced over at Megan. She was busying herself looking out the window at the passing buildings.

Paul came up to a traffic light and made a left before answering. "Things are good here. Work is keeping me busy."

She paused. "And how's Megan?"

Megan glanced over and met his gaze. "She's good, too."

"Paul, please tell me you aren't fooling around . . . with that girl." Cindy lowered her voice for the last part, presumably to keep Chloe from overhearing.

He watched as Megan's eyes widened in shock at the obvious disapproval. "Cindy, my relationship with Megan—whatever it may be—is between me and her. I know you're concerned, and I appreciate it, but I'm asking you to please butt out."

Cindy was quiet for longer than was natural. "What if—"

"There will always be what ifs, Cindy."

He heard sniffling from the other end of the line. "I have to go give Chloe her bath. Good night, Paul. Stay safe."

"Cindy?"

His question was met with dead air.

Megan lowered the phone and placed it back in the center console where

Paul always kept it while driving. "Well, that was interesting."

"I'm sorry about that. I thought she and I had already had this discussion. I didn't realize she'd bring it up again."

"So you knew she disapproved of us?" Megan asked.

Paul glanced over at her. He didn't like that Megan was frowning. They'd been enjoying themselves. He wanted to see her smiling again, but he figured it was best to get it out in the open. They'd agreed to be honest with each other, after all. "It's not that she disapproves. She's worried."

"About what?"

There was no easy way to say it, so he decided to spit it out. "Chloe. Cindy is afraid that you'll . . . get bored."

Megan turned in her seat. "Bored? With what? You? Chloe? Having a place to call home? Someone I can trust won't walk out on me as soon as things get tough?"

He knew she was upset, and it wasn't what he wanted. They were supposed to be on a date. Having fun. "Yes. She's worried about all those things."

"Are you?" He heard the challenge in her voice.

"Not as much as I used to be."

Anger turned to hurt. "That means you still are. At least, some part of you is."

Paul reached out and took hold of one of Megan's hands. She pulled it out of his reach.

Frustrated because driving limited his actions, he found the closest parking spot, and pulled over. Once his hands and attention were free, he released both their seat belts, and reached for her.

She resisted a little, but after he persisted, she allowed him to pull her into his arms. It was awkward, given they were in his car, but he had to do something. Ten minutes ago, they had been laughing and teasing, and then one phone call with his mother-in-law and her feelings were hurt.

"I'm sorry. Cindy didn't say those things to hurt you," he whispered.

Megan shook her head against his shoulder. "I don't care about what Cindy says or thinks. I care about what you think—how you feel."

He sighed. "I'm not going to lie and say I don't have doubts. I do. But every day we're together, they get quieter. I'm starting to believe this can work."

She sat up so that he could see her face. "Really? You're not just telling me what I want to hear?"

Paul brushed the hair away from her face. "Really."

A second later, Megan's lips were covering his, and her tongue was inside his mouth. He kissed her soundly for several minutes, and then forced them apart. They were both breathing hard again, and the semi-erection he'd been sporting since the restaurant was tenting his pants.

"We should get going." He had no idea how he managed to get the words out or sound so rational.

Megan licked her lips and lowered herself back into her seat.

She was smiling once more.

When he continued to sit there, she smirked, and ran her hand from his knee to his thigh. "Were you planning to get to the club at some point tonight, or did you want to go straight home?"

He removed her hand to a safe distance and took a deep breath. "Behave."

She pouted. "Where's the fun in that?"

Paul laughed and started driving again. "You don't make it easy, you know."

"Easy is boring."

It was his turn to frown.

"Oh, stop looking like that. You are anything but easy, and neither am I. We both have baggage out the wazoo."

Megan was right. He was still dealing with the loss of his wife, and she had a rocky past that tainted her outlook on life and relationships. "I think we're doing pretty good so far. Don't you?"

She didn't answer right away, but he felt her gaze on him. "Yeah, I do."

Paul laced their fingers together, and brought the back of her hand up to press against his lips. "Good. Now, where exactly is this club?"

***

Megan was trying her best to let what Cindy said roll off her back, but it was nagging at her. Was Paul right? Was Cindy only worried about Chloe? Or was it more than that?

They drove by the club and found a place to park a few blocks away. Paul walked around the car and helped her out of the vehicle.

He must have realized something was still bothering her. "Hey, are you all right?"

"Yeah, I'm good." She gave him the best smile she could manage.

Paul wasn't buying it. "You're still upset by what Cindy said."

She nodded.

He crushed her against his chest and brushed the side of his cheek against hers. It was completely smooth—smoother than she'd ever felt it. And he smelled divine. She'd have to ask him sometime what cologne he was wearing so she could stock up.

His voice vibrated against her ear. "Don't be. What she thinks doesn't matter. This is about us."

Megan held on tight, not wanting to let him go. "You don't care that she doesn't approve?"

Paul shrugged. "She didn't approve of me at one point, so no."

She leaned back and quirked an eyebrow at him. "Cindy didn't approve of you?"

"Neither did George. Although, I don't think it was me, specifically. I think it was more they didn't like the fact that their sixteen-year-old daughter was dating. Since having Chloe, I'm beginning to understand. I'm fairly certain I'm not going to enjoy her teenage years."

Paul grimaced, and Megan laughed.

They began walking hand in hand toward the entrance to the club.

"I'm sure you'll do fine. Somehow, I imagine you being a cop will make any of Chloe's suitors think twice about doing anything stupid."

He kissed the top of her head as they approached the door. "I hope you're right."

Megan had done a lot of research to find a club she thought they would both enjoy. This one was a little more subdued than some she'd found, but she didn't think Paul would be able to relax and have a good time at one of the more trendy locations.

As they made their way inside, she recognized various parts of the club from the online pictures. The walls were painted a dark blue, but there were lighter accents throughout. To their right was a long bar that stretched almost the entire length of the wall. On the left there were tables and booths—most of which were occupied. The center of the room was dedicated to a large dance floor with a stage at the back. An all-male band was currently playing an upbeat dance track she recognized from about five years ago.

"Come on, let's see what kind of dance moves you have."

She dragged him by the hand through several groups of people until they were near the center of the dance floor. Ignoring convention, Megan rested her arms on Paul's shoulders, and began swaying her hips to the beat.

Following her lead, Paul placed his hands on her hips, and matched her movements.

By the end of the song, Megan was no longer worrying about Cindy. "You're not bad."

He laughed. "I never said I was bad, only that it had been a while."

The next song was a little slower, so Megan took the opportunity to press their bodies together. It was still a dance beat, but it almost reminded her of the steady rhythm of lovemaking. She took advantage and ground her pelvis into his.

Paul looked around frantically, but when he realized that no one was paying the least bit of attention to them, he dug his fingers into her ass and mimicked the motion. They danced like this for several songs, adjusting the timing of their movements to the beat. It was one of the sexiest things she'd ever done.

By the time the band finished their set, Megan was about to crawl out of her skin for want of him. The more they danced, the less it became about dancing and more about touching and rubbing against one another. All that was left was to shed their clothes and they would have been going at it like two rabbits in the middle of the dance floor.

Paul guided her over toward the bar. "I need something to drink."

Megan couldn't agree more. She was parched. Problem was she didn't think anything at the bar was going to quench her thirst—not entirely, anyway.

Since he was driving, Paul ordered himself a coke. Megan got a margarita. They took their drinks across the room and found a table.

The club was noisy, but not so much that you couldn't hear the person next to you. It was another reason she'd chosen this particular club. It seemed classier than some of the others. That, and it wasn't marketed to college students. Most of the people present were in their twenties and early thirties, but the club didn't give off that sorority/fraternity vibe.

"Are you having a good time?" Megan asked.

He took a drink of his coke and leaned in close to whisper in her ear. "I can't believe you're asking me that."

She ran a hand along his thigh, and this time he didn't stop her. "Well, I didn't want to assume . . ."

Paul shocked her when he grabbed hold of her wrist and placed her hand over his crotch. He was hard and pulsing against her palm.

Megan swallowed and met his heated gaze. "I'll be back."

Removing her hand from his lap, she stood, and made a beeline for the bathroom. Once inside, Megan splashed some water on her neck so as not to ruin her makeup. She needed to cool down. The whole point of tonight was for them to get out and have some fun. In public. To see if they could be a couple outside the confines of Paul's house.

She took a deep breath and waltzed back out into the main room of the club. Halfway back to their table, Megan caught sight of Paul. He looked somewhat lost sitting there all alone. She knew exactly how to remedy that.

"You ready to take another go at the dance floor?"

"Don't you want to finish your drink first?" he asked.

Megan picked up her margarita, took a long sip, and then reached for his hand. "I can multitask."

The floor was more crowded this time, so Megan and Paul stuck to the outside of the designated dance floor. They swayed their hips to the music, commenting every now and then on the song or the original artist. She was having fun, and he was, too.

After a second full set from the band, Megan was ready to call it a night. They'd been teasing each other for almost two hours. All she wanted was to find a flat surface, lift up her skirt, and have him buried deep inside her. Paul was a cop, though, so she knew better than to suggest they find a dark corner to slake their lust.

It took almost forty minutes for them to get home. By then, Megan was rubbing her legs together in an attempt to stave off the need to jump him. As it was, as soon as he'd parked the car in the driveway, Megan popped the button on her seat belt, and crawled across the console into Paul's lap.

Her ass hit the steering wheel, beeping the horn. She shifted a little, and then she heard Paul release his own seat belt and felt him slide the seat back as far as it would go.

"I want you," she murmured against his lips.

His response was a strangled moan.

Paul snaked his hands beneath her skirt, pushing it up around her waist. With the newfound freedom of movement, Megan parted her legs, and straddled him. He took hold of her hips and rotated his pelvis, giving her the friction she desired.

"W-we should go inside." His voice was strained as Megan

continued to move against him. Her dress was up around her waist, and one of her breasts was exposed. They were making out like teenagers.

But they weren't teenagers, and what Megan wanted to do to him was anything but childish.

After a long kiss, Megan reluctantly removed herself from Paul's lap. His hair was sticking up in spots, and half his shirt was unbuttoned. She also thought she saw a wet spot on his slacks.

He moved first. "Come on. Let's get inside before I forget all common sense and take you here, despite the consequences."

Megan would have laughed, but she felt the same way. She needed him, and she was past caring about their surroundings.

They made it as far as the kitchen. He shut the door, flipped the lock, and then reached for her.

Clothes disappeared quickly after that. They were inside their home with no one else around. All that mattered was her and Paul.

He laid her flat out on the kitchen table and spread her legs. She was naked and more than ready for him. Paul had the patience of a saint, though. No matter how much she tried to hurry him along, he was determined to pleasure her first.

Megan threaded her fingers through his hair as he knelt between her legs. She closed her eyes and let the feelings overwhelm her. *I love you.*

Her world shattered, and her heart beat with every bit of love she felt for him. As he moved up her body, covering her, Megan wanted more than anything to tell him how she felt. But she wasn't sure he was ready for that yet.

So instead of declaring her love for him, Megan let her body do the talking. She plunged her tongue inside his mouth, tasting herself on him. Paul hummed in response, meeting every thrust of her tongue with one of his own.

"Upstairs," he said in between kisses. "No condoms . . . down here."

The last thing on Megan's mind was condoms. She wanted him, and she wanted him now. "I'm on birth control. And I'm . . . I'm clean."

He stopped, and she groaned.

"Are you sure?" he asked.

Megan ran her fingers along his face and met his gaze. "I'm

sure."

Paul appeared to debate with himself for half a second. Then he reached between them and positioned himself at her entrance. She pushed her hips forward, encouraging him.

As he slid inside her for the first time without protection, Megan had to bite her lip not to scream out. It was the best feeling.

"You okay?" Beads of sweat dotted Paul's forehead.

She raised up to lick his lips with the tip of her tongue. "I'm more than okay. You?"

He closed his eyes and started to move. "You feel amazing. I want . . ."

Megan was trying not to get lost in how good everything felt. "You want what?"

"I don't want to stop. Ever."

Paul picked up his pace, and she knew he wouldn't be able to hold on much longer. They'd been teasing each other all night. It was one of the things she loved about dancing. When done right, it was the perfect aphrodisiac.

Suddenly, he was pulling out of her, and she felt bereft. "What—"

Without saying anything, Paul led her up the stairs. She had no idea what was going on. Maybe he'd changed his mind about the condom, although she really hoped that wasn't the case. Megan had gotten a taste of what making love to him was like without anything between them, and she wasn't sure she ever wanted to go back.

He surprised her when he bypassed her room and continued on to his.

She looked at him with a startled expression. "Paul, we don't—"

"Shh," he said as he pulled her flush against him once more.

Paul kissed her thoroughly until she was barely able to remember her own name, let alone whatever it was she was going to say.

He guided her over to the bed and eased her down onto the mattress. As he hovered over her, Megan saw something change in him. For the first time, she believed that Paul might actually be able to love her.

Chapter 23

Megan lay sprawled out on her back, trying to catch her breath. She'd had great sex before, but the last few hours had completely blown her previous experiences out of the water. And that didn't even count the added sensation of him not wearing a condom.

Once Paul brought them to his bedroom, it was as if he'd wiped the slate clean, and they'd started from scratch. She couldn't remember how many times she'd climaxed. Six times? Maybe it was seven. The amount really didn't matter. What did matter was how attentive he'd been. By the time he found his own release, her entire body was vibrating with pleasure, and it felt as if all her bones had been liquefied. Maybe it was because he was older, but it seemed he knew exactly where to touch her to make her body sing.

She felt the mattress move beside her, and then the next thing Megan knew Paul's arm wrapped around her stomach. He pulled her flush against his chest, and she rolled over so that he could spoon her from behind. Megan knew things would be different with Paul—she loved him. What she hadn't expected was how overwhelming it would feel. If something happened and she lost him, she didn't know what she would do.

The deep rise and fall of Paul's chest told her he'd fallen sleep. It took much longer for sleep to claim Megan. Before, she hadn't fully understood what he must have gone through when he lost his wife, but she did now. She wondered how he'd survived it.

But she knew the answer to that, too. Chloe. She had been his reason for living—what kept him going for so long.

Megan's heart broke for all the pain he must have endured. More than anything, she wanted Paul to be happy, and she wanted to be part of that happiness.

Eventually sleep claimed her, and she woke up to something tickling her cheek. Blinking open her eyes, Megan turned to see Paul propped up behind her, smiling. He had a tiny feather—most likely gleaned from one of the pillows—pinched between two fingers.

He leaned down to give her a brief kiss. "I was wondering if you were going to sleep the day away."

She craned her neck to the side and stretched. Her muscles ached in a very good way. "What time is it?"

"After ten."

That surprised her. "Aren't you going in to work today?"

Paul shrugged. "I need to go in at some point for a few hours. It can wait, though."

He kissed her again, but this time there was nothing quick about it. When he tried to deepen the kiss, however, she turned her head. "I should go brush my teeth."

"I don't care about that," he grunted into her neck.

She laughed. "Yes, well, I do."

He sighed and released her. "Fine. Go brush your teeth and get dressed. I'm taking you out for breakfast. Or I guess it might be lunch by the time we get there."

Megan punched him lightly on the arm before hopping out of bed. "I'll meet you downstairs in fifteen minutes."

The sound of his laughter echoed down the hall after her as she dashed into her room to get ready. She gathered her hair up into a ponytail and took one of the quickest showers of her life. Throwing on some underwear, a pair of jeans, and a fitted T-shirt, Megan added a pair of flats and she was set. She arrived downstairs with a minute to spare.

Paul was already in the kitchen. His eyes nearly bugged out of his head when he saw her.

"What?" she asked, thinking maybe she'd forgotten something important.

He shook his head. "You look about sixteen with your hair pulled up like that."

Megan grinned. "Afraid someone will think you're robbing the cradle, Detective?"

She was expecting him to come back with some sort of an affirmative, but he didn't. Instead, Paul backed her up against the wall, and kissed the daylights out of her.

When he released her, he had a smug look on his face. "There. I've been waiting to do that since I woke up this morning."

Megan was still trying to get her bearings when they climbed into his car. "Our age difference doesn't bother you anymore?"

She had to ask. In the past, it had bothered him a great deal.

"No." He shot her a glance as he pulled into the restaurant parking lot.

Paul turned off the engine, but neither made any move to go inside.

"What changed?" she asked.

She felt something shift in the atmosphere around them.

He reached for her hand and met her gaze. "I realized that you were right. We're both adults, and as long as it's what we both want, then the rest shouldn't matter."

"Wow."

Paul cupped the back of her head with his free hand, and brought her mouth to meet his. The kiss was slow, and it reminded her of the night before when he'd all but worshipped her body from head to toe.

She held tight to him, not wanting to let go. Her thoughts from the night before came back to the forefront, and she wanted so badly to tell him how she felt.

He rested his forehead against hers. "Let's go eat. Something tells me I'm going to need my energy later."

Megan laughed and scraped a manicured nail down the back of his neck. "I think you might be psychic."

They ended up sitting side by side in a back corner booth. The food was good, but it was made better when Paul started feeding her bites of his Belgian waffle. He always made sure his aim was slightly off so she'd get whipped cream on her face. She couldn't really complain, since he was right there to lick it off for her. Megan had never imagined Paul with a playful side, but she loved every minute of it.

Nearly two hours later, they were on their way home. She knew he would be leaving for work soon, but the selfish part of her didn't want him to go.

"Something wrong?" he asked as he pulled into the driveway.

She shook her head. "Not really. I'm just enjoying our time together so much I don't want it to end."

He entwined their hands, and squeezed. "I'll be gone three . . . four hours at most."

"I know. Don't mind me. I'm being silly."

Paul was quiet for a long moment. "You're not being silly. It's different now."

She knew he was talking about them. "Yeah, it is."

They sat there holding hands until Paul broke the silence. "I'm not sure how things will be once Chloe comes home. I don't know how she'll react. To us being together, I mean."

"I think she'll be fine. She was worried about you having a girlfriend, after all."

"What? When?" Paul demanded.

Megan laughed. "Don't look so shocked. Chloe picks up on things like how all her friends' parents are either married or they have girlfriends or boyfriends."

"She asked you about this?" He sounded as if she'd knocked his legs out from under him.

"She did."

Paul shook his head. "Why didn't you tell me?"

"Would it have changed anything? She asked me months ago, and I explained it to her the best way I could."

"I still should have known." He was upset.

"Paul, you can't know everything." He started to interrupt her, but she pushed on, cutting him off. "Are you more upset that I didn't tell you or that she asked in the first place?"

He opened his mouth and then closed it. "I don't know."

Megan leaned her head on his shoulder, and he rested his cheek against her hair. "You don't have to have all the answers, you know."

"Then why does it feel like I should?" he asked.

She tilted her head so she could look up into his face. Megan's eyes drifted to his lips, and she pulled his mouth down to hers. "You don't have to do it all on your own anymore."

They kissed until his phone started vibrating. He seemed reluctant to burst the bubble they were floating in. "I should get that."

"You should," Megan said, putting some distance between them.

He picked up the phone and answered it. "Daniels."

After a few seconds, Megan realized it was his partner.

"I'll be leaving the house in a few minutes. Yes, I know. Can it, Davis. I'll see you when I get there."

When he hung up the phone, Megan could have sworn he was blushing. "Everything okay?"

He sighed. "Everything's fine. Janey's just giving me a hard time because I told her we had a date last night. She's letting her imagination run wild."

Megan perked up. "You told her about our date?"

"Yeah. Although now I'm rethinking the wisdom of that decision."

She ran her fingers along his jaw before letting her hand fall. "Don't be. She wouldn't be giving you a hard time if she didn't care. I'll let you get to work."

Paul caught her hand as she was stepping out of the car. He didn't say anything—just met her gaze and held it for a long moment before letting her go.

***

As Paul drove toward the station to meet Janey, he couldn't get what Megan had said out of his head. *You don't have to do it all on your own anymore.* He'd been doing it on his own for a long time. But then he realized that ever since Megan entered their lives, that had begun to change. She was so much more than a nanny—she always had been. Even from the beginning.

Her revelation about Chloe asking about him having a girlfriend was eye- opening. It hadn't crossed his mind that his daughter would worry whether or not he had a woman in his life. What else didn't he know about?

Janey was waiting outside for him when he pulled into the parking lot. She opened his passenger side door and got in. No words were spoken, but he could tell she was dying to say something.

"Spit it out already."

"I think you're getting paranoid. I wasn't going to say

anything," Janey said, acting all innocent.

Paul eyed her skeptically. "Sure you weren't."

"I'll just say this—"

"There it is."

She stuck her tongue out at him.

He laughed.

"As I was saying, before I was so rudely interrupted." Janey tilted her head forward, giving him one of those you-better-listen-if-you-know- what's-good-for-you stares. "You'd better not let her get away."

Paul flexed his fingers against the steering wheel. Something had occurred to him that morning as he and Megan were lying in his bed. He was in love. It had hit him out of the blue as he watched the sunlight dance across her face.

Something had prompted him to take her to his bed the night before. He hadn't understood it then, but when he'd woken up and felt her warm and soft beside him, he'd known. All his crazy arguments were gone. For whatever reason, Megan wanted to be with him, and he wanted that, too.

"Earth to Paul?"

He blinked and glanced over at his partner. "What?"

She smiled knowingly. "I asked you if Chloe's having a good time with her grandparents."

"Oh. Yeah. She's loving it. Ma's going to have her hands full, I think. Cindy and George are spoiling her rotten."

Janey laughed. "I'm sure she'll be fine. Your mom can always call your brothers if she gets desperate. Chloe's always been a sucker for her uncles."

"True," Paul said as he pulled up in front of Scott Parker's apartment. They'd debated on whether or not to show up at his place of employment, but decided maybe a one-on-one visit without an audience would be best.

Paul and Janey exited the vehicle and strolled up the short path to Parker's apartment. It was in a decent neighborhood—completely average. It was a direct contrast to the flashy persona their suspect presented online.

Janey knocked and they waited patiently for Parker to answer the door.

When the door was opened, however, they came face-to-face

with a young woman with a baby on her hip. Although it was an unexpected development, he and Janey didn't react outwardly.

Paul showed the woman his badge. "Hello, ma'am. Is Scott home?"

The woman adjusted the baby, turned her back on them, and walked into the apartment. She left the door cracked open, and they could hear voices coming from inside.

Janey glanced in his direction, and he shrugged. Paul had no idea what was going on. After ten years on the force, not much surprised him anymore. That's also why he made sure not to let down his guard. People did weird things like run, jump out two-story windows . . . you name it, and he'd probably seen it.

Luckily, the only thing they got this time was a groggy-looking man in his mid-twenties who looked as if he'd had one too many the night before.

"Scott Parker?" Janey asked.

"Yeah. Who wants to know?"

They both flashed their badges this time, and he squinted like he was looking into the sun. "What did I do?"

"May we come inside?"

Parker shifted his gaze to Paul, and backed into the apartment. It appeared neither Parker nor the woman were overly talkative.

When Paul and Janey entered the apartment, the first thing they noticed were the toys scattered around the living room floor. It was obvious from what he could see that the baby lived in the apartment, or had at least been there for an extended period of time.

Once they were all seated, Janey started in on the questioning. "Mr. Parker, last year you received some tutoring for a math class, is that correct?"

Parker rubbed his eyes and blinked. "Yeah. That's right."

"Was your tutor's name Jessica Chase?" Paul asked.

The young woman hovered in the background, curious, but not participating. Parker didn't seem bothered by her presence. "Yeah. She helped me get through my class. Why?"

They ignored his question. "And how long did you meet with Ms. Chase?"

Parker appeared to do some calculations in his head before he answered Janey. "About two months."

"So you stopped meeting with her in . . ."

"August? Yeah. It was August."

"Do you remember when exactly in August? Janey prompted.

"Hmm. I'm not sure. It was hot. I remember that. She wore this white tank top that showed off her tits."

"Thank you for that *detailed* description of Ms. Chase, Mr. Parker. Could you tell us where you used to meet Ms. Chase?" Paul was hoping it was somewhere on campus. That would positively put her in the same location as the other victims.

"In the library. I tried to get her to meet somewhere a little more . . . romantic, you know. I mean, the library?" His revulsion was evident. "Hey. Why are you asking all these questions about Jessica?"

Paul and Janey looked at each other, and then Paul shrugged. Letting the cat out of the bag wasn't likely to hurt anything at this point. "Jessica Chase was murdered."

That sobered him some.

"Is there anything else—besides Ms. Chase's physical appearance—that you can remember about your last few meetings?" Paul asked.

"Oh, there was this dude. Yeah."

"What *dude*?"

Parker leaned forward in his seat to answer Paul's question. "Didn't get his name. He was some book nerd. I think he worked at the library or something."

"And what was it about this guy that makes you think we should talk to him?"

"Because he was weird. I mean he would hang around all the time. And I think he even asked her out." Parker's nose scrunched up in distaste.

Janey took down a description—or what Parker could remember, at least—of the man in question. They would have to take a trip to the library and see if they could locate him. As it was, they'd gathered as much information as they could from Scott Parker.

Twenty minutes after leaving Parker's apartment, they arrived back at the station. They both went inside to make a report of their activities.

It didn't take long for Paul to finish his paperwork. There wasn't all that much to report, after all. Parker had been moved way down on their suspect list, and the information they had on this library employee was sketchy at best.

Paul logged off his computer, and made sure he had both his cell phone and his keys. His mind was already on ways he and Megan could spend their evening.

Janey looked up from the report she was still working on. "Tell Megan I said hi."

Paul paused for a second before reaching for his jacket. "I will. See you Monday, Janey."

"You're not coming in tomorrow?" she asked. Then she shook her head. "Of course you're not. Go enjoy your new girlfriend. I'll be thinking of you while I'm sitting at home all alone eating bonbons."

He laughed and patted her on the shoulder as he went by. His partner had a very active social life. It was the main reason she always gave him such a hard time about his lack of one. "Enjoy your bonbons."

By the time Paul made it home, he was almost giddy. It was a strange way to describe a grown man, but that was how he felt. He was in love— something he never thought would happen to him a second time. It scared him to death, but he was through fighting it. He had a second chance at happiness, and he was going to take it.

Chapter 24

Paul stepped out of the shower on Monday morning with a smile on his face. Of course, that probably had a lot to do with how he'd been awakened. Not by an alarm clock, but by Megan. He'd opened his eyes to find her poised between his legs. It was one of those things wet dreams were made of, and he hadn't been dreaming.

When he arrived home late Saturday afternoon, they'd worked side by side in the kitchen to make dinner, and then spent the rest of the evening curled up on the couch watching a movie. It was a stark contrast to the high energy of the dance club, but that hadn't seemed to matter to either of them.

That night they once again slept in his bedroom—as they did Sunday night. Megan hadn't asked him about the change in venue, but he hoped she understood the significance. It was a big step for him, letting her into his personal space.

He was also trying to open up more and let her into his life. Although the thought of messing up again still haunted him, Paul was determined to give this relationship a go. Megan made him feel alive. When he saw that teasing glint in her eye, his heart skipped a beat. He was, beyond a shadow of a doubt, in love.

As Paul continued getting ready for work, he mused over the rest of their weekend. They'd spent Sunday working outside in the backyard. Megan and Chloe had started a flower garden along the back of the house, so Megan worked on that while he did the mowing and trimming. It was incredibly normal, and yet in some ways it felt extremely intimate to him.

After a long day outside, they'd ended up in his shower together. Megan had introduced him to shower sex. It might sound strange, but he and Melissa had never showered together, with the exception of her last two weeks of pregnancy. She'd had difficulty washing, and so he'd stepped in and helped. There hadn't been anything sexual about it, however. His wife had been miserable at the time as she counted down the days until Chloe was born.

Lifting his shirt collar, Paul situated his tie, and secured it around his neck. He flipped the collar down, and reached for his belt and holster.

Sometimes it felt odd to compare Melissa and Megan. They were complete opposites. But Paul supposed it was natural. Melissa had been the only other woman in his life. Outside of his parents, his relationship with her was the only thing he could use as a guide.

Although Megan was night and day different in personality to Melissa, there were similarities. He and Melissa used to stay up late into the night talking. It didn't matter the subject. More than once they'd both gotten in trouble with their parents for staying up well after midnight chatting on the phone when they were supposed to be asleep. Obviously with Megan, it was different—he was no longer a teenager sneaking around to talk to his girlfriend, but conversation came as easily with Megan as it had with Melissa.

There was also the chemistry. With Melissa, it had been a slow burning fire that would consume him. Megan drew from that same fire, but it was more of a flash flame. Every time he touched her, he wanted everything she had to offer and then some.

Slipping his jacket on, Paul made his way downstairs. When he strolled into the kitchen, Megan was flipping eggs, and humming to herself. She turned to smile at him when she heard him enter the room. "Did you enjoy your shower?"

That glint in her eye was back, and it had his body reacting despite the recent release it had. He walked over to where she was standing in front of the stove, and pulled her back against him with more force than necessary. "Yes, I enjoyed my shower. But not nearly as much as my wake-up call."

She giggled, and pushed him away with her hips. "Go pour yourself some coffee. Breakfast will be ready soon."

Normally he grabbed a muffin or some cereal before heading

out to work, but he wasn't going to turn down a hot breakfast.

Doing as he was told, he went to retrieve his mug from the dishwasher. His hand covered the mug, and he froze.

Megan noticed. "Is something wrong?"

He shook his head and removed his hand. "No. Nothing's wrong."

Closing his eyes, he took a moment to let the conflicting emotions flow through him, and then searched in the cabinets for another mug for his coffee.

She didn't comment until she brought their food to the table and sat down beside him. "You're not using your regular coffee mug. Was there something wrong with it? Did the dishwasher not get it clean or something?"

Paul breathed deep and took a sip of his black coffee. It was bitter. He'd gotten used to having it doctored up with sugar and cream. He didn't look at Megan as he spoke. "It was Melissa's mug. She used it every morning for her coffee. I-I found it in the dishwasher the morning after the funeral."

Megan placed her hand over his. It was the only reaction she made to the information he shared.

"I don't know why, but I took it out and started using it. I even made my coffee the way she used to—three quarters coffee, two sugars, and fill the rest of the mug with milk. It was strangely comforting, so I kept doing it."

He looked up to find moisture in Megan's eyes. It wasn't the reaction he'd been expecting. But then again, Megan usually surprised him.

She blinked. "It made you feel close to her."

Paul nodded.

Their eggs were getting cold, but neither of them seemed to care.

They stared at each other for what felt like an eternity before Megan broke the silence. "You don't have to stop. Not because of me."

He glanced down at their hands—now clasped together on the table between them. "Yes, I do. This morning I realized that I was holding on to the past. Melissa isn't ever coming back, and no matter what I do, or how I drink my coffee, there is nothing I can do to change that. I can't give Chloe her mother back."

There was a catch in his voice as he said that last part. It was what he'd felt guilty about more than anything. His choices five years ago had stolen Chloe's mother away from her. That was something he would never forgive himself for.

"Paul, you didn't kill Melissa." Megan's voice was soft and soothing. She was more than he deserved.

"I did."

Megan opened her mouth again to contradict him, but he cut her off.

"That's why I want you to know that I'm going to try my best not to make the same mistake again."

He looked her in the eye and took a deep breath. "I love you, Megan. I don't deserve this second chance, but for some reason you think I'm worth it, and I'm tired of fighting. You make me feel whole again."

Tears ran freely down her cheeks, and Megan didn't bother brushing them away. "You love me?"

Paul scooted his chair away from the table and knelt down beside her. He took her hands in between both of his and gazed up at her. "I'm sorry I pushed you away for so long. I know I must have hurt you."

She sniffed. "Say it again, please."

He rose up on his knees, bringing their faces level, and brushed her lips with his. "I love you."

Megan made a sound somewhere between a laugh and a cry. "I love you, too."

Their lips met in a heartfelt kiss.

"I don't deserve you," he mumbled.

She pressed her lips to his again. "Yes, you do."

***

He'd said it. Paul had told her he loved her. Megan had no idea what it would mean for their future, but she did know it meant Paul wanted one—a future—with her. He wouldn't have said it otherwise.

They had to warm up their breakfast in the microwave, but it was worth it. She kissed him goodbye, and started in on some housework. With Chloe gone, there wasn't much to do. Paul was surprisingly neat for a bachelor.

Megan was practically skipping as she got into her car around midday and drove into town. Since Chloe wasn't with her, she stopped off at the mall to pick up a few non-food items at her favorite department store. One could never have too many bra and panty sets, especially when there was someone to show them off to.

It turned out the store was having a sale, so Megan took her time going through all the items and picking out the ones she liked the best. She couldn't wait to see Paul's face when he saw them. One set was made of a very thin see-through material. She'd tried the bra on in the fitting room, and delighted at how it left very little to the imagination. It almost reminded her of those wet T-shirt contests, without the need for water.

As Megan was checking out, she had the distinct feeling that someone was watching her. She glanced behind her, but didn't see anyone looking in her direction. Everyone in her line of sight was busy shopping.

Taking her purchases, Megan walked back out into the main area of the mall. She didn't need anything else, but since it was rare she had the time to shop without a five-year-old in tow, she decided to browse. The whole time she felt as if something was off, but when she couldn't spot any valid reason for it, Megan pawned it off as paranoia.

After a relaxing lunch in one of the mall restaurants, she headed back to her car. She still had grocery shopping to do, and she wanted to make sure she had plenty of time to get home and cook dinner.

The grocery store was a little more crowded than she was used to. That was probably because it was later in the day. When she brought Chloe along with her, they typically came early in the morning. It was already after two.

Driving home was another exercise in patience. There was an accident and one of the main roads had been closed off. They were detouring everyone five miles out of their way in order to get around it. Megan was hoping the ice cream she'd bought wouldn't melt, considering it was nearly eighty degrees out. Air conditioning helped, but there was little she could do about the sun beating down in the backseat.

Eventually, she made it on the other side of the detour. The rest of the drive was, thankfully, uneventful.

She brought the food into the house and got it all put away

before starting on dinner. There was a recipe she'd found online that she wanted to try, but it meant marinating the meat for at least two hours.

With that task completed, Megan grabbed her shopping bags, and started upstairs to put her new lingerie away. As she reached the top of the stairs, the phone rang. Not knowing who it was, but hoping it was Paul, Megan ran the few remaining feet into her room, and snatched the receiver out of its cradle. "Hello?"

"You sound like you're out of breath." Her sister's voice held a note of concern.

Megan felt a bit of disappointment that it wasn't Paul. "I just got back from the store."

"Get anything good?" Rebecca asked.

Setting her bags down on her bed, Megan began removing the items and laying them out on the mattress. She'd need to wash them before she could wear any of them. They'd all been in a large bin for people to sort through. It was hard to tell how many hands had been on them. "Just some new undies."

Her sister was too quiet.

"What?" Megan asked.

"You went to the store specifically to buy underwear?"

Megan wasn't getting what the big deal was. "Yeah."

She heard Rebecca release a heavy sigh.

"Would you just spit it out already?" Her sister didn't normally beat around the bush like this.

"Your shopping trip wouldn't have anything to do with that guy you were telling me about, would it?" Rebecca asked.

Why was it that her sister could make her feel as if she were twelve years old again and getting in trouble for eating a cookie before dinner? "Not entirely."

"Oh, Megan."

She could hear Rebecca's disappointment, but Megan refused to act ashamed of her relationship with Paul. Even though her sister had no idea Paul was the guy in question. "Don't say it like that. You can't tell me you've never bought sexy underwear to wear for Gage."

"That's different."

"How's it different?" Megan demanded.

"He's my husband."

"So you didn't dress sexy for him until *after* you married him? Please. You may be a stick in the mud sometimes, Becca, but even I know better than that." She hated fighting with her sister, but she wasn't going to back down on this. Rebecca needed to stop treating her like a child.

Her sister didn't answer immediately, and Megan was beginning to fear that Rebecca had run off in tears again.

"I don't want to see you get hurt again."

Megan sighed and sat down on the edge of the bed. "He won't hurt me. Not intentionally, anyway. You don't have to worry."

"So does that mean you and he are . . ."

"Yes." Megan smiled thinking back to earlier that morning when Paul told her he loved her.

"I see. So does that mean I get to meet him?" Rebecca asked.

"It's still new, but yeah. I think maybe we can arrange something soon." Although she and Paul hadn't talked about it in detail, they both knew that once Chloe returned home there would be no keeping their relationship secret. Given how their family was already connected, it would probably be better to come clean to everyone sooner rather than later.

"What's he like? Tell me about him."

Megan chuckled. "So the interrogation is about to start?"

"No interrogation. I promise. I'm just curious."

This was going to be tricky. Her sister was a private investigator. Megan knew Paul wanted to keep things quiet to their families for a little while longer, but she also knew that if she didn't give Rebecca something, her sister had the resources to start digging up info on her own. That wasn't how she wanted Rebecca or the rest of Paul's family to find out.

"Well, he's a lot different from the other guys I've dated. He has a job, for one thing."

Rebecca laughed. "That's a good start. What does he do?"

"I thought you said this wasn't an interrogation?"

"What? I can't even ask a question?" Megan could almost hear her sister rolling her eyes.

"No. You can't."

"All right. Fine. Go ahead. I'll try not to ask you anything," Rebecca said.

"Thank you."

Megan waited for several moments to see if her sister was going to keep her end of the deal before she continued. "He's good to me. And he can be really sweet. Friday night we went to a Japanese restaurant and I got him to try sushi for the first time. I don't think he liked all of it, but he tried everything because I asked him to."

"You're right. He does sound different from the others." Her sister almost sounded impressed. Or shocked. Either way, it meant that maybe Rebecca would cut her some slack.

"After that, we went dancing. It was a great date." Megan tried to keep the dreaminess out of her voice.

"You love him." Rebecca didn't ask it as a question. It was her sister's job to read between the lines.

Megan didn't bother to deny it. "Yeah. I do."

"And he feels the same way?" The worry was back.

"He does."

"Okay."

Megan's eyes widened with shock. "Okay? That's all you're going to say?"

"I'm going to try and trust you, all right? That's what you want, isn't it?" Rebecca asked.

"Thank you." Megan couldn't express how grateful she was to her sister. Rebecca had always been there for her, no matter how screwed up Megan's life got.

Figuring it was time to redirect the conversation, Megan brought up the one subject sure to get her sister talking. "So tell me about the nursery. Have you finished decorating yet?"

Sure enough, Rebecca began telling Megan about all the new additions to the nursery they'd made since she left. Even though it had only been a week, her sister described each new item, along with several other ideas she had for the baby's room. Apparently, Rebecca had found the perfect rocking chair at a flea market but hadn't been able to fit it in her car, so she'd sent Gage to pick it up in his SUV after practice.

In many ways, Gage and Rebecca were a lot like her and Paul. Not that Megan was anything like her sister, or even that Paul was remotely similar to Gage. It was more that Gage and Rebecca were very much opposites, and the same could be said for her and Paul. On the outside, they didn't seem to fit. But in reality, they were each other's perfect balance.

Megan and Rebecca continued to talk about babies and nursery decorations until Gage arrived home around four. Rebecca said goodbye with a reminder that she couldn't wait to meet Megan's mystery guy. Megan had no idea how her sister would react when she found out Paul was the guy, but she was hoping it would be a good thing. Paul was a good man. Rebecca knew that. Megan only hoped all that knowledge didn't go out the window when the truth came out into the open.

After hanging up with her sister, Megan took the time to wash her new acquisitions before going back downstairs to start dinner. She'd just put the chicken in the oven when there was a knock on the front door.

Wrinkling her nose, Megan wiped off her hands, and went to see who it was. She wasn't expecting anyone. Maybe it was one of the neighbor kids.

She rounded the corner and came face-to-face with the last person she thought she'd see on the other side of her door. Walking the few remaining steps, Megan pulled open the door, and smiled. "Jay. What are you doing here?"

Chapter 25

Paul and Janey spent Monday morning going through the list of students and faculty the college finally sent over to them. Given the information they'd gotten from Scott Parker, they focused on the male library employees and student volunteers. It was a longer list than they would have liked, but by the time they left for the college, they were armed with some basic knowledge about each of their suspects.

It was after one by the time they arrived at the library. The college was currently in between sessions. Paul was hoping that didn't mean their killer had taken some time off due to the break.

When they walked inside the building, they split up. Janey went to take a look around—get a lay of the land—while Paul strolled over to the main desk. "Hello."

The young woman behind the desk glanced up from her computer. "May I help you find something?"

He smiled, attempting to put the young woman at ease. If she sensed something was wrong, she might attempt to alert the other members of the library staff, and that would only make his job harder. "I was wondering if you could point me in the direction of Mr. Chaney."

"The library director?"

"Yes. I was told I could find him here?" Again, Paul tried to keep his tone light and conversational.

"Um. He should be up in his office."

"And where is that exactly?" he asked.

"Oh. Up the stairs and to your right, there's a hallway. Follow that, and his office is the last door on the left. Did you want me to call up and see if he can come down to meet you?"

Paul shook his head. "No, that's all right. I'm sure I can find it."

As he headed toward the staircase, Paul locked eyes with his partner, and nodded toward the second floor. Janey tilted her head in assent and held her position. If the killer was on the premises, they might spook him. Having Janey remain near the entrance was a precaution. If someone suddenly made a beeline for the door, she'd be in a better position to intercept him.

Finding the director's office wasn't difficult. The hallway only had a total of six doors—three on each side—all with nameplates. Paul stood in front of Phillip Chaney's door and knocked.

A few seconds later a man not much older than Paul himself opened the door. "May I help you?"

"Mr. Chaney?" Paul asked.

"Yes?"

Paul showed the man his badge. "May I come in?"

The library director's eyes widened at the sight of Paul's badge, and he quickly motioned him inside. Mr. Chaney took a seat behind his desk, and Paul lowered himself into the chair nearest the door.

"Thank you for your time, Mr. Chaney. My name is Detective Paul Daniels."

It was always good to be polite in situations like these. Phillip Chaney, while not completely off their list of suspects, was a good way down the list. He was married with three kids, and he'd been the director at the college library for nearly ten years. There was nothing in his background that screamed "serial killer". He did, however, have direct contact with all the other library staff, and could be valuable in helping them narrow down their focus. It had already been a month since the last victim was found. If the killer held to his pattern, they had less than a month left before he killed again.

"What can I help you with, Detective?"

"Sir, I'm looking for a person of interest in a case I'm working on, and I believe he either works or volunteers here."

Shock crossed Mr. Chaney's features. "Who?"

"Well, Mr. Chaney, that's where I need your assistance. All I have is a description."

Mr. Chaney swallowed nervously. "And you want me to tell you who I think it is?"

"Exactly."

"But . . . but what if I get it wrong? I wouldn't want to point the finger at someone who's innocent," Phillip Chaney said.

"I only wish to ask this person some questions. He may have information on a murder investigation I've been working on."

"Murder?" Chaney's eyebrows disappeared above his hairline.

Paul kept his tone even and polite. "Yes. So will you help me?"

"Y-yes. Of course."

After giving Mr. Chaney the description Scott Parker had provided, Paul could tell the library director had a specific person in mind.

"Do you know who this might be, Mr. Chaney?"

"I-I think so."

Paul leaned back in his chair, feigning nonchalance. "Who, Mr. Chaney?"

The library director reached up to straighten his tie, almost as if it were suddenly too tight. "Adam Stalz."

"And is Mr. Stalz working today?"

Mr. Chaney turned to his computer, and after a few keystrokes, he nodded. "He's scheduled to work from three to nine."

Paul looked at his watch. It was almost two. They had an hour to kill before Adam Stalz made his appearance, so Paul decided to use the time wisely. "What can you tell me about Adam?"

By the time he left Mr. Chaney's office forty-five minutes later, Paul had a much better understanding of his suspect. Adam Stalz was a sophomore at the college. He'd gotten a job at the library roughly ten months ago to help pay for tuition. The timeline fit.

As Paul made his way downstairs to the main floor, he spotted his partner loitering in front of a bookcase not far from the library entrance. She met his gaze.

"I was beginning to think I'd have to send a search party in after you."

He smirked and shook his head. "Just getting some intel."

"A productive meeting, then, with the library director?"

"Very." Paul tilted his head, motioning toward a more isolated corner of the library.

Instead of saying the suspect's name, Paul found it on the list they'd been provided, and pointed it out to Janey. The chances they would be overheard were minimal, but he wasn't taking any chances. "Three o'clock."

Janey glanced down at her watch and nodded.

"I'm going to take up a position in the store, in case he enters from that end. I'll call if I spot him first. The director was kind enough to offer us his office if we need it," Paul said.

"Very generous of him." His partner never took her eyes off the door.

"Yes. Very."

Once everything was in place, Paul walked over to the other side of the building. It was more crowded than the library, but he supposed that made sense.

At two fifty-six, a young man meeting the description they'd been given entered the bookstore. Paul double-checked the picture they'd found off the Internet, and with the exception of his glasses and a slightly different hair color, it matched. He dialed Janey's number to let her know as he continued to follow the young man.

Stalz stepped behind the counter and retrieved what looked to be one of the aprons all the library staff wore, and then he crossed the room, walking right past Paul, and disappearing into a side room marked *Staff*.

Janey appeared from the adjoining building, and they closed in on the door their suspect walked through. No one seemed to be paying them any attention, which was good. The fewer people who knew what was going on, the better.

They were two feet away when Stalz reappeared. He noticed them, and although Paul could tell he was startled, Stalz grinned, and greeted them.

"Is there something I can help you with today?"

"Are you Adam Stalz?" Janey asked.

A look of apprehension crossed Stalz face. "Y-yes. That's me."

"We were wondering if we could speak to you in private. Maybe a manager's office? We wanted to ask you a few questions about a few of your library patrons that we wouldn't want overheard." His partner used her most nonthreatening voice. Janey could be menacing when she chose to be. Right now, that wouldn't get them what they wanted.

Stalz swallowed, and Paul could see the vein at his neck pulsing wildly. The guy was nervous. "Is something wrong?"

This was the tricky part. Not to lie, but not give anything away at the same time. Paul continued to remain silent and allow Janey to do what she did best. "We're hoping you can help us with something we're working on. Do you think you could spare a few minutes?"

Stalz looked around, unsure. "I-I guess. I mean I'm supposed to be working now, helping customers."

"I'm sure it will be fine. Maybe your boss' office, that way you could clear it with him?"

The suspect still looked torn. "I guess so."

"Great. Which way?"

"Um. Upstairs . . ."

Not giving Stalz time to change his mind, Janey turned on her heel, and headed back into the library.

The man hesitated for a moment, glancing over at Paul.

"After you," Paul said.

***

Once the three of them were in Mr. Chaney's office, Paul offered Stalz a chair and took up position to the left of the door. Janey pulled up another chair that had been against the wall, and positioned it a couple of feet in front of the suspect.

"Adam, my name is Detective Davis, and this is Detective Daniels. Do you have any idea why we wanted to talk to you today?"

Stalz shook his head. "No, ma'am."

Polite. That was a point in Stalz's favor. They'd see if it held once they began questioning him in earnest.

Paul opened the folder he had tucked under his arm, and pulled out the pictures of the four victims. "Do you recognize any of these women?"

Adam Stalz looked intently over each picture. "I-I don't know. Maybe."

"Come now, Adam. We know you asked at least one of these young women out several times while you were working. Does Mr. Chaney know you've been harassing the library's patrons?"

"No. I haven't been harassing anyone. No. That's not true." Stalz was getting agitated. "Okay, I asked them out, but when they said no, that was it. I would never do that."

"So you asked all of these women out?"

He didn't answer right away.

"I'm sure we could find other women you've harassed to come forward, Adam. All we have to do is ask around, and—"

"No! I mean, yes, I ask a lot of girls out. But like I said, when they say no, that's it. I leave them alone. Honest."

Paul continued to scowl at the suspect while Janey leaned forward. "We'd like to believe you, Adam, but you see, we have a problem. All of these women, they were found dead in their homes after they refused to go out with you."

It wasn't a lie.

"Did you follow them home, Adam? Did you stalk them, waiting for the right time, and then kill them?" Paul demanded.

Stalz shook his head violently. "No. No. I wouldn't do that. I couldn't kill anyone. I faint at the sight of blood."

"And why should we believe you?" Paul asked.

"Ask any of my friends. They'll tell you." Stalz turned to Janey. "Please. You have to believe me. I didn't kill anyone."

Paul took a step forward.

Stalz sat up straighter in his chair, pushing against the back, trying to put distance between him and Paul.

"Don't you think it's a bit of a coincidence that all of these women wound up dead after they turned you down? Why do you think that is?"

"I don't know. A lot of pretty women come to the library."

"And do you ask all of them out?" Janey asked.

His eyes flickered to her and then back to Paul. "Yeah. Most of them."

Paul crossed his arms. "So you only kill the ones that say no."

"I told you. I didn't kill anyone."

Janey jumped in, redirecting Stalz's attention to her. The two of them had done this song and dance routine many times since they'd become partners. Paul's size made it easy for him to play the gruff bad cop role, while his partner would turn on the charm—a direct contrast to what Paul was projecting. Suspects would often begin pleading their case to Janey and let something valuable slip.

"Maybe he's telling the truth. Maybe he was just being friendly. The women are pretty," Janey said to Paul before turning to their suspect. "Adam, you have to understand that we're trying to find out who did this, don't you?"

He nodded.

"So were you *maybe* watching them? Before you asked them out?" she asked.

Adam lowered his head, broadcasting his guilt.

Janey softened her voice. "Adam? You watched them, didn't you?"

"Sometimes. It wasn't anything, though. I promise. I just paid attention when they came into the library. Offered to help them find stuff. I didn't do anything wrong," he insisted.

His partner glanced up at him, and Paul nodded. Stalz's responses were consistent. Other than his initial response when asked about the women, and that could be chalked up to embarrassment or fearing for his job, he reeked more of desperation than anything else. Serial killers usually had huge egos. Paul wasn't getting that impression from Stalz.

"Is there anything you could tell us about these women that might help us find out who killed them? Maybe you saw something that would help us. Was there something they had in common?" Janey asked.

They were grasping at straws, but considering their best lead had dried up, it was worth a shot.

Stalz was quiet for an extended period of time. Although Paul was tempted to break the silence with another question, he remained patient. It paid off.

"There was this guy," Stalz said.

He was looking at Paul when he said it, but Janey was the one who responded. "What guy, Adam?"

Stalz shrugged. "I don't know his name. He hangs out at the library sometimes."

"And why do you think this guy may have something to do with these women?" Paul asked.

"Because I see him hanging around talking to girls all the time."

Stalz had their complete attention. "What can you tell us about him? Do you remember what the guy looked like?" Janey asked.

"Tall. Not as tall as you, though," he said to Paul. "And he has blond hair."

Paul opened the folder to make notes. "Bleach blond or more of a sandy blond?"

"Sandy."

"Anything else about him you can remember?" Paul asked.

"I think he might be campus security or something."

Paul jotted that down. "Why do you think that?"

"Because sometimes he'd come in wearing a uniform."

"Anything else?" Paul asked.

Stalz shook his head. "No. But he was here last Friday."

Janey stood. "Do you know if he spoke to anyone?"

"I didn't see anyone, but I was helping someone at the time so I wasn't paying close attention."

Paul and Janey glanced at each other, and he knew they were both thinking the same thing. There had been a thief at the store two years ago. The detective that usually handled burglaries was on vacation, so he and Janey had drawn the case. It turned out to be some sort of prank, but after that, the library put in security cameras. Hopefully, their mystery man had been caught on camera.

Janey thanked Adam Stalz and walked him out. When she reentered the room, Paul was leaning against Chaney's desk facing the door.

"We've got to get our hands on those security tapes."

He pushed himself away from the desk and joined her at the door. "Agreed. Let's just hope Mr. Chaney is in a giving mood and doesn't require we get a warrant first."

His partner chuckled as they strolled out the door. "Well, maybe if we ask real nice."

***

It took a little while to find Mr. Chaney. Since Paul and Janey had taken over the library director's office, he'd gone down to the basement to get some archival work done. One of the library volunteers eventually remembered seeing him head toward the stairs, and had gone down to search.

They got lucky, and after calling the dean, Mr. Chaney agreed to pull the security footage from Friday. The catch was they couldn't remove it from the premises without a warrant.

As a compromise, the three of them set up shop in Mr. Chaney's office to go through the footage. It was a long process, since they didn't exactly know who they were looking for.

Roughly an hour in, something caught Paul's eye. "Go back."

"What? What did you see?" Janey asked.

Paul didn't answer until he had what he was looking for on the screen. "Is that who I think it is?"

Janey stood and walked closer to the monitor. "Is that Officer Rollins?"

"You know this man?" Mr. Chaney asked.

Both Paul and Janey ignored him.

"Is his name on the student list?" Janey asked. "I don't remember seeing it."

Flipping through the folder with the list of student and faculty names the dean had sent over, Paul confirmed that Rollins was not on the list. "We need to get Stalz back in here to see if this is the guy he saw."

Before Janey could comment, Paul was out the door in search of Stalz. There was no sign of him on the second floor, so Paul bounded down the stairs as quickly as he could. If Rollins was the man Stalz saw, there was a very real possibility that he was their killer. They'd been racking their brains trying to figure out how the man managed to get into the victims' houses without any sign of forced entry. It was all beginning to make sense. Rollins could have used his badge and most likely preyed on the women's fears.

Paul found Stalz in the connecting building. He was with a customer. "I'm sorry to interrupt, but we need to speak to you again."

Stalz paled slightly. After the grilling Paul had given him earlier, he supposed he couldn't blame the young man for being a little skittish. "Can it wait until I'm finished helping her—"

"No. I'm sorry. It can't. Maybe another one of the staff could be of assistance?" Paul was trying really hard not to drag Stalz kicking and screaming up the stairs. They were close to solving the case. He could feel it. Paul only needed Stalz's positive ID.

It took a little longer than Paul had hoped, but less than five minutes after finding Stalz, they were on their way back up the stairs.

As soon as Stalz saw the footage, Paul knew by his reaction they had their man. "Yeah. Th-that's him. That's the guy."

Knowing they would need a warrant not only for the footage they'd reviewed, but also all the library's security surveillance for the last twelve months, Paul put in a call to get the process started. "Mr. Chaney, the warrant should be here in a few hours. We're going to need everything you have for the last twelve months."

"Everything?"

"Yes. I'm afraid so," Janey said.

"When do you think you could have it to us?"

"Most of our footage is stored digitally off-site. I'd have to make a request to have it pulled. Maybe a week? A few days, if I pull a few strings."

Janey placed a reassuring hand on Mr. Chaney's shoulder. "Pull a few strings, please. Someone else's life could be in danger."

After leaving Mr. Chaney with a few more details, Paul and Janey practically ran to the car. While Paul started toward Rollins' house, his partner put a call in to the captain to let him know what was going on.

Rollins was off duty until midnight, which meant he could be anywhere.

Chapter 26

Jay sat at the kitchen table while Megan poured both of them a cup of freshly made coffee. She wasn't averse to him stopping by, but she was slightly thrown by it. Sure, they'd agreed to be friends, but other than running into him outside the campus library, she hadn't spoken to him since Paul had tried to set them up. Had Jay ever been to Paul's house before? Megan didn't think so.

She brought the steaming coffee over to the table and took a seat opposite him. "Are you sure you don't want cream or sugar?"

He shook his head. "No. Black's fine. So how have you been?"

"Good. You?"

"Keeping busy. You know how it is," Jay said.

"And you're going to school, too. I can't imagine how tough that would be on top of a full-time job."

Jay lifted his coffee to his mouth, but lowered it back to the table before taking a drink. Maybe it was still too hot for him. "You're taking classes, too, though, you said. That can't be easy with a child running around."

Megan shrugged and sipped her coffee. It was the perfect temperature for her, but then again she'd added some cream. "Chloe's great. All I've got to do is sit her down with a book and she's content. If that wasn't the case, then I don't think I could do it."

He glanced around the room. "Is she in her room or something?"

"No. She's with her grandparents. It's just me and Paul at the moment."

"So did he ever get his head out of his ass?" Jay grinned and wiggled his eyebrows.

She laughed. "Maybe."

"Ah. So the great Detective Daniels isn't above chasing a pretty girl."

Megan grinned, but otherwise remained silent, tilting her head down toward her drink.

Jay cleared his throat. "Speaking of the good detective, you didn't tell him about the other day, did you? That you saw me, I mean."

"No. You asked me not to. Although, I don't really understand what the big deal is. I mean, Paul wouldn't begrudge you an education. He's been really supportive of me going back to school."

"That might be the case, but you don't know how it is at the station. Guys can be brutal if stuff like that gets out." Again, he raised the cup to his lips but didn't drink. Megan wondered if maybe he really didn't like coffee but had only accepted to be polite.

She shook her head. "Men. I will never understand the lot of you."

He laughed with her, but for some reason Megan felt it wasn't genuine. Had she offended him?

Before she could think it through too much, her cell phone rang. Knowing it might be Paul, she set her mug on the table, and stood. "Excuse me."

Unfortunately, she only made it halfway across the room before an arm wrapped around her waist, and a hand covered her mouth. "I'm sorry, Megan. You're a sweet girl—not like the others—but I can't take a chance on you blabbing your mouth."

Megan's eyes widened in horror. What was going on? Why was Jay . . .

"Don't struggle, and I'll make it quick. I promise," he whispered.

Her heart was pounding in her ears, but Megan knew she had to stay focused—look for an opportunity.

Jay began moving them back toward the table. She had no idea why, other than it put more distance between her and her phone—her phone that had quieted for only a few seconds before it started ringing again.

Knowing she needed to get him to let his guard down, Megan didn't fight him. She didn't help him move her, but she didn't prevent him either.

Breathing in and out as evenly as she could, she waited. Hoping, praying he made a mistake.

Her opportunity came a few seconds later when he let go of her waist and reached for something on the table. She stepped forward with her left foot, and with all the energy she could muster, Megan bent at the waist, pulling Jay over her shoulder.

She didn't quite manage to completely flip him—he was a big guy, after all—but her move landed him on his back.

Not giving him time to recover, Megan made a beeline for the back door. Unfortunately, he caught up to her before she was able to step outside.

Jay pulled her kicking and screaming by the ankles back into the main part of the kitchen. She no longer had the element of surprise, so she knew anything she tried he would be anticipating. Megan couldn't stop fighting, however. It wasn't in her nature.

Once he got her back near the table, Megan saw what she'd missed before. A knife. It was small, maybe six or seven inches in total. The small metal blade reflected the sunlight, almost as if taunting her.

The wheels began turning in Megan's head, and she remembered the bits and pieces she'd seen on the news about the serial killer—how the women's throats and wrists had been cut.

And then there was what Jay had said before about the other women.

"You're him. The serial killer."

He grinned, and it sent a chill up her spine.

She swallowed. Jay had pulled her arms above her head and held her wrists captive with a single hand. He straddled her waist, putting pressure on her hipbones, making it almost impossible to move. Her only hope was to get him talking. Megan had to either reason with him or get him to drop his guard again. Given he'd killed four women already, she didn't put much stock in the former, so she was hoping for the latter.

"Figured that out, did you?" he asked.

He picked up the knife and held it mere inches from her neck.

She tried not to move. "I don't understand. Why? I mean . . . you're a cop."

To her dismay, Jay pressed the blade against her throat. He didn't puncture the skin, but she got the message loud and clear.

"Sometimes people need to be punished. And if the law won't do it, then someone has to."

Every word coming out of his mouth was making her skin crawl. How could she have missed this side of his personality? Surely there had to have been a sign. Something.

All she knew was she had to keep him talking. That's what Rebecca always told her. Even if there was no way to talk the person down, buying time was always the best option. Megan only hoped it was Paul who'd tried to call her and he'd realize something was wrong when she didn't answer.

"What did the other women do wrong, then?" Her voice was shaking. She couldn't help it.

"Ah, ah, ah. No more questions. I promised to make things quick if you didn't struggle. Now I'm going to have to make you pay."

She gasped as he ran the knife blade along the width of her neck. It cut into her skin, and a few moments later she felt blood trickling down to stain her shirt.

He chuckled as she struggled against his hold. She opened her mouth and was surprised she was still able to speak. The cut must not be that deep. He was toying with her. "Please, don't do this, Jay. Please."

With the back of his hand, he slapped her across the face. "I said be quiet!"

His eyes were blazing with fury, and Megan knew the end was coming. There was nothing she could do to stop him, and talking only seemed to make it worse.

He ran his nose along the edge of her face. In another circumstance, it would have been rather intimate. As it was, bile rose in Megan's throat. She closed her eyes and prepared herself to die.

She yelled out in pain as the knife sliced through one of her wrists.

***

Paul and Janey drove straight from the library to Rollins' house. Neither he nor his vehicle was there. Normally, Paul would begin tracking down the suspect's friends in an attempt to narrow down his whereabouts. That didn't sit well with him as an option. If he was right, Rollins was their serial killer. He was also a cop, which meant he had advantages above that of the average criminal.

When Paul was unable to reach Megan, he began to get a sickening feeling in his gut. Megan always answered her phone when he called. He'd known her to climb out of the shower when her phone rang. This wasn't like her. He wanted to warn her about Rollins. Although Paul knew that wasn't standard protocol, he didn't care. Megan had become extremely important to him, and he didn't know if he'd be able to stand it if something happened to her.

Especially since it would be all his fault. He'd introduced her to Rollins, after all.

"Do you want me to keep trying?" Janey asked, sensing his worry.

Paul shook his head. "If she hasn't answered by now, she isn't going to."

"You don't think . . ."

"I don't know. Do you mind if we—"

"Of course not. Let's go."

Turning around in the nearest driveway, Paul worked his way through traffic as quickly as he could to get to his neighborhood. Rollins only lived about ten minutes from Paul's house. Paul made it there in six.

The minute they turned onto Paul's street, they spotted Rollins' car. It wasn't parked in front of the house, but it was well within easy walking distance. Any optimism Paul had felt before went out the window. If Megan was hurt . . .

He didn't even want to think of the other possibility.

Paul pulled up along the curb. He jumped out, not bothering to turn off the engine, and sprinted toward the house.

He was almost to the garage when he heard Megan scream. If there'd been any doubt Rollins was inside the house before then, it was entirely gone. Releasing his gun from its holster, Paul raced toward the back of the house where he'd heard her scream originate.

Janey was hot on his heels. He knew she'd heard Megan as well. The scene that greeted them when they burst through the back door turned his stomach. Megan was laid out on the floor with Rollins on top of her. There was blood coming from her wrist, and from her neck.

Without thinking, Paul launched himself across the room, and knocked Rollins back. They both went tumbling and hit the tile floor hard. Paul's gun went flying, but that was the least of his worries. Rollins recovered quickly from the unexpected hit, and Paul felt something sharp puncture his leg. Without seeing what it was, he knew it had to be whatever Rollins had used on Megan and the other women he'd killed.

The struggle seemed to last forever, but in reality it was probably only a few minutes. Rollins was younger, and stronger, but Paul was driven by rage. He hadn't been able to take out his anger on the drunk driver who'd killed Melissa, but Rollins was there in the flesh in front of him.

Somewhere along the line, Rollins wiggled his way free, and Paul had to tackle him again. They ended up in the hallway, rolling around on the floor grasping for the knife. Rollins managed to get the blade between them, and Paul used all the strength he had to kick Rollins away. If he was able to stab something vital, Paul knew it would be all over for him.

Rollins hit the wall, jarring the knife from his hand.

Paul went for it. So did Rollins.

One minute they were fighting over the knife, and then the next, Rollins gasped and went limp. Paul pushed him away, and saw the blade of the knife sticking out of Rollins chest.

Before he could check to see if Rollins was still alive, Janey yelled from the other room. "Paul, you need to get in here."

Scrambling to his feet, Paul ran back into the kitchen. Janey was sitting at Megan's head with a kitchen towel wrapped tight around her wrist.

"I called for backup and an ambulance. She's losing a lot of blood. He only got one wrist, but it's deep and right along the vein," Janey said.

Paul lifted Megan onto his lap, and took over holding her wrist above her head to slow down the blood loss while Janey went out to meet the paramedics.

The cut along her neck didn't look deep. He wasn't a doctor, but he could tell there wasn't any immediate danger there. Her wrist, however, was another matter. The towel was drenched in blood, and if they didn't get it to stop soon, Megan would die.

He brushed his lips along her hairline. Megan was pale, and her eyes were closed. "Hold on, all right? You're going to be okay."

A minute later, Janey clamored back through the door followed by two paramedics. He knew he should move out of the way and allow them to do their job, but he couldn't let Megan go.

Janey put a hand on his shoulder and whispered in his ear. "It's okay, Paul. Let them do their job. They'll take care of her."

Reluctantly, he surrendered her to the paramedics, and let them load her onto a stretcher.

"I'm going with her," he said to no one in particular.

Janey answered him. "Go. I'll take care of things here, and keep you informed."

Paul was grateful the paramedics didn't give him a hard time about riding in the ambulance with Megan. He and Megan weren't family—not in the way that would normally make any difference to medical personnel. Whether it was because he was a cop, or because they knew him, he couldn't say, but either way he would owe them. Letting Megan out of his sight wasn't an option.

The ambulance ride was short. On the way to the hospital, they'd been able to stop most of the bleeding at her wrist. They'd cleaned up the cut on her neck as well. It would need to be bandaged, but Paul thought it would eventually heal completely. He didn't even think there would be a scar.

When they arrived at the ER, it was a slightly different story. At first, they weren't going to allow him to go with her, but the paramedic said something to the nurse and she waved Paul back.

He stood off to the side while the nurses worked to hook Megan up to all the necessary monitors. It was almost comforting when he saw her steady heartbeat on the screen.

They gave her an IV and took a sample of her blood. Everything happened extremely fast.

As the nurses were finishing up, a doctor appeared and began taking stock of her injuries. He asked Paul a few questions, and he answered them. At least, he thought he did. There was only one other time in his life when he'd felt this helpless. He'd hoped he'd never feel that way again, but here he was.

Before the doctor finished bandaging up her wrist, a nurse he'd seen before reentered the room, this time with a pint of blood. She hung it behind Megan's hospital bed and attached it to the IV tubes already in the uninjured arm.

The doctor turned to Paul. "She's lost at least a couple pints of blood, so we're giving her some O negative until we get the test results back on her blood type."

"Will she be all right?" Megan still hadn't regained consciousness, but her heartbeat was steady. He knew that was a good sign, but Paul needed reassurance.

"She's stable, and after we get some blood back into her system, she should wake up. After that, we'll have a better gauge of her condition."

Paul nodded.

"Is there someone you can call for her? Family?"

He blinked several times, staring at the doctor as if he were speaking a foreign language.

"Mr. Daniels?"

The doctor clearly thought Paul was losing his mind. Maybe he was. "Yeah. Her sister. I-I'll call her as soon as she wakes up."

"Mr. Daniels, we really like to have . . ."

Paul looked the doctor in the eye and lowered his voice. "I'm not leaving her side until she wakes up."

Sighing, the doctor lowered his gaze to Paul's leg. "We should probably take a look at that."

He looked down at the dark stain on his pants. Paul had completely forgotten about being stabbed. "I'm fine."

The doctor ignored him and waved one of the nurses over.

The wound wasn't deep and it was clean. They disinfected and cleaned the area, and the doctor sewed him up with five stitches before he backed out of the room. The nurse finished bandaging Paul up and then left him alone with Megan.

He scooted his chair closer and took hold of her hand. It was tricky with the IV and all the other tubes, but he worked around them. Paul needed to touch her. He needed that connection.

"I'm so sorry, Megan. I would never have introduced the two of you if I . . . if I . . ." A sob caught in his throat. He'd warned her that he feared he'd mess up again—that he didn't deserve her.

Paul rested his head beside her on the mattress, stroking her fingers. He would make sure she was okay and then send her back to

Nashville with her sister. It was the only way. The only way to keep her safe.

He didn't know how he'd make it no longer having her in his life, but he didn't have a choice. There was no way he could lose her like he had Melissa. He'd rather she lived a long and happy life without him than have her life end prematurely. Rebecca would help Megan move on and see that she was taken care of.

It was the only way.

Chapter 27

Megan's head was pounding. There was also this buzzing sound that wouldn't seem to go away. Her arm felt unusually heavy, and it ached.

She tried to lift it, but a hand stopped her.

"You need to lie still." The voice was firm, yet gentle—and one Megan recognized immediately.

"Paul?"

He squeezed the fingers of her other hand. "I'm right here."

"My arm . . ."

"Is it hurting you? I can ask them to get you some medicine." There was something in Paul's voice she didn't understand.

Forcing her lids open, Megan turned her head to the side. The first thing she noticed were Paul's eyes. They were bloodshot and puffy as if he'd been crying.

Everything was coming back to her as the fog of sleep left her brain. "What happened?"

He frowned. "You don't remember?"

"Yes. I meant what happened to Jay?" The last thing she remembered was the searing pain of him cutting her wrist, and then a loud bang. After that, things started getting fuzzy.

"He can't hurt you anymore."

She could have asked Paul to clarify, but the hard set of his jaw told her what he meant. Twisting her wrist slightly, she cupped the side of his face. He leaned into it for a second and then pulled back.

It was her turn to frown. "What's wrong?"

Paul stood, and her arm fell onto the mattress. "I need to call your sister. Will you be okay alone for a few minutes?"

"Of course, but—"

"I'll be right back."

Megan watched as he disappeared through the hospital curtain. What the hell just happened?

She was still mulling it over when a nurse pushed aside the curtain. "It's good to see you awake. How are you feeling, Miss Carson?"

"All right."

The nurse looked at something over Megan's shoulder. "Your vitals look good. How's the pain?"

Megan glanced down at her wrist. It hurt but she figured, given the circumstances, it could be worse. "It's tolerable."

"Well, everything is looking good so far. You lost a decent amount of blood, though, so we're going to want to keep you hooked up to an IV." The nurse patted Megan's shoulder. "If all goes well, we should be able to send you home in a few hours."

After checking the bandage on Megan's arm, the nurse exited the room, pulling the curtain closed behind her. With a few minutes alone, Megan's thoughts drifted back to Paul and his strange reaction to her gesture. It was the first time since she'd returned from visiting her sister that he'd shied away from her touch.

Was he repulsed by her injuries? Megan didn't think so. She knew he saw far worse on a regular basis being a homicide detective.

Maybe he was attempting to remain professional. Jay had admitted to being the serial killer, and that was Paul's case.

But even that didn't make sense. They were alone. If anyone had walked in on them, it would most likely have been one of the nurses. She couldn't imagine the hospital staff would have said anything. It wasn't as if he were crawling into bed with her in the middle of the ER.

She was still trying to figure things out when a hand poked through the fabric, and Paul slipped back inside the confined area. He smiled, but it looked forced.

"Rebecca will be here in the morning. I'm not sure if Gage is coming with her or not. He was going to call his coach and see if he could skip tomorrow's practice."

"What? Why?"

He lowered himself back into the chair he'd been sitting in earlier, but unlike before, he kept space between him and the bed. "She couldn't get a flight out until then."

Megan shook her head. "No. I meant, why is she coming? I'm fine."

"Megan, you could have . . . died." Paul averted his gaze as he said that last word, and something clicked in her brain.

"Why did you pull away from me earlier?"

To his credit, he didn't deny it. "I think once you're feeling better, you should go home with your sister. With the baby coming, I'm sure she'd love to have some help."

She couldn't believe what she was hearing. Okay, she could. That didn't mean she had to like it. "I'm not going to go live with Rebecca."

He met her gaze, and his mask was back. All the tenderness she'd seen in his eyes over the past week was gone. "I want you to go."

"Why?" she demanded. If he thought she was going to pack her bags and go willingly, then he sorely underestimated her. She'd gotten a glimpse of what they could have, and she wanted it.

Paul tilted his head down, no longer looking at her. "It's the right thing. The best thing."

"For who?"

"You." He still wasn't looking at her.

The urge to scream made her head ache worse. She probably should have accepted the nurse's offer for pain medication. It was too late for that, however, and there was no way she wanted anyone interrupting their conversation. "You're what's best for me."

"I'm not."

She released a heavy sigh, trying to keep her temper in check. "Is this about Melissa again? About you not feeling good enough? I thought we'd gotten past that."

Paul looked up, but he kept his shoulders hunched over. "You could have died."

Was that it? Did the fear of losing someone else he cared about spark some sort of buried trauma? "But I didn't. I'm going to be fine."

He stood abruptly and began pacing in the small space next to her bed. "Don't you understand? You could have died, and it would have been my fault. This is why I knew a relationship would be a bad idea. I'm not good for you, Megan. I'm not good for any woman."

At that moment, Megan really wished she could shake him. "What in the world are you talking about?"

Paul stopped moving and stared several feet above her head. "If I hadn't introduced you to Rollins, he never would have known who you were."

"That's absurd."

He lowered his gaze to meet hers. "Is it?"

"Yes. The whole reason Jay came to the house was because I ran into him outside the library Friday, and he wanted to make sure I hadn't said anything to you about it. Me running into him had nothing to do with you."

Paul seemed to consider that. "But if you'd never met, he might have walked right on by you."

"*Might.*"

He shook his head. "It doesn't matter. Your sister is going to need you, and—"

"And I'm not going. First of all, I won't leave Chloe like that. I promised her I had no plans to leave anytime soon, and I won't have her thinking I lied to her."

"Chloe will get over it," he said, interrupting her.

She ignored him. "Second, Rebecca and Gage will be fine on their own. If she needs my help for a couple of weeks after the baby's born, I can go then. But honestly, I'm guessing your mom is probably going to be all over that. She hasn't had a new grandchild in five years."

Paul didn't have a rebuff for that one.

Megan decided to press forward. "And third. I love you."

He began shaking his head. "You don't. It's just a crush. It's just . . ."

"Paul, I've been in love with you for a while now. So the question is how do you feel about me?"

"Megan, I . . ." He looked torn.

Pushing through the pain, she reached for him. The move nearly ripped the IV out of her hand, but she didn't care. This was important. "I don't care about the past. This isn't about Melissa, or

Chloe, or anything else besides you and me."

He gazed down at where she was gripping his wrist. "I want you to have a long and happy life."

She smiled. "I want that, too. With you."

"That's not possible." Paul was shaking his head again. She really wished he would stop that.

"Paul, just answer the question. Do you love me?"

He took her hand in his and began playing with her fingers. As much as she wanted him to get on with it—to answer her question already—she tried to be patient and give him time.

Before he could answer, the nurse returned. She made a clicking sound with her tongue when she saw how Megan was putting strain on her IV leads. Without a word, the nurse retracted Megan's arm, and Paul released her. It felt as if any ground they'd gained had been lost with the physical separation.

"There. Everything looks to be in working order. How's the pain?" Although the nurse was speaking to Megan, she sent several reproachful looks in Paul's direction.

"I'm fine," Megan answered, not taking her eyes off Paul.

"All right. I'll be back to check in on you in a bit." The nurse sounded doubtful.

Megan waited until they were alone again. "Paul?"

He closed his eyes. "Please, don't ask me that."

"Why not?"

"Because I don't want to lie to you."

She swallowed. "I just want the truth. Please."

***

Why was she doing this? He was trying to do the right thing.

Megan shifted, and he realized she was going to reach for him again. He couldn't have that. Stepping closer, he placed a stilling hand on her forearm.

She wouldn't let it go otherwise—he knew she wouldn't.

There was noise all round them in the ER. The only thing that separated it from them was a thin layer of fabric. Even still, it seemed as if the world around them faded away.

He looked into her young, beautiful face. "Yes. I love you."

She smiled.

"Which is exactly why you need to go with your sister. Megan, I can't lose you like I did Melissa. I'd rather you live your life away from me than have it cut short. I wouldn't survive it." He sounded desperate, and he was. Paul had to get her to understand. He was doing this for her.

Megan's eyes filled with moisture. "Paul, you didn't kill Melissa. Should you have picked up the diapers on your way home like you said you were going to? Probably. But you'd just come from a murder scene. No one expects you to be unaffected by that. You *are* human."

"That doesn't excuse—"

"Shut up and listen to me," she snapped.

If the situation weren't so serious, Paul would have laughed.

"Melissa is the one who made the choice to go out that night, not you. She could have waited until morning. I'm sure Chloe would have survived a few hours with a wet diaper."

This was the first time Megan had said anything negative about Melissa, and Paul wasn't sure he liked it.

"And what about the drunk driver? Does he not have any responsibility in her death? He chose to drink and then get behind the wheel. They made those choices, Paul, not you." Megan's voice trailed off.

What she said made sense, but that didn't change the guilt he felt.

Before he could say anything, she continued. "I know you think you should have somehow been able to foresee what would happen and save her, but you're not perfect, Paul. None of us are. I love how protective you are of those you love, but I don't need you pushing me away because you somehow think that's what's best for me. I'm a grown woman. I will make my own decisions on who I want, where I want to live, and anything else. Clear enough for you?"

Despite their surroundings and the fact that he knew she had to be weak from her recent blood loss, Megan looked as fierce as a mother lion defending her cub. If he didn't know any better, he would think she was ready to pounce at any second.

"Well?"

"Well, what?" He'd been so caught up in studying her reactions, he must have missed something she said.

"I love you, and you love me, too. I'm not letting you get away that easily."

"I never should have told you."

"Why?" she asked.

Paul took a step back and lowered himself into the chair once more. "Because it doesn't change anything. I'm still bad for you, Megan."

She scowled at him. "And what about Chloe? Are you going to send her away, too?"

That surprised him. "What are you talking about?"

"Well, if people being in close proximity to you is such a bad thing, then I'd think you'd want your daughter as far away from you as you can get her. It's only *logical*, after all."

He blinked. "You think I should send Chloe away?"

"No. That's my point."

Paul sighed, and leaned forward, resting his forearms on his knees. "I see what you're trying to do, but it's different. Chloe is my daughter—my responsibility. She already lost her mother. It wouldn't be fair for her to lose me as well."

"You realize how crazy that sounds, don't you?"

He shrugged, not really sure what she wanted him to say. The situation with Chloe was different. Making sure she was taken care of and loved was the last thing he could give Melissa.

"Will you do me a favor?"

He looked up at Megan, afraid of what she might say next. "What?"

"Stop trying to do what you think is best for me."

"I don't know if I can do that." It was the truth. Paul had always been the protector—for as long as he could remember.

"Try."

Neither of them said anything for several minutes.

"You really aren't going to leave, are you?" He wasn't sure if he was happy about that or not. It would be better for her to go, but selfishly he wanted her to stay.

"No."

Resigned, Paul leaned back in his chair. Despite everything, he felt himself grin.

"Care to share what's so funny?" she asked.

"I honestly don't know."

Megan smiled. "Will you come closer? I want to be able to

touch you, and I don't think the nurse will like it much if I try to tear the needle out of my hand again."

He hesitated and then scooted his chair closer. Taking hold of her hand, he laced their fingers together. Even something as simple as touching her made him feel better. He was still scared for her, although he wasn't sure anything would ever take that away completely.

"So Becca's coming tomorrow."

Paul nodded. "Yeah. She was pretty hysterical on the phone when I first told her. Once she knew you were going to be all right, she calmed down."

Megan rolled her eyes. "That isn't surprising. My sister has a tendency to overreact. Especially when it comes to me."

"You almost died, Megan. If I hadn't gotten there when I did . . ."

She squeezed his fingers. "But you did."

He didn't argue with her. What would be the point?

Deciding to redirect the topic of conversation a little, he shared what he hoped she'd consider good news. "I spoke to the doctor before I called your sister. He says you should be able to go home in a few hours."

"That's what the nurse told me, too. So did you tell Becca to come to the house, then?" she asked.

"Yes. That helped to calm her as well. I'm sure she figured you really were going to be okay if they were sending you home." Paul lifted her hand and placed a light kiss in the center of her palm.

"She's asked about you."

He raised his eyebrows in question.

"Becca's curious about the guy I'm seeing."

"Oh." For some reason that made him nervous.

"Paul?"

He must have lowered his gaze involuntarily, because he had to force himself to look up to see her. She had a serious expression on her face.

"Do you want to be with me? I know you're afraid of what might happen, but aside from that, what is it you want?" she asked.

That was easy. He wanted her. Megan brought a joy into his life he never thought he'd experience again after Melissa was taken from him.

When he didn't answer, she placed her hand on the side of his face like she had earlier. This time, he didn't pull away. "Do you want to be with me?"

"Yes." He couldn't deny it.

She smiled, and it stirred something in the pit of his stomach. "Forever?"

He closed his eyes and nodded. "Heaven help me, but yes."

"Good. I'm glad."

When he opened his eyes again, she was grinning from ear to ear. "Megan, I—"

"Paul, I want to ask you something."

She stroked her fingers along the line of his jaw, making it difficult for him to concentrate on anything else. She had his full and undivided attention.

"I love you. I love being with you. This past week, I've been happier than I can ever remember being. Even before then, when we were only friends, you brought things into my life I'd never had before. You accepted me into your home—into your family. I'd never had that. Becca has always been the only one I could count on, and then there you were. After knowing me for a day, you brought me home with you to start a new life. I will never be able to thank you enough for that."

He wasn't sure what to say, so he said nothing.

"I know you think my life would be better without you in it, but I know for a fact it wouldn't. I've been there before. I know what it's like. I don't want that again. Every morning, I wake up excited to find out what cute thing Chloe will do that day. Plus, who would I get to play poker with me?"

He chuckled, remembering their late night poker games.

"You make me feel part of something, Paul. I don't want to ever give that up. I want to stay with you and Chloe. Forever."

She took a deep breath, and he knew something big was coming. "Will you marry me?"

Paul sat there stunned for a long moment. "You-you want to marry me?"

"Yes."

He sat there unmoving.

"But the question is do you want me to be your wife?" she asked.

All the reasons why he wasn't right for Megan swirled through his mind. Was she being serious? Had she lost more blood than they'd thought?

Looking at her, he knew the answer. She was completely serious.

"This is really what you want?" He had to be sure.

"You're not supposed to answer a question with a question, Detective, but yes, it's what I want. I wouldn't have asked, otherwise."

He removed her hand from his face—her left hand—and rubbed his thumb over her ring finger. "The guy is supposed to be the one who asks, you know."

She snorted. "Well, you know me. I'm not exactly traditional."

Paul laughed. "No. That you're not."

"Well?" She was still waiting on an answer.

"Only if you agree that I'm the one that gets to buy you an engagement ring. We have to stick to some traditions."

Megan beamed. "So is that a yes?"

He smiled back. "Yes."

Chapter 28

It was after four in the morning before Megan was released from the emergency room. They were both exhausted, and all Paul could think about was getting her home. He knew they wouldn't get more than a few hours' sleep with Rebecca coming, but some was better than none.

The doctor told Megan to get as much rest as possible over the next few days so her body could heal. She was supposed to follow up with her family doctor in two days. The cut along her neck wasn't more than a scratch, and Rollins had only cut one of her wrists. She'd more than likely have a scar for the rest of her life, but all things considered, she'd been lucky.

Janey stopped by the hospital a little after midnight to drop off his car and to let him know that the forensic unit had released the house, and Rollins' body had been removed. She'd called in a favor and had a bio unit come do a quick cleanup of the area. They would only have removed any visible signs of blood, but he was glad Megan wouldn't have to see it.

They were also getting more information filtering in regarding Rollins. He'd served as an army medic for four years after high school, before joining the police force. It explained the precise cuts on the women. He'd known exactly how and where to cut in order to inflict the damage he wanted. They still weren't sure why he'd targeted them.

Paul pulled into the driveway and glanced over at Megan. She was asleep. As much as he didn't want to wake her, he doubted he'd be able to pick her up and carry her upstairs to bed.

"Megan? We're home, sweetheart. Do you think you can walk? We need to get you into bed."

She fluttered her eyes open. "Paul?"

He limped around to the passenger side and opened the door for her. "Come on, let's get you inside so you can rest."

It took some effort, but he managed to help her out of the car and into the house through the front door. He was glad she was out of it because they had to walk through the small hallway that connected the living room to the kitchen. The same area where Rollins took his last breath.

Paul had a momentary stab of indecision when they reached the top of the stairs. Should he take her to her bedroom, or his?

Megan sagged against him, and he decided to throw caution to the wind. She was his fiancée, after all. Of course, that was assuming she didn't change her mind once she was feeling better. He didn't think she would, though. Megan was never fickle. Once she made up her mind about something, she didn't back down.

Bypassing Megan's bedroom, he walked the extra steps to his. Everything was exactly as they'd left it earlier that morning, including the lingering scent of sex in the air.

Guiding her to the bed, Paul sat her on the mattress, and bent to take off the slippers the hospital had provided. She smiled down at him. The doctor had given her some pain medication before they left. It wasn't terribly strong, he said, but whatever it was, it had knocked her out almost as soon as they got into his car.

When Paul had her slippers removed, he began working on the rest of her clothes. Along with the footwear, the hospital had supplied a pair of scrubs for both of them. Given they'd both come into direct contact with Rollins, their clothing had been taken as evidence.

The top was easy enough to lift over her head. The bottoms, however, were another matter. He had to help her lie back on the bed, shimmy them over her hips, and then down her legs. It might sound simple, but Megan was dead weight in her current condition.

Leaving her side for a minute, Paul rushed into her bedroom to grab one of her more chaste nighties. The last thing he needed was to be more tempted than he already was.

When he reentered his bedroom, he found Megan sitting up and trying to unclasp her bra.

"What are you doing?"

She looked up at his approach. "I can't get it off."

"Here. Let me help." He brushed her hands away and released the hooks holding her bra in place.

Megan sighed.

Paul snatched up the nightie he'd brought from the other room and slipped it over her head. The sooner he got her covered up, the less distracted he would be.

Getting her under the covers proved to be another challenge. Even after she was tucked securely under the blankets, he wasn't sure how they'd accomplished it. There had been rolling and lifting and pulling. If he hadn't already been ready to pass out, that would have done it.

Shedding his own borrowed scrubs, Paul checked the clock beside his bed, and set the alarm for ten. Rebecca wasn't due to arrive until sometime after ten thirty, and he wanted to have time to wake up and shower.

Rolling onto his side, Paul wrapped his arm loosely around Megan's waist. Although he knew he should keep his hands to himself, he needed to feel her near him. It was the only way he could convince himself she was safe.

It hadn't taken him long to fall asleep. With Megan's warmth pressed against his chest, he'd sunk into a deep slumber. Unfortunately, it was short-lived. Paul woke up a few hours later in a cold sweat. It was the same dream he always had from the night Melissa died—with one exception. When he'd been called over to identify the body, it wasn't Melissa's face he'd seen. It was Megan's.

He sat up, holding his head in his hands, trying to breathe through the nightmare. His heart was pounding a mile a minute in his chest.

"Are you okay?" a sleepy voice mumbled beside him.

Paul glanced over and saw Megan gazing up at him. He tried to smile. "I'm all right. Go back to sleep."

"Not until you talk to me."

He tried to calm his thundering heart.

"Come here."

Paul shook his head. "Your arm."

She inched closer. "My arm's fine. Just be careful you don't bump my wrist."

He debated for a long moment, but decided not only was it not worth the effort arguing with her, he also needed her comfort.

Resting his head gently on Megan's shoulder, he let her warmth penetrate all the way down to his soul.

"Do you want to tell me about it?" she asked.

Did he? Outside of the department psychologist, he'd never told anyone about his nightmares. Even then, he'd downplayed them. "It's the same nightmare I always have. Sort of."

She laid her cheek against his head, drawing him closer.

"The night she died. The state highway patrolman knocked on my door to tell me what had happened and that they needed me to come down to the morgue to identify the body."

He heard Megan suck in a breath, but other than that, she didn't react.

"I couldn't leave Chloe alone, so I packed her up and drove her the few miles to George and Cindy's house. Of course, I had to explain why I was there. Cindy fell to the floor and began sobbing uncontrollably. George didn't fare much better, but he kept it together enough to comfort his wife.

"Once she calmed down a little, I promised them I'd be back as soon as I could, and left Chloe with them while I drove to the morgue. It was the longest drive of my life. I'd driven back and forth to my in-laws' house many times over the years, but this felt ten times as long, even though it took me no more than ten minutes. Me going to identify the body was a technicality. The woman driving matched Melissa's description, and she'd been driving her car. Her purse and ID were in the vehicle as well. There wasn't likely to be a mix-up."

Although talking about it was hard, this was the first time he'd been able to do so without going into a panic. "In the dream, I'm walking down to the morgue. I pass my colleagues—their faces full of pity. Then I step into the viewing room, and the coroner pulls the sheet down."

He was quiet for several moments. "Usually I see Melissa's face staring back at me. This morning, it was yours."

She hugged him, and he wondered if it was putting too much

pressure on her wrist. He went to pull away.

"Don't. Please," she begged.

Unable to deny her, he settled back down against her warmth. "I can't lose you like that, Megan. I can't."

"You won't."

"How can you be so sure?" he asked.

Paul felt her smile against his forehead. "Because if you haven't figured it out, I'm pretty stubborn. You can't get rid of me that easily."

He grinned and tilted his head up to look into her eyes. "Were you serious about being my wife?"

"You better believe it."

Reaching up, he ran his thumb along her cheek, down across her lips. "I love you."

***

Their moment was interrupted by his alarm. Paul groaned. "I need to get up and shower before your sister gets here."

Megan reluctantly let him go. "Are you picking her up?"

"No. I offered, but she insisted she could grab a cab."

She nodded and tried to get up.

Paul rushed to her side to help her. "You really should stay in bed and rest."

"I know they cleaned me up some at the hospital, but it still feels like I have a layer of . . . something on me. Do you think you could help me shower? There should be some plastic wrap downstairs to cover my bandage." If need be, Megan could manage a shower on her own, but it would be easier with his help. Plus, she was always up for opportunities to see Paul naked.

"Sit down on the bed, and I'll see what I can find." She could tell he wasn't keen on the idea, but at least he wasn't going to fight her.

He returned a few minutes later with the roll of plastic wrap. They wound the clingy material around her wrist until everything was covered completely.

The shower was uneventful, for the most part. Paul and Megan shared some kisses, but that was where it ended. Although she would have been up for a little more, he was firmly in caregiver mode.

Megan accepted it, and was content to know he was no longer pushing her away.

Paul helped her to dry off and get dressed. Megan didn't want to greet her sister lying in bed, so she asked him if he'd help her downstairs. He got her set up on the couch, and after giving her a soft kiss, he headed into the kitchen to make them something to eat.

He was still in the other room when Rebecca and Gage arrived. As soon as he let them in the door, her sister pushed him aside to join Megan on the couch. Rebecca surveyed Megan's injuries, and fawned over her like a mother hen.

"What happened?"

Megan wrinkled her brow. "Paul didn't tell you?"

Rebecca waved her hand dismissively. "He told me, but I want to hear it from you. Megan, why did you let that man in the house? How many times have I told you—"

"Maybe you should go easy on her, Rebecca. She did just get out of the hospital," Gage said.

Her sister looked at her husband and then back to Megan. Rebecca reached up to brush Megan's hair back behind her shoulders. "You scared me, you know that, don't you?"

"I know. But I'm fine. Honestly. The doctor said all I need is to rest for a few days." Megan hoped that would pacify her sister.

"Well, I'm going to stay and take care of you. Gage has to fly back tonight, but I'm here for as long as you need me." Rebecca hadn't stopped touching her since she sat down.

Paul cleared his throat. "I'm going to go finish getting our lunch ready. Gage, did you want to join me?"

"Yeah. Sure. We'll leave you two alone for a few minutes."

Megan watched Paul and Gage disappear into the kitchen. There must have been something that gave her away because when she turned back to her sister, Rebecca had a "deer in the headlights" look. "Becca? Are you feeling all right?"

Rebecca's expression went from shock to anger in a matter of seconds. "Something you want to tell me?"

"About?" Megan asked.

"Paul's your mystery man, isn't he?"

Megan refused to lie. "Yes."

"Oh, Megan." By the look on Rebecca's face, Megan would have thought someone had died, not that she'd confessed to being in a relationship with the man she'd been living with for the last seven-and-a-half months.

"Please don't do that," Megan pleaded.

"He's going to break your heart." Rebecca said it as if it were a foregone conclusion.

"No, he won't."

Before her sister could berate her some more, Paul strolled into the room with a tray of food. Rebecca waited until he set it down on the coffee table before laying into him.

"I thought I could trust you. Gage assured me you weren't the type to take advantage of a woman, and I believed him."

Paul met Megan's gaze, and she knew he realized the gig was up. Instead of retreating, or getting defensive, he shifted her a little to the side, and sat down behind her. He pulled her against his chest, and wrapped his arm protectively around her. His solid form behind her gave Megan strength.

"Becca, he didn't take advantage of me."

Her sister wasn't listening to her. Rebecca was staring Paul down. But he didn't seem bothered by her disapproval.

"Paul?" There was a note of disbelief and confusion in Gage's voice. He'd ambled into the room to find Paul and Megan cuddled together on the couch and Rebecca shooting daggers at his brother with her eyes.

Paul never took his eyes off Rebecca. "Let's get this all out in the open, shall we?"

Gage moved to stand behind his wife. "Would someone please tell me what's going on?"

"Paul is Megan's mystery man," Rebecca said through gritted teeth.

"What?" Gage's loud voice reverberated off the walls of the living room.

If there'd been any doubts, they were dashed when Paul tilted Megan's head back and placed a chaste kiss on her lips. She smiled up at him. Megan knew her sister would be upset with the news, but knowing Paul was there beside her, supporting her, she knew she could tackle anything. Including Rebecca.

After giving Paul another quick kiss, Megan turned back to face her sister. "Becca, I love you, but you need to get over it. Paul loves me, and . . ."

Megan glanced up at Paul, and he nodded.

She took a deep breath, and met her sister's furious gaze. "We're getting married."

Both Gage and Rebecca's mouths dropped open.

"Married?" Rebecca asked once she regained the ability to speak.

Paul jumped in. "That's right. We're getting married. I love your sister, Rebecca, and I hope you can learn to accept us. You're the only family Megan has, and I know she'll want you to be part of everything."

There were no words to describe the look on Rebecca's face.

Gage noticed his wife's distress. "Why don't we go get some air?"

Rebecca went with him reluctantly.

Alone again, Paul reached for the sandwich he'd made, and handed it to her.

"Thank you."

He smiled and kissed her forehead. "You're welcome. Now, eat. You need your strength."

Megan took a bite, chewed, and swallowed. It was her favorite—baloney, cheese, and mustard. "I'm sorry it came out like that. Becca's always been able to pick up on subtle things. I guess I must have been ogling you or something when you left the room."

Paul chuckled. "It's fine. We would have had to tell her soon, anyway. If she's going to be staying here for the next few days, I doubt we would have been able to hide it from her for long."

"You're not upset?"

He shook his head. "Why should I be?"

"I don't know. I guess I assumed you might want to keep it quiet until we talked to Chloe. You know, to make sure she approves and all." It wasn't that Megan was having doubts exactly, but Chloe's endorsement meant more to Megan than anyone else's.

"I don't think you have to worry about Chloe. Something tells me as long as it means you aren't going anywhere, she'll be all for it."

Megan forgot about her sandwich and pulled his head toward her for a kiss. "Nope. Not going anywhere."

He kissed her back and smiled. "Good."

A throat cleared, and they looked up to find Gage and Rebecca standing across the room right inside the doorway. Rebecca appeared calmer, but her eyes still held uncertainty.

"May we come in?" Gage asked.

Megan dropped her hand from around Paul's neck. "Sure."

Rebecca took a seat in the high-backed chair a foot or so away from where Paul and Megan were sitting. Gage retook his position behind his wife, resting his hands on her shoulders. As anxious as Megan was to find out what her sister had to say, she held her tongue and waited.

"You two are really getting married?" Rebecca asked.

Megan nodded. "We are."

Her sister turned her attention to Paul. "You really love her?"

"Yes, I love her."

Rebecca released a deep breath. "Okay."

"Okay?" Megan asked.

Her sister shook her head. "I don't understand it, but Gage reminded me how odd a match we appeared to be at first."

Megan smiled. "This is true. Trent thought I was Gage's girlfriend instead of you."

They both laughed, and Rebecca nodded. "He did."

Everyone was quiet for a long moment.

"So are we good?" Megan asked.

"Yeah. As long as he treats you right, we're good."

Megan wrapped her arm around Paul's waist and rested her head on his shoulder. "I don't think you have to worry about that."

Paul brushed his lips over her hair. "No, you don't. I plan on doing everything I can to make sure Megan is happy. That's a promise."

With the tension resolved, Gage rubbed his hands together. "Do you have any champagne around here, big brother? This is cause for a celebration."

Paul laughed. "No, but I think I've got some beers in the fridge."

Gage strolled into the kitchen and returned with three bottles of beer and a glass of water for Rebecca. He handed them all out and proposed a toast. "To my brother and my sister-in-law."

They all tipped their beverages and drank.

"So when is the big day?" Gage asked.

Megan looked to Paul. "We hadn't really discussed it."

"Ah. Well, I recommend you do it soon. When Mom gets wind of this, you aren't going to be able to contain her."

"We want to tell Chloe first," Megan said.

Gage smiled. "Somehow, I don't think she'll object."

Epilogue

A knock on his bedroom door caused Paul to jump. He wasn't normally so on edge, but it wasn't a run-of-the-mill kind of day.

"Are you decent?" Chris called from the hallway.

Paul chuckled. "I guess it depends on what you consider decent."

The door opened, and all three of his brothers walked in. Trent whistled when he got a good look at Paul in his new suit. "You clean up pretty well, big brother. I'd almost forgotten."

"I was in a suit for Chris' wedding. And Gage's. It hasn't been that long," Paul said.

Trent laughed.

Gage stepped forward and placed a hand on Paul's shoulder. "Since Megan and Rebecca's father isn't a part of their life, I figure it falls to me to lay down the law and tell you that you better treat her right, or else."

Although he knew Gage said it in jest, he also knew his little brother meant every word. The Daniels family had embraced both Rebecca and Megan from the beginning. They were part of the family, and the devil help any person who hurt them.

"Hey, stop giving Paul a hard time. He'll do right by Megan. Won't you?" Chris prompted.

Their father strolled through the door with a small box. "Stop giving your brother grief. How are you holding up, son?"

Paul ignored his brothers and concentrated on his dad. "I'm good. Is everything ready?"

"Yep, we're all set. You ready?" he asked, handing Paul the ring he'd asked his dad to pick up at the jewelers that morning.

Tucking the ring in the inside pocket of his jacket, Paul nodded.

He and his brothers followed their father downstairs and out to the backyard. Paul and Megan had discussed it, and decided on a simple wedding in their backyard at the end of July. She didn't want anything overly fancy, although Paul was more than willing to have a church wedding. Plus, Megan insisted she didn't want to wait the months it would take to organize such a thing.

The biggest unknown had been Chloe's reaction. They shouldn't have been worried, though. When they explained that he and Megan getting married would mean Megan would be Chloe's stepmom, she began jumping up and down screaming *"Megan's going to be my mommy"* over and over again.

After that, it was time to tell the rest of the family. His mom and dad didn't sound all that surprised. Neither did Chris, Elizabeth, or Trent. Maybe Paul and Megan's feelings for each other had been more obvious at Chris and Elizabeth's wedding than Paul thought.

The hardest sell, of course, had been Cindy. Because of her earlier comments, they decided to deliver the news face-to-face. He was extremely proud of Megan. She could have laid in to Cindy for what she'd said, but Megan took the high road and tried to reassure Cindy she loved Paul and Chloe, and was committed to both of them. By the end, both Cindy and Megan were crying and hugging each other.

To prove how much Cindy's feelings had changed regarding his and Megan's relationship, Cindy and George were in attendance for the wedding. The only other people were his family, her sister, and his partner, Janey. Small, but in their opinion, perfect. They didn't need, or want, anything flashy.

Paul said hi to each of them as he made his way up to the front of the makeshift aisle. So much had happened in the last month and a half. Megan had moved all her things into the master bedroom the day after they told Chloe the good news.

He'd also been busy at work tying up the loose ends on the

serial killer case. It turned out there'd been an incident with a young woman overseas a few months prior to Rollins being discharged. The woman had ended up dead, her murder unsolved. It now appeared that Rollins had killed her, and whatever had prompted her murder had followed him home. The powers that be were blaming it on PTSD.

The minister waited underneath a cluster of trees along the fence that surrounded the yard. Paul pushed the thoughts of Rollins and work out of his mind. This wasn't the day for those thoughts. In a few minutes, his bride would be walking toward him. Megan had kept her dress hidden from him, but he knew it was white. He couldn't wait to see it. To see her in it. And then to peel it off her later that night.

Paul took his place beside the minister and turned to face the house where Megan would make her entrance. Everyone took their seats and waited.

In addition to keeping the guest list small, Paul and Megan had also decided not to have anyone other than Chloe stand up with them. As if in tune with his thoughts, the back door opened, and his daughter tiptoed outside in her fancy white dress. She made it about halfway across the yard before she lost all sense of decorum and ran toward him with her little basket of flowers.

He caught her and swung her up into his arms.

"Did I do it right, Daddy?" she asked.

Paul laughed. "You did perfect, sweetpea."

Giving her a kiss on the cheek, he set Chloe on her feet, and positioned her in front of him.

Everyone stood as Megan entered the backyard. She wore a simple white dress that flared a little at the waist. It only came down to her knees, which showed off her legs—a definite plus in his opinion.

The closer she got, the bigger her smile seemed to get. Paul was sure his expression mirrored hers. His cheeks ached with how much he was grinning.

"Hi," he said when she finally stood in front of him.

She giggled. "Hi."

Their vows were simple and traditional. Chloe stood in front of the minister while they exchanged their rings and as the minister pronounced them husband and wife.

Threading his fingers through her hair, Paul kissed his new bride. "I love you, Mrs. Daniels."

"And I love you, Mr. Daniels. Forever."

"Forever."

Keep reading for a preview of
What Might Have Been

To learn about Sherri's upcoming releases, sign up for her newsletter at http://eepurl.com/J4vDb

Preview – What Might Have Been

SHERRI HAYES

WHAT MIGHT HAVE BEEN

THE DANIELS BROTHERS   BOOK 4

Chapter 1

Trent Daniels double-checked to make sure he had all the paperwork he might need. He had no idea why Frank and Lillian Baxter wanted to see him. As far as he knew, they were happy with the work his landscaping crew was doing, but the vague call he'd received the day before asking if he could meet with them at one o'clock was ominous. Like it or not, he had to consider that he might be losing his biggest client.

Satisfied everything was in order, he closed his briefcase and straightened his tie. He hated suits and did his best to wear them as little as possible. Give him jeans and a T-shirt any day over the noose he currently had wrapped around his neck.

"Got everything you need, Boss?" He glanced over his shoulder to find his office manager, Trinity, smirking at him.

"Everything I can think of, at least."

She crossed her arms over her chest and leaned on the doorframe. "Too bad Mrs. Baxter isn't twenty years younger. You could charm your way to securing the contract. You're looking pretty smokin' in that suit."

That made him grin and some of the tension dissipated. "Thanks. But I'm hoping talent brings this one home."

"You don't know what it's about, though, right? I mean it could be nothing." Joking aside, Trinity knew more than anyone did how big a blow it would be if they lost this account. She'd been with him since the beginning and had helped him build the company from the ground up. If things went badly with the Baxters, he might have to lay some people off and that was the last thing he wanted to do.

Trent picked up the briefcase and headed toward Trinity. She pushed herself away from the wall and took a step out of the room as he drew closer. The look on her face told him she was as worried as he was. He came to a stop in front of her and did his best to reassure her. "You're right. It could be anything. No reason to think the worst."

She smiled, but he could still see the worry in her eyes.

He placed a comforting hand on her arm. It was bad enough one of them was stressed out over this. "We'll be okay. We always are."

Trinity nodded and took a deep breath. "Go get 'em."

He gave her arm a reassuring squeeze. "Exactly what I plan to do."

As he passed Joss and Kevin, they didn't bother to look up from whatever they were working on. To them it was just a normal day at the office.

The drive to the Baxters' corporate office seemed to take longer than usual. He was sure that was only because of the lead weight that had settled in his stomach. Landing the Baxter account five years ago had put him and his company on the map. Before, he'd had a small crew made up of four guys and himself with a handful of regular accounts around the city. It wasn't bad, but he had bigger plans for himself and his company.

Trent parked in one of the guest spots near the front of the building then strolled up the steps toward the main entrance. As he passed by the flower beds, he couldn't help but take a quick survey of their condition. Everything looked great, in his opinion. The hedges were neatly trimmed and the beds well maintained. His crew did good work.

Shaking his head, Trent pushed everything out of his mind except for the task at hand. He had to be prepared for anything. Even if they lost the account, it wouldn't do any good to leave a bad impression.

A security guard sat behind a circular desk not far from the entrance. The middle-aged man glanced up as Trent walked in the glass doors.

"I'm here to see Mr. and Mrs. Baxter."

The security guard, looking somewhat bored, passed him a sign-in sheet. "Name?"

"Trent Daniels."

Nodding, the man picked up the phone, effectively ignoring Trent as he put his name and time of arrival on the paper attached to the clipboard.

When the man hung up the phone, Trent handed the sign-in sheet back to him. The security guard took it and placed it on the desk without looking at it. "You can have a seat over there. Mr. Baxter's assistant will be down to get you shortly."

Trent had been dismissed. He knew it wasn't personal and went to take a seat on the modern-looking sofa.

Less than five minutes after he sat down, Melinda, the Baxters' assistant, exited the elevator. She had a sly smile on her face as she approached him. "Frank told me you were going to be stopping by today. It's good to see you again. It's been a while."

"It hasn't been that long. I was here last month." Trent stood and followed her as she pivoted on her heel and strode toward the elevator. He didn't miss the extra swing in her hips as she walked that drew his attention directly to her backside. Melinda was a beautiful woman and she knew it.

He'd considered asking her out, but decided it wasn't a good idea. If something went wrong, he didn't want to put himself and the Baxters in an awkward position. However, that didn't mean he couldn't enjoy the view.

The elevator doors closed. She glanced over her shoulder, meeting his gaze.

"Nice dress."

Melinda beamed at the compliment. "Thank you. It's new."

She took a step toward him and ran a hand down the side of her dress in a way that had him wondering what those curves of hers would feel like pressed up against him.

"You don't think it's too much for work? I was thinking of going out later tonight and didn't want to go home first to change."

He grinned, trying to keep it casual. "Not at all. I'd say it's perfect for a girls' night out on the town."

Her confidence faltered a little at his response, but she recovered quickly. When they reached the top floor, Melinda sashayed out of the elevator, giving him another perfect view of her ass. Interested or not, Trent was a guy and it was hard to ignore something like that when it was right there in front of you.

She exaggerated every movement as she made her way over to her desk and sat down. It was like this every time he visited.

Trent cleared his throat. "Should I go in?"

Melinda looked a little disappointed, but nodded. "Yes. He's expecting you."

"Thanks."

Trent paused outside Mr. Baxter's door and took a deep breath. The one thing Melinda's flirting had done was help get his mind off this meeting. If he didn't know she'd take it the wrong way, he'd send her flowers or something.

He raised his hand and knocked.

"Enter." Despite the closed door, Mr. Baxter's voice rang out loud and clear.

Trent straightened his shoulders, opened the door, and walked in.

Mr. Baxter smiled when he saw Trent and waved him inside. "Come in, come in. How have you been?"

Seeing Mr. Baxter's upbeat attitude, Trent relaxed some. Surely if they were going to fire him, Mr. Baxter wouldn't be so welcoming.

"I've been well, Mr. Baxter. Thank you for asking."

He motioned for Trent to take a seat and waited until he was settled before continuing. "I'm so glad you could make it in today."

"Of course." Mr. Baxter was pushing sixty, but it was hard to tell. He dyed his hair and worked out regularly. If not for the lines around his eyes, he could easily pass for someone in his forties.

Hearing a noise behind him, Trent glanced toward the door. A man around his age, wearing a very expensive-looking suit, entered followed by Mrs. Baxter.

"I was beginning to think you two weren't coming," Mr. Baxter said, rising from his seat to give his wife a peck on the cheek.

Mrs. Baxter grinned at her husband, and then lowered herself into the empty chair next to Trent. "Lunch took longer than expected. I do believe the waitress had a small crush on Maxwell."

The other man, who Trent assumed to be Maxwell, took a seat on the couch along the wall and rolled his eyes. "I think you're making too much of it, Aunt Lillian. She was just trying to be nice."

His comment received a look of disbelief from Mrs. Baxter, but she didn't reply.

Mr. Baxter cleared his throat. "Let's get started, shall we?" He turned his attention to Trent. "As you've probably already surmised, this is our nephew, Maxwell Collins."

Trent nodded in Maxwell's direction. The man leaned forward and extended his hand in greeting. Trent took it and smiled politely.

"Good. Now that the introductions are settled," Mr. Baxter said when their handshake was over, "we can get down to business."

"We have something we'd like to ask you," Mrs. Baxter began, before being cut off by her nephew.

"What my aunt means to say is that I'm in need of some help and they feel you might be able to assist me."

"What is it that you need?" Trent asked. He was still trying to shift gears from thinking he was going to lose the account to being asked for help.

Maxwell sat forward, clasping his hands in front of him. "My father was diagnosed with pancreatic cancer and has recently taken a turn for the worse. He kept it from all of us until recently. Now that I know, I've come home to take care of things and to run the family business."

Trent waited for him to go on, since that still didn't explain what they needed from him.

"My father's assistant, Emily, knew about his condition and helped him hide it from the family," Maxwell continued. "As he got worse, she took over more and more of the daily operations."

He stood and walked over to the bank of windows along the wall. When he came into the room, he'd looked to be in his early thirties, the same as Trent himself. But now, talking about his father's declining health, Maxwell seemed to have aged ten years before his eyes.

Stuffing his hands in his pockets, Maxwell turned around to face Trent. "Long story short, some bad decisions were made. One of those was to trim the budget so it didn't include outside maintenance for any of our properties. It's no wonder sales are declining when the grass hasn't been cut in weeks and there are weeds everywhere."

It sounded like a mess. Lawns left unattended that long were likely to have seeded. It would take weeks, if not months to get them back to where they should be. "How many properties?"

"Ten. And I need them looking presentable as soon as possible.

I'm willing to pay for overtime or whatever else is needed. My family has put a lot of work into building this company. I won't allow it to crumble under my watch."

Trent needed to see firsthand what he was dealing with. "I would have to take a look at all the properties and come up with an action plan."

"Good. When can you get started?"

"I have some time tomorrow if that would work for you."

Maxwell grinned and handed Trent two business cards from inside his jacket. "I'll have my assistant, Abigail, meet you in front of our corporate office at nine. She can take you around to each of the properties and answer any questions you may have."

Trent glanced down at the two cards. One had Maxwell Collins, Attorney at Law written in fancy lettering along with a Manhattan address. The second card was for Collins and Baxter Property Management Corporation with a local address.

"If you need anything before tomorrow, you can reach me on my cell."

Standing, Trent tucked the cards in his pocket. "If I can get a look at everything tomorrow, I should be able to have some figures for you by the end of the week."

"I look forward to it." Maxwell extended his hand again to Trent.

After a brief goodbye to Mr. and Mrs. Baxter, Trent left the office and made his way back down the elevator. His head was spinning. Not only had they not lost the Baxter account, but it looked as if they were gaining another big client.

Trent strolled past the security guard in the lobby and out into the parking lot. He climbed into his truck, shut the door, and reached for his cell.

Two rings later, Trinity picked up. "How'd it go?"

Trent tilted his head back against the seat and chuckled. "You're not going to believe it."

***

Abigail Hoffman took a seat on the stone bench outside the Collinses' corporate office. She glanced up at the sky and frowned. It was going to be hot and humid once the sun worked its way higher in the sky. Just her luck she'd be spending the day driving around town showing the new landscaper all the Collinses' properties. Abby prayed his vehicle had air conditioning.

Max had returned from his meeting the day before and gleefully informed her of how she'd be spending her day today. She was glad he'd solved one of the hundreds of issues they'd inherited upon his return to Cincinnati, Ohio. Instead of spending time with his ailing father, Max was stuck trying to fix the months of bad decision-making his father's assistant, Emily, had made.

Emily had no experience running a business and it showed. She'd cut spending in an effort to save the company money, but she hadn't understood that sometimes you have to spend money in order to make it. Now it was up to Max, and Abby, to get things back on track. If they didn't, Collins and Baxter Property Management wasn't going to last much longer.

She glanced at her watch. It was already five minutes after nine and there was no sign of the landscaper.

Her phone buzzed and she dug in her purse to check the message. It was from Max, of course.

Didn't scare him off, did you? - Max

She rolled her eyes. **No. He hasn't shown up yet. - Abby**

He didn't reply immediately. **Don't worry. He'll be there. Aunt Lillian says he's the best landscaper in town. - Max**

High praise coming from your aunt. - Abby

I know. Call me tonight? - Max

Sure. - Abby

Sighing, she put her phone back in her purse. When Max told her about his dad and asked for her help, Abby couldn't say no. Max was her best friend and he'd been there for her more times than she could count over the years.

That didn't mean she was feeling all warm and fuzzy about being back in her hometown. There were too many memories here. Too many chances of running into someone she knew.

Abby checked her watch again. Ten minutes after nine. Maybe Aunt Lillian had been wrong about this guy of hers.

"Excuse me?"

She looked up at the large figure looming over her. The sun was behind him and she was having trouble seeing his face. "Hi."

"Hi." He sounded amused. "Would you happen to be Abigail?"

Right then he moved a little to the right, blocking the sun, and she got a good look at his face. Abby blinked. She had to be seeing things. It couldn't be—

"Are you all right?" His amusement had turned to concern when she didn't respond.

Abby stood and attempted to hide her unease. She didn't need to be at any more of a disadvantage than she already was. "Yes. I'm fine."

A second later, she saw recognition cross his face. "Abby? Is that you?"

"Hi, Trent."

"Wow. I can't believe it. When I was told I'd be meeting Abigail, I had no idea it would be you."

"Yep. It's me." She knew what was coming and the last thing she wanted to do was take a trip down memory lane. "And I'm guessing you're the landscaper."

"Landscape architect, actually. But my company does everything from design to implementation and maintenance."

She was impressed, despite everything else that was going through her head at that moment. "Sounds like a lot of work."

"It is. But I love it."

Standing there, Abby realized how easy it would be to slip into the effortless friendship they'd had before. A part of her longed for that, but she had to remember why that wasn't a good idea—why she needed to keep her distance. "Word on the street is that you're the best."

Trent lifted a single eyebrow and one side of his mouth tilted up. "By the street you mean Mrs. Baxter."

She couldn't help the bubble of laughter that escaped. "Max's aunt thinks highly of you and she doesn't dole out praise lightly."

Abby knew that much from personal experience. The first time she'd met Lillian and her husband, Frank, she'd been peppered with questions from the woman. Even though Max had explained that he and Abby were merely friends, Lillian was convinced there had to be more to it. She wanted to make sure her nephew wasn't having the wool pulled over his eyes.

"You must be talking about another Mrs. Baxter. She's always been quite pleasant to me." He was teasing her and it brought back a lot of memories . . . memories she really wanted to keep buried.

"Lucky you." Abby smiled and picked up the paperwork on all the properties she'd brought with her, trying to ignore the churning in the pit of her stomach. "We have a lot of ground to cover today. Are you ready to get started?"

He motioned toward the parking lot. "Ready when you are."

They made their way down the walkway to where he'd parked his vehicle—a silver pickup truck. It looked new, but when Abby climbed inside she noticed a few signs of wear on the interior. There were also several notebooks and a stack of papers on the seat between them.

Trent put the key into the ignition, started the engine, and put the vehicle in gear. "Where to first?"

Abby flipped open the folder in her lap. The first property on the list was another office building. It was as good a place to start as any. "Gavin's Ridge. We'll start there."

"Gavin's Ridge it is."

He backed out and maneuvered his way through the parking lot and onto the main road. Abby told herself to stay calm. It would be okay. This was Trent. Her childhood friend.

While that was true, a lot had changed since they'd sat on the steps outside his home and played *I spy*.

She chanced a glance at him before looking away.

Pressing her lips together, she ordered herself to breathe. It would be okay. She'd do her job, he'd do his, and then they'd go their separate ways.

Yeah. Who was she trying to kid? There was no way Trent would leave it at that. Not with their history.

Available Now!

About the Author

Sherri spent most of her childhood detesting English class. It was one of her least favorite subjects because she never seemed to fit into the standard mold. She wasn't good at spelling, or following grammar rules, and outlines made her head spin. For that reason, Sherri never imagined becoming an author.

At the age of thirty, all of that changed. After getting frustrated with the direction a television show was taking two of its characters, Sherri decided to try her hand at writing an alternate ending, and give the characters their happily ever after. By the time the story finished, it was one of the top ten read stories on the site, and her readers were encouraging her to write more.

Since then Sherri has published several novels, many of which have hit the top 100 in their category on Amazon. Writing has become a creative outlet that allows her to explore a wide range of emotions, while having fun taking her characters through all the twists and turns she can create. You can find a current list of all of Sherri's books and sign up for her monthly newsletter at www.sherrihayesauthor.com.

21423437R00157

Made in the USA
Columbia, SC
18 July 2018